About the Authors

USA Today Bestseller **Lucy Monroe** finds inspiration for her stories everywhere as she is an avid people-watcher. She has published more than fifty books in several subgenres of romance and when she's not writing, Lucy likes to read. She's an unashamed book geek, but loves movies and the theatre too. She adores her family and truly enjoys hearing from her readers! Visit her website at: http://lucymonroe.com

Susanna Carr has been an avid romance reader since she read her first Mills & Boon at the age of ten. She has written sexy contemporary romances for several publishers and her work has been honoured with awards for contemporary and sensual romance.

Susanna lives in the Pacific Northwest with her family. When she isn't writing, she enjoys reading romance and connecting with readers online. Visit her website at susannacarr.com

Mills & Boon novels were **Julia James'** first 'grown up' books she read as a teenager, and she's been reading them ever since. She adores the Mediterranean and the English countryside in all its seasons, and is fascinated by all things historical, from castles to cottages. In between writing she enjoys walking, gardening, needlework and baking 'extremely gooey chocolate cakes' and trying to stay fit! Julia lives in England with her family.

The Hidden
COLLECTION

Hidden Motives

LUCY MONROE

SUSANNA CARR

JULIA JAMES

MILLS & BOON

First Published in Great Britain 2020
By Mills & Boon, an imprint of HarperCollins*Publishers*
1 London Bridge Street, London, SE1 9GF

HIDDEN MOTIVES © 2020 Harlequin Books S.A.

Prince of Secrets © 2013 Lucy Monroe
Her Shameful Secret © 2013 Susanna Carr
The Dark Side of Desire © 2012 Julia James

ISBN: 978-0-263-28144-6

MIX
Paper from
responsible sources
FSC® C007454

This book is produced from independently certified FSC™ paper to ensure responsible forest management.

For more information visit: www.harpercollins.co.uk/green

Printed and bound in Spain
by CPI, Barcelona

PRINCE OF SECRETS

LUCY MONROE

For Debbie, my sister and my friend. God blessed our family immeasurably when He brought you into it. And for Rob, a dear brother of the heart. Together, you have brought so much generosity, love, faith and joy to our family and to me personally. Much love to you both, now and always!

PROLOGUE

"WHAT AM I looking at?" Demyan asked his uncle, the King of Volyarus.

Spread before him on the behemoth antique executive desk, brought over with the first Hetman to be made Volyarussian king, was a series of photos. All were of a rather ordinary woman with untamed, curly, red hair. Her one arresting feature was storm-cloud gray eyes that revealed more emotion in each picture than he would allow himself to show in an entire year.

Fedir frowned at the pictures for several seconds before meeting Demyan's matching espresso-dark gaze.

Those who mistook Demyan for Fedir's biological son could be forgiven—the resemblance was that strong. But Demyan was the king's nephew and while he'd been raised in the palace as the "spare heir to the throne," three years older than his future king, he'd never once gotten it confused in his own mind.

Fedir cleared his throat as if the words he needed to utter were unpalatable to him. "That is Chanel Tanner."

"Tanner?" Demyan asked, the coincidence not lost on him.

"Yes."

The name was common enough, in the United States, anyway. There was no immediate reason for Demyan to assume she was related to Bartholomew Tanner, one of the original partners in Tanner Yurkovich.

Except the portrait of the Texas wildcatter hanging in the west hall of the palace bore a striking resemblance to the woman in the pictures. They shared the same curly red hair (though Bartholomew had worn it shorter), high forehead and angular jaw (though hers was more pleasingly feminine).

Her lips, unadorned by color or gloss, were a soft pink and bow-shaped. Bartholomew's were lost beneath the handlebar mustache he sported in the painting. While his eyes sparkled with life, hers were filled with seriousness and unexpected shadows.

Bartholomew Tanner had helped to found the company on which the current wealth of both Volyarus and the Yurkovich family empire had been built. At one time, he had owned a significant share in it as well.

"She looks like Baron Tanner." The oilman had been bequeathed a title by King Fedir's grandfather for his help in locating oil reserves and other mineral deposits on Volyarus.

Fedir nodded. "She's his great-great-granddaughter and the last of his bloodline."

Relaxing back in his chair, Demyan cocked his brow in interest but waited for the king to continue rather than ask any questions.

"Her stepfather, Perry Saltzman, approached our office in Seattle about a job for his son." Another frown, which was unusual for the king, who was no more prone to emotional displays than Demyan. "Apparently, the boy is close to graduating university with honors in business."

"Why tell me? Maks is the glad-hander on stuff like this." His cousin was also adroit at turning down requests without causing diplomatic upset.

Demyan was not so patient. There were benefits to not being raised a Crown Prince.

"He is on his honeymoon." Fedir's words were true, but Demyan sensed there was more to it.

Otherwise, this could have waited. "He'll be back in a couple of weeks."

And if Mr. Saltzman was looking for a job for his son, why were there pictures of his stepdaughter all over the conference table?

"I don't want Maks to know about this."

"Why?"

"He will not agree to what needs to be done." Fedir ran his fingers through hair every bit as dark as Demyan's, no strands of gray in sight. "You know my son. He can be unexpectedly…recalcitrant."

For the first time in a very long while, Demyan had to admit, "You've lost me."

There was very little his cousin would not do for the country of his birth. He'd given up the woman he wanted rather than marry with little hope for an heir.

Fedir stacked the pictures together, leaving a candid shot on top that showed Chanel smiling. "In 1952, when Bart Tanner agreed to help my grandfather find oil on or around the Volyarussian islands, he accepted a twenty-percent share in the company in exchange for his efforts and provision of expertise, a fully trained crew and all the drilling equipment."

"I am aware." All Volyarussian children were taught their history.

How Volyarus had been founded by one of Ukraine's last Hetmans, who had purchased the chain of uninhab-ited and, most believed, uninhabitable islands with his own personal wealth from Canada. He and a group of peasants and nobles had founded Volyarus, literally meaning free from Russia, because they'd believed it was only a matter of time before Ukraine fell under Russian rule completely.

They had been right. Ukraine was its own country again, but more people spoke Russian there than their native tongue. They had spent too many years under the thumb of the USSR.

Hetman Maksim Ivan Yurkovich the First had poured his wealth into the country and become its de facto monarch. By the time his son was crowned King of Volyarus, the House of Yurkovich's monarchy was firmly in place.

However, the decades that followed were not all good ones for the small country, and the wealth of its people had begun to decline, until even the Royal House was feeling the pinch.

Enter wildcatter and shrewd businessman Bartholomew Tanner.

"He died still owning those shares." Fedir's frown had turned to an all-out scowl.

Shock coursed through Demyan. "No."

"Oh, yes." King Fedir rose and paced the room, only to stop in front of the large plate glass window with a view of the capital city. "The original plan was for his daughter to marry my grandfather's youngest son."

"Great-Uncle Chekov?"

"Yes."

"But…" Demyan let his voice trail off, nothing really to say.

Duke Chekov had been a bachelor, but it wasn't because Tanner's daughter broke his heart. The man had been gay and lived out his years overseeing most of Volyarus's mining interests with a valet who was a lot more than a servant.

In the 1950s, that had been his only option for happiness.

Times had changed, but some things remained static. Duty to family and country was one of them.

King Fedir shrugged. "It did not matter. The match was set."

"But they never married."

"She eloped with one of the oilmen."

That would have been high scandal in the '50s.

"But I thought Baron Tanner left the shares to the people of Volyarus."

"It was a pretty fabrication created by my grandfather."

"The earnings on that twenty percent of shares have been used to build roads, fund schools… *Damn.*"

"Exactly. To repay the funds with interest to Chanel Tanner would seriously jeopardize our country's financial stability in the best of times."

And the current economic climes would never be described as that.

"She has no idea of her legacy, does she?" If she did, Perry Saltzman wouldn't bother to ask for a job for his son—he'd be suing Volyarus for hundreds of millions. As one of the few countries in the world that did not operate in any sort of deficit, that kind of payout could literally break the Volyarussian bank.

"What's the plan?"

"Marriage."

"How will that help?" Whoever she married could make the same claims on their country's resources.

"There was one caveat in Bartholomew's will. If any issue of his ever married into the Volyarussian royal family, his twenty percent would revert to the people less a sufficient annual income to provide for his heir's well-being."

"That doesn't make any sense."

"It does if you know the rest of the story."

"What is it?"

"Tanner's daughter ended up jilted by her lover, who

was already married, making their own hasty ceremony null."

"So, she still could have married Duke Chekov."

"She was pregnant with another man's child. She'd caused a well-publicized scandal. He categorically refused."

"Tanner thought he would change Great-Uncle Chekov's mind?"

"Tanner thought *her* son might grow up to marry into our family and link the Tanner name with the Royal House of Yurkovich for all time."

"It already was, by business."

"That wasn't good enough." King Fedir sighed. "He wanted a family connection with his name intact, if possible."

"Family was important to him."

"Yes. He never spoke to his daughter again, but he provided for her financially until she remarried, with only one caveat."

"Her son keep the Tanner name." It made sense.

"Exactly."

"And he presumably had a son."

"Only one."

"Chanel's father, but you said she was the only living Tanner of Bart's line."

"She is. Both her grandfather and father died from dangerous chemical inhalation after a lab accident."

"They were scientists?"

"Chemists, just like Chanel. Although they worked on their own grants. She's a research assistant."

The woman with the wild red hair in the pictures was a science geek?

"And no one in the family was aware of their claim to Tanner's shares?"

"No. He meant to leave them to the people of Volyarus. He told my grandfather that was his intention."

"But he didn't do it."

"He was a wildcatter. It's a dangerous profession. He died when his grandson was still a young boy."

"And?"

"And my grandfather provided for the education expense of every child in that line since."

"There haven't been that many."

"No."

"Including Chanel?"

"Yes. The full ride and living expenses scholarship she received is apparently what gave Perry Saltzman the idea to approach Yurkovich Tanner and trade on a connection more than half a century old."

"What do you want me to do? Find her a Volyarussian husband?"

"He has to be from the Yurkovich line."

"Your son is already married."

"You are not."

Neither was Demyan's younger brother, but he doubted Fedir considered that fact important. Demyan was the one who had been raised as "spare to the throne," almost a son to the monarch. "You want me to marry her."

"For the good of Volyarus, yes. It need not be a permanent marriage. The will makes no stipulations on that score."

Demyan did not reply immediately. For the first time in more years than he could remember, his mind was blank with shock.

"Think, Demyan. You and I both know the healthy economy of Volyarus sits on a precarious edge, just like the rest of the world's. The calamity that would befall us were we to be forced to distribute the funds to Miss Tanner would be great."

"You are being melodramatic. There's no guarantee Maksim the First's duplicity would ever be discovered."

"It's only a matter of time, particularly with a man like Perry Saltzman in the picture. His kind can sniff out wealth and connections with the efficiency of ferrets."

"So, we deny the claim. Our court resources far exceed this young woman's."

"I think not. There are three countries that would be very happy to lay claim to Volyarus as a territory, and the United States is one of them."

"You believe they would use the unclaimed shares as a way to get their hands on a part of Volyarus."

"Why not?"

Why not, indeed. King Fedir would and, come to it, Demyan wouldn't hesitate to exploit such a politically expedient turn of events himself.

"So I marry her, gain control of the shares and dump her?" he asked, more to clarify what his uncle was thinking than to enumerate his own plans.

He would marry one day. Why not the heir to Bartholomew Tanner? If she was as much a friend to Volyarus as her grandfather had been, they might well make an acceptable life together.

"If she turns out to be anything like her grasping stepfather, yes," Fedir answered. "On the other hand, she may well be someone you could comfortably live with."

The king didn't look like he believed his own words.

Frankly, Demyan wasn't sure he did, either, but his future was clear. His duty to his country and the well-being of his family left only one course of action open to him.

Seduce and marry the unpolished scientist.

CHAPTER ONE

DEMYAN SLID THE black-rimmed nonprescription glasses on before pushing open the door to the lab building. The glasses had been his uncle's idea, along with the gray Armani cardigan Demyan wore over his untucked dress shirt—no tie. The jeans he wore to complete the "geeky corporate guy" attire were his own idea and surprisingly comfortable.

He'd never owned a pair. He'd had the need to set the right example for his younger cousin, Crown Prince to Volyarus, drummed into Demyan from his earliest memory.

He'd done his best, but they were two very different men.

Maksim was a corporate shark, but he was also an adept politician. Demyan left politics to the diplomats.

For now, though, he would tone down his fierce personality with clothes and a demeanor that would not send his prey running.

He knocked perfunctorily on the door before entering the lab where Chanel Tanner worked. The room was empty but for the single woman working through her lunch hour as usual, according to his investigator's report.

Sitting at a computer in the far corner, she typed in quick bursts between reading one of the many volumes spread open on the cluttered desktop.

"Hello." He pitched his voice low, not wanting to startle her.

No need to worry on that score. She simply waved her hand toward him, not even bothering to turn around. "Leave it on the bench by the door."

"Leave what, precisely?" he asked, amused in spite of himself by her demeanor.

"The package. Do you really need to know what's in it? No one else ever asks," she grumbled as she scribbled something down.

"I do not have a package. What I do have is an appointment."

Her head snapped up, red curly hair flying as she spun her chair to face him. "What? Who? You're Mr. Zaretsky?"

He nodded, impressed by the perfect pronunciation of his name.

"You aren't expected for another half an hour." She jumped to her feet, the pocket of her lab coat catching the edge of a book and knocking it to the floor. "And you're going to be late. Corporate types interested in funding our research always are."

"And yet I am early." He crossed the room and picked up the book to hand to her.

Taking it, she frowned, her small nose scrunching rather charmingly. "I noticed."

"Eventually, yes."

Pink stained her cheeks, almost washing out the light dusting of freckles. "I thought you were the delivery guy. He flirts. I don't like it, so I ignore him if at all possible."

The woman was twenty-nine years old and could count the number of dates she'd had in the past year on less than the fingers of one hand. Demyan would think she might welcome flirting.

He did not say that, of course. He gave her the smile

he used on women he wanted to bed. "You have no filter, do you?"

"Are *you* flirting with me?" she demanded, her gray eyes widening in shock.

"I might be." Awkward and this woman were on very friendly speaking terms.

Her brows furrowed and she looked at him with evident confusion. "But why?"

"Why not?"

"I'm hospitably inept, not desperate."

"You believe you are inept?"

"Everyone believes I'm *socially awkward,* particularly my family. Since not one of them has trouble making friends and maintaining a busy social life, I bow to their superior knowledge in the area."

"I think you are charming." Demyan shocked himself with the knowledge that he spoke the truth.

An even bigger but not unwelcome surprise was that he found the geeky scientist unexpectedly attractive. She wasn't his usual cover model companion, but he would like very much if she would take off her lab coat and give him the opportunity to see her full figure.

"Some people do at first, but it wears off." She sighed, looked dejected for a few short seconds before squaring her shoulders and setting her features into an expression no doubt meant to hide her thoughts. "It's all right. I'm used to it. I have my work and that's what is really important."

He'd learned that about her, along with a great deal else from the investigation he'd had performed on top of the dossier his uncle had provided. "You're passionate about your research."

"It's important."

"Yes, it is. That is why I am here."

The smile she bestowed on him was brilliant, her gray

eyes lighting to silver. "It is. You're going to make it possible for us to extend the parameters of our current study."

"That is the plan." He'd determined that approaching her in the guise of a corporate investor was the quickest way to gain Chanel's favor.

He'd obviously been right.

"Why are you here?" she asked.

"I thought we'd been over that."

"Most corporations donate without sending someone to check our facility over."

"Are you offended Yurkovich Tanner did not opt to do so?"

"No, just confused."

"Oh?"

"How will you know if this is a good setup or not? I mean, even the most fly-by-night operation can make their lab look impressive to a layman."

"The University of Washington is hardly a fly-by-night operation."

"No, I know, but you know what I mean."

"You really have no filter, do you?"

"Um, no?"

"You as good as called me stupid."

"No." She shook her head for emphasis.

"The implication is there."

"No, it's not. No more than I consider myself stupid because I could stare at my car's engine from dawn to dusk and still not be able to tell you where the catalytic converter is."

"It's under the engine."

"Is it?"

"Point taken, but you knew your car exhaust system has one. Just as I know the rudimentary facts about lab research."

"I know about the catalytic converter because my mother's was stolen once. I guess it's a thing for young thugs to steal them and sell them for the precious metal. Mom was livid."

"As she had a right to be."

"I suppose, but getting a concealed weapons permit and storing a handgun in her Navigator's glove box was taking it about sixty million steps too far. It wasn't as if she was in the car when they stole the thing."

Demyan felt his lips twitching, the amusement rolling through him an unusual but not unwelcome reaction. "I am sure you are right."

"Is English your second language?"

"It is." But people rarely realized that. "I do not speak with an accent."

"You don't use a ton of contractions either."

"I prefer precise communication."

Her storm-cloud gaze narrowed in thought. "You're from Volyarus, aren't you?"

He felt his eyes widen in surprise. "Yes."

"Don't look so shocked. My great-great-grandfather helped discover the oil fields of Volyarus. Did you really think I wouldn't know that the Seattle office of Yurkovich Tanner is just a satellite? They paid for my university education. It was probably some long-ago agreement with Bartholomew Tanner."

She was a lot closer than was comfortable to the truth. "He was bequeathed the title of baron, which would make you a lady."

"I know that, but my mom doesn't." And from Chanel's tone, she didn't want the older woman finding out. "Besides, the title would only pass to me if I were direct in line with no older sibling."

"Do you have one?" he asked, knowing the answer but following the script of a stranger.

"No."

"So you are Dame Tanner, Lady Chanel, if you prefer."

Her lovely pink lips twisted with clear distaste. "I prefer just Chanel."

"Your mother is French?" he asked, continuing the script he'd carefully thought out beforehand.

Demyan was always fully prepared.

"No. She loves the Chanel label, though."

"She named you after a designer brand?" His investigators had not revealed that fact.

"It's no different than a parent naming their child Mercedes, or something," Chanel replied defensively.

"Of course."

"She named me more aptly than she knew."

"Why do you say that?" he asked with genuine surprise and curiosity.

He would have thought it was the opposite.

"Mom loves her designers, but what she never realized was that Coco Chanel started her brand because she believed in casual elegance. She wore slacks when women simply did *not*. She believed beauty should be both effortless and comfortable."

"Did she?"

"Oh, yes. Mom is more of the 'beauty is pain' school of thought. She wishes I were, too, but well, you can see I'm not." Chanel indicated her lab coat over a simple pair of khaki slacks and a blue T-shirt.

The T-shirt might not be high fashion, but it clung to Chanel's figure in a way that revealed her unexpectedly generous curves. She wasn't overweight, but she wasn't rail thin either, and if her breasts were less than a C cup, he'd be surprised.

That information had not been in her dossier, either.

"You're staring at my breasts."

"I apologize."

"Okay." She sighed. "I'm not offended, but I'm not used to it. My lab coat isn't exactly revealing and the men around here, well, they stare at my data more than me."

"Foolish men."

"If you say so."

"I do."

"You're flirting again."

"Are you going to try to ignore me like the delivery man?"

"Am I going to see you again to ignore you?"

"Oh, you will definitely see me again."

As hard as Chanel found it to believe, the gorgeous corporate guy had meant exactly what he said. And not in a business capacity.

He wanted to see *her* again. She hadn't given him her number, but he'd called to invite her to dinner. Which meant he'd gone to the effort to get it. Strange.

And sort of flattering.

Then he'd taken her to an independent film she'd mentioned wanting to see.

Chanel didn't date. She was too awkward, her filters tuned wrong for normal conversation. Even other scientists found her wearing in a social setting.

Only, Demyan didn't seem to care. He never got annoyed with her.

He didn't get offended when she said something she shouldn't have. He didn't shush her in front of others, or try to cut off her curious questioning of their waiter on his reasoning behind recommending certain meals over others.

It was so different than being out with her family that

Chanel found her own awareness of her personal failings diminishing with each hour she spent in Demyan's company.

She'd never laughed so much in the company of another person who wasn't a scientist. Had never felt so comfortable in a social setting with *anyone*.

Tonight they were going to a dinner lecture: *Symmetry Relationships and the Theory of Point and Space Groups*. She'd been wanting to hear this particular visiting lecturer from MIT for a while, but the outing had not been her idea.

Demyan had secured hard-to-come-by tickets for the exclusive gathering and invited her.

She'd been only too happy to accept, and not just because of the lecture. If he'd invited her to one of the charity galas her mother enjoyed so much, Chanel would have said yes, too.

In Demyan's company, even she might have a good time at one of those.

Standing in front of the full-length mirror her mother had insisted Chanel needed as part of her bedroom decor, she surveyed her image critically.

Chanel didn't love designer fashion and rarely dressed up, but no way could she have been raised by her mother and *not* know how to put the glad rags on.

Tonight, she'd gone to a little more effort than on her previous two dates with Demyan. Chanel had felt the first two outings were flukes, anomalies in her life she refused to allow herself to get too excited over.

After all, he would get that glazed look at some point during the evening and then not call again. Everyone did. Only, Demyan hadn't and he had—called, that is.

And maybe, just maybe, she and the corporate geek had a chance at something more than the connection of two bouncing protons.

He understood what she was talking about and spoke in a language she got. Not like most people. It was the most amazing thing.

And she wanted him. Maybe it was being twenty-nine or something, but her body overheated in his presence big-time.

She'd decided that even if their relationship didn't have a future, she wanted it to have everything she could get out of it in the present.

Both her mother and stepfather had made it clear they thought Chanel's chance of finding a lifelong love were about as good as her department getting better funding than the Huskies football program.

Nil.

Deep inside, Chanel was sure they were right. She was too much like her father—and hadn't Beatrice said she'd married him only because she was pregnant with Chanel?

Chanel wasn't trapping anyone into marriage, but she wouldn't mind tripping Demyan into her too-empty bed.

With that in mind, she'd pulled out the stops when dressing for their dinner tonight. Her dress was a hand-me-down Vera Wang from her mother.

It hadn't looked right on the more petite woman's figure, but the green silk was surprisingly flattering to Chanel's five feet seven inches.

The bodice clung to her somewhat generous breasts, while the draping accentuated her waist and the line of her long legs.

It wasn't slutty by any stretch, but it was sexy in a subtle way she trusted Demyan to pick up on. She would usually have worn it with sensible pumps that didn't add more than an inch to her height.

But not tonight. Demyan was nearly six-and-a-half feet

tall; he could deal more than adequately with a companion in three-inch heels.

Chanel had practiced wearing them on and off all day in the lab.

Her colleagues asked if she was doing research for a physics experiment. She'd ignored their teasing and curiosity for the chance to be certain of her ability to walk confidently in the heels.

And she'd discovered it *was* like riding a bike. Her body remembered the lessons her mom had insisted on in Chanel's younger years.

The doorbell rang and she rushed to answer it.

Demyan stood on the other side, his suit a step up from his usual attire on their dates, too.

He adjusted his glasses endearingly and smiled, his mahogany gaze warm on her. "You look beautiful."

Her hand went to the crazy red curls she rarely did much to tame. Tonight she'd used the full regimen of products her mother had given her on her last birthday, along with a lecture about not getting any younger and looking like a rag doll in public. "Thank you."

"Do we have time for a drink before we leave for the dinner?" he asked, even as he herded her back into the small apartment and closed the door behind him.

"Yes, of course." Heat climbed up her neck. "I don't keep alcohol on hand, though."

The look in his eyes could only be described as predatory, but his words were innocuous enough. "Soda will do."

"Iced green tea?" she asked, feeling foolish.

Her mother often complained about the food and drink Chanel kept on hand, using her inadequacies as a hostess to justify the infrequent motherly visits.

Demyan's eyes narrowed as if he could read Chanel's thoughts. "Iced tea is fine."

"It's green tea," she reiterated. Why hadn't she at least bought soda, or something?

"Green tea is healthy."

"Lots of antioxidants," she agreed. "I drink it all the time."

He didn't ask if the caffeine kept her up, but then the man drank coffee with his meals and had gotten a large-size fully caffeinated Coca-Cola at the movie.

"I keep both caffeinated and decaf on hand," she offered anyway.

"I'll take the caffeine. I have a feeling we'll be up late tonight." The look he gave her was hot enough to melt magma.

Suddenly, it felt as if all the air had been sucked out of her apartment's cheerfully decorated living room. "I'll just get our tea."

He moved, his hand landing on her bare arm. "Don't run from me."

"I'm not." How could two simple words come out sounding so breathless?

His hand slid up her arm and over and down again, each inch of travel leaving bursts of sensation along every nerve ending in its wake, landing proprietarily against the small of her back. "I like this dress."

"Thank you." Somehow she was getting closer to him, her feet moving of their own volition, no formed thought in her brain directing them.

"You're wearing makeup."

She nodded. No point in denying it.

"I didn't think you ever did."

"I stopped, except for special occasions, after I moved away from home."

"An odd form of rebellion."

"Not when you have a mother who insists on image

perfection. I wore makeup from sixth grade on, the whole works."

"And you hated it."

"I did."

"Yet you are wearing it now." The hand not resting on her back came up to cup her nape. "For the visiting MIT professor?"

"No."

"I didn't think so." Then Demyan's head lowered, his mouth claiming hers with surprisingly confident kisses.

And she couldn't think at all.

Sparks of pleasure kindled where their lips met and exploded through her in a conflagration of delight. It was only a kiss. He was barely touching her, just holding her, really. And yet she felt like they were in the midst of making love.

Not that she'd actually done the deed, but she'd come close and it hadn't been anything as good or intimate as this single kiss. She'd been naked with a man and felt less sensation, less loss of control.

Small whimpers sounded and she realized they were coming from her. There was no room for embarrassment at the needy sounds. She wanted too desperately.

She'd read about this kind of passion, but thought it was something writers made up, like werewolves and sentient beings on Mars. She had always believed that this level of desire wasn't real.

Before meeting Demyan.

Before this kiss.

The hands on her became sensual manacles, their hold deliciously unbreakable. She didn't *want* to break it. Didn't want to take a single solitary step away from Demyan.

Their mouths moved together, his tongue barely touching hers in the most sensual kind of tasting. He used his hold on her nape to subtly guide her head into the position he wanted and she found it unbearably exciting to be mastered in this small way.

Demyan was one hundred percent in control of the kiss, and Chanel reveled in it with every single one of her sparking nerve centers.

The hand on her waist slid down to cup her bottom. He squeezed. The muscles along her inner walls spasmed with a need she'd never known to this intensity.

She'd been tempted to make love before, but never to the point of overcoming the promise she'd made to herself never to have sex—only to ever make love. In her mind, that had always meant being married and irrevocably committed to the man she shared her body with.

For the first time, she considered it could well mean giving her body to someone she loved.

Not that she loved Demyan. How could she? They barely knew each other.

The feelings inside her had to be lust, but they were stronger than anything she'd ever considered possible.

He kneaded her backside with a sensual assurance she could not hope to show. She tilted her pelvis toward him, needing something she wasn't ready to give a name to. Her hip brushed the unmistakable proof of his excitement; they moaned into one another's mouths, the sounds adding to the press of desire between them.

The knowledge he wanted her, too, poured through her like gasoline on the fire of her desire.

Her hands clutched at his crisp dress shirt as she rocked against him, wanting more, needing something only he could give her. He rocked back against her, the sounds coming from him too feral and sexy for the "normal corporate guy" he was on the outside.

The disparity so matched her own newly discovered

sexual being inside the science geek, the connection she felt with him quadrupled in that moment.

Without warning, he tore his mouth from hers and stepped back, his breathing heavy, his eyes dark and glittery with need. "Now is not the time."

Her own vision hazy with passion, all that she saw in focus was his face, the expression there an odd mixture of confusion and primal sexual need that could not be mistaken.

Even by someone as socially inept as she was.

Why was he confused? Didn't he realize how much she wanted him, too?

"We don't have to go to the dinner." She stated the obvious.

CHAPTER TWO

"NO. WE WILL GO." He took a deep breath, like he was trying to rein in the passion she so desperately wanted him to let loose.

On her.

What would it be like to be the center of the storm she could see swirling in his intent gaze?

Shivering, she knew with absolute certainty that was one query she wanted answered.

"Do not look at me like that," he ordered.

"Like what?"

"You want to be naked," he gritted out as if it was an accusation.

Though how could it be? With the erection pushing so insistently against his dinner trousers, there could be no question his body was on board with hers in the desire department.

More to the point, *she* wanted *him* naked, but she didn't have the moisture in her mouth to say so. She simply nodded a hazy agreement.

"No. We have the dinner. Sex…" He shook his head as if finding something difficult to comprehend. "Sex will come later."

"Please tell me you aren't into delayed gratification." She'd found her voice and cringed at how blunt she'd been, not to mention needy sounding. "It's just that I don't get a lot of gratification at all. I don't want to put it off."

She snapped her mouth shut, biting her lips from the inside to stop any more untoward words from escaping.

Instead of reassuring her that it would be perfectly okay to miss the lecture, and dinner, and anything else that stood between them and making love, he seemed amused by her words. Darn it.

Demyan's mouth curved slightly and the need in his eyes receded a little. "Rest assured when we make love, you will not feel in any way ungratified."

Chanel usually objected to the euphemism of lovemaking for what was essentially a physical act between two people. An act she had heretofore refused to indulge in completely. They weren't in love, so how could they make love?

Only, she found the words of objection stuck in her throat. In fact, she could do nothing but agree with his assertion. "I'm sure."

He might be something of a corporate geek, but his confidence in his sexual prowess was too ingrained not to be well based.

Demyan helped Chanel into her seat, his head still reeling from how quickly he'd lost control with her back at the apartment.

He'd very nearly taken her right there in the living room. No finesse. No seduction. Just raw, consuming, *needy* passion.

Demyan did not do consuming. He did not do need.

Raw exposure of desire was for other men. He didn't hold back, but he didn't lose control either. He was known for showing maximum restraint in the sexual realms, bringing his partners to levels of pleasure they showed great appreciation for.

He did not lose it over a simple kiss.

His tongue had barely penetrated Chanel's mouth. With two layers of clothing between them, their bodies had not been able to touch intimately. He'd still been so close to coming, he'd had to pull away before he shamed himself with a reaction he'd never even evinced in adolescence.

The plan had been to give *her* a small taste of passion before leaving the apartment, to flirt with Chanel in subtly sexual ways over dinner and then leave her after a make-out session that left her wanting more.

Gaining her acquiescence to a hasty marriage with the prenuptial agreement the royal family's lawyers had already drawn up required strict adherence to his carefully thought out strategy.

The plan was to keep her reason clouded by emotion, unfulfilled lust built into consuming desire being the primary element.

He didn't plan to consummate their relationship for another week, at least. He wanted her blinded by her own physical wants, ready to commit to him sexually and emotionally.

Instead, he felt like an untried boy gasping for the chance to feel up under her skirt.

"Are you okay?" Chanel asked, worry in her tone.

Shaking off the disturbing thoughts, he gave her his most winning smile. "Of course. I am here with you, aren't I?"

"Don't say things like that." Her frown was far too serious for his liking.

"Why not, when they are true?"

"They don't *sound* true." There was too much knowing

in her gray eyes for his comfort. "That smile you give me
sometimes, it's just like a plastic mannequin."

How odd that she should claim to know the difference.
No one doubted his sincerity.

A smile was a smile. Except when it wasn't. As he well
knew but had not expected his less-than-socially-adept
companion to. Taken aback, he sat down, noting as he did
so the interested looks of their neighbors.

He turned the smile on them. "What do you say? Am
I sincere?" he asked an older woman wearing something
he was sure fit a lecture hall better than a formal dinner
hosted in the Hilton ballroom.

Her returning smile was the besotted one he was used
to getting from women. Even academics. "Very. Perhaps
your companion can't help her insecurities. Women like
us don't usually snag such lovely escorts."

Chanel made a small, almost wounded sound next to
him.

Before he could respond to it, the short, rather round
man beside the older woman puffed up like a rooster. "Is
that meant to imply that I am not as imposing?"

The woman looked at her date, and the smile she gave
him shone with the kind of emotion Demyan found incomprehensible. "No, you are not, and that's exactly the way I
love you. I would not have married you nearly forty years
ago and stayed this long otherwise."

Feathers suitably smoothed, the man relaxed again in
his chair, even deigning to give a somewhat superior smile
to Demyan before turning to his wife. "Love you, too,
m'dear."

The older couple became obviously lost in a moment
Demyan felt uncomfortable witnessing. He turned his attention to Chanel, only to find her frowning, her expression sad and troubled.

"What is it?"

"She's right. You don't belong with me."

"That is not what she said, Chanel." He put his hand on the green-silk-clad thigh closest to him. "I would say there is great evidence to the contrary."

"What do you mean?"

He did not answer, but his expression was as meaningful as he could make it.

He could tell the exact moment all the tumblers clicked into place in Chanel's scientific brain.

Her eyes widened, color surging up her neck into her face. "That's just chemistry. A kiss hardly constitutes a claim."

On that, he could not agree. Loss of control or not, their kiss had been a definite claim-staking on his part. "I'm surprised a woman of your education would declare there was anything *mere* about chemistry."

"We're *here*."

"And?"

"And if the chemistry was so amazing, we wouldn't be."

He couldn't believe she'd said that. He'd damn near ruined a pair of Armani trousers because of the heat between them.

They were not back at her apartment making love for two important reasons only, and neither had a thing to do with how much he'd wanted what she offered so innocently.

Making love tonight wasn't according to plan. Even if it had been, Demyan would have changed the plan because he'd needed the distance from his passion.

He couldn't tell her that, though. Not even close. "I thought you wanted to hear this lecture."

"I did."

He let one brow quirk.

"I do," she admitted with the truculence of a child, made

all the more charming because he was fairly certain she had not been a truculent child.

Just a very different one than her mother had expected her to be.

From everything he'd learned about her, both from the investigative dossier and herself, Chanel Tanner took after her father, not her mother. Not even a little. Mrs. Saltzman had clearly found that very trying when raising her daughter.

An hour later, Chanel looked up from the furious notes she'd been taking for the past twenty minutes on her smartphone. "I'm enjoying myself. Thank you."

A genuine smile creased his lips. "You're welcome."

He liked seeing her like this, enthusiastic, clearly in her element.

"Dr. Beers has made at least two points I hadn't considered before. They're definitely worth additional consideration and research." Chanel glowed with satisfaction Demyan found oddly enticing.

He liked this confident side of her.

Afterward, Demyan made sure she got the opportunity to talk to not only the visiting lecturer but also the head of the university department overseeing her lab's research.

Her boss, who had attended the dinner as well, kept shooting her accusing glances from across the ballroom.

Demyan observed, "The head of your research is not happy to see you here."

"He doesn't like any of his assistants to make connections outside the department." Chanel didn't sound particularly bothered by that fact.

"That is very shortsighted."

"He's a brilliant scientist, but petty as a human being." She shrugged. "I have no aspirations to run my own lab."

"Why not?"

"Too much politics involved." She looked almost guilty. "I like the science."

That sounded like what Demyan knew of her father. "Why the frown?"

"My mother and stepfather would be a lot happier if I had more ambition, or any at all, really."

"Yes?"

"When Yurkovich Tanner offered my schooling scholarship, they made it clear I could attend any school I wanted to."

This was not news to Demyan, but perhaps she would explain why she'd opted for a local state school when she'd had the brains, the grades and the SAT scores to attend MIT, or the like.

"You graduated from Washington State University."

"It was close to home. I didn't want to move away."

Pity. It might have done both Chanel and her mother a world of good. "You were still looking for a relationship with your mother."

He understood that, though he'd never told another soul. His parents had given him up in everything but name, but he'd never cut ties completely with them.

He'd spent his angst-ridden teen years waiting for them to wake up and realize he was still their son. It hadn't happened and by the time he left to attend university in the States, he'd come to accept it never would.

"I think I still am," Chanel answered with a melancholy he did not like.

"You are very different people."

"I'm the odd one."

"You are not odd." Unique, but not in a bad way.

"I wasn't the daughter she wanted. My younger sister is the much-improved model."

"That's ridiculous. You are exactly as you should be."

"Sometimes even I think you're being sincere."

Once again, she'd startled him. Because she was right. In that moment, he'd been speaking nothing but the truth with no thought of his final agenda.

Chanel wasn't sure of the proper way to go about inviting a man up to her apartment for sex.

Demyan wasn't making it easy, either. She wasn't entirely sure, despite the kiss earlier, that he would accept. He'd been attentive over dinner, made sure she enjoyed herself to the fullest. She'd even caught him giving her that look, the one that said he wanted her.

Only, she got this strange sense that he was holding back.

And not for the same reason she was so uncertain about this whole sex thing. No way was Demyan a virgin.

She couldn't help it—no matter how much her body was clamoring for sexual congress with this man, there was still a part of her that insisted that *act* was supposed to be a special one. Not very scientific of her, she knew.

Everyone from her mother, who had given up on Chanel's nonexistent love life, to friends who could not comprehend her "romanticized view of sex," agreed on one thing. Chanel's virginity was just another sign of how she did not fit into the world around her.

But making love was supposed to be something more than two bodies finding physical release, she was sure of it.

Chanel had never wanted just sex. Wasn't sure what effect it would have on her sense of self if she indulged in it now.

Things looked different at twenty-nine than they had at nineteen, though.

She should be more relaxed about the prospect of casually sharing her body with another person. She wasn't.

If anything, the older she got the more important she realized each human connection she made was. Sex was *supposed* to be the ultimate act of intimacy.

She had to admit she'd never felt the bone-deep connection with the few men in her past that she'd felt in that single kiss with Demyan.

She wasn't stupid. She knew losing the two people in her life who had loved her unconditionally at the tender age of eight had made her reticent about opening up to others, particularly men.

Her father and grandfather.

Chanel's stepfather hadn't loved her at all, never mind without limits. As for her mother, Chanel was twenty-nine and the jury was still out on that one.

Which, as an adult woman, had nothing to do with the question of if and how Chanel should offer her invitation to Demyan.

His car slid to a halt by the curb outside her apartment building. He cut the engine, reaching to unclip his belt in one smooth move.

Maybe she wouldn't have to figure it out, after all.

"You're coming up?"

"I will see you to your door."

"It's not necessary." She could have smacked herself. "I mean, only if you want to."

Oh, that was so much better.

One dark brow lifted as he pushed his door open. "Have I ever left you to see yourself inside?"

"It's only our third date." Hardly enough time to set a precedent in stone.

Her own words hit her with the force of a solid particle mass traveling beyond the speed of light. What was she thinking? *Sex with him when they'd barely spent more than a minute in each other's company?*

Still remembering the pleasure of his kiss earlier, her body screamed *yes* while her mind sounded a warning Klaxon of *nos.*

No closer to a verdict about how to handle the rest of the night, she stalled in frozen indecision.

Her door was opened and Demyan bent toward her in his too-darn-sexy dinner suit, his hand reaching toward her. "Are you coming?"

She fumbled with her seat belt, getting it unbuckled after the second try.

The knowing look in his dark eyes said he knew why she was so uncoordinated.

"Don't," she ordered.

The knowing glance turned into a smirk. "Don't?"

"You're smug," Chanel accused as she climbed from the car, eschewing the help of his hand.

Ignoring her attempt to keep her distance, he put his hand around her waist, tucking her body close to his as they approached her building. "I am delighted by your company."

Heat arced between them and, that quickly, she remembered why after only three dates she was ready to break a lifetime habit of virginity.

"I'm still not sure why we're here."

"You live here?" Amusement laced his voice as he led her into the unsecured building.

The lack of a doorman was a bone of contention between Chanel and her mother. If the older woman had been concerned for her safety, Chanel might have considered moving, but the issue was in how it *looked* for her to live in an unpretentious, entirely suburbanite apartment complex.

"I do not like the fact that the entrance to your home is so accessible. This dark cove outside your door is not entirely secure, either," Demyan complained as he took her keys and unlocked the door.

She hadn't quite decided if the action was some throwback to old-world charm or simply indicative of his dominating nature when he ushered her inside.

They moved into the living room and he shut the door behind them. There was meaning in that, right? The shut door. If he'd wanted only to see her inside, he could have left her on the landing.

"Would you like a drink or something?" Like her?

Was she really going to do this? Chanel thought maybe she was.

"Not tonight." The words implied he planned to leave, but the way he stepped closer to her gave an entirely different meaning.

She didn't reply, his proximity stealing her breath just that fast. For the first time in her life, she began to understand *how* her mother, Beatrice, had ended up pregnant by a man so very different from herself.

Sex *was* a powerful force. "Body chemistry is so much more potent than I ever believed." She sounded every bit as bewildered as she felt.

"Because you have never felt it so strongly with someone else." There was no question mark at the end of *that* sentence.

Chanel would take umbrage at the certainty in his tone if Demyan didn't speak the absolute truth.

"I'm sure *you* have."

Something strange moved across his features. Surprise? Maybe confusion. "No."

"You stopped earlier, not me."

"It was not easy."

Was that supposed to make her feel better about the fact he'd been more determined to go to the lecture than *she'd* been? Sarcasm infused her voice as she said, "I'm glad to hear that."

His eyes narrowed, a spark of irritation showing before it disappeared. She wasn't surprised. Demyan might not be the corporate shark her stepfather was, but he was not a man who liked to lose control, either.

Not that he had. Now, *or* earlier.

He had stopped after all, and right now, as much as she could read desire in his dark gaze, he wasn't acting on it.

She, on the other hand, was seconds away from kissing him silly. She, who had never initiated a kiss in her life.

"Do you want to stay?" she asked baldly.

Subtlety was all well and good for a woman who found the role of flirt comfortable, but that woman wasn't Chanel.

He smiled down at her. "Do you want me to?"

"I don't know."

Shock held his face immobile for the count of three seconds. *"You don't know?"*

She shook her head.

"You didn't seem unsure about what you wanted earlier tonight." Disbelief laced his voice.

She nodded, making no attempt to deny it. Subterfuge was not her thing. "I barely know you."

"Is that how it feels to you?"

She experienced that strange sense of disparity she'd had with him before. The words were right, the expression concurrent and yet, she felt the lack of sincerity.

Only, unlike at the dinner, there was a vein of honesty in his words that confused her.

"You already know you could take me to bed with very little effort."

"I assure you, the effort will not be minimal." Sensual promise vibrated in every word.

Chanel felt his promise to her very core and her thighs

squeezed together in involuntary response, not because she feared what he wanted but because it made her ache with a need she'd never known.

"That's not what I meant." Her voice cracked on the last word, but she pretended not to notice.

The slight flaring of his nostrils and the way his eyes went just that much darker said he had, though. "What did you mean then, *little one?*"

"I'm hardly little." At five foot seven, she was above average in height for a woman.

"Do not avoid the question."

"I wasn't trying to." She'd just been trying to clarify, because that was familiar territory.

The rest of this? Was not.

Only he knew how tall she was, so if he wanted to call her *little one,* maybe that was okay. "I suppose I do seem kind of short to you. You're not exactly average height for a man in North America, though maybe I should be comparing you to Ukrainians, as that's your country's formative gene pool."

In fact, he was well above average height, certainly taller than most of the men in her life, and that gave her a peculiar kind of pleasure. Which, like many things she'd discovered since meeting him, surprised her about herself.

She'd never thought she would enjoy feeling *protected* when she was with a man, or that the difference in their height would even succeed in making her feel that way. Maybe it wasn't just that difference but something else about Demyan entirely.

Something intangible that didn't quite match his casual designer sweaters and dark-rimmed glasses.

"You do not seem *short.*" He tugged at one of her red curls, a soft smile playing about his lips as if he could read her thoughts and was amused by them. "You are just right."

This time there was no conflict between the words and sincerity in his manner.

But it put the times there was in stark relief in her mind. "I can't make you out."

"What do you mean?" He looked surprised again and she got the definite impression that didn't happen a lot with him.

"Sometimes I think you mean everything you say, but then there are times, like at dinner tonight, when it seems like you're saying what you think I want to hear."

"I have not lied to you." Affront echoed through his tone.

"Haven't you?"

"No." Dead certainty, and then almost as if it was drawn from him without his permission, "I have not told you everything about myself."

"I didn't expect you to bring along an information dossier on our first date." Of course she didn't know everything about him; that was part of the dating process, wasn't it? "You don't know everything about me, either."

His gaze turned cold, almost ruthless. Then he adjusted his glasses and the look disappeared. "I know what I need to."

Sometimes there was a glimmer of another man there— a man that even a shark like Perry would swim from in a frantic effort to escape. Then Demyan would smile and the impression of that other man would dissipate.

CHAPTER THREE

DEMYAN DIDN'T SMILE now, but she knew the man in front of her wasn't a shark.

Not like the overcritical Perry, and definitely not like someone even more ruthless than her stepfather. There was too much kindness in Demyan, even if he was wholly unaware of it, as Chanel suspected he was.

"What did you mean earlier?" he asked, pulling her back to the original question.

Oh, yes…right.

"It's just…you must realize I'm a sure thing. Even if I'm not sure I *want* to be."

"Why aren't you sure?" he asked, deflecting himself this time.

Or maybe he just really wanted to know. Being the center of someone else's undivided attention when she wasn't discussing her work wasn't something Chanel was used to.

When she was with Demyan, he focused solely on her, though, as if nothing was more important to him. He wanted to know things others reacted to with impatience, not interest. It was a heady feeling.

Even so, peeling away the layers to reveal her full self to him wasn't easy. "You'll laugh."

"Is it funny?"

"Not to me." Not even a little.

"Then I will not laugh."

"How can you be so perfect?"

"So long as I am perfect for you, that is all that matters."

"Do you mean that?"

"Yes." There could be no doubting the conviction in his tone or handsome features.

"Why?"

"Are you saying you feel differently?" he asked in a tone that implied he knew the answer.

"Love at first sight doesn't happen."

"Maybe for some people it does."

All the breath seemed to leave the room at his words. "Are you saying..." She had to clear her throat, suck in air and try again. "Are you saying you feel the same?"

"I want to be your perfect man."

"You mean that." And maybe it was past time she stopped doubting his sincerity.

How much of her feeling he was saying what she wanted to hear stemmed from her own insecurities? Why was it so hard for her to accept that this man didn't need her to be something or someone different to want to be with her?

The answer was the years spent in a family she simply didn't fit, the daughter of a mother and stepfather who found constant fault with a child too much like her own father for their comfort.

"I do."

She nodded, accepting. Believing. "I've never had sex."

Once again she'd managed to shock him. And this time she didn't have to look for subtle signs.

His whisker-shadowed jaw dropped and dark eyes widened comically. "You are twenty-nine."

"I'm not staring retirement in the face, or something." She had eleven more years of relatively safe childbearing, even.

Not that she thought she was going to marry and have children. She'd given up on that idea when she realized that even in the academic world, Chanel was a social misfit.

"No, I didn't mean that." But his voice was still laced with surprise and his superior brain was clearly *not* firing on all cylinders. "You're educated. *American.*"

"So?" What in the world did her PhD in chemistry have to do with her virginity?

"Are you completely innocent?"

Man, did he even realize how that sounded?

And people thought she was old-fashioned. "Even if I'd had sex, I would still be innocent. Sex isn't a crime."

"You know that is not what I was referring to."

"No, I know, but *innocent?* Come on."

The look he was giving her was way too familiar.

"I'm awkward," she excused with a barely stifled sigh. "I told you." Had he forgotten?

"You are refreshingly direct." That wasn't disappointment in his tone and the look she thought she recognized.

Well, it wasn't. He almost looked admiring. If she believed it, and hadn't she diced to do just that? "Mother calls it ridiculously blunt."

"Your mother does not see you as I do."

"I should hope not."

They both smiled at her small joke that did nothing to dissipate the emotional tension between them.

He put his big hands on her shoulders, his thumbs brushing along her collarbone, the hold possessive like before. And just like earlier, she found a new unexpected part of her that liked that. A lot.

"Demyan." His name just sighed out of her.

She didn't know what she meant by it. What she wanted from him.

He didn't appear similarly lost, his gaze direct and commanding. "You say you've never had sex. I want to know what that means."

It took two tries to get words past her suddenly constricted throat. "Why does it matter?"

"You can ask that?"

"Um, yes." Hadn't she just done?

"You are mine."

"Three dates," she reminded him.

"Love at first sight," he countered.

"You… I…"

"We are going to make love. What I want to know is what you have done to this point." His thumbs continued the sensual caress along her collarbone. "You are going to tell me."

"Bossy much?"

"Only in bed."

She wasn't sure she believed him, was even less sure if it mattered. She wasn't worried about standing up for herself. She'd never conformed when it counted, no matter how much easier it would have made her life—especially with her family.

Right now she found she wanted to answer his question, needed to. Still, she kept it general. "Heavy petting, I guess you'd say."

"Be more specific."

"No." Heat crawled up her neck.

He shouldn't care, should he? Virginity wasn't an issue for modern men. *Or modern women,* her inner voice mocked her, *and yet you are a virgin.*

He bent so close their lips almost touched. "Oh, yes."

Thoughts came and went, no words making it past her lips until she made a sound she'd never heard from her own vocal cords before. It was something like surrender, but more.

It was sexual.

The air between them grew heavy with the most primal kind of desire, pushing against her, demanding her acquiescence.

In a last-ditch desperate bid for space, she shut her eyes, but it did no good. She could feel his stare. Could feel his determination to get an answer.

She was super sensitive to his nearness, too, her body aching to press against his, her lips going soft in preparation for his kiss.

The kiss didn't come.

"Tell me," puffed across her lips.

The sound of his voice whispered through her, increasing the sensual fire burning through her veins.

"It wasn't anything."

"Were you naked?"

"Once."

"Good." He kissed her, his lips barely there and gone before she could lose herself in the caress she wanted more than air or research funding. "When?"

"In college."

He just waited.

"He told me he loved me." She'd wanted to be loved so badly, she realized later.

"You didn't let him into your body."

"No."

"Why?"

"It didn't feel right." Old pain twisted through her heart.

She turned her head away, stepping back when a few seconds before she would have said she wasn't capable of moving at all, much less away from him.

"He hurt you." The growl in Demyan's voice made Chanel's eyes snap open, her gaze searching for him, for visual proof of what had been in his tone.

The anger in his eyes wasn't directed at her, but it still made Chanel shiver. "He broke up with me."

Her ex had called her a dried-up relic, a throwback woman who belonged in a medieval nunnery, not a modern university. Chanel had a lot of experience with disappointing her family, so her ex-boyfriend's words should not have had the power to wound.

She should have been inured.

But they'd cut her deeply, traumatically so.

She'd never shared with another person the experience that had left her convinced her mother and stepfather were right, had never admitted her ultimate failure.

"I'm hopeless with men." What was she doing here, wanting to give her body to a man destined to eviscerate her heart?

He wasn't ever going to stay with her. He said they were going to make love, but they couldn't. He didn't love her, no matter what his words had implied. He couldn't.

She wasn't that woman.

Chanel wasn't a bubbly blonde beauty like her sister, Laura. She wasn't a cool sophisticate like her mother. Chanel was the awkward one who could make perfect marks in chemistry courses but utterly fail at the human kind.

She shook her head, her hands cold and shaking. "You should leave."

Another primal sound of anger came out of him before he crossed the small distance between them and yanked her body into his with tender ruthlessness. "I'm not going anywhere. Not tonight. Not ever."

"You can't make promises like that." His breaking them was going to destroy something inside her that her parents and ex had been unable to touch.

The belief that she was worth *something*.

"I can."

"What? You're going to marry me?" she demanded with pain-filled sarcasm.

"Yes."

She couldn't breathe, her vision going black around the edges. Words were torn from her, but they came out in barely a whisper. "You don't mean that."

He cupped the back of her head, forcing her gaze to meet his. "I do."

"You can't."

"I am a man of my word."

"Always?" she mocked, not believing.

No one kept all their promises. Especially not to her. Hadn't her father told her he'd always be there for her? But then he'd died. Her mother had promised, in the aftermath of Jacob Tanner's death, that she and Chanel would always be a team, that she wouldn't leave her daughter, wouldn't die like her husband.

Beatrice *hadn't* died, but she'd abandoned Chanel emotionally within a year of her marriage to Perry, making it clear from that point on that the only team was the Saltzmans'. Chanel Tanner had no place on it.

"Try me," Demyan demanded, no insecurity about the future in *his* words.

"You'll destroy me."

"No."

"Men like you…" Her words ran out as her heart twisted at the thought of never seeing him again.

"Know our own minds." There was that look in his eyes again.

As if he was a man who always got what he set out to, no matter what he had to do to get it. As if she might as well give in because he *never* would.

"I wanted to wait until I got married. I didn't want to trap someone into a lifetime they would only resent."

"There are such things as birth control."

"My mom was on the Pill when she got pregnant with me. I was not part of her future plans. Neither was my father."

"She didn't have to marry him."

"She loved him. At first." Chanel didn't know when that had changed.

She'd been only eight when her dad died, but she'd believed her parents loved each other deeply and forever. It was her mother's constant criticism and unfavorable comparisons later that made Chanel realize Beatrice had not approved of her husband any more than she did their daughter.

"They were not compatible." Demyan said it like he really knew—not that he could.

"I thought they were, when I was little. I was wrong," she admitted.

"We aren't them. We are compatible."

"You don't know that."

"I know more than you think I do. We belong together." There was a message in his words she couldn't quite decipher, but his dark gaze wasn't giving any hints.

"I told you I was a sure thing." Though she wasn't sure that was true. Part of her was still fighting the idea of total intimacy, especially at the cost of opening herself up like this. "You don't have to say these things."

"I am not a man who makes a habit of saying things I do not mean."

"You never lie." He'd as good as said so earlier.

Something passed across his handsome features. "I have not lied to you."

His implication was unbelievable. "You really plan to marry me. After three dates?"

"Yes." There was so much certainty, such deep conviction in that single word.

She could not doubt him, but it didn't make sense. Her scientific brain could not identify the components of the formula of their interaction that had led to this reaction.

In her lab she knew mixing one substance with another and adding heat, or cold, or simply agitation resulted in identifiable and documented results.

Love wasn't like that. There was nothing predictable about the male-female interaction, especially for her.

But one thing she knew—a man could not hide his true reaction to a woman in bed. It was why she'd refused her ex back at university. He hadn't been completely into it.

Oh, he'd wanted to get off, but she could tell that it didn't matter it was *her* he was getting off with.

"Show me," she challenged Demyan now. "Make me believe."

His eyes narrowed, but he didn't pretend not to understand what she wanted.

Demyan could not let Chanel's challenge go unmet.

Whatever the cretin who had turned her off sex had done to her, at least part of her thought Demyan would do the same thing. He could see it in the wary depths of her gray eyes.

"You will see, *sérdeńko.* I am not that guy."

"You keep calling me little." She didn't sound as if she was complaining, just observing.

He noticed she did that when the emotions got too intense. She retreated behind the barrier of her analytical mind.

When this night was over there would be no barriers between them.

"You speak Ukrainian." Her dossier had mentioned she studied the language, but not how proficient she was.

To translate the endearment, which was a diminutive form of heart, implied a far deeper knowledge of his native tongue than the investigative report had revealed.

"I studied it so I could read scientific texts by notable scientists in their native tongue."

"And *sérdeńko* came up in a scientific text?" he asked with disbelief.

"No." She sighed as if admitting a dark secret. "I like languages. I'm fluent in Ukrainian, Portuguese and German."

"So you could read scientific texts."

"Among other things." She blushed intriguingly.

"What things?" he asked, his mouth temptingly close to hers.

He wanted to kiss her. She wanted the kiss, too—there could be no doubt.

"Erotic romance."

"In Ukrainian?" he asked, utterly surprised for the third time that night.

This woman would never be a boring companion.

"Yes."

"I am amazed."

"Why?"

"If you like reading about sex so much, how are you still a virgin?"

"I like reading murder mysteries, too, but I haven't gone out and killed anybody."

He laughed, unable to remember the last time he'd been so entertained by a female companion.

This marriage he had to bring about would not be a hardship. Chanel Tanner would make a very amiable wife.

With that thought in mind, he took the first step in convincing her that they belonged together.

He kissed her, taking command of her mouth more gently than he might have before her revelation.

She couldn't know it, but her virginity was a gift to him in more ways than one.

First, that he was the only man who would ever share her body in this way was not something to take lightly. Not even in this modern age.

But second, and more important to his efforts on behalf of Volyarus, once Demyan had awakened her passions for the first time, Chanel would be more likely to accept his proposal of marriage.

It meant adjusting his schedule up for her seduction, but he wasn't leaving her tonight. Doing so might cause irreparable harm to the building of trust between them. She needed to know he wanted her, and he did.

Unlikely as he would have considered it, he desired this shy, bookish scientist above all other women.

She didn't want to believe in forever with him, but she would learn. He had spoken the truth earlier. Prince Demyan of Volyarus did not break his promises.

And he had promised King Fedir that Demyan would marry Chanel Tanner.

She whimpered against his lips, her sexual desire so close to the surface he thought she needed her first climax to come early so she could enjoy the lead-up to the next one.

With careful precision, he built the kiss until the small sounds of need were falling from her lips to his in a steady cascade. Control starting to slip, he deepened the kiss, wanting more of her taste, more of her response...more of everything Chanel had to give.

A small voice in the back of his mind prompted that the time had come to pull back and lead her into the bedroom.

Only, his lips didn't want to obey, and for the first time in memory Demyan found himself lost in a kiss, his plans for a suave seduction cracking under the weight of his more primitive need.

He had just the presence of mind to move her backward toward the sofa. Unbelievably, *neither* of them was going to be able to stay vertical much longer.

Demyan maneuvered them both so Chanel sat sprawled across his lap, her dress hiked up, her naked thighs pressing against his cloth-covered ones.

He never let her lips slide so much as a centimeter away from his.

Demyan liked sex. According to Maks, he'd had more than his fair share of partners. Some of them were very experienced in the art of seduction, women who knew exactly how to use their bodies for maximum effect. None of them had turned him on as much as the uncalculated and wholly honest way Chanel responded to his kiss.

She moved with innocent need against him, her body undulating in unconscious sensuality that drove him insane with the need to show her what those types of movements led to.

He brought his hand down and cupped her backside, guiding those untutored rolls of her hips into something that would give them both more pleasure and fan the flames of desire between them into an all-out inferno.

She jolted and moaned as her panty-clad apex rubbed over his trapped hard-on. He couldn't hold back his own sounds of raw sexual desire and keep from arching his hips to increase the friction.

The kiss went nuclear and he did nothing to stop it, demanding entrance into her mouth with his tongue and getting it without even a token resistance.

This woman did not play the coquette. Her honest passion was more exciting than any practiced seduction could be. She couldn't know, though; she was too unused to physical intimacy. For that ignorance, at least, he could be glad.

She could not take advantage of a weakness she did not recognize in him, and damned if he would point it out. He might not be able to control himself completely this first time with her, but no doubt that was a big part of the reason why.

It *was* her first time and he found that highly erotic.

The one benefit was that it was clear Chanel was completely out of control and definitely imprinting on him sexually.

Equally important, after what she'd revealed, was for her to realize *he* wanted *her*.

As she'd demanded, he would show her.

She would never again doubt her feminine appeal to him, not after tonight. And perhaps that, even more than her virginity, would lead her to accept his speed-record-breaking proposal when it came.

That it might no longer be completely about his duty to country was a thought he dismissed as unimportant.

He would have her. She would have him and whether she knew it or not, she needed him. He was good for her.

It started with now, giving her what she hadn't realized she was missing.

After insuring she kept the rhythm that made her body shake, he mapped her body with his hands through the soft green silk of her dress, caressing her in ways reserved for a lover.

He enjoyed this part of sex, touching a woman in ways no one else was allowed and, in Chanel's case, never had been.

Knowing a woman had put her body in his very-capable-to-dole-out-pleasure hands turned him on. Demyan liked *that* control, too. For reasons he didn't feel the need to dwell on, that knowledge was even more satisfying with Chanel than it had been with other women.

She might not realize it, but the kind of response she gave meant she would let him do *anything.* That acknowledgment came with a heady kind of enjoyment destined to undermine his self-control further if he wasn't very careful.

It was important for her pleasure, particularly this first time, that he not let that happen. He had to maintain some level of premeditation, or he could hurt her.

That reminder sobered him enough to think—at least a little—again.

Touching her was good, though. Too damn good.

He cupped her breasts, reveling in the catch of her breath as his thumbs brushed over turgid nipples. He wanted to feel them naked, but even this was incredible.

His sex pressed against the placket of his trousers in response to the feel of her in his hands.

He pinched, knowing the layers of silk and her bra would be no true barrier between those buds and the sensation he gave her.

She tore her mouth from his, her eyes opening, pupils blown with bliss almost swallowing the stormy irises. "I… That…"

"Is good." He did it again, increasing the pressure just enough to give maximum pleasure that might border on pain but would never go over. "Say it."

CHAPTER FOUR

CONFUSION FLITTED ACROSS the sweet oval of Chanel's face. "What?"

"Say it feels good."

She didn't have to speak her refusal—it was there in the way her body stiffened and she averted her gaze.

"Look at me," he demanded, his fingers poised to give more pleasure but not offering it. "Look at me and say it."

Her storm-cloud gaze came back to his, her mouth working, no words coming out.

"You are a woman. You can acknowledge your own pleasure, Chanel. I believe in you."

"It's not that." The word cut off as if her air had run out. She took a deep breath and let it out, her tongue coming out to wet her lips. "I know sex is supposed to feel good."

"Do you?"

"I've read books."

"Erotic books."

"Yes."

"So, say it."

"You want to strip me bare," she accused.

He saw no point in denying it. "Yes."

"Why?"

"You have to let go."

"You never let go."

"I am the experienced one here. If I let go of my control, we'd both be in trouble."

"That doesn't make sense."

"Only because you haven't done this before."

She didn't deny his words. "I like it."

"I know." He pressed just slightly, giving her a taste of what was to come.

She moaned, her head falling back, her eyelids sliding down to cover the vulnerability in her gaze. "So, why do I have to say it?"

"For me. Say it for me."

"It feels good." The words came out in a low, throaty whisper infused with sincerity.

Oh, yes, this woman would learn to hold nothing back.

He rewarded her with more pleasure until she was rocking against him with gasping breaths. "Demyan!"

"What, *sérdeńko?*"

"You know! You have to know."

"This?" he asked as he pushed up to rub his hardness against her, pinching her nipples at the same time.

"Yes."

He did it again, making sure to continue the friction against that bundle of nerves through the damp silk of her panties. "Let go, Chanel."

"I…"

He didn't want arguments. He wanted her surrender. "Come for me, Chanel. You are mine."

And unused to this level of pleasure, she came apart, her body arching into a stiff contortion of delight while a keening wail sounded from her throat.

Oh, yes, this woman belonged to him. Her body knew it, even if her mind was still in some doubt.

He let the shivers of aftershock finish, concentrating on gaining his own breath and a measure of mental fortitude. When he was sure he could do it without his own limbs giving way, he tucked one arm under her bottom and the other against her back and stood with her secure in his hold.

Her head rose from where it had come to rest against his shoulder, her face still flushed with pleasure, her gray gaze meeting his. "What… Where?"

"Your first time will not happen on a sofa, no matter how comfortable."

"It already did."

He shook his head. "That was not sex."

"But it was my first orgasm with another person."

Perhaps that small fact helped to explain why she was still a virgin, too.

He didn't repeat his shock at her age, or his disgust with her previous partners. "It will be the first of many, I promise you."

She swallowed audibly, but nodded with appreciative enthusiasm.

He felt his mouth curve into a very rare and equally genuine smile.

How had she remained untouched so long?

This woman was sweetly sensual and engagingly honest. Far from socially inept. Demyan found her fascinating.

It did not bother him at all, though, that she would be giving her body to him and only him. He would honor the gift and she would find no reason to regret it.

He made the vow to himself, and Demyan never broke his word. Chanel was still trying to catch her breath when Demyan laid her oh so carefully on the bed after yanking back the covers.

Sexual demand radiated off him like heat from a nuclear reactor. Yet there was no impatience in the way he handled her.

The bedding? Yes. It lay in disarray on the floor, his powerful jerks pulling the sheet and blanket that had been tucked between the mattress and box spring completely away.

But her?

He settled with a gentle touch that belied his obvious masculine need.

"I was going to wait." He shrugged out of his suit jacket, letting the designer garment drop to the floor without any outward concern about what that might do to it.

"Why?"

"It seemed the thing to do."

"Because things are moving so fast between us," she said rather than asked.

He only loosened his tie and undid the top buttons on his shirt before pulling the whole thing over his head in one swift movement. "We will not be waiting."

His torso was chiseled in that way really fit men with natural strength were. Dark curls covered his chest, narrowing into a V that disappeared into the waistband of his trousers. She wanted to see where that trail of sexy hair led.

She might be a virgin, but she was pretty sure she wasn't a shy one.

"You are beautiful," she breathed.

"Men are not beautiful." But his eyes smiled at the compliment.

"The statue of David is beautiful."

"That is art."

"So are you."

He shook his head, his hands going to his trouser button. "I am a flesh-and-blood man, never doubt it."

How could she, with all that flesh staring her in the face?

His trousers slid down his legs, revealing CK black knit

boxers that conformed to every ridge of muscle and the biggest ridge of all. His erection.

Her mouth went dry, the moisture going straight to her palms. "You're big, aren't you?"

"I've never compared myself to other men." With that he shucked out of his boxers, leaving his very swollen, very rigid length on display.

"According to scientific studies, the average penile length is five to five-point-seven inches in length when erect." And Demyan was definitely longer, unless her eyes were deceiving her.

But Chanel was a scientist who had conducted enough measurements she could usually guess within a centimeter's accuracy.

He frowned and stopped at the side of the bed, his erection bobbing with the movement even as it curved upward toward his belly. That wasn't usual, either, she'd read. Most men erected perpendicularly with a slight leaning toward one side. Some even had a small downward angle.

For Demyan's hardness to be curving upward, it had to be *extremely* ready for intercourse.

"How do you know that?" he demanded with amusement in his voice.

"I read. A lot."

"You cannot believe everything you read in your Ukrainian erotica."

"Of course not."

His brow rose, the mockery there.

"I read that particular fact in a scientific journal."

His dark gaze pinned her to the bed, though he had yet to join her with his incredibly gorgeous naked body. "We have better things to do than discuss frivolous scientific research."

"It isn't frivolous to the tens of thousands of men who

have been feeling inadequate because of the supposed average lengths gleaned from self-measurement."

"What you are telling me is that men measure themselves as larger than they are?" He definitely sounded amused now.

"I don't think *you* would."

"I would not measure myself at all." From his tone, he found the idea of doing so absolutely ridiculous.

"I think I'd like to measure you."

"No."

"With my hand."

The erection in question jumped at her words and it was her turn to smile.

"Do not tease," he warned.

"I'm not teasing."

"You are smiling."

"I'm just really happy that you react to me so strongly." So strongly in fact that despite the fact she'd led them down one of the conversational byways that always annoyed others, his visible response to her had not dimmed in the least.

"You are a very sexy woman."

She couldn't help laughing at that assertion, but she didn't accuse him of lying. Honest desire burned in the brown depths of his eyes.

"It is time I did something about your lack of focus." He didn't sound mad about it, though.

She just nodded, wanting more of what they'd done in the living room, more kisses, more touching, more of that amazingly intimate connection.

"First we need to get you naked, too."

She'd already kicked her heels off in the living room and she wasn't wearing panty hose. That didn't leave much to get rid of.

She started tugging her skirt up, only to have his hands

join her in the effort. Only somehow he made the slide of silk up her body into a series of sensual caresses, so she was shivering with renewed passion by the time he pulled the green fabric over her head.

He tossed it away.

"My mother would be very annoyed if she saw you treating clothes the way you do." Especially high-end designer ones.

"Your mother has no place in our bedroom."

"It's not *our* bedroom."

"You belong to me. This room belongs to you. Therefore, it is ours."

She couldn't push a denial of his claim through her lips. There was too much truth to it.

It was almost scary, but she wasn't afraid.

In fact, that part of her that had felt alone in the world since her mother's marriage to Perry Saltzman warmed with an inexplicable sense of belonging.

"She's still my mother," was all Chanel could think to say.

"And she always will be, but her views and opinions about you are skewed by grief and a lack of understanding. Therefore, they have no place in our life together."

"We don't have a life together," she said with more vehemence than she felt.

But it was insane, this instant connection, his claim he planned a future with her. It just wasn't real. Couldn't be.

"We do. It starts with this." His hands reached behind her to unhook her bra clasp, sight unseen.

Her nipples, already tightened into hard points from his earlier manipulations, contracted further from the cooled air brushing across them.

There was no stifling the shiver that went through her in response to the extra stimulation.

His smile was predatory. "You have very sensitive breasts."

"Nipples," she couldn't help correcting. It wasn't her entire boob responding, was it?

He brushed his fingertips along the side of her breast, sliding forward, but not touching the nipple.

Desire coiled low in her belly, her body arching toward his.

He did it again. "Very responsive."

"You don't like to be wrong, do you?" she asked in a voice that hitched every other syllable with her gasping breaths.

"It is a rare occurrence."

"Arrogant."

"Certain."

"Same thing."

"It is not." Then he kissed her, preventing any more words.

It was a sneaky way to end an argument, but she couldn't make herself mind. Not when it felt so wonderful. It might be only their lips that were connected, but she felt as if he was touching her to the very depths of her soul.

He pulled back, their breath coming in harsh gasps between them. "One thing left."

"What?" she asked, nothing but his lips making any sense in that moment.

"Your panties."

Were surplus to requirements. She got the picture but found she was hopeless in the face of doing something about it.

It was okay, though. His long masculine fingers were sliding between her hips and the silk and then it was being tugged down, baring the last bit of her to him.

"There will be nothing between us," he growled, as if he could read her mind.

She looked up at him, their gazes locking, and what she saw in his left her in no doubt he *wasn't* just talking about clothing.

He'd pushed her in the living room, demanding she acknowledge her own pleasure, her own desires, this crazy thing happening between them.

He was going to push her further now.

"It's just sex," she claimed with a desperate attempt to believe her own words.

"We are making love, locking our lives together."

"This isn't real."

"It is very real."

"Please…"

He cupped her face, the move one she was becoming quite familiar with and incidentally learning to love. "Please, what?"

"Just tonight? Can it just be about tonight?"

He lowered his head until their lips almost brushed. "No."

This time, she kissed him. Couldn't help herself and was glad she hadn't when he took control and drew forth a response from her body that shouldn't have been possible. Not after she'd just climaxed.

Only it was.

It was as if they were connected by live electric current, energizing, transforming every synapse in its wake, so that her body was uniquely tuned to him. The way that big body blanketed hers, his hardness rubbing against the sensitive curls at the apex of her thighs indicated he was being tuned to the same frequency.

A frequency she thought would rule her body's responses for the rest of her life.

And if she could believe his words, it would.

The kiss pulled her out of time, suspending them in an intimacy that had no limits, not in hours and minutes, or in emotional connection.

It was beyond anything she thought two people could feel together.

His hands were everywhere, bringing pleasure, teaching her body his touch, making that indescribable pleasure spiral tighter and tighter inside her again.

She touched him, too, letting her fingertips learn his body, and just doing that gave her a level of delight she'd never known. She could caress this man, touch his naked skin and he wanted it, wanted *her* touch. Not just any woman's. *Hers.*

An empty ache started, making her body restless for what it had never known.

As if he knew exactly what she needed, he nudged her thighs apart and adjusted his body so the head of his erection pressed against the opening to her body. However, he made no move to enter her.

The moment felt so momentous that tears washed into her eyes and trickled down her temples. He broke the kiss, lifting his head, his expression knowing.

He touched the wetness, wiping at the tears with one finger. "It is not just about tonight."

"It's not supposed to be this big."

"You have waited twenty-nine years, *krýxitka.*"

She wasn't a baby, not by any stretch, but having him call her one didn't feel wrong. "But women don't, anymore."

"You had your reasons."

"I want this."

"I know."

"You do, too."

"Yes."

"With *me*," she confirmed, maybe needing a little more reassurance than she'd realized.

"Only *you* from this point forward."

"You do not believe in infidelity?" A lot of businessmen thought it was their right when they flew out of town to leave their wedding ring in the bedside drawer of their hotel rooms.

Or so she'd read. Honestly, as awful as Perry might be toward Chanel, she couldn't imagine him cheating on her mother. It was one of the reasons she respected him, even if she didn't like the business shark.

She could never respect a man who didn't understand and adhere to the true meaning of loyalty and faithfulness.

"It is too damaging to everyone involved." There was something about Demyan's tone that said he knew exactly what he was talking about.

She would have asked about it, but right now all she could really focus on was how much she needed him inside her. "It's time."

"Not yet."

Unexpected anger welled up. "You're not going to get bossy about this. I'm not begging."

"I don't want you begging. Tonight."

"But—"

He smiled down at her, indulgence and tenderness she wasn't even sure he was aware of glowing in his dark gaze. "You are a virgin. A certain amount of preparation will make the difference between a beautiful experience and one you never want to have to remember."

"You make it sound so dire."

"It can be."

"Much experience deflowering virgins?" she asked with sarcasm and maybe just a hint of jealousy.

"Tonight is not the time for discussing past sexual encounters."

"That isn't what you said earlier."

His jaw hardened but he said, "Fine. She was young. I was young. It was a disaster."

"Did you love her?"

"Not even a little."

"Did she love you?"

"No." No doubt there.

"You decided to figure out how to fix the problem." She could so see him doing that.

She might not know everything there was to about this man, but some of his basic characteristics she understood very well.

He nodded even as he shifted again so there was room for his hand to get between them. A single finger gently rubbed along her wet folds.

"That feels good," she whispered.

"It is supposed to."

The touch moved up, circling her clitoris. It felt so delicious she gasped with the pleasure of it.

He kissed her and then lifted his head. "Touching you is such a pleasure. You hide none of your responses from me."

"Am I supposed to?"

"No." Very definite. Unquestionably vehement.

"You're kind of a control freak in bed, aren't you?"

"Giving you pleasure takes a lot of concentration. Why would you try to hinder my efforts by lying to me?"

"I never…" She gasped as his fingers moved a certain way. "Didn't say I would."

"Never?" he asked.

She could have accused him of taking unfair advantage, but really? It wouldn't have mattered if he'd asked her in the middle of the street standing ten feet away.

Her answer to that question would always be the same. "Never."

"Thank you." Demyan continued to touch her until she was moving restlessly beneath him.

"Please…" She wasn't even sure what she was asking for.

Intercourse? Maybe, but what she really wanted was resolution to the storm building inside her and Chanel didn't really care how she got it.

Even so, she was shocked when he shifted down her body, his intention clear. She'd read about this. Of course she had. Her ex-boyfriend had even wanted to do it to her, but he'd told her she'd have to shave her hair off first.

She'd refused.

Demyan didn't seem in the least put off by the damp curls between her legs, his tongue going with unerring accuracy right to where his finger had been.

She cried out, her hips coming off the bed. His mouth followed, his ministrations with lips and tongue never pausing.

This was oral sex? This intimate kiss that led to feeling so close to someone else that there was nothing embarrassing about it?

She always thought it would bother her to have a man's mouth *there*. She hadn't refused to shave her nether region just because she was a prude back then.

Only it didn't bother her. Not at all.

It felt so good, so perfect.

Demyan's fingers came back to play, this time with one of them sliding just inside her as his tongue swirled over her most sensitive spot. He moved the finger in and out, going a little deeper each time until he pressed gently against her body's barrier.

It didn't hurt; it was not too much pressure, but it would be different when he was inside her. Wouldn't it?

He would have to break through the barrier then. With his longer-than-average erection. That's what had to happen next.

Only, he didn't seem to have the script, because he kept licking, sucking and nibbling at her clitoris until she was on the verge of climax. His finger inside her continued sliding in and out of her channel, pressing just a little bit harder against the thin barrier every few times.

His other hand came up to play with her breasts and tease at her nipples, increasing the sensations below by a factor of ten. It was incredible. Amazing.

And she felt that precipice draw closer and closer. She didn't think she was supposed to climax again before they were joined, but she didn't worry about it. He knew what he was doing and wouldn't let her.

Only, he didn't seem concerned when she warned him it was getting to be too much. He only renewed his efforts, sucking harder on her clitoris and nipping it ever so gently with his teeth.

Without warning, her body splintered apart in glorious pleasure again, this time so intense she couldn't even get enough air to scream. He didn't stop the intimate kiss, but he gentled it, bringing her prolonged ecstasy that went on and on even as his finger pressed more insistently against that thin membrane of flesh inside.

Until, as she floated on a cloud of sensual bliss, she felt the sharp sting of pain and realized he'd broken through the barrier of her body. With his finger.

"What? Why?" she asked, the hazy peace cracking a little.

"It hurts less." He gently withdrew his finger before placing a single soft kiss against her nether lips.

It felt like a benediction.

He moved off her and she saw him grab a corner of the sheet from the floor to wipe his face and hand before he rejoined her on the bed.

Demyan pulled her body into his still-very-aroused one, his expression very satisfied. "You are beautiful in your passion, Chanel."

"We… Aren't you going to…"

"Oh, yes. But only when you are ready to begin building toward climax again."

She didn't know what he meant, but he showed her, after cuddling her and telling her how amazing and lovely she was. After his touch and nearness once again began to draw forth need to be joined with him.

When he finally pressed inside her, she cried for the second time that night. He didn't look in the least worried he'd hurt her, though. In fact, his expression was one of understanding overlaying utter male satisfaction.

She didn't begrudge him one iota of it, either.

He might have had a debacle with his first virgin, but he'd made this one's initiation into intimacy unbelievably good.

Once she started to move against him, his control slipped its leash and his passion turned harsh and exciting. She screamed her pleasure this time even as his body pounded into hers, and his shout was loud enough to make her ears ring.

Afterward he was quiet, his expression impossible to read. "You'll want a shower."

"Couldn't we shower together?" she asked.

"Your bathroom isn't meant for shared intimacies."

She hadn't been propositioning him, couldn't believe he thought she had any energy left for *that,* but she didn't say so.

While she was in the shower she tried to go over what had happened, but couldn't figure out why he'd withdrawn and wondered if he'd even still be there when she came out.

CHAPTER FIVE

HE WAS, THOUGH, and he'd remade the bed with fresh sheets.

"Thank you," she said, feeling unsure.

"We will be more comfortable sleeping on clean bedding."

That one small word washed through her like life-giving oxygen. *We.* He'd said *we.*

Before she could remark on it, or say anything at all, he started toward the bathroom. "I'll have my shower now. Get in bed."

"You said you were only bossy in the bedroom."

He stopped at the doorway to the bath and looked at her over his shoulder. "We are in the bedroom."

"Why don't you just admit you have oldest-child syndrome?"

His expression turned somber, though she didn't understand why. "Noted."

She would have teased that wasn't an admission, but Demyan disappeared into the bathroom.

Chanel didn't understand what was going on with him, but he wasn't leaving. She'd take that as a good sign.

Did he regret the implications toward the future he'd made before they had sex? Was he realizing now that he'd gotten his rocks off how ludicrous they'd been?

Maybe he thought she'd try to hold him to his words as if he'd made promises. She wouldn't.

Perhaps she needed to tell him that.

She crossed the room, but when she tried the door to the bath, it was locked.

She let her hand drop away. Okay, then.

Maybe she just needed to go to bed. Any talking could happen in the morning.

After only a few moments' deliberation, she opted to wear pajamas to bed. The mint-green jersey knit wasn't exactly sexy, but it was comfortable.

She was still awake when he joined her some indeterminate time later.

He didn't pause before pulling her into his arms, though he made a sound of surprise when his hands encountered fabric. "Why are you wearing this?"

Because she'd needed a barrier between them, a level of armor, even if it was just her favorite pair of pj's. "Why not?" she answered rather than admit that, though.

"Because I prefer naked skin and I think you do, too."

"I wouldn't know. I've never slept with another person," she replied a tad acerbically.

"Perhaps it is for the best tonight. You will be too sore tomorrow if we make love again in the night."

"Oh." He still wanted her?

That was good, right?

"Do not sound so disappointed. We will make love again. Many times."

As promises for the future went, that was one she could live with. "I'm glad."

They were silent for several seconds before she offered, "Thank you for making my first time so special."

"I lost control." And there it was.

What was bothering him. She *knew* it.

"I liked it."

"I could have hurt you."

"But you didn't and I think it *would* have hurt me if you hadn't lost yourself just as badly as I did."

"Yes?" he asked, as if the concept was foreign to him.

"Absolutely."

"I am very glad to hear it." He'd turned out the light, but she could still hear the smile in his voice.

"Go to sleep."

"Your wish is my command."

She would have said something sarcastic about that blatant fabrication, but her mouth didn't want to work and she slipped into sleep, comforted by their banter.

Chanel was astonished by how easily she grew used to sleeping with someone else.

Not to the sex, though. She wasn't sure she'd ever grow *used to* the level of pleasure she and Demyan found in one another's bodies.

He *was* bossy in bed, just like he'd told her, but it was all targeted toward her enjoyment. Every directive, every withholding of one instant gratification for something more was so that her final satisfaction was so incredibly overwhelming, she lost her mind with it.

But the sleeping together, that was different. That was all-night-long intimacy of another sort.

She, who had never even cuddled a bear in bed, found it difficult to sleep now when Demyan's arms weren't wrapped around her, his heartbeat a steady, comforting sound against her ear.

Hence her yawning this morning as she crunched the new data, despite three cups of coffee made in the new Keurig machine Demyan had gotten her.

He liked to buy her things, she'd noticed. Things *she* would like.

Her entire life, gifts had come with a subtle message to her to become something different. Designer clothes in a style unlike the one she favored, athletic shoes that were supposed to encourage her to take up running when she was perfectly happy with her tae kwon do training. Golfing gear, though she hated the game, a tennis racket despite the fact she'd never played.

But Demyan's pressies were different. They were all targeted to the woman she was now, with no eye to making her into someone else. He showed an uncanny ability to tap in to her preferences, even when she'd never shared certain things with him.

Like her addiction to flavored coffees in direct opposition to her frustration over the complicated business of making a good cup of the beverage. So Demyan had found a way to feed the one while minimizing the other.

And the coffee? Delicious. And so darn easy.

She couldn't mess it up even when she got sidetracked by a new algorithm she wanted to try.

Even when she was sleepy from waking every couple of hours, reaching for him in the bed only to find empty space.

Demyan had left Seattle in the wee hours of the previous morning for what Chanel assumed was a business trip. She hadn't asked what it was about and he hadn't offered the information.

What she did know was that he wouldn't be back for two more days and an equal number of nights. Forty-eight more hours without him.

In the time line of life, it was hardly a blip.

So why did it feel longer than a particularly depraved man's purgatory to her?

Chanel already missed him with an ache that made absolutely no sense to her scientific brain. Okay, so they'd been dating a month now, not just three days. Making love and sleeping together every single night of the past three weeks of that month.

Still. How could she have become more addicted to his company than caffeine?

Because Chanel knew without any doubts she could go without coffee a heck of a lot more easily than she was finding it to be without her daily dose of Demyan.

She didn't know if she'd fallen in love at first sight like he'd hinted at three weeks ago, but she was in love with him now.

And that scared her more than a weekend at the spa with her mother.

"How close are you to closing the deal?" Fedir asked without preamble once he and Demyan were alone in the king's study.

Demyan's cousin and Gillian had returned from their honeymoon, and Queen Oxana wanted *family time.* That meant everyone in their small inner circle had come to the palace for a few days of "bonding."

Since his own parents would cheerfully go the rest of their lives without seeing Demyan, he never took Oxana's desire to spend time as a *family* for granted.

Though on this particular occasion, his mother and father and siblings were also staying at the palace in order to get to know their future queen, Gillian, better.

His father wouldn't make any effort to spend one-on-one time with Demyan, though. For all intents and purposes, Demyan's younger brother was his acknowledged oldest son.

Pushing aside old wounds Demyan no longer gave the

power to hurt him, he answered his uncle's question. "She's emotionally engaged."

"When will you propose?"

"When I return."

Fedir nodded. "Smart. The time apart will leave her feeling vulnerable. She'll want to cement your bond. Women are like that."

Demyan didn't reply. His uncle was the last man, bar none, he would ask for advice on women.

"She'll sign the prenuptial agreement?"

"Yes." The more Demyan had gotten to know Chanel, the more apparent it had become that money was not a motivating factor for her.

She'd sign even the all-contingency prenuptial agreement Fedir's lawyers had drawn up simply because the financial terms would not matter to her.

"Good, good."

"I'll want changes made to some of the provisions before I present her with it, though."

Fedir frowned. "What? I thought the lawyers did a good job of covering all the bases."

"I want more generous monetary allowances for Chanel in the event our marriage ends in divorce or my death."

"What? Why?" Fedir's shock was almost comical. "Has a woman finally gotten under the skin of my untouchable nephew?"

Of course his uncle would immediately assume an emotional reason behind Demyan's actions. His sense of justice was a little warped by his all-consuming dedication to the welfare of Volyarus.

"I will do whatever I need to in order to protect this country, but I will do it with honor," Demyan replied.

"Of course, but your integrity is in no way compromised by your actions to insure the healthy future of our country."

Demyan wasn't sure he believed that. Regardless, he would minimize how much tarnish it took. "The terms will be changed to my requirements, or I won't offer the document to Chanel to sign."

As threats went, it wasn't very powerful. Baron Tanner's will had been clear and airtight. Chanel lost all claim to the baron's shares in Yurkovich Tanner upon marriage to any direct relation to the king.

"And without a prenup, there will be no wedding," Demyan added after several seconds of silence by his uncle.

"You don't mean that."

"When have you ever known me to bluff?" Demyan asked.

Fedir frowned. "She really does mean something to you."

"My integrity certainly does."

He was a ruthless man. Demyan knew that about himself. He could make the hard choices, but he was an honest man, too. And he didn't make those choices without counting the cost.

"A man has to make sacrifices, even in that area for the greater good."

Demyan shrugged. "I'll contact the lawyers with the changes I want made to the agreement."

He wasn't going to debate his uncle's choices. The other man had to live with them and their consequences. It might be argued that everyone in the palace did, too, but Demyan wasn't a whiny child, moaning how his uncle's decisions had cost him his family.

The truth was, his own parents and their ambition were every bit as culpable.

"I'll trust you to be reasonable in your demands."

"I appreciate that."

"Demyan, you will never be king, but you are no less a

son to me than Maksim." Fedir laid one hand on Demyan's shoulder and squeezed.

The words rocked through Demyan. His uncle was not an emotionally demonstrative man, in word or deed. Nor was he known for saying things he did not mean, at least not to family.

However, Demyan's cynicism in the face of life's lessons drove his speech. "A son you call nephew."

"A son I and all of Volyarus call prince."

"You never adopted me." According to Volyarussian law, which the king could change should he so desire, doing so would have made Demyan heir to the throne, not the spare.

He understood that, but it was also a fact that if he were truly every bit as much a son to Fedir, his place in the right of succession wouldn't have been a deterrent.

"Your parents refused."

Was Fedir trying to imply he'd asked? "I find that difficult to believe. They gave me up completely."

"But so long as you were legally their son, your father had leverage for his interests. He and your mother categorically refused to give that up."

His uncle's words rang true, particularly when weighed against how few of Demyan's father's efforts had met with support of the king since he'd become an adult. "I get my ruthlessness from him."

"But your honor is all your own. You are a better man than either of your fathers, the one by birth and the one by choice."

Fedir was not a man who gave empty compliments. So, Demyan couldn't help that the older man's words sparked emotion deep inside, but he wasn't about to admit that out loud.

"Oxana feels the same. She is very proud of both of her sons."

He thought of the excitement the queen had shown when Demyan had warned her that he'd found the one. "She wouldn't be proud of me if she knew why I'm pursuing Chanel."

"You're wrong. I am very proud of you." Oxana came into the room from the secret passageway entrance. "You have put the welfare of our people and your family ahead of your own happiness. How can I be anything but proud of that?"

Fedir started, clearly shocked his wife had been listening in.

"She's a special woman. She deserves a real marriage." It wasn't a sentiment Demyan would have expressed to Fedir without prompting, but this was Oxana.

She'd sacrificed her entire life for their country and her family. Yet she was not a bitter woman. She loved them all deeply, if not overtly. She deserved to know that Demyan wasn't going to play Chanel for the sake of her inheritance.

"So, give her one." Oxana smiled with the same guarded approval she'd given him since he was a boy, though as he'd grown older he'd learned to look deeper for the true emotion. It was there. "She is a very lucky woman to have you."

Since he wasn't about to comment on the latter and the former was Demyan's plan, he merely nodded.

"That's not a reasonable request," Fedir said forcefully.

"For you, we all know that is true. But Demyan is a different man. A *better* man, by your own admission."

Fedir scowled at his wife of more than three decades. "He is our son. How can you demand he sacrifice the rest of his life for the sake of this girl's feelings?"

"How can you ask him to sacrifice his personal integrity to save our country?" Oxana countered, deigning to look at Fedir.

"He is not being dishonest."

"Oh, so you've told Chanel about her inheritance?" Oxana asked Demyan.

But he knew she wasn't talking to him, not really, so he didn't answer with so much as a shake of his head.

"How do you know about it?" Fedir asked Oxana, with shock lacing his usually forceful tones.

"It is in the historical archives for anyone to read."

"Anyone with access to the private files."

"I am queen. I get access."

Fedir opened his mouth and then shut it again without a word being uttered, his face settling into a frown.

Oxana turned to face Demyan, effectively cutting Fedir out of the conversation. "Promise me one thing."

"Yes." He didn't have to ask what it was. He trusted Oxana in a way he didn't trust anyone besides Maks.

If she wanted a promise, he would give it to her.

"Don't tell this woman, Chanel Tanner, that you love her unless you mean it. Love isn't a bartering tool."

"She loves me." Chanel hadn't said so, but he was sure of it.

It's what he'd been working toward since he'd first walked into her office.

"No doubt. You are an eminently lovable man, but you owe it to her and to your own sense of honor not to lie about something so important."

"I never lied to you," Fedir inserted.

"Nothing has ever hurt as much as realizing Fedir had only said the words to convince me to give him the heir he needed for the throne."

"I did love you. I do love you."

Oxana spun to face her husband, but *not* her lover. "Like

a sister. The few times you shared my bed, you called out *her* name at the critical moment."

This was so much more than Demyan wanted to know, but he saw no way of extricating himself from the situation. He could walk out easily enough, but he wouldn't leave Oxana to face the aftereffects of the emotional bloodletting that had been decades in the making.

"You knew about Bhodana from the beginning."

"You told me you loved me. I thought that meant you were going to let her go."

"I never promised you that."

"No, you were very careful not to."

"Oxana."

She waved her hand, dismissing him and his words as she turned back to Demyan. "You promise me, be the better man. Do not make declarations you don't mean."

"You have my word."

"I look forward to meeting her."

"I didn't plan to bring her here before the wedding."

"You don't want to scare her away."

"No." Unlike many women, Chanel was less likely to marry a prince than a normal man. "I've taken great care not to frighten her off."

"Does she know the real you?" Oxana asked.

He thought about their time in bed, intimacy during which his plans flew straight to heaven in the face of his body's response to Chanel. He'd try to convince himself that it would only be the first time, but subsequent sessions of lovemaking had proven otherwise.

"Yes," Demyan said. "She may not realize it, but definitely."

"Then all will be well. She is marrying the man you are at your core, Demyan, my son, not your title or the corporate shark who runs our company's operations so efficiently."

He hoped once Chanel saw his true persona and position, she would agree with her future mother-in-law. It was the one element to his plan that he could not be absolutely sure about.

With another woman, maybe, but with Chanel…learning he was a de facto prince could turn her right off him.

Excited anticipation buzzed through Chanel as the limousine taking her to meet Demyan rolled through the wet streets of Seattle.

His flight had arrived that morning, but he'd had a full day of meetings. Thankfully he'd told her about them before she offered to take a vacation day to spend with him.

Needy much?

She cringed at how much she'd missed him and was fairly certain allowing him to see the extent of it might not be the best thing to do. Even someone as socially inept as Chanel realized that.

Still, it had been hard to play it cool and agree to let him send a driver for her without gushing over the idea of seeing him tonight and not having to wait until tomorrow.

They were attending an avant-garde live theater production downtown. No dinner. Demyan's schedule had not permitted.

Chanel was just glad he hadn't put off seeing her, but he'd seemed almost as eager to be with her as she felt about seeing him again. Considering the number of times their short phone call had been interrupted, she knew he'd had to force a slot into his schedule for her.

Knowing she was going to see him had made focusing on her work nearly impossible. Chanel had ended up taking the afternoon off and calling her sister for a last-minute shopping trip. Laura had helped Chanel pick out an outfit that was guaranteed to *drive the guy crazy.*

The sapphire-blue three-quarter-length-sleeve top was deceptively simple. With a scoop neckline outlined by a double line of black stitching and mock tuxedo tucking in the front, it was tailored in along her torso to emphasize her curves. The semi-transparent silk was worn over a bra in the same color. Not overtly slutty with the pleats in front, it still did a lovely job of highlighting Chanel's femininity.

The black silk trousers appeared conservative enough. Until she sat down, bent over or walked. Then the slit from midthigh to ankle hidden by the tuxedo stripe when she was standing gave intriguing glimpses of naked skin.

She'd never worn anything so revealing, but Laura insisted the peek-a-boo slit was interesting and not cheap. At the prices Chanel had paid for each piece of the outfit, she supposed *cheap* would not be a term that would ever apply to the clothing.

It had looked sophisticated in the boutique's full-length mirror, a little more scandalous in her own.

Laura had insisted on styling Chanel's ensemble as well, adding a demure rope of pearls knotted right below her breasts in an interesting juxtaposition that drew attention to the curves as effectively as the blue silk.

Her heels were strappy black sandals with what Laura called a *do-me-baby* heel. Chanel hadn't bothered to admonish her sister about the description.

She'd decided years ago that Laura was light-years ahead of Chanel in the girl-boy department. She didn't know if her baby sister was still a virgin like Chanel had been when she met Demyan, and honestly she had absolutely no desire to know.

The limousine slid to a halt and Chanel took a calming breath that did exactly no good.

She resisted the urge to pull at the carefully styled curls her sister had worked so hard to effect and waited for the driver to open the door.

It wasn't the chauffeur's hand reaching in to help her out of the limousine, though.

It was Demyan's, and his dark eyes glittered with lust as he took in her exposed thigh before meeting her gaze. "Hello, *sérdeńko*. I am very happy to see you."

She made no effort to stifle the smile that took over her features as she surged forward to exit the limo. If he hadn't been there with a steadying hand and then his arm around her waist, she would have fallen flat on her face.

But he *was* there and part of her heart was beginning to believe maybe he always would be.

He tucked her into his body protectively before leaning down to kiss her hello, right there in front of the crowd making their way into the theater.

She responded with more enthusiasm than probably was warranted, but he didn't seem to mind.

The kiss ended and he smiled down at her. "You look beautiful tonight. Very sexy."

"Laura played stylist."

"Your younger sister?"

"Yes. She's got even more acute fashion sense than Mom."

"Tell her I approve."

"She said you would."

His gaze skimmed her body. "Though I am not sure how I feel about everyone else seeing your body."

"They're just legs."

"Nice ones."

"It's the tae kwon do." Chanel's mother had heard somewhere that taking martial arts could improve Chanel's grace.

It hadn't done much for her poise and composure, but Chanel had discovered she *enjoyed* the classes. She'd insisted on continuing when her mother would have preferred she take a dance class.

Just one of many arguments between her and Beatrice during Chanel's formative years marked with parent-child acrimony.

"Then I am very grateful for your interest in Korean martial arts."

"You've never asked what color belt I am," she observed as he led her into the theater.

His thumb brushed up and down against her waist as if he couldn't help touching her. "What color?"

"Third-level black belt."

"Sixth-level black in judo," he said by way of reply.

"Want to spar?" she teased breathlessly.

The silk of her shirt transmitted the heat from his skin to hers and she wondered if she was the one who was going to end up teased to distraction by her outfit tonight.

"I spar with my cousin. I prefer less competitive physical pursuits with you."

She looked up into the side of his face, loving the line of his jaw, the way he held himself with such confidence. "Me, too."

He groaned.

"What?"

He stopped in the lobby and pulled her around so their gazes locked.

His was heated. "How can you ask what? You are dressed in a way guaranteed to keep my thoughts off the play and on what I plan to do to you once we get back to my condo."

CHAPTER SIX

HE SHOOK HIS HEAD as if trying to clear it. "What do you think has me groaning? It has been three nights."

She tried not to look as pleased as she felt, but was afraid she wasn't doing a very good job.

So she averted her head and met the envious gaze of another woman. Chanel ignored it, the envy having no power to pierce the bubble of happiness around her.

Demyan was with her and showed zero interest in being with, or even looking at, another woman.

She looked up at the sound of his laughter. He was watching her.

"I'm funny?" she asked.

"You are very pleased with yourself."

"I am happy with life, and you most of all," she offered.

She wasn't one to share her feelings easily, but Laura hadn't spent the afternoon just coaching Chanel on fashion choices. Her little sister had told Chanel that if she really liked this man, she needed to open up to him.

"You can't do that thing you do with Mom and Dad and everyone else besides me and Andrew," Laura had said.

Even though Chanel thought she knew, she'd asked, "What thing?"

"The way you hold the real you back so no one can hurt her."

"You're pretty insightful."

"For a teenager, you mean."

"For anyone." Their mother was nearly fifty and Beatrice had less understanding of her oldest daughter's nature.

Demyan's hand slid down her hip, his fingertips playing across her exposed flesh through the slit.

Chanel gasped and jerked away from the touch.

His look was predatory. "I don't like to be ignored."

"I wasn't ignoring you."

"You weren't thinking about me."

"How can you tell?"

"I know."

"You're arrogant."

"So you have said, but you know I do not agree."

And the more she knew of him, the less she believed the accusation herself. There was a very hard-to-detect strain of vulnerability running through the man at her side. You had to look very closely to see it, but she watched him with every bit of her formidable scientist's brain focused entirely on one thing. Deciphering the data that made up Demyan Zaretsky.

"I'm thinking about you now," she promised.

"I know."

She laughed, feeling a light airiness that buoyed her through the crowd.

"Demyan!" a feminine voice called.

There was no mistaking the way his body tensed at the sound, not with him so close to Chanel as they walked.

He was coiled tightly, even as he turned them toward the woman who had called his name, with one of those fake smiles Chanel hadn't seen since their very first dates on his face. "Madeleine."

Madeleine's fashion sense and poise was everything Chanel's mother wished for her daughter.

Unfortunately, Chanel refused to make it a mission in life to live up to such hopes. She'd learned too young that nothing she did would ever be enough; therefore, what would be the point in trying to be someone she was not?

Madeleine's blond hair probably wasn't natural, but there were no telltale indicators. She wore her Givenchy dress with supreme confidence, her accessories in perfect proportion to the designer ensemble.

Chanel couldn't tell the other woman's age by looking at her but guessed it was somewhere between thirty and a well-preserved forty-five.

The look she gave Demyan said *he* knew her age, intimately.

If this had happened a month ago, Chanel would have withdrawn into herself and given up the playing field.

But what she'd denied on their third date was a certainty now. She was head over heels in love with Demyan Zaretsky, though she hadn't had a chance to tell him yet. Wasn't sure exactly when she wanted to.

While he'd never said the words, either, he hinted at a future together almost every time she saw him.

That love and his commitment to their future gave her strength.

Drawing on a bit of her mother's aplomb, Chanel stepped forward and extended her hand. "Chanel Tanner. Are you an *old* friend of Demyan's?"

Madeleine didn't miss Chanel's slight emphasis on the word *old,* her eyes narrowing just slightly with anger but no righteous indignation. So, she was older than she looked.

"You could say that." Madeleine put her hand on Demyan's sleeve. "We know each other quite well, though I admit I *didn't* know he wore glasses."

Demyan adroitly stepped away from the touch while keeping a proprietary arm around Chanel. "Is your husband here tonight, Madeleine?"

Stress made Chanel's body rigid. Had Demyan and this woman had an affair? He'd said he didn't believe in infidelity.

Had he been lying?

"He couldn't get away from the Microsoft people. I'm quite on my own tonight." Madeleine smiled up at Demyan, her expression expectant.

It was clear she was angling for an invitation to join them, though Chanel wasn't sure how that was supposed to happen.

Their tickets had assigned seats.

Demyan ignored the hint completely. "The cost of being married to a man with his responsibilities."

The older woman frowned again, this time genuine anger lying right below the surface. "Does your little friend here know that? Or is she still in the honeymoon phase of believing you'll make her a priority in your life?"

"She is a priority." He pulled Chanel closer.

She didn't know if the move was a conscious one, but Madeleine noticed it, too.

That made Madeleine flinch and Chanel felt unexpected compassion well up inside her. "I'm sure you're a priority to your husband. He works to make a good life for you both."

That's what she remembered her father saying to her mother.

"I knew what I was getting when I married him." Madeleine gave a significant look to Demyan. "And what I was giving up. I liked my chances with Franklin better."

"He married you. You read the situation right." There was a message in Demyan's voice for the other woman.

He was telling her *he* wouldn't have married her, and her words had put Chanel's mind at rest about the affair. Oh, it was clear the two had shared a bed at one time, but it was equally obvious that circumstance had ended before Madeleine married Franklin.

"How long were you two together?" Chanel asked with her infamous lack of tact but no desire to pull the question back once it was uttered.

It might be awkward, but it struck her how very little she really knew about Demyan.

"Didn't he tell you about me?" Madeleine asked, her tone just this side of snide.

And still Chanel couldn't feel anything but pity for her. She didn't look happy with her choices in life.

"No."

The other woman didn't seem happy with the answer. Maybe Madeleine had thought she'd made a bigger impact on Demyan's life than she had. "You're a blunt one, aren't you? Did your mother teach you no tact?"

"To her eternal disappointment, no."

That brought an unexpected but small smile to Madeleine's lips.

Demyan leaned down and kissed Chanel's temple, no annoyance with her in his manner at all. "She is refreshingly direct," he said to Madeleine while looking at Chanel. "There is no artifice in her."

"So, she does not see the artifice in you," Madeleine opined, sounding sad rather than bitter.

"He holds things back," Chanel answered before Demyan could, but she did the older woman the courtesy of meeting her gaze to do so. "But if I know that, he's not hiding anything. I understand how hard it can be to share your true self with someone else."

"Heavens, don't you have *any* filters?" Madeleine demanded.

"No."

It was Demyan's turn to laugh, the sound genuine and apparently shocking to the other woman. Madeleine stared at him for a count of five full seconds, her mouth agape, her eyes widened comically.

Finally, she said, "I've never heard you make that sound."

"He's just laughing." Okay, so he didn't do it often, but the man had an undeniable sense of humor.

"*Just,* she says. This young thing really doesn't know you at all, does she?" Madeleine was the one looking with pity on Chanel now.

"It was a pleasure to run into you, but we need to find our seats. If you will excuse us," Demyan said, his tone brooking no obstacles and implying the exact opposite to his words.

Madeleine said nothing as they walked away.

When they reached their seats Chanel understood how the other woman had thought she might be included in their evening. Demyan had a box.

Although there was room for at least eight seats in it, there were only two burgundy-velvet-covered Queen Anne-style chairs. A small table with a bottle of champagne and two-person hors d'oeuvres tray stood between them.

Demyan led her to one of the seats, making sure she was comfortable before taking his own.

He looked out over the auditorium, stretching his long legs in front of him. "She's wrong, you know."

"Madeleine?"

"Yes."

"About what?"

He turned his head, looking at her in that way only he

had ever done. As if she was a woman worthy of intense desire, of inciting his lust. "You know the man at the base of my nature."

"I hardly know anything about you." The words came from the scientist's nature even as her heart knew he spoke the truth.

That man who lost his control when he tried so hard not to, that man was the real Demyan.

Demyan shook his head, his dark eyes glowing with sensual lights she now recognized very well. "You know the most personal things about me."

"So does she."

"No."

"You had sex with her." And even though she now knew that Madeleine hadn't been married at the time, Chanel realized it still bothered her a little.

She knew he'd been with other lovers. Probably lots of them, but she really didn't want to keep running into them.

"She never saw the more primal side of my nature. No other woman has seen it."

"You think I know you better than anyone else because you don't show absolute control in the bedroom?" It's what she'd thought only seconds before, but saying it aloud made the very concept seem unreal.

"Yes."

"I want to know about your past. Not names of every woman you've been with. I hope I never meet another one, but I don't know *anything* about you." Except that to him, she was special.

She kept that to herself. She wanted more.

"It's the future that counts between us."

"But without a connection to the past, there is no basis for understanding the future." Historians made that claim all the time and scientists knew it to be true as well, for different reasons.

"I thought scientists were all about progress."

"Building on the discoveries of the past."

"Not making something entirely new?"

"Nothing is new, just newly discovered."

"Like your sexy fashion sense?" he teased.

"That's all Laura."

"I don't see Laura here now."

"I'd like you to meet her." If they had a future, they had to share their present lives.

Even the less-than-pleasant bits, which meant he'd have to meet her mother and Perry, as well.

"I would enjoy that very much."

"You would?"

"Naturally. She is your sister."

"A part of my past."

"And your present and your future."

"Yes, so?" she prompted.

He gave her a wary look she didn't understand. "You want to meet my family?"

"Very much. Unless… Do you not get on?" Maybe his relationship with his parents was worse than hers with Beatrice and Perry.

"I get on very well with the aunt and uncle who raised me."

"What happened to your parents?"

"Ambition."

"I don't understand."

"They gave me to be raised by my aunt and uncle to feed their own ambition."

There had to be more to the story than that, but she understood this was something Demyan didn't share with everyone. "Do you ever see them?"

"My aunt and uncle? Often. In fact, that's where I spent the last three days."

"I thought it was business."

"I did not say that."

"You didn't say anything at all."

"You did not ask."

"Do I have the right to ask?"

"Absolutely."

That was definitive and welcome. "Okay."

"My parents come to family social occasions," he offered without making her ask again, proving he'd known what she meant the first time around.

"And?"

"They do not consider me their son."

"Or their beloved nephew."

"Not beloved anything." His expression relayed none of the hurt that must cause him.

"I am sorry."

"You don't have it much better with your mother and Perry."

"I'm not sure I have it better at all," she admitted.

"Your parents do not understand you."

"They don't approve of me. That's worse, believe me." It would have been so much easier for her if her mother and Perry simply found her an enigma.

Instead, they considered her a defective model that needed constant attempts at fixing.

"I approve of you completely."

"Thank you." She grinned at him, letting her love shine in her eyes. She had a feeling the words weren't far from her lips, either. "I approve of you, too."

"I am very glad to hear that." He picked up the champagne bottle and poured them each a glass.

"Why champagne?" she asked.

If it was his favored wine of choice, she wouldn't ask, but he'd shared with her he drank champagne on only very special occasions.

He handed her a glass. "I'm hoping to have something to celebrate in very short order."

Goose bumps broke out over Chanel's skin, her heart going into her throat. "Oh?"

He reached into his pocket and brandished a small box that was unmistakable in size and intent.

"Isn't this supposed to happen after a five-course dinner and roses, and..." Her breath ran out and so did Chanel's words.

"I am not a man who follows other people's dictated scripts."

She had no trouble believing that. "Just your own."

Something passed through his eyes, almost like guilt, but that didn't make any sense. He might be bossy outside the bedroom a bit, too, but it was nothing to feel guilty about.

Chanel was no shrinking violet that she couldn't stand up to him if need be.

He moved, and suddenly he was on one knee in front of her, the ring box open and in his palm. "Marry me, Chanel."

"You... I... This... How can you want... It's only been a month..."

"Is longer than three dates. I knew I wanted to marry you from the beginning." There could be no questioning the truth of that statement.

It was there in his eyes and voice. Nothing but honesty. He'd known he wanted her, had never wavered in that belief.

"What about love?"

"Do you love me?" he countered.

She nodded.

"Say it."

She glared. "You first."

"I may never say the words. You will have to accept that."

"If I want to marry you."

"Oh, you want to."

She did, but she didn't understand. "Why can't you say the words?"

"I can promise you fidelity and as good a life together as it is within my power to make for us. Is that not enough?"

The syntax change was odd and then she realized that as a native Ukrainian speaker, he was using the sentence structure of his first language. Did that mean he was nervous despite how calm and assured he appeared?

She looked at him closely and saw it, that small strain of vulnerability she knew he'd rather she never witnessed. "I do love you."

"And I will always honor that."

"I don't know."

He flinched, uncertainty showing in his expression for a brief moment before his face closed. "You need time to consider it. I understand."

He stood up, pocketing the ring. "Lights will be going down momentarily for the play."

The gulf between them was huge, but she didn't know what to do to bridge it. She couldn't say *yes* right then. She didn't know if it was enough to never hear the words. Did not saying them mean he didn't feel the sentiment?

Maybe if he'd tell her *why* he couldn't say them, but clearly he didn't want to.

Still. He wanted to marry her. "Tell me why."

"Why, what?"

Was he playing dense, or did he really not know? "Why you won't say the words."

"I made a promise."

"To who?"

"The mother of my heart."

Chanel tried to understand. "She doesn't want you to get married?"

"Of course she does. She's very eager to meet you."

"But she doesn't want you to love me?" That didn't sound promising.

"She does not want me to use the words to convince you to marry me. It must be your decision entirely."

"Is this a Ukrainian thing?"

"We are not Ukrainian. We are Volyarussian."

Unlike their Ukrainian brothers, the Volyarussians had not been subject to Russian rule and loss of identity. Their ties to the old ways of doing and thinking from their original homeland were probably stronger than in the current Ukraine, but she understood what he was saying.

"Okay, a Volyarussian thing."

"It is a Yurkovich family thing."

"Your last name is Zaretsky."

"My parents never gave up legal rights."

"You could change your name now." He was an adult. There was nothing stopping him.

He jolted as if the idea had never occurred to him. Then he smiled. "Yes, I could."

"Maybe you should."

"Maybe if you agree to share it, I will change my last name to the one of my heart."

Those words played through Chanel's mind as the lights dimmed and the play began. She couldn't follow what was happening on the stage; she was too busy trying to figure out what was going on in Demyan's mind.

He'd asked her to marry him. He'd as good as told her he planned to, but she hadn't let herself believe.

She cast one of many glances in his direction, but his attention seemed riveted by the performance. He'd backed off so quickly, given up so easily.

That wasn't in character for him. Her certainty on that matter pulled her thoughts short. She'd claimed not to know him. He'd said she knew the man he was at his most basic nature. And she'd taken that to mean sexually.

But the truth was she knew him well in a lot of areas. He was a man driven by his own agenda, even ruthless in achieving it. The way he brought her pleasure, withholding both hers and his own until they'd reached *the* place indicated as much.

Demyan didn't give up easily, either. He pushed for what he wanted. Like convincing her to try making love while her hands were tied with silk scarves. She'd been leery and unwilling to do it, but he'd convinced her.

And it had been amazing.

Which begged the question: Did he not want her badly enough to fight, or was he sitting in that chair right now plotting how to get her while pretending to watch the actors on the stage?

She was pretty sure she knew the answer and it wasn't a disheartening one, though it was kind of alarming.

He was plotting, but she *wasn't* ready to give him an answer. Which meant she had to orchestrate a preemptive strike to prevent whatever it was he was planning. Probably to make love to her until she was an amenable pile of happy goo who would say *yes* to anything.

Not letting herself think about it too long and lose her nerve, Chanel scooted off her chair and onto the floor. Demyan's head snapped sideways so he could see her, proving he was highly attuned to what she was doing.

Definitely plotting.

"What are you doing?" he whisper-demanded.

She knee-walked the couple of feet between her chair and his. "You know, you could have opted for a more romantic setting. This would be easier if you'd had a settee brought in."

He stared at her, shock showing with flattering lack of artifice on every line of his handsome face. "What?"

"This." She reached for his belt.

He grabbed her wrist. "What are you doing?"

"You're repeating yourself and I would have thought it was obvious."

"Here?" he demanded, not sounding like himself at all.

She liked that. Very much.

In answer, she tugged her wrist free so she could undo the buckle on his belt. Once it was apart, she unbuttoned the waistband and then slowly and, as quietly as she could, she began to lower the zipper on his trousers in the darkened theater box.

No one could see her, though there were literally hundreds of people mere feet away.

The backs of her fingers brushed over an already erect shaft and a small laugh huffed out of her.

"What is funny?"

"I was wrong."

"About?"

"I thought you were over here plotting, but the truth is, you were thinking about sex, weren't you?"

"Yes."

"Or were they one and the same?" she asked, realizing belatedly the one did not necessarily preclude the other.

He didn't answer, which was answer enough.

"We've done a lot of things."

His head nodded in a jerky motion.

"But not this."

"No."

"Why?"

"I did not know if you wanted to."

"You decided I wanted a lot of other things I wasn't sure about."

"This is different."

Maybe it was. Maybe this had to come at her instigation. "This is me, instigating."

"I do not understand."

She smiled at the confusion in his tone. "Here I thought you could read my mind."

"Not even I can do that."

Not *even* him. She almost laughed. "But you're not arrogant."

CHAPTER SEVEN

"CONFIDENT. NOT THE SAME." His words came out gritty and chopped, not at all like him.

Understandable and welcome in the circumstances.

"No, maybe it's not." She worked his hot shaft out through the slit in his boxers, thankful they were made from stretchy fabric. "I've never done this before."

"Do whatever you want. I promise to enjoy it."

She smiled. She believed him. There was one area of their relationship she was absolutely certain about and that was the amount of pleasure he took from their physical intimacy.

The man could not get enough of her.

So she didn't let herself worry if she was doing it right when she bent forward and licked around the head of his erection. It was wide and she knew she'd have to stretch her lips to get him inside. No way was much of him going to fit into her mouth, though.

She didn't worry about that right now, but concentrated on enjoying the taste of him. It was salty and kind of bitter, but sort of sweet, too. His skin was warm and clean and hot against her lips and tongue.

She liked it. A lot.

He didn't try to rush her, though a steady stream of pre-ejaculate was now weeping from his slit and his thighs were rock-rigid with tension. She jacked the bulk of his shaft with her hands while sucking on the end.

He made small, nearly nonexistent noises, letting her know he was enjoying this as much, or more, than she was.

Suddenly he grabbed her head and pulled it back, messing up the curls Laura had taken such effort to tame. "You have to stop."

"No."

"I'm going to come," he said fiercely.

"That's the point," she whispered back.

He shook his head. "You're not swallowing your first time. You don't know if you'll like it."

"You're being bossy again and this is not the bedroom."

Ignoring her less-than-stern admonition, he pulled her into his lap, maneuvering her so she could continue to touch him. Then he handed her a napkin from the table.

She grinned and almost asked what it was for to tease him, but the light in his eyes had gone feral. And really, she wasn't looking to get arrested for public indecency, which might well happen if his control slipped his leash completely.

So she finished him with her hand, catching his ejaculate with the napkin and his shout with a passionate kiss.

When he was done, he slumped in the chair, though his hold on her remained tight. "You did that on purpose."

"To give you pleasure?"

"That, too."

She snuggled into him. "I'm not giving you an answer tonight."

"Okay."

"Really?" She kissed under his chin, a little startled by the reality of his suit and tie still pristinely in place.

"Yes, but that will not stop me taking you back to my condo and showing you what our married life will be like."

"I've got no doubts about the great sex."

"We will make sure of that by morning."

"Should I call in at work tomorrow?" She didn't want to try to do the complicated calculations for their current phase on no sleep.

And the look in his dark eyes said while she might get to know his bed very well, she wasn't going to be doing a lot of resting there.

"I think perhaps you should."

She did. In the early hours of the morning after he made love to her through the night in his condo that turned out to be a penthouse taking up the entire top floor of one of the more historic Seattle buildings.

Demyan woke her with kisses and caresses a few hours later.

Their lovemaking was slow and almost torturous in its intensity. He seemed set on proving something to her, but Chanel wasn't convinced it was what she needed to know to agree to marry him.

When she was once again sated and relaxed, he informed her he'd called her sister and arranged to invite Chanel's entire family, including Andrew, whom he was flying up for the weekend in his private jet, for dinner the following evening.

"My parents are coming here?" Postcoital bliss evaporated like water pooled on a rock in the desert as she jumped out of his king-size bed and started pacing the darkly masculine bedroom. *Tomorrow?*

"Yes."

"Didn't you think you should ask me first?" she demanded.

Looking smug and certain of his answer, he said, "You were asleep."

"You could have waited until I woke up."

"I was bored."

"Right. And you had nothing else to occupy your time but calling my sister. How did you even get her number?" Had he gone snooping through her phone?

He averted his gaze without answering.

She sighed. "You got sneaky and underhanded, didn't you?"

It wasn't exactly a challenging conclusion to draw. As if there was any other way to get her sister's private cell number without waking and asking Chanel.

"The prospect does not make you angry?" he asked with a cautious look.

Nonplussed, she stared at him. "You aren't worried about how annoyed I am that you made plans with my family, just how irritated I am about your method for getting my sister's number?"

He shrugged.

"News flash—I find it a lot less upsetting that you scrolled through my phone's contacts while I was sleeping than the fact you used said contacts to set up a dinner with my family." She shook her head. "Well, this ought to be interesting."

With that, she went into the bathroom for a shower. It was her turn to lock the door.

Being the sneaky, underhanded guy he was, Demyan found his way inside regardless. Chanel hadn't expected anything else.

So she didn't jump when his hand landed on her hip and his big body added to the heat behind her from the shower. "You told me you wanted me to meet your family."

"I said my sister," Chanel gritted out.

The man was far too intelligent not to have made the distinction.

He turned her in his arms, his expression more amused than concerned. "You know I will have to meet all of them eventually. Why not now?"

"Because I'm not ready!" She made no effort to control her volume, but she wasn't a yeller by nature, so the words came out sounding only about half as vehement as they did in her head.

The argument might have escalated, but he had the kissing-to-end-conflict technique down to a fine art.

They made love, moving together under the cascading water, his body behind hers, his arms wrapped around her so his hands could reach her most sensitive places.

As he brought her the ultimate in pleasure, he promised, "It will be all right, sérdeńko."

She desperately wanted to believe him, but a lifetime of experience had taught her otherwise. "You'll see me through their eyes."

"Or I will teach them to see you through mine."

Maybe, just maybe, his supreme self-confidence would guide his interactions with her family down that path.

She could hope.

The following night, her entire family showed up at Demyan's condo right on time.

Chanel was so happy to see Andrew and Laura that her stress at seeing her mother and stepfather didn't reach its usual critical levels instantly. That might also be attributed to the way Demyan kept one comforting arm around her throughout introductions and the launch into the usual small talk.

He'd brought in catering with servers so Chanel didn't have to cook or play hostess getting drinks. Somehow he'd known that those domestic social niceties had always been a source of criticism and failure with her family in the past.

She hadn't invited her parents to her apartment since moving out as a fresh-faced nineteen-year-old. Chanel had thought that having her own place would make a difference in how Beatrice and Perry responded to her efforts at cooking.

She'd learned differently quickly enough when they'd made it clear she fell short in every hosting department. The meal was too simple, the drinks offered too narrow in choice and even her bright stoneware dishes from a chain department store were considered inferior.

As could be inferred by her mother's gift of appropriate understated chinaware on Chanel's next birthday. She'd donated it to Goodwill and continued using her much less expensive, bright and cheerful dishes.

Since then, Chanel had assiduously avoided her mother's inferences and even direct suggestions that Chanel might like to host one of the smaller family get-togethers over the years. In the ten years since that first debacle, Chanel had made sure there were no situations in which she'd have to invite her mother or stepfather into her home for so much as a drink of water.

Perry was clearly impressed by Demyan as a host, though, the older man's expression shining with approval over the high-end penthouse and being offered his highball by a black-clad server.

Demyan kept them occupied with small talk, redirecting the conversation any time it looked like it would go into the familiar *let's-criticize-Chanel* direction. He was also overtly approving, verbalizing his appreciation for Chanel in ways that could not be mistaken or overlooked by her parents.

His protective behavior touched her deeply and Chanel found herself relaxing with her family in a way she could not remember doing in years.

"So, you work for Yurkovich Tanner?" Perry asked Demyan over dinner.

"I do."

Chanel added, "In the corporate offices."

A vague answer never satisfied her stepfather and she wasn't sure her addition would, either, but she could hope. She didn't want to spend the rest of the evening listening to Perry grill Demyan about his connections and job prospects.

She realized moments later that she needn't have worried.

Demyan adroitly evaded each sally until Perry gave up with a rather confused-sounding "Well, maybe you can put a good word in for Andrew. I tried contacting them on his behalf, you know, because of Andrew's connection to one of the original founders."

Andrew wasn't the one connected to Bartholomew Tanner. That was Chanel and her connection was tenuous at best, but trust Perry to dismiss her blood relationship to the founder and receipt of a Tanner Yurkovich university scholarship as unimportant altogether.

"I haven't heard back." Perry shrugged. "It was a long shot, but business is all about contacts."

Demyan nodded and then looked away from Perry to smile at Chanel. "I'm always happy to put a good word in for family."

Oh, the fiend. Chanel kicked Demyan's ankle under the table, but he didn't even have the courtesy to flinch.

So, that's why the dinner tonight. He'd said he was okay with waiting for her answer on his proposal, but really he had every intention of getting her family on his side. He had to realize it wouldn't take much.

Beatrice Saltzman had given up hope her oldest daughter would ever marry, and had never had any that it would be advantageously. She would be Demyan's biggest supporter once she realized the plans he wanted to make.

Chanel was going to kill him later, but right now she had to deal with the fallout of his implication.

It wasn't her mother or Perry who picked up on it, either. They wouldn't

"You're getting married?" Laura gasped, her eyes shining. She grinned at Chanel. "I told you that outfit was going to hook him."

"I wasn't looking to *hook* anybody. We're not engaged."

"But I have asked Chanel to marry me."

Chanel's mother stared at her agape. "And you haven't said *yes?* No, of course you haven't." She shook her head like she couldn't expect anything else from her socially awkward eldest.

"I'm thinking about it." Chanel glared daggers at Demyan, but he smiled back with a shark's smile she was now convinced was *not* her imagination.

"Don't think too long. He's likely to withdraw the offer," Perry advised in serious, almost concerned tones. "You're not likely to do better."

"It's not a business deal." Chanel ground out the words, refusing to be hurt by her stepfather's observation.

Because it was true. She couldn't imagine anyone *better* than Demyan ever coming into her life, but that wasn't what was holding her back, was it?

"No, it's not," Andrew chimed in, giving his dad a fierce scowl. "Leave her alone about it. Demyan would be damn lucky to have Chanel for a wife and he's obviously smart enough to realize it."

Their mom tut-tutted about swearing, but Andrew ignored her and Chanel just gave her little brother a grateful smile. He and Laura had never taken after their parents' dim view of Chanel. Their extended family, other friends and colleagues of the Saltzmans might, but not her siblings.

For that, Chanel had always been extremely thankful. Because she loved Andrew and Laura to bits.

Instead of looking annoyed by Andrew taking Chanel's part, Demyan gave him an approving glance before turning a truly chilling one on Perry. "Neither of us is likely to do better, hence my proposal."

"Well, of course," Perry blustered, but no question—he realized he'd erred with his words.

Chanel wanted to agree to marry Demyan right then, but she couldn't. There was too much at stake.

Chanel was sitting down to watch an old-movie marathon on A&E when her doorbell rang the next evening.

She'd turned down Demyan's offer of dinner and a night in at the penthouse, telling him she wanted some time alone to think.

He hadn't been happy, insisting she could think as easily in his company as out of it. Knowing that for the fallacy it was, she'd refused to budge. No matter how many different arguments he brought to bear.

Chanel had taken the fact she'd gotten her way as proof she could withstand even the more forceful side of his personality. *And* that he respected her enough to accede to her wishes when he knew she was serious about them.

If he was the one ringing the bell, both suppositions would be faulty and that might be the answer she needed.

As painful as it might be to utter.

It wasn't Demyan through the peephole, though. It was Chanel's mom.

Stunned, Chanel opened the door. "Mother. What are you doing here?"

"I wanted to talk to you. May I come in?"

Chanel stepped back and watched with some bemusement as her mother entered her apartment for the first time since she'd moved in years ago.

Beatrice sat down on the sofa, carefully adjusting the skirt of her Vera Wang suit as she did so. "Close the door, Chanel. The temperature has dropped outside."

"Would you like something to drink?" Chanel asked as she obeyed her mother's directive and then hovered by the door, unsure what to do with herself.

"No, thank you." With a slight wave of her hand toward the other end of the sofa she indicated Chanel should sit down. "I... You seemed uncertain about your relationship with Demyan last night. I thought you might want to talk about it."

"To you?" Chanel asked with disbelief as she settled into her seat.

Her mother grimaced, but nodded. "Yes. I may not have been the best one these past years, but I am your mom."

"And he's rich." His penthouse showed that even to someone as oblivious as Chanel could be. Beatrice would have noticed and probably done a fair guesstimate of Demyan's yearly income off it.

"That's not why I'm here."

"He has corporate connections Perry and Andrew might find useful, too. I suppose that might carry even more weight with you." After all, scientists could be rich, but Beatrice had never made any bones about not wanting another one in the family.

Her mom sighed. "I am not here on behalf of your brother or my husband, either."

"You're here for my sake," Chanel supplied with full-on sarcasm.

But her mother nodded, her expression oddly vulnerable and sincere. "Yes, I am. The way you two are together. It's special, Chanel, and I don't want you to miss that."

"We've only been dating a month," Chanel said, shocking herself and voicing her biggest concern.

Beatrice nodded, as if she understood completely. "That's the way it was for me and your dad. We knew the first time we met that we would be together for the rest of our lives."

"You stopped loving him." What would Chanel do if Demyan stopped wanting her?

Her mother's eyes blazed with more emotion than Chanel could ever remember seeing in them. "I never did."

"But you said…" Pain lanced through Chanel as her voice trailed off.

There were too many examples to pick only one.

"He was *it* for me."

"You married Perry."

"I needed someone after Jacob died."

"You had me. You promised we would always be a team." That broken promise had hurt worst of all.

"It was too hard. You were too much like him. I tried to make you different, but you refused to change." Her mother sighed, looking almost defeated. "You are so stubborn. Just like him."

For the first time, Chanel heard the pain in those words her mother had never expressed.

Some truths were just as hurtful to her. "Perry hates me."

"He's a very jealous man."

"He wasn't jealous of me. You weren't affectionate enough to me to make him jealous."

Sadness filled Beatrice's eyes. "No, I haven't been. He was jealous of Jacob."

"Because you never stopped loving him." Despite all evidence to the contrary.

"How do you stop loving the other half of your soul?"

Finally Chanel understood a part of her childhood she'd always been mystified by. She'd tried with Perry at first. Really tried. "Perry blamed me. He took his jealousy out on me."

"Your father wasn't around to punish."

"You let him."

Beatrice looked away and shrugged. As if it didn't matter. As if all that pain was okay to visit on a child.

"You let him," Chanel said again. "You knew and you let him hate me in effigy of my father."

Her mom's head snapped back around, her expression dismissive. "He doesn't hate you. He wanted you to be the best and all you wanted was your books and science."

"It's what I love. Didn't that ever matter to you?"

"Of course it mattered!" Beatrice jumped up, showing an unfamiliar agitation. "Science stole your father from me. Do you for one second believe I wanted it to take you, too?"

"So, you pushed me away instead."

"That wasn't my intention."

"I don't fit with the Saltzmans."

Beatrice didn't deny it, but she didn't agree either. Should Chanel be thankful for small mercies?

"I did fit with the Tanners."

"Too well, but they're all gone, Chanel. Can't you see that?"

"And you think I'll die young like Dad did because of my love for science?"

"You're too much a Tanner. You take risks."

"I don't!" She'd been impacted by the way her father and grandfather had died, too. "I'm very careful."

"If you are, then I've succeeded a little, anyway."

"You succeeded, all right. You succeeded in picking away at our relationship until there wasn't one anymore." Chanel nearly choked on the words, but she wouldn't hold them back anymore. "You couldn't handle how much having me around reminded you of Dad, so you pushed me away with both hands."

"And now you can barely bring yourself to see me even once a month."

"Visits with you are too demoralizing."

"Your sister and brother see you more often."

Even Andrew. He was away at university, but Chanel went to visit her brother at least once a term. She always made sure she got time with him when he was home. While she'd done her best to nurture her relationships with her siblings, Chanel had avoided her mother with the skill of a trained stunt driver.

"You have your sister date with Laura every week, but somehow you manage to avoid seeing me or Perry."

"Can you blame me?" Chanel demanded and then shook her head. "It doesn't matter if you do, or don't. I know whose fault it is we don't have a relationship and it's *not* mine."

Finally, she truly understood that. It wasn't that Chanel wasn't lovable. Unless she'd been willing to become a completely different person, with none of her father's passions, mannerisms or even affections, Chanel had been destined to be the brunt of both her mother's grief and Perry's jealousy.

There was no way she could be smart enough, well behaved enough or even pretty enough to earn their approval.

Not with hair the same color as her dad's and eyes so like his, too. Not with a jaw every Tanner seemed to be born with and her bone-deep desire to grow up and be a scientist.

Beatrice's eyes filled with grief that slowly morphed into resolution. "No, it's not. You deserved better than either Perry or I have given you. You deserve to be loved for yourself and by someone who isn't wishing every minute in your company you would move just a little differently, speak with less scientific jargon…"

"Just be someone other than who I am."

"Yes. You deserve that." Her mom's voice rang with a loving sincerity Chanel hadn't heard in it since she was eight years old and a broken vulnerability she *never* had. "That's why I'm urging you with everything in me not to push Demyan away because how you feel about him scares you. I wouldn't trade the years I had with your father for anything in the world, not even a life without the constant pain of grief that never leaves."

"You think Demyan loves me like Dad loved you?"

"He must." In a completely uncharacteristic gesture, Beatrice reached out and took both Chanel's hands in her own. "Sweetheart, a man like that, he doesn't offer you marriage when he could have you in his bed without it, not unless he wants all of you, but especially the life you can have together."

Her mother hadn't called her sweetheart in so long that Chanel had to take a couple of deep breaths to push back the emotion the endearment caused. "He's really possessive."

And bossy in bed, but she wasn't going to share that tidbit with her mom.

"He needs you. For a man to need that deeply, it's frightening for him. It makes him hold on tighter."

"Did Dad hold on tight?"

"Oh, yes."

Chanel had a hard time picturing it. "Like Perry?"

"Nothing like Perry. Jacob wasn't petty. Ever. He wasn't jealous. He trusted me and my love completely, but he held on tight. He wanted every minute with me he could get."

"He still followed his passion for science."

"Yes. I used to love him for it."

"You grew to hate him, though, didn't you?" That made so much sense.

Chanel hadn't just spent her childhood as scapegoat to Perry for a man who couldn't be reached in death. Her mom had punished her for being too like her father, too.

"I did." Tears welled and spilled over in Beatrice's eyes. "I betrayed our love by learning to hate him for leaving me."

Chanel didn't know what to do. Not only had she not seen her mother cry since the funeral, but they didn't have the kind of relationship that allowed her to offer comfort.

"He doesn't blame you." Chanel knew that with every fiber of her being. Her dad's love for her mom had had no limits.

"For hating him? I'm sure you're right. He loved so purely. But if he were here now to see the damage I've done to you, to our bond as a family, he'd be furious. He *would* hate me, too."

CHAPTER EIGHT

CHANEL COULDN'T RESPOND.

Her throat was too tight with tears she didn't want to shed, but her mom was probably right.

Jacob Tanner had loved his daughter with the same deep, abiding emotion he'd given his wife. He'd expected a different kind of best from both of them than Perry ever had.

The good kind. The human kindness kind.

Beatrice sighed and swiped at the tears on her cheek, not even looking around for a tissue to do it properly. "I wish I could say I would do it all differently if I could."

"You can't?" Chanel asked, surprised at how much that hurt.

"As I have grown older and watched your brother and sister mature, had the opportunity to observe the way you are with them, it's opened my eyes to many things. I have come to realize just how weak a person I am."

"If you see a problem you have the power to fix and do nothing to change it, then yes, I think that does make you weak."

"So pragmatic. Your father would have said the same thing, but you both would have assumed I had the power to change myself. If I did, do you think I would have worked so hard at changing you?"

"So, that's it? Things go on like always?"

"No," Beatrice uttered with vehement urgency. "If you'll give me another chance, I will do better now."

"So, you *have* changed." Could Chanel believe her?

"I've acknowledged the true cost of my weakness. The love and respect of my daughter. It's too much."

"I don't know if I can ever trust you to love me."

"I understand that and I don't expect weekly mother-daughter dates."

"I don't have time." Chanel realized how harsh that sounded after she said the words, and she winced.

Her mom gave her a wry smile. "Your time is spoken for, but maybe we could try for more often than once every couple of months."

"Let's see if we can make those visits more pleasant before we start making plans for more." Words were all well and good, but Chanel had two decades of her mother's criticisms and rejections echoing in her memories.

Beatrice nodded and then she did yet another out-of-character gesture, opening her arms for a hug. When Chanel didn't immediately move forward to accept, her mother took the initiative.

Chanel responded with their normal barely touching embrace, but her mom pulled her close in a cloud of her favorite Chanel No. 5 perfume and hugged her tight. "I love you, Chanel, and I'm very proud of the woman you've become. I'm so very, very sorry I wasn't a better mother."

Chanel sat in stunned silence for several seconds before returning the embrace.

"You don't think I'm too awkward and geeky for Demyan?" she asked against her mother's neck.

Still not ready to see the older woman's expression in case it wasn't kind.

But Beatrice moved back, forcing Chanel to meet her

eyes. "You listen to me, daughter. You are more than enough for that man. You are *all* that he needs. Now *you* need to believe that if you're going to be happy with him."

"It's only been a month, Mom."

"Your dad proposed on our third date."

The synergy of that took Chanel's breath away. Demyan hadn't proposed on their third date, but he'd told her then that they were starting something lifelong, not temporary. "I thought you got married because you were pregnant with me."

"I was pregnant, yes, but we'd already planned to get married. Only, our original plan was to do it after he finished his degree."

"You said…"

"A lot of stupid things."

Chanel's mouth dropped open in shock at her mother's blunt admission.

Beatrice gave a watery laugh. "Close your mouth. You'll catch flies."

"I love you, too, Mom."

"Thank you. That means more than you'll ever know. I know I don't deserve it."

"I didn't say I liked you," Chanel offered with her usual frankness and for once didn't regret it.

Their relationship was going to work only if they moved through the pain, not try to bury it.

"You will, sweetheart. You loved your daddy, but I was your favorite person the first eight years of your life."

"I don't remember." She didn't say it to belabor the point. She just didn't.

"You will. I'm stubborn, too. You didn't get it all from Jacob."

"What about Perry?"

"I'll talk to him. I guess I never realized how bad it was

in your mind between you. He really doesn't hate you. He's even told me he admires you."

Chanel made a disbelieving sound.

"It's true. You're brilliant in your field. I think it intimidates him. He's a strong businessman, but if he had your brains he'd be in Demyan's position."

With a penthouse with a view of the harbor? Her parents lived in the suburbs and she couldn't imagine them wanting anything different.

Her mother left soon thereafter, once she'd promised again to change and make sure Perry knew he had to alter the way he interacted with Chanel, too.

No one could have been more shocked than Chanel when she got a call from the man himself later that night. He apologized and admitted he'd thought she had always compared him unfavorably to her dad, just like her mom did.

Chanel didn't try to make him feel better. Perry did compare unfavorably with Jacob Tanner. Her dad had been a much kinder and loving father, but Chanel agreed to try to let the past go if the future was different.

How had Demyan affected such change in her life in so little time? She wasn't going to kid herself and try to say it was anything else, either.

Somehow Demyan had blown into her life and set it on a different path, one in which she didn't have to be lonely or rejected anymore.

If she could let herself trust him and the love she felt for him, the rest of her life could and would be different, too.

She picked up the phone and called him.

"Missing me, little one?" he asked without a greeting.

"Yes." There was a wealth of meaning in that one word, if he wanted to hear it.

"*Yes* as in yes, you miss me, or *yes* as in you will marry me?" he asked, sounding hopeful but cautious.

"Both."

"I will be there in ten minutes."

It was a half-hour drive from his penthouse, but she didn't argue.

Demyan knocked on Chanel's door with a minute to spare in the ten he'd promised her.

What he hadn't told her when she called was that he was already in the area.

The door swung open, and Chanel's eyes widened with disbelief. "How did you get here so fast?"

"I was already on the road." Had been for the better part of an hour, driving aimlessly, with each random turn taking him closer and closer to her apartment complex.

She frowned. "On your way here?"

"Not consciously." He'd argued with himself about the wisdom of calling or stopping by after she'd told him she wanted the night to think.

So far, respecting her wishes had been winning his internal debate.

"Then what were you doing over here?"

He gently pushed past her, not interested in having this discussion, or any other, on the stoop outside her door. "I was out for a drive."

"On this side of town?" she asked skeptically.

"Yes."

"But you weren't planning to come by."

"No." And that choice had clearly been the right one, though more difficult to follow through on than he wanted to admit.

"Do you go out for drives with no purpose often?" she asked, still sounding disbelieving.

"Not as such, no." He went through to the kitchen, where he poured himself two fingers of Volyarussian vodka before drinking half of it in two swallows.

He'd brought the bottle with him one night, telling her that sometimes he enjoyed a shot to unwind. She'd told him he could keep it in the freezer if he liked.

He did, though he rarely drank from it.

"Are you okay, Demyan?" she asked from the open archway between her living room and kitchen. "I thought you'd be happy."

"I didn't like the emptiness of my condo tonight." He should have found the lack of company peaceful.

A respite.

He hadn't. He'd become too accustomed to her presence in the evenings. Even when she only sat curled up with one of her never-ending scientific journals while he answered email, having her there was *pleasant*.

Had almost become necessary.

"I missed you, too."

"You wanted your space. To think," he reminded her, the planning side of his facile brain yelling at him that his reaction wasn't doing his agenda any favors.

"It was fruitful. Or have you forgotten what I told you on the phone?"

He slammed the drink onto the counter, clear liquid splashing over the sides, the smell of vodka wafting up. "I have not forgotten."

Her gray eyes flared at his action, but she didn't look worried. "And you're happy?"

"Ecstatic."

"You look it." The words were sarcastic, but an understanding light glowed in her lovely eyes.

"You are a *permanent fixture* in my life. It is only natural I would come to rely on your companionship to a certain extent." He tried to explain away his inability to remain in his empty apartment and work, as he'd planned to.

A small smile played around her mobile lips. "So, you considered me a permanent fixture before I agreed to marry you?"

"Yes." He was not in the habit of losing what he went after.

"I see. I wasn't nearly so confident, but I missed you like crazy when you were in Volyarus."

"And yet you refused my proposal at first."

"I didn't. I told you I had to think."

"That is not agreement."

"Life is not that black-and-white."

"Isn't it?"

"No." She moved right into his personal space. "I think you're even more freaked out by how fast everything has gone between us than I am."

"I am not." It had all been part of his plan, everything except this inexplicable reaction to her request for time away from him.

"You're acting freaked. Slamming back vodka and driving around like a teenager with his first car."

"I assure you, I did not peel rubber at any stoplights."

"Do teens still do that?"

"Some." He never had.

It would have not been fitting for a prince.

"I said yes, Demyan." She laid her hands on his chest, her eyes soft with emotion.

His arms automatically went around her, locking her into his embrace. "Why?"

Her agreement should have been enough, but he needed to know.

"My mom came by to talk. She told me not to give up on something this powerful just because it scares me."

"Your mother?" he asked, finding that one hard to take in.

"Yes. She wants to try again, on our relationship."

"She does realize you are twenty-nine, not nineteen?"

Chanel smiled, sadness and hope both lurking in the storm-cloud depths of her eyes. "We both do. It's not happy families all of a sudden, but I'm willing to meet her partway."

"You're a more forgiving person than I am."

"I'm not so sure about that, but one thing I do know. Holding bitterness and anger inside hurts me more than anyone who has ever hurt me."

A cold wind blew across his soul. Demyan hoped she remembered that if she ever found out the truth about her great-great-grandfather's will.

She frowned up at him. "You were driving without your glasses?"

"I don't need them to drive." He didn't need them at all but wasn't sure when he was going to break that news to her.

"You always wear them, except in bed."

"They're not that corrective." Were in fact just clear plastic.

"They're a crutch for you," she said with that analytical look she got sometimes.

"You could say that."

"Do you need them at all?"

He didn't even consider lying in answer to the direct question. "No."

He expected anger, or at least the question, *why did he wear them?* But instead he got a measured glance that implied understanding, which confused him. "If I can step off the precipice and agree to marry you, you can stop wearing the glasses."

The tumblers clicked into place. She saw the glasses

as the crutch she'd named them for him. Being who she was, it never occurred to her that they were more a prop.

"Fine." More than. Remembering them was a pain.

She grinned up at him and he found himself returning the expression with interest, a strange, tight but not unpleasant feeling in his chest.

"Want to celebrate getting engaged?" she asked with an exaggerated flutter of her eyelashes.

The urge to tease came out of nowhere, but he went with it. "You want a shot of my vodka?"

He liked the man he became in this woman's presence.

"I was thinking something more *mind-blowing* and less about imbibing and more about experiencing." She drew out the last word as she ran her fingertip across his lips, down his face and neck and on downward over his chest, until she stopped with it hovering right over his nipple.

He tugged her closer, his body reacting as it always did to her nearness. "I'm all about the experience."

"Are you?" she asked.

He sighed and admitted, "Not usually, no. My position consumes my life."

"Not anymore."

"No, not anymore." He hadn't planned it this way, but marrying Chanel Tanner was going to change everything.

He could feel it with the same sense of inevitability he'd had the first time he'd seen her picture in his uncle's study. Only now he knew marrying her wasn't going to be a temporary action to effect a permanent fix for his country.

And he was glad. The sex *was* mind-blowing, but that didn't shock him as much as it did her. What *he* hadn't anticipated was that her company would be just as satisfying to him, even when it came without the cataclysm of climax.

Right now, though? He planned to have both.

* * *

Chanel adjusted her seat belt, the physical restraint doing nothing to dispel the sense of unreality infusing her being.

Once she'd agreed to marry Demyan, he'd lost no time setting the date, a mere six weeks from the night of their engagement. He'd told her that his aunt wanted to plan the wedding.

Chanel, who was one of the few little girls in her class at school who had not spent her childhood dreaming of the perfect wedding, was eminently happy to have someone else liaise and plan with her mother. Beatrice was determined to turn the rushed wedding into a major social event.

And the less Chanel had to participate in that, the better. If she could have convinced Demyan to elope, she would have, but he had this weird idea that she *deserved* a real wedding.

Since she'd made it clear how very much she *didn't* want to be the center of attention in a big production like the type of wedding her mother would insist on, Chanel had drawn the conclusion the wedding was important to Demyan.

So, she gave in, both shocked and delighted to learn that her mom had agreed to have the wedding take place in Volyarus with no argument.

Beatrice had been vague when Chanel had asked why, something about Demyan's family being large and it only being right to have the wedding in his homeland. Chanel hadn't expected that kind of understanding from her mom and had been glad for it.

She'd even expressed genuine gratitude to Beatrice for taking over the planning role with Demyan's aunt. Chanel had spent the past weeks working extra hours so she could leave her research in a good place to take a four-week honeymoon in Volyarus.

She hadn't been disappointed at all when Demyan had

asked her if she'd be willing to get to know his homeland for their honeymoon.

She loved the idea of spending a month in his company learning all she could about the small island country and its people, not to mention seeing him surrounded by family and the ones who had known him his whole life.

There was still a part of Chanel that felt like Demyan was a stranger to her. Or rather a part of Demyan that she did not know.

Her mother had flown out to Volyarus two weeks before to finalize plans for the wedding with Demyan's aunt. Perry, Andrew and Laura were on the plane with Chanel and Demyan now.

Perry *had* made a determined effort not to criticize her, but Chanel couldn't tell if that was because of her mother's talk with him or out of deference for Demyan. She'd never seen her stepfather treat someone the way he did Demyan, almost like business royalty, or something.

It made Chanel wonder.

"What is it you do at Yurkovich Tanner?" she asked as the plane's engines warmed up.

Demyan turned to look at her, that possessive, content expression he'd worn since the morning after she agreed to marry him very much in evidence.

"Why do you ask?"

"Because I realized I don't know."

"I am the Head of Operations."

"In Seattle?" she asked, a little startled his job was such a high-level one, but then annoyed with herself for not realizing it had to be.

Only, wasn't it odd for the corporate big fish to personally check out the recipients of their charitable donations?

"Worldwide," he said almost dismissively. "My office is in Seattle."

"I knew that, at least." Worldwide, as in he was Head of Operations over all of Yurkovich Tanner?

She'd done a little research into the company after they gifted her with a university education. It wasn't small by any stretch. They held interests on almost every continent of the world and the CEO was the heir apparent to the Volyarussian throne.

That Demyan was Head of Operations meant he swam with some really exalted fish in his tank.

"You are looking at me oddly," Demyan accused.

"I didn't realize."

He brushed back a bouncy curl that had fallen into her eye, his own expression intent. "Does my job title matter so much?"

"I know your favorite writer, the way you like your steak and how many children your ideal family would have, but I don't know anything about your job."

"On the contrary, you know a great deal. You have sat beside me while I took conference calls with our operations in Africa and Asia."

"I tuned you out." Corporate speak wasn't nearly as interesting as science…or her erotic readings.

Now that she had practical experience, they were even more fascinating.

He smiled with a warm sincerity she loved, the expression almost common now. At least when directed at her. "You did not miss anything that would interest you."

"I figured." She sighed. "I just feel like I should understand this side of your life better. You work really long hours."

So did she, but it occurred to her that maybe his long hours weren't going to go away like hers now that she'd caught up on work for her extended honeymoon.

"It is a demanding job."

"Do you enjoy it?"

"Very much."

"Will you continue working twelve- to sixteen-hour days after we get back from Volyarus?"

"I will do my best to cut my hours back, but twelve-hour days are not uncommon."

"I see. Okay, then."

"Okay, what? You have that look you get."

"What look?"

"The stubborn one." His brows drew together. "The same one you got when you insisted on buying your wedding dress without your mother's or my aunt's input."

Demyan's aunt, Oxana, had offered a Givenchy gown. Chanel had turned her down. Demyan hadn't been happy, wanting to save Chanel the stress and expense of searching for the perfect dress. He knew clothes were not usually her thing, but Chanel refused to compromise on this issue.

While she couldn't really care less about the colors for the linens, what food would be served or even the order of events at the reception, there were two things Chanel did care about.

What she wore and who officiated.

On the officiate, she'd agreed to have Demyan's family Orthodox priest perform the service so long as the pastor from the church she'd attended since childhood, a man who had known and respected both her father and grandfather, led them in their personally written vows and spoke the final prayer.

Her dress she wasn't compromising on at all. Chanel and Laura had spent three weeks haunting eBay, vintage and resale shops, but they'd finally found the perfect one.

An original Chanel gown designed by Coco herself.

Because while her mother had named Chanel after her favorite designer, she'd also named her after the designer she'd been wearing when Chanel's dad proposed. Chanel had wanted a link to her dad on her wedding day and wearing the vintage dress was it.

The rayon lace overlay of magnolia blossoms draped to a demure fichu collar. However, the signature Coco Chanel angel sleeves with daring cutouts gave the dress an understated air of sexiness she liked.

The dress was designed to enhance a figure like Chanel's. Clinging to her breasts, waist and hips only to flare slightly from below the knee, the gown made her look and feel feminine without being flouncy and constrictively uncomfortable.

Buying it had nearly drained Chanel's savings account and she really didn't care. Her job paid well and Demyan wasn't exactly hurting for cash.

Demyan's mouth covered Chanel's and she was kissing him before she was even conscious he'd played his usual *get-Chanel's-attention-when-her-mind-is-wandering* card. She had to admit she liked it a lot more than the sharp rebukes she got from others because of her habit of getting lost in thought.

After several pleasurable seconds, he lifted his head.

Dazed, she smiled up at him even as she was aware of her brother making fake gagging gestures in his seat across the aisle.

Perry shushed him, but Chanel paid neither male any heed.

She was too focused on the look in Demyan's eyes. It was so warm.

"That's better," he said.

"Than?"

"You thinking about something else. You're only thinking about me, now."

She laughed softly. "Yes, I am."

CHAPTER NINE

"WHAT PUT THAT stubborn look on your face before?"

She had to think and then she remembered. "You said you worked twelve-hour days, usually."

"I did and you said that was okay."

"No, I said *okay* in acknowledgment."

"You do not approve of twelve-hour days."

She shrugged. "That's not really the issue."

"It's not?"

"No."

"What is the issue?"

"Children."

His brows drew together like he was confused about something. "We agreed we wanted at least two."

He'd figure it out. He was a smart man.

"We also agreed that because of health considerations and family history, I wouldn't get pregnant after thirty-five."

"So?"

"So, we may have to adjust for an only child, or no children at all."

"Why?" he asked, sounding dangerous, the expression on his gorgeous face equally forbidding.

"Children need both parents' attention."

"Not all children have two parents."

"But if they do, they deserve both of those parents to make them a priority."

"I will not shirk my responsibility to my children."

"A dad does more than live up to responsibilities. He takes his kids to the beach in sunny weather and attends their soccer games. You can't do that if you're working twelve-hour days five days a week."

Something ticked in his expression.

Her heart sank. "You work weekends."

"Thus far, yes."

Was this a deal breaker? No.

But she didn't like figuring it out now, either. "I'll volunteer with after-school programs," she decided. "I don't have to have children to have a complete life."

"You are threatening not to have children if I do not cut my hours?"

"I'm not threatening. I'm telling you I'm not bringing any children into this world who are going to spend their childhoods wondering how important they are to their dad, if at all."

"And you accuse me of seeing the world in only two colors."

"I see lots of shades and shadows. That doesn't mean my children are going to live under one or more of them."

"Have you never considered the art of compromise?"

"I suck at it." Hadn't he realized that already?

She gave in on what didn't matter, and on what did? Well, she could be a bit intransigent.

"This may be a problem. I am not known for giving in on what matters to me." He said it like she might not know.

"It's a good thing we agree on this issue, then."

Demyan didn't look comforted. "How is that?"

"You said you wanted to be the best father possible,

that you never wanted your children to doubt their place in your life."

"Yes."

"Then you agree it is better not to have them if your work schedule isn't going to change."

He looked tired suddenly, and frustrated. "It is not that simple."

"It can be."

"What do you suggest? That I let Yurkovich Tanner run into the ground?"

"I suggest you hire three assistants, one for each major market, men and women who know the company, who care about it and that you trust to make minor decisions. They're the first line for policy and decision making, leaving you open to spend your time on only the most high-level stuff."

"And if that's all I work on already?"

"It's not."

"You told me you tuned out my calls."

"That doesn't mean I can't access the memories."

"You're scary smart, aren't you?"

She shrugged, but they hadn't even bothered finishing her IQ test in high school after she completed the first three exercises before the tester even got the timer going. The teacher hadn't wanted her to feel like a freak.

If only he'd been able to coach her parents.

"You just found out what my job is and you're already giving advice on it." Far from annoyed, Demyan sounded admiring.

"I'm a quick thinker."

"You'd be brilliant in business."

"No interest." Much to both her mother's and Perry's distress.

"I'll talk it over with my uncle."

"Is he your business mentor?"

"He's my boss."

"He works for Yurkovich Tanner?"

"He's the King of Volyarus."

She waited for the rest of the joke, only it didn't come, and the look Demyan was giving her said it wasn't going to.

She knew that ultimately the ownership of Yurkovich Tanner resided with the monarchy of that country. However, the thought that Demyan's uncle and the king were one and the same person had never entered her mind.

"Your uncle is a king."

"Yes."

"Oxana?"

"Queen."

"She told me to call her Oxana."

"That is her privilege."

Chanel felt like she was going to be sick. "You never said."

"I didn't want to scare you off."

"Holding back important information is like lying."

"I'm called Prince Demyan, but I'm no knight in shining armor. At heart I am a Cossack, Chanel. You must realize that. Any armor I have is tarnished. I am a human man with human failings." He said it as if admitting a darkly held secret.

Another time, she would have teased him about his melodrama and the arrogance behind it. Right now? She needed to think.

"I wasn't expecting this. You're this corporate guy who wears sweaters." Only, he hadn't been wearing them, or the jeans, so much lately.

She hadn't really noticed, until now. Clothing didn't matter much to her. She wasn't her mother, or even Laura in that regard. But looking back, she realized there had been a lot of subtle changes over the past six weeks.

He dressed in suits so sharp they could have come out of the knife drawer. She hardly ever saw the more casual attire he'd been wearing when they first met. Sometimes in the evenings, but he never left the house in the morning wearing a sweater.

She never noticed him reaching to adjust glasses that weren't there anymore, either.

Which meant what? That he was a lot more confident than she'd thought.

Okay, anyone who thought Demyan Zaretsky lacked confidence needed to take a reality check. Her included.

She didn't know why he'd worn the glasses, but they weren't a crutch for some deep-seated insecurity.

And honestly, did that matter right now?

"Chanel," he prompted.

She stared at him, trying to make the difference between *who* he was and *what* he was make sense through the shock of his revelation. "You're a prince."

"It's a nominal title only."

"What does that even mean?" What she knew about royalty wouldn't fill a page, much less a book.

"Officially, I am a duke, but I am called prince at the pleasure of my uncle, the king."

"The one who raised you?" Still not making sense, and getting cloudier rather than clearer.

"He and Oxana raised me as a brother to Maksim, the Crown Prince. I was spare to the throne."

"Was?"

"My cousin's wife is expecting their first child."

"Next in line to the throne now?"

"Yes."

"It's just all so strange."

She looked around the plane, which had taken off at

some point but she couldn't have said when. Her family were all staring, making no effort to hide their interest.

Perry didn't look surprised at all, but Andrew's and Laura's eyes were both saucer wide.

"Mom and Perry knew," she guessed.

"Yes."

"They never said."

"They agreed my position might scare you off me. I wanted time to show you *I* am the man you promised to marry."

"But *you* are a prince."

"Does that change how you feel about me?" he demanded, no give for prevarication in his voice.

There were a lot of conflicting things going on inside Chanel, but this wasn't something she was in any question about. "No. I love you, not what you are."

"I am glad to hear it." The relief in his tone couldn't be faked.

"This is so cool," Andrew said, reminding Chanel of their audience.

She frowned at her little brother. "You might think so."

"I do, too," Laura said.

"The only thing that matters is what you think," Demyan said from beside her.

"The jury is still out on that one."

"Don't be flip."

She glared up at him. "I'm not. I mean it. Give me some time to process."

"Chanel—"

"No. I don't want to talk about it right now."

She didn't want to talk at all, and shut down every attempt either he or her family made on the rest of the flight, going so far as to feign sleep to get them all to just leave her alone for a bit.

Life had changed so fast and she'd thought she'd come to
terms with that, but Demyan was still throwing her curve-
balls and Chanel had never been good at sports.

Their arrival in Volyarus was less overwhelming than she
might have expected given Demyan's position.

Thankfully, there was no fanfare, no line of reporters
with oversize cameras. Of course if there had been, she
would have shown them all just how she'd gotten her black
belt in tae kwon do, with Demyan as her unwitting assistant in the endeavor.

However, other than some official-looking men who
looked like they were straight off the set of *Men in Black,*
there were only two other people—Chanel's mother and
a beautiful woman with an unmistakable regal bearing.
Queen Oxana.

Demyan guided Chanel toward the two women with his
hand on the small of her back. He stopped when they were
facing his aunt and he introduced them all.

The queen put her hand out to Chanel. "It's a pleasure
to meet you. Demyan speaks very highly of you, as does
your mother."

Chanel did her best not to show her surprise.

She knew Beatrice was trying, but the idea she had actually *complimented* Chanel to the other woman was still
too new to be anything but startling. Oxana had spent the
past two weeks in Beatrice's company. In the past, Chanel
would have been sure the results would be catastrophic for
any hopes she might have of gaining the queen's regard.

From the look of both women, that wasn't something
she had to worry about anymore.

Unexpected and warm pleasure poured through Chanel's heart, filling it to the brim, and she smiled at her
mother before squeezing the queen's hand. "Thank you for

making Demyan a part of *your* family. Someone taught him how to protect the people he cares about and I think that was you."

The lovely dark eyes widened, Oxana's mouth parting in shock and then curving into an open smile. "I believe he will be in very good hands with you, Chanel."

The king was waiting at the palace when they arrived, his manner more reserved and less welcoming to Chanel. She didn't mind.

She thought she understood.

Everyone else was acting as if it was perfectly normal for a prince to get engaged after a month and married six weeks later.

Obviously, King Fedir had his qualms about it.

Since Chanel still had her own fears, she had no problem with the fact he might have some, as well.

Wedding plans made it impossible for Chanel and Demyan to have any time alone for the rest of the day. She was not surprised to find him in her room late that night after she left her mother and the indefatigable Oxana still discussing seating charts.

Demyan pulled Chanel into his arms and kissed her for several long seconds before stepping back. "That is better."

"You missed me."

"I spend all day without you at work."

"But it was different here."

"Yes."

"Worried the mom of your heart would let slip too many of your secrets?" she teased, unprepared for the clearly guilty look that crossed his features. "What?"

He shook his gorgeous head. "Nothing."

"Demyan?"

"She is the mother of my heart."

"Have you told her and the king you filed for an official name change?"

"They will hear when the priest names me during the ceremony."

"You're a closet romantic, aren't you?"

"I am no romantic, Chanel."

"You just go on thinking that." Then a truly horrific thought assailed her. "Are people going to call me Princess after we are married?"

"Are you going to refuse to marry me if I say yes?" he asked, sounding way too serious.

"I'm not going to refuse to marry you, but Demyan, it's not easy, this finding-out-you're-royalty thing."

He nodded, as if he understood, but how could he? He'd grown up knowing what he was.

"So, about the princess thing…" She wasn't willing to let this go. Chanel wanted an answer.

He'd left enough out up to this point.

"That depends on my uncle."

"If he calls me princess…"

"Then others will."

"Oh." Considering the cool reception she'd received from King Fedir, she didn't think he was going to call her princess anytime soon.

"You look relieved."

"I'm not a princess in his eyes." As she said the words, she knew them to be absolute truth. And she didn't blame King Fedir for feeling that way. "I'm not nobility."

"You are. You inherited the title from your great-great-grandfather—you are a dame. Marrying me will make you a duchess."

"So?"

"So, even if you are not called princess, most will call you by your title." His expression and tone said he was perfectly aware she wasn't going to see that truth as a benefit to marriage.

"That's medieval."

"No. Trust me, the nobility system is alive and well in many modern countries."

"But…" She didn't want to be called duchess.

"The correct term is Your Grace."

"That makes me sound like, like… What do they call them, a cardinal or something in the Catholic church."

He laughed, like she'd been joking.

She wasn't. "I'm… This is…"

He didn't let her keep floundering. Showing he knew exactly what Chanel needed—him—Demyan pulled her into his arms and kissed her.

All thoughts of unwanted titles and unexpected ties to royalty went flying from her head in favor of one consuming emotion. Love for the man so intent on making her his wife.

Over the next few days, Chanel hardly saw Demyan—except when he came to her room at night and made passionate, almost desperate love to her.

She didn't understand, but it felt like he was avoiding her. Not sure that wasn't her old insecurities talking, she refused to voice her concerns aloud.

He didn't seem inclined to anything serious for pillow talk either, but she understood that. Chanel certainly didn't want to talk about the wedding and its never-ending preparations and plans. Nor was she interested in discussing her fledgling closer relationship with her mother and stepfather.

Beatrice was in her element planning a wedding for her daughter to a prince. A cynical part of Chanel couldn't help wondering how much of her mother's newfound approval stemmed from this unexpected turn of events.

Perry wasn't nearly as overtly critical as he had been in the past, but he didn't go out of his way to extend even pseudo fatherly warmth, either.

As they had been for the majority of her life, Laura and Andrew were two bright beacons of sincere love and affection for Chanel. Their steady presence reminded her that no matter how her life might change by marrying royalty, some things—the truly important things—remained.

Though she saw little of him during the day, Demyan arrived in her room every night—sometimes very late and clearly exhausted. Apparently when he was in Volyarus, his duties extended beyond the company business into the family business: the politics of royalty.

Sometimes they didn't make love before falling into exhausted slumber, but those nights he woke her in the wee hours in order to bring amazing pleasure to her body.

He'd found time to sit with her today, though, while she and her stepfather's lawyer went over the prenuptial agreement. Perry had offered his expertise as well, but honestly?

Chanel trusted Demyan to watch out for her best interests more than her stepfather.

Once she'd read it through, though, she didn't think she needed anyone else's interpretation. For a legal document, the language was straightforward and to the point.

There was some serious overkill in her opinion, but nothing that bothered Chanel to sign.

Upon her marriage, she and her heirs gave up any and all rights might have in Volyarus, its financial and political endeavors and anything specifically related to the business enterprises of the Yurkovich family.

The fact that particular paragraph was followed by one giving any children she had with Demyan full interest as *his* heirs, she felt was particular overkill.

Clearly, the royal family was very protective of their interests, though. King Fedir's influence, no doubt.

The man had not warmed up to her at all, but he'd never been unkind, either. After her years with Beatrice and Perry, Chanel was practically inured to anything less than overt hostility.

Even with what she was sure were the king's stipulations, the terms of the agreement were very generous toward Chanel, considering the fact she wasn't bringing any significant accumulated wealth to the marriage. The agreement guaranteed an annual sum for living expenses that Chanel couldn't imagine spending in five years, never mind one.

Unless it was on research, but she didn't see Demyan approving using their personal finances to fund her scientific obsessions. Yurkovich Tanner had been generous in that regard already.

One thing the prenup spelled out in black and white, oversize and bolded print to her heart was that Demyan wanted their relationship to be permanent. If she'd been in any doubt.

Which she wasn't.

The financial provision did not decrease in the event of his death. The annual income was Chanel's and her children's for her lifetime and theirs.

There were some other pretty stringent requirements that would insure she didn't divorce Demyan or be unfaithful to him, though. Not that she would ever do either.

But the agreement spelled out quite clearly that any children born of a different father had absolutely no financial interest through her or any other source in the Yurkovich, Zaretsky or Volyarussian wealth.

Oddly, if she divorced Demyan, or he divorced her for anything other than *her* infidelity, she would still be well taken care of. Until she remarried. If she were ever to marry someone else, or have irrefutable evidence of infidelity brought against her, she lost all financial benefits from her marriage to Demyan.

It wasn't anything less than she expected, but having it spelled out in black and white sent a shiver along her spine that was not exactly pleasant.

Demyan laid his hand over hers before she signed. "You are okay with all the terms?"

"They are more than generous."

"I will always make sure you have what you need, no matter what the agreement says."

"I believe you." And she did. With everything in her.

CHAPTER TEN

THE MORNING OF Chanel's wedding was every bit as tediously focused on beauty, fashion and making an impact as she'd feared it might be with Beatrice in charge.

Strangely, for the first time in her life, Chanel found she didn't mind her mother's fussing over her appearance.

For once, going through the paces of having her legs waxed, her hair done and makeup applied resonated with an almost welcome familiarity in this strange new situation that had become her life.

It had been years since Chanel had sat through one of her mother's preparation routines for a social function, but the sound of Beatrice's voice giving instruction to the stylists resonated with old memories.

Memories were so much easier to deal with than the reality of the present. She was marrying a prince.

It was beyond surreal.

"Your fingers are like ice." The manicurist frowned as she took Chanel's hand out of the moisturizing soak. "Why did you say nothing? The water must be too cold."

Beatrice was there in a second, testing the water with her own finger and giving Chanel a look filled with concern. "Are you all right, sweetheart?"

Chanel nodded.

Her mom did not look comforted. "The argan oil solution is warm enough, but the manicurist is right. Your hands feel like they've been wrapped around an icicle."

Chanel shrugged.

"Mom, she's marrying a prince. That's not exactly Chanel's dream job," Laura said in that tone only a teenager could get just right. "She's stressed out."

"But he's perfect for you."

"You've barely seen us together. How would you know?" Chanel asked, with little inflection.

"You love him."

Chanel nodded again. There was no point in denying the one thing that would prompt her to marry a man related to royalty.

"He adores you."

Laura grinned at Chanel, her eyes filled with understanding. "I agree with Mom on that one, at least."

"I think he does," Chanel admitted. Demyan acted like a man very happy with his future.

Beatrice reached out and put her hand against Chanel's temple, frowning at whatever she felt there. "You're in shock."

"Sheesh, Mom, way to state the obvious." Laura didn't roll her eyes, but it was close.

Beatrice frowned. "I do not appreciate your tone, young lady."

"Well, you're acting like Chanel should be all excited and happy when it's probably taking everything in her not to run away. She's a scientist, Mom, not a socialite."

"I am well aware of my daughter's chosen profession." Beatrice was careful not to frown—that caused wrinkles—but her tone conveyed displeasure.

The interaction fascinated Chanel, who hadn't realized her mother and Laura had anything less than the ideal mother-daughter relationship.

Beatrice looked at Chanel. "Do you need some orange juice to bring up your blood sugar?"

Chanel shook her head. "It just doesn't feel real."

"Believe it or not, I threw up twice before walking down the aisle to your father," Beatrice offered with too much embarrassment for it not to be sincere.

Laura snorted. "You were preggers, Mom. It was probably morning sickness."

"I was not morning sick. I was terrified. I nearly fainted when I was getting ready for my wedding to *your* father."

Chanel couldn't imagine her mother agitated to that level. "Really?"

"It's a huge step, marriage. No matter how much you love the man you're marrying."

"I don't know what the big deal is. If it doesn't work out, they can get divorced," Laura said with the blasé confidence of youth.

Their mother glared at her youngest daughter. "That is not the attitude women of this family take into marriage."

"You and Chanel can get all stressed about it, but I'm not going to. If I get married at all. It all seems like a lot of bother over something that ends in divorce about fifty percent of the time. I think living together makes a lot more sense."

Chanel almost laughed at the look of absolute horror crossing their mother's features. She would have, if she could feel anything that deeply.

Right now the entire world around her was one level removed.

"Stop looking like that, Mom. You and Chanel take everything so seriously. I'm not like you."

It was a total revelation to Chanel that Laura considered her like their mother.

"You're more like us than you realize, young lady. Regardless, there will be no more talk of divorce on your sister's wedding day."

Chanel had never heard her mother use that particular tone with her golden-child sister.

And Laura listened, but her less-than-subdued expression implied she *had* heard it before and didn't find it all that intimidating.

How much had Chanel missed about the world around her? She hadn't realized Demyan was a corporate king, much less a real-life prince. She'd had no idea her mother still loved her father and she'd been sure Beatrice no longer loved *her*.

Chanel had been wrong on all counts.

It was a sobering and hopeful realization at the same time.

Nevertheless, she continued through the rest of her personal preparations for the wedding in the fog of shock that had plagued her since waking without Demyan in her bed.

As the makeup artist finished the final application of lip color, a knock sounded at the door.

"The driver is here. Are you both ready?" Beatrice asked, managing to the look the part of the mother of the bride for a prince, anyway.

Laura looked like a blond angel in her ice-blue Vera Wang maid-of-honor dress that was a perfect complement to Chanel's vintage designer gown.

Chanel hoped her mother had worked some kind of magic and she looked her part, as well. She hadn't looked in the mirror since the hair stylist had shown up.

"It's not the driver," Laura announced after opening the door. Then she dropped into a curtsy and Chanel's throat constricted.

Had the king come to tell her he didn't want Chanel

marrying his quasi-adopted son? No, that was an irrational thought.

But…her thoughts stopped their spin out of control in the face of the majesty that was Queen Oxana in full regalia. The Queen of Volyarus swept into the room, making the huge chamber feel very small all of a sudden.

"Good morning, Chanel. Beatrice." The queen gave Chanel's mother a small incline of her head and then a smile to Laura. "Laura, you look lovely."

"Thank you, Your Majesty," Laura replied with her irrepressible smile.

"And you, my dear," the queen said as she focused her considerable attention on Chanel. "You look absolutely perfect. That's an original by Coco Chanel herself, is it not?"

"Yes."

"She was a brilliant and innovative designer who changed the face of female haute couture almost single-handedly. I find your choice to dress in one of her gowns singularly appropriate as I am sure you will be equally as impacting in your field."

It was the first time anyone who mattered to Chanel emotionally had made such a claim. Bittersweet joy squeezed at her heart, even through the layer of numbness surrounding that organ. "Thank you."

Oxana smiled. "You are very welcome." She offered Chanel a medium-sized dark blue velvet box meant for jewelry. "I would be honored if you would wear this."

Expecting pearls, or something of that nature, Chanel felt her heart beat in a rapid tattoo of shock at the sight of the diamond-encrusted tiara. It wasn't anything as imposing as the crown presently resting on the queen's perfectly coiffed hair, but it *was* worthy of a princess.

"I'm not… This is…" Chanel didn't know what to say, so she closed her mouth on more empty words.

"Part of my own wedding outfit," the queen finished for her. "It would please me to see it worn again."

"Didn't Prince Maksim's wife wear it?" Laura asked, managing to verbalize at least one of the questions swirling through Chanel's brain.

"King Fedir gave her his mother's princess tiara. It was decided between us that mine would be reserved for the wife of our eldest."

Chanel's heart warmed to hear Demyan referred to as the eldest child of the king and queen.

Somehow, though the stylist had been unaware that a tiara would be added later, the updo she had designed for Chanel lent itself perfectly to the diamond-encrusted accessory.

Or so her mother told Chanel.

"Here, see for yourself," Oxana insisted.

Both Laura and Beatrice gave her a concerned look. So, they had noticed she hadn't looked in the mirror since that morning.

But Chanel didn't want visual proof that she didn't look like a princess.

"I trust your judgment," Chanel hedged.

"Then you will trust my instruction to look at yourself, my soon-to-be daughter." Oxana's expression did not invite argument.

Oh, gosh…she'd never even considered this woman would truly consider herself Chanel's mother-in-law.

"You look like a princess," Beatrice said with far more sincerity than such a trite statement deserved.

"You're going to knock Demyan on his butt," Laura added with a little less finesse, but no less certainty.

Far from offended, the queen laughed and agreed. "Yes, I do believe you will."

Taking a breath for courage, Chanel turned to face the impartial judge that could not be gainsaid. The mirror reflected only what was—it made no judgments about that image.

The woman staring back at Chanel with wide gray eyes did not look like a queen. No layers and layers of organza to look like any princess bride Chanel had ever seen in the tabloids, either, but in this moment she *was* beautiful.

The vintage Coco Chanel design fit her like it had been tailored to her figure, the antique lace clinging in all the right places. The single-layer floor-length veil and tiara added elegance Chanel was not used to seeing when she looked in a mirror.

The makeup artist had managed to bring out the shape and pink tint of Chanel's lips while making her eyes glow. Her curls had been tamed into perfect corkscrews and then pinned up so that the length of her neck looked almost swanlike.

This woman would not embarrass Demyan walking up the aisle.

Chanel turned to her mother and hugged Beatrice with more emotion than she'd allowed herself to show in years with the older woman. "Thank you."

"It was my pleasure. It has been a very long time since you allowed me to fuss over you. I enjoyed it." Beatrice returned the embrace and then stepped back, blinking at the moisture in her eyes.

Chanel and her mother would probably never agree on what it meant to *fuss* over someone else, but she began to see that, in her own way, her mother hadn't abandoned Chanel completely as a child.

* * *

Wearing the gold-and-dark-blue official uniform of the Volyarussian Cossack Hetman, Demyan waited at the bottom of the palace steps, as it was his country's royal tradition that he ride with Chanel in the horse-drawn carriage to the cathedral.

His dark eyes met hers, his handsome face stern and unemotional. Yet despite wearing what she'd come to think of as his "corporate king" face, there was an unmistakable soul-deep satisfaction glimmering in his gaze.

He put his hand out toward her. The white-glove-covered appendage hung there, an unexpected beacon. He wasn't supposed to take her hand yet; he wasn't supposed to touch her at all. They had been instructed to enter the carriage separately. She was to sit with her back toward the driver and he was to face the people on the slow procession to the Orthodox cathedral.

According to the wedding coordinator and royal tradition, she and Demyan were not supposed to touch so much as fingertips until the priest proclaimed them man and wife.

So this one gesture spoke volumes of her prince's willingness to put Chanel ahead of protocol.

Without warning, the mental and emotional fog surrounding Chanel fell away, the world coming into stark relief for the first time that day. Though it was early fall, the sun shone bright in the sky, the air around them crisp with autumn chill and filled with a cacophony of voices from the crowds lining the palace drive that were suddenly loud.

Love for Demyan swelled inside Chanel, pushing aside worry and doubt to fill her with a certainty that drove her forward toward the hand held out to her.

Their fingers touched, his curling possessively and decisively around her cold ones. He tugged her forward even as electric current arced between them despite the barrier of his glove.

Devastating emotion shuddered through her, completely dispelling the last of the strange, surreal sensations that had plagued her since waking.

His eyes flared and then he was pulling off the cape from his uniform and wrapping it around her. Several gasps sounded around them and the king said something that Chanel had no doubt was a protest.

She couldn't hear him, though, not over the blood rushing in her ears. The long military cloak settled around her shoulders. She didn't argue that she wasn't really cold, because it carried the fragrance of Demyan's cologne and skin, making her feel embraced by him.

He helped her into the open landau carriage, further eschewing protocol to sit beside her.

Cameras flashed, people cheered and while all of it registered, none of it really impacted Chanel. She was too focused on the man holding her hand and looking at her with quietly banked joy.

"It's just you and me," she said softly, understanding at last.

"Yes."

He didn't relate to her as a prince, though he was undeniably that. Demyan related to her as the man who wanted to share his life with her.

That life might be more complicated because of his title, but at the core, it was the life she wanted. Just as at the core, she knew this man and connected to him soul to soul.

The deep happiness reflecting in his gaze darkened to something more serious. "Always believe that, no matter what else might come up, our marriage is about you and me. Full stop."

"Period," she finished, her heart filled to bursting with such love for this man.

It didn't have to make sense, or be rational, she realized. She had fallen for him immediately and she was wholly and completely *in love* with him now.

They could have waited another year to marry and she wouldn't be any surer of him than she was right now.

As her mom had said, this man was *it* for Chanel, the love of her life, and he felt the same. Even if he hadn't said the words.

Even if he never did.

"I love you," she said to him, needing to in that moment as much as she needed to breathe.

"I will treasure that gift for the rest of my life, I promise you."

He made the vow official less than an hour later when he said it in front of the filled-to-capacity cathedral as part of the personal vows they'd agreed to speak. He also promised to care for her, respect her and support her efforts to make the world a better place through science.

Chanel, who never cried, felt hot tears tracking down her cheeks—thank goodness for her mother's insistence on waterproof makeup—as she spoke her own personal promises, including one to love Demyan for the rest of her life.

It wasn't hard to promise something she didn't think she had a choice about anyway.

His name change was also acknowledged for the first time publicly during the wedding ceremony, when the Orthodox priest led them in their formalized vows before pronouncing them married.

A murmur rippled through the crowd, but Demyan seemed oblivious, his attention wholly on Chanel.

The king's expression was filled with more emotion than Chanel thought the rather standoffish King of

Volyarus capable of as he made his official acknowledgment of his *son's* new married state.

Crown Prince Maksim and his wife were both gracious and clearly happy about the name change when Chanel finally met them for the reception line after the ceremony.

She'd thought it odd she hadn't yet met Demyan's *brother* and was relieved when Princess Gillian remarked on it, as well.

It had been clear from several remarks Demyan made that the two men were close. The fact Chanel hadn't been introduced before had had her wondering if maybe the Crown Prince had disapproved of the wedding.

Only now it was obvious he hadn't even known about the upcoming nuptials until he'd been summoned back to Volyarus by his parents. Chanel didn't understand it, but she was the first person to admit that most politics of social interaction and even family relationships went right over her head.

Prince Maksim seemed nice enough and quite willing to accept Chanel into the family. His own wife wasn't royalty or even nobility, so he had to have a fully modern view of marriage within his family.

Though a comment, or two, made by his wife implied otherwise.

Once they'd finished greeting those allowed into the formal reception line, the entire Yurkovich family addressed the people of Volyarus from the main balcony at the front of the palace. The king gave a speech. They all waved and smiled for what felt like hours before everyone but she and Demyan retreated inside.

He addressed the crowd, telling them how honored he was that Dame Chanel Tanner had agreed to be his wife, that he knew her ancestor Baron Tanner would have been very happy, as well.

Then he kissed Chanel.

And it wasn't a chaste, for-the-masses kiss. Demyan took her mouth with gentle implacability, showing her and everyone watching how very pleased he was she was now officially *his*.

Chanel found herself separated from Demyan during the reception, but she wasn't surprised.

He'd prepared her for the way the formal event would unfold, during which they would have very little time together. He had promised to make up for that on their wedding night and the extended honeymoon that was to follow.

What did surprise Chanel was to find herself completely without any of the people who had seemed intent on making sure she was never on her own in the highly political gathering.

Queen Oxana was occupied talking to Princess Gillian. Chanel's mother had been waylaid by an elderly duke, while Andrew flirted with the man's granddaughter under the watchful and not-very-happy gaze of the teen's eagle-eyed mother. Perry was talking business in a corner somewhere—not that he was one of Chanel's self-appointed minders.

Even Laura had lost herself in the crowd.

Chanel thought now would be the ideal time to find a quiet place to regroup a little. The crush of people was overwhelming for a scientist who spent most of her days in the lab, the mixture of so many voices sounding like a roar in her ears.

Seeing a likely hallway, she ducked out of the huge ballroom. The farther she walked along the hallway, the more muted the cacophony of voices from the ballroom became and the more tension drained from her until even her hands, which had been fisted unconsciously at her sides, uncurled.

Only as her fingers straightened did she realize how very hard she'd been holding them.

She could hear voices ahead, one whose tones she recognized with a smile. Demyan.

Delighted by the opportunity to see him amidst the chaos of her wedding day, she quickened her steps, only slowing down when she realized who he was with.

King Fedir.

The one person who intimidated Chanel and brought out her barely resolved and all-too-recent insecurities. There were two other voices as well, a woman and a man.

They were all speaking Ukrainian, thinly veiled anger resonating in at least two of the speakers' tones.

As Chanel slowed her progress, their conversation resolved itself into actual words she could understand.

The unknown woman demanded, "How dare you humiliate us this way?"

"My actions were not intended as an insult toward you." Demyan did not sound particularly worried the woman had taken whatever he'd done as such, though.

"How could they be taken any other way?" a man who was not the king said. "You have repudiated us before all of Volyarus."

"I didn't repudiate you. I aligned myself with my true family."

"I gave you birth," the woman said in fury.

And the identity of the other two people became clear to Chanel: Demyan's birth parents.

"You also *gave* me to your brother, abdicating any responsibilities and all emotional connections to me. I am no longer your son."

"You are not a child." The man speaking had to be Demyan's biological father. "You know why that was necessary."

"I know that you traded your son for the chance at leverage over your brother-in-law, the king. I know that Fedir and Oxana needed a secondary heir to the throne, but they have always treated me as more than an expedience."

"I'm very pleased you took our house's name, Demyan," the king said with sincerity. "Your parents could have avoided this surprise today by allowing Oxana and me to adopt you as a child. It was their choice not to, as you said...for their own expedience. I, for one, was joyfully surprised and I know your mother feels the same."

Chanel smiled, pleased the outwardly cold man so obviously cared about his adopted son. Demyan said something she did not catch.

"You think you are more than an expedience to the king and queen?" Duke Zaretsky sneered. "He has just ensured you sacrificed the rest of your life for the sake of his family's wealth. You are far more his tool than you were ever mine."

Chanel didn't understand what the duke meant by his words, but there was no question they were intended to wound. And she wasn't about to stand by while anyone tried to hurt Demyan.

She pushed open the door to what turned out to be a very impressive masculine study and crossed to Demyan's side quickly.

His dark gaze flared with something that looked like worry before pleasure at her presence sparked to life, as well. "Hello, *sérdenko*."

"What are you doing here?" the king asked with his usual less-than-warm attitude toward her.

"The reception was getting too loud."

"You cannot abandon your responsibilities as a hostess on a whim."

"Really? Then what are you doing back here?" she asked with enough sarcasm to be mistaken for her sister. "Correct me if I'm wrong, but wasn't it *your* name on the invitation listed as host of this party?"

Demyan laughed, taking her hand and pulling her to his side. "You make an excellent case, little one."

Everyone in the room except Chanel showed differing levels of surprise at his humor. The king recovered first, giving her a grudging look of respect when she'd expected a frown and polite dressing-down.

She had a lot of experience with both and a lifetime realizing she was no good at taking the path of least resistance, even if it meant avoiding them.

"Point taken," King Fedir said. "We should *all* be getting back."

"Does she know yet?" the duke asked, his expression calculating, his tone undeniably malicious.

CHAPTER ELEVEN

CHANEL DIDN'T ASK what he meant, or even acknowledge the man had spoken.

He'd done it in Ukrainian. Somehow she doubted Demyan had been into sharing confidences with the older man, which meant the duke had no idea she understood the language. That made his choice to converse in it pointedly without courtesy.

"You will be silent," the king replied in the same language to his brother-in-law, his tone harsh.

Ignoring both posturing men, Chanel smiled up at Demyan. "I missed you."

"Oh, how sweet," Princess Svitlana said in a tone that made it clear she thought it was anything but.

Demyan's expression was an odd mixture of tenderness and a strange underlying anxiety as he looked down at Chanel. "I am very proud of you. Not many science geeks would do so well at an affair of state with so little training."

"You assigned a very potent group of babysitters."

His nostrils flared as if her words surprised him.

"You didn't think I realized you'd asked them to watch over me?" Once she had, she'd felt very well cared for.

Demyan would never leave Chanel to sink or swim in the shark-infested waters of his life.

"I could not be with you the entire time," he said by way of an explanation.

Not that she'd needed one. "Because you're a prince."

"It's a nominative title only," his birth mother said with more venom, in English this time. "He's no more a prince than you are a well-bred princess."

Chanel gave the older woman a measure of her attention, but kept her body and clear allegiance toward Demyan. "I am not a horse and I wasn't born in a breeding program. While I won't claim to be a princess, Demyan is definitely a prince."

"He won't inherit. Not now that Princess Gillian is carrying the next heir to the throne."

"But he is the king and queen's son. That makes him a prince."

"I gave birth to him," the duchess said.

Chanel found it odd that the duke never verbalized his claim at fatherhood. "Congratulations."

"Are you mocking me?"

"No. I don't know what your other children are like. Hopefully more like their older brother than their parents, but I do know you gave birth to an amazing man in Demyan. I'm sure you are very proud of that accomplishment, but you aren't his mother any more than I am a princess."

"Oxana is my mother," Demyan asserted with absolute assurance.

"And you would do anything for her and the man you consider your father, even marry some socially backward American *scientist* to protect the Yurkovich financial interests." She said scientist as if it was a dirty word.

Chanel almost smiled. She'd never considered her vocation as beyond the pale before.

"That is enough, Svitlana." The king's tone was again harsh, his expression forbidding.

"Oh, so you *haven't* told her?" Duke Zaretsky asked snidely, clearly ignoring his king's evident wrath and this time taking evident pleasure in speaking English. "I could almost feel sorry for her. She gave up hundreds of millions of dollars by marrying you and she doesn't even know it."

There could be no doubt the duke was talking about Chanel, but the words made absolutely no sense.

"I didn't give up anything and gained everything marrying Demyan," she fiercely asserted.

The duchess looked at her pityingly. "You have no idea, but no matter what kind of prenuptial agreement these two convinced you to sign, until you spoke your vows three hours ago, you were a twenty-percent owner in Yurkovich Tanner."

"I wasn't. My great-great-grandfather left his shares to the Volyarussian people." He'd told her great-grandmother so in a letter still in Chanel's possession, along with the family Bible.

"And they have been used to finance infrastructure, schools and hospitals since then," the king assured her.

She smiled at him, holding no grudge for his unwelcoming demeanor. "I know. I did some research when I got the scholarship. Your country is kind of amazing for its progressive stance on the environment and energy conservation."

"I am glad you think so."

"That money was yours," the king's sister insisted. "Until you married my son."

The claims were starting to make an awful kind of sense, but Chanel had no intention of allowing the two emotional vultures in front of her to know about the splinters of pain slicing their way through Chanel's heart.

She simply said, "He's not your son."

"Would you like to see your grandfather's will?" the duke asked, clearly unwilling to give up.

Two things were obvious in that moment. The first was that there had to be some truth to what the duke and his wife were saying. If there wasn't, Demyan and the king would have categorically denied it.

Also, they were both way too tense now for the claims to be entirely false.

Second, whatever the duke and Princess Svitlana's motives for telling Chanel, it had nothing to do with helping or protecting *anyone*. Her least of all.

In fact, she was fairly certain their intention was to hurt the son who had finally made a public alliance with the family who had raised him.

She turned away from the duke and duchess to face Demyan. "Tell me your siblings don't take after your egg and sperm donors."

Duplicate sounds of outrage indicated the Zaretskys had heard her just fine.

Demyan didn't respond, an expression she'd never seen in his eyes. Fear.

She wasn't sure what he was afraid of. Whether he was afraid she would mess up whatever plan he'd made with King Fedir, or worried she would go ballistic at their very politically attended reception, or something else really didn't matter.

Whatever Demyan felt for her, Chanel loved him and she wasn't going to let the two people whose rejection had already caused him a lifetime of pain hurt him anymore.

"I think it's time we all returned to the reception." She couldn't quite dredge up a smile, but she did her best to mask her own hurt.

He spoke then, the words coming out in a strange tone. "We need to talk."

She didn't want him showing vulnerability in front of the Zaretskys. Chanel wasn't giving them the satisfaction of believing they'd succeeded in their petty and vindictive efforts.

She reached up and cupped his face, like he did so often with her, hoping it gave him the same sense of comfort and being cared for it had always done her, no matter how much of a lie it might have been at the time. "Later."

"You promise?"

"Yes."

"She is a fool," the duke said in disgusted Ukrainian.

Chanel looked at him over her shoulder, her expression a perfect reflection of her mother's favorite one for disdain. "The only fool here is you if you think for one second you have the power to influence my prince's life for good or ill today, or any time in the future. You simply don't matter."

She had also spoken in his native language and enjoyed the shock that produced in the overweening nobleman.

The duchess gasped. "You're American."

"Which does not equate to uninformed, stupid or uneducated." Chanel met eyes so similar in color but different in expression from Demyan's. "My heritage in this country may not be royal, or as long-standing, but when it comes to the welfare of Volyarus, it is equally as important as yours."

Her grandfather had helped this nation stay afloat financially three decades ago and his efforts were still benefitting the Volyarussians.

"You already knew," the duchess said, almost as if she admired Chanel's acumen. "But then why did you marry him?"

"Because she loves me," Demyan said, his voice gravelly.

Chanel turned back to him without agreeing or giving his parents another single solitary moment of her time. She hadn't known about the will being different than what her great-grandmother had believed, or what that had to do with Chanel's marriage to Demyan, though she could make a pretty educated guess based on the prenuptial agreement.

She wasn't about to admit that to the Zaretskys, though.

Demyan was searching her face as if trying to read Chanel's thoughts. So far in their relationship, she'd been an open book. She had little hope of hiding what was going on in her head right now.

But she didn't have to talk about it. Especially in front of the older generation of the royal family.

"Leave," the king said to his sister and brother-in-law.

The Zaretskys started for the door of the study.

"No," the king instructed. "Out through the secret passage. You will not return to the reception and you will be out of the palace within the hour."

"What? You cannot be serious. How would that look?" his sister demanded.

"Like you threw a temper tantrum when your son chose to change his name to reflect his true parentage," the king replied, his tone arctic.

Princess Svitlana crossed her arms, but stopped just shy of stomping her feet. "I won't do it."

"You will. Do not presume to forget that this is not a nominal King of Volyarus. I hold the power to revoke your citizenship and deport you. Do not tempt me to use it."

The duke and his wife both paled at the king's words, Princess Svitlana doing a fair imitation of a gasping fish, though no words passed her lips.

The expression in her brother's eyes suggested she keep it that way.

Showing she was marginally more intelligent than evidence might suggest, the princess left without another word. Through the secret passageway. Her husband followed close behind her.

Chanel stepped back from Demyan, intending to return to the reception. The crowds of people and litany of voices that fifteen minutes ago had seemed so overwhelming now called like a beacon for escape from the thoughts that were multiplying by the second in her head.

And with every new thought came a shard of pain Chanel had no idea how long she could contain.

The king blocked her exit, his gaze searching hers as much as his adopted son's had done. However, the level of ruthlessness behind his perusal chilled her; she'd felt only confusion mixed with hurt at Demyan's look.

She said nothing, simply waited for the King of Volyarus to move.

He frowned. "You will not return to the reception only to cause a scene."

She was doing her best to hold back an emotional devastation she hadn't experienced since her father's death. Did he really think his display of bossiness was helping the situation?

"Let me give you a small piece of advice, Your Majesty."

His brows rose in obvious shock at her tone.

She went on, "Right this second, all I see when I look at you is a man who would use whatever underhanded means are necessary to rob a woman and her family of a legacy they knew nothing about."

"There was nothing underhanded about your marriage to my son. It is legal in every sense. You cannot undo it."

She said a word that rarely passed her lips, but called the lie for what it was. Oh, he might be correct in that she could not undo whatever legality the wedding had wrought, but as for nothing about it being devious?

That was an ugly bit of nonsense. "All I've done so far is tell you my opinion, not offered my advice. If you're smart, you will take it."

"Chanel, you cannot speak to him like that," Demyan said, sounding tired rather than corrective. "He is your king."

"Not *my* king." Any more than Demyan was *her* prince.

King Fedir asked before Demyan could reply to that claim, "What is your advice?"

"Do not attempt to tell me what to do. Because though my intention is *not* to embarrass my family, or Queen Oxana who has been nothing but kind to me, your very instruction not to cause a scene is nearly overwhelming impetus to do so."

"You love my son."

She didn't deny it. What would be the point? Everyone in that room knew the truth about her emotions. And his now, no matter how misled she'd been that morning.

"But I don't even like you," she told Demyan's adopted father very succinctly.

The king flinched, his face slackening in shock as if he'd never had anyone speak to him in such a way before. Maybe he hadn't.

"Chanel…" That was Demyan, the tone in his voice not one she wanted to hear or could even begin to trust right then.

Definitely not admonishment for her rudeness to his father, but what it was, she refused to name.

She spun to face him, her heart in a vise that brought pain with each indrawn breath. "Don't. Just *don't,* Demyan. However horrible their intentions, the duke and duchess were more honest with me than you've been."

"No." He lurched forward, as if he'd been yanked by a string attached to his chest.

She stepped back quickly, sure of one thing. She could not allow him to touch her right now. "Stop. I said later. I meant *later*."

"Perhaps you two should speak *now*," the king said, sounding less certain than he had to this point.

Chanel made no attempt to hide the utter dislike she felt when she faced him. "You're doing it again. You say maybe we should talk and all I can think is how much more certain I am that there isn't going to be any more talking."

"You are a contrary woman."

"You have no idea how contrary I can be, but spend a few minutes talking with my stepfather and he'll fill you in."

"I have spent some time in his company already."

And heard an earful, Chanel was sure. For the first time in her life, she simply didn't care if Perry had managed to turn someone right off her. "I'm sure he enjoyed that."

"He's an opportunistic man."

"He is." Something clicked in her mind, two memories coming together to form a single conclusion. "He's the one, isn't he, the reason you had to act now?"

The king's face smoothed over into an emotionless mask, but not before she saw the flare of surprise at her guess.

Because she was right.

"My great-great-grandfather Tanner died, apparently with a very different will to the one my great-grandmother believed to have been in existence. Yet no one from your family has approached mine in four generations to secure Baron Tanner's shares in your precious company."

"It is not just a company—it is the financial cornerstone of an entire country."

"Your country."

"Yours now, too."

"That remains to be seen."

"Chanel—" Demyan tried to say something.

She put her hand up. "No. Not you. Not now. Trust me when I tell you it is better for everyone if you show that ruthless patience you are so well-known for in business."

"How do you know about that?"

"I've spent six weeks learning you." Too bad he hadn't done the same.

He would have realized there was no worse way she could have learned of his subterfuge than to be told by an outside party. But then maybe he had realized and it simply didn't matter.

He wouldn't risk upsetting whatever scheme he and his father had set in motion to protect their precious wealth and thereby their country.

She focused on the king again. "My stepfather approached your company trying to trade on connections he didn't really have, but it got you all worried."

"He is a resourceful man."

"He's a shark, though I think maybe Demyan is a bigger, and much meaner, one."

"Without doubt." The king sounded proud.

But then he would be, wouldn't he? His son's ruthless resourcefulness had netted him full interest in Yurkovich Tanner for the first time in four generations.

She didn't know how, or what the details were, but that much she had gleaned from what had and had not been said in this room tonight.

"There are half-a-dozen moderately accessible chemical compounds that would eat the flesh from a shark's body in less than a minute, did you know that?"

The king shook his head, his expression almost bemused.

"I did. I know every single one of them."

"Are you threatening him?"

"I am reminding you that even sharks get eaten if they aren't careful and it doesn't always take a bigger shark to do it."

"I believe there is a strand of ruthlessness in you, too."

"Would you like to find out?"

The king opened his mouth and then closed it, giving Demyan a look of concern before his expression turned thoughtful. "No."

"Good."

"What do you plan to do?"

"Throw the bouquet."

"You know that is not what I meant."

"I care?"

The king's mouth tightened, but he stepped aside, having seemingly finally gotten the message that his admonitions were more effective goads to bad behavior than preventers of it.

Chanel threw the bouquet.

She even managed to dredge up a photo-op-worthy smile when Laura caught it and tossed it away again immediately. Her sister's attitude toward the institution of marriage couldn't have been more obvious.

Chanel had to wonder if the teenager had caught the bouquet just so she could throw it away again. The entire ballroom erupted into laughter and even Beatrice was smiling.

She should be.

Her disappointment of a daughter had managed to land a prince. No wonder she'd come to Chanel's apartment with stories of undying first love.

Chanel couldn't believe she'd thought her mom was

finally showing a vested interest in her oldest daughter's happiness.

But then she'd let herself be convinced that Demyan *wanted* to marry *her*. Not Bartholomew Tanner's only surviving heir.

Smile still fixed firmly in place, Chanel looked out over the ballroom full of people. Her gaze settled on Queen Oxana. The older woman looked pleased, her normally controlled expression filled with unmistakable happiness.

Was that because she knew the Yurkovich fortune was secure, or was she happy at what she thought was her son's marriage to someone she believed was his one true love?

Another memory clicked into place and the smile fell away from Chanel's face. Oxana was the one who had made Demyan promise not to use protestations of love to convince Chanel to marry him.

The queen knew about the will. She must, but she had scruples where her husband and son did not. She might be the only person Chanel could trust to tell her the truth.

She was tempted to leave the reception early, but every time she let her gaze find Demyan, he was watching her. He would only follow her, but she wanted a chance to talk to his mother, to get some answers on her own first.

She got her chance unexpectedly when Oxana came up to her and laid a hand on her arm. "Are you all right, Chanel?"

Chanel looked toward Demyan. He returned her regard, his dark-eyed expression unreadable, but something in the way he watched Chanel and his mother told Chanel he had sent the older woman to her.

"You know," Chanel said instead of answering.

"That you and my husband had something of an altercation earlier? Yes."

Interesting that the queen considered the argument to

be between Chanel and the king, not Chanel and Demyan. "Did he tell you?"

"Demyan did."

Even the sound of his name on Oxana's lips hurt Chanel in some indefinable way. "You were aware of their plans because of my great-great-grandfather's will."

Oxana nodded.

"You made him promise not to lie about loving me. Thank you." She wasn't sure how much worse the pain inside her would be if she'd believed false words of love. "I want to read the will."

"If you ask Demyan, he will tell you everything."

"I don't want to hear from him. He had his chance to tell me. He chose not to."

"He was trying to protect our nation."

Chanel couldn't help mocking. "Because I'm such a huge security risk."

Oxana looked around them, obviously concerned someone might overhear. No one was in range of their subdued tones, but that could change any second.

"I don't want to be here," Chanel admitted hopelessly.

There was nowhere else she could be without someone she didn't want to talk to following her, which included pretty much everyone but Oxana at the moment.

The queen sighed, looking at her sadly. "He cares for you."

Maybe Oxana wouldn't be the best company either. Chanel just shook her head, moving to turn away.

But Oxana's hand on her arm stopped her from putting distance between them. "Come, I will take you someplace away from the scrutiny and company of others."

Chanel thought it a bit obvious when the queen led her to the retiring room for the ladies, but they didn't stop in the outer room as she expected. The queen led her into one of the three small chambers with toilets, closing the door behind them.

While the room was larger than the usual commode stall, it wasn't exactly meant for two people and Chanel didn't think talking about sensitive subjects with only a door between them and anyone who walked into the lounge was a good idea.

But Oxana did not ask any questions, or make any attempts at comfort. She simply pushed up on a section of wainscoting and then the wall behind the commode swung backward.

Oxana put her hand out to Chanel. "Come, I'll take you to the private papers library for the House of Yurkovich. Your great-great-grandfather's will has been stored there."

CHAPTER TWELVE

DARKNESS SURROUNDED CHANEL as she stood on the balcony overlooking the now-silent grounds of the palace. The reception was long over, the last guest's car having left the drive thirty minutes before.

Temperatures had dropped since that morning and she shivered in the cold air, but she did not go back inside.

Before leaving her to read over the will and relevant places in Bartholomew Tanner's diaries the queen had marked for Chanel, Oxana had told her that her favorite place for solitude was this balcony.

"The bedrooms do not have security cameras in them, but they do have infrared monitoring. The public rooms and hallways are all covered with video feed, though. The only two places in the palace where you can relax unmonitored in any way are the public address balcony and the one outside Fedir's rooms."

"Isn't that a security risk?" Chanel had asked.

But Oxana had shaken her head. "The walls and every approach are covered."

Which meant that Demyan would eventually find her because Chanel's path to the balcony would have been tracked by video monitoring once she left the secret passageway.

She could have left the palace completely. Chanel was

a resourceful woman and there had been dozens of cars departing the grounds over the past few hours.

But she wasn't a coward and she'd never hidden from the truth, no matter how much it might hurt to face.

What that truth was, however, wasn't entirely clear. Not after reading the will. Not after remembering Demyan's words in the carriage that morning.

Not after having Oxana tell Chanel exactly what promise she'd extracted from her son over the *love* thing.

Not until Chanel asked Demyan the only question that really mattered.

"Chanel."

She turned at the sound of her name on Demyan's lips.

He stood framed by the light from the hall. He reached and flipped a switch. More golden light flooded the balcony.

"Turn it off," she said, angling her head away so he could not see the damage tears had done on even the indelible makeup job her mother's professional artist had applied.

"No. We do not need more shadows in our relationship."

She swung back to face him head-on, anger making her muscles rigid with tension. "The shadows are all you."

He nodded, his expression as tortured as she felt, if she could believe the evidence of her eyes.

She wasn't sure she trusted her own perceptions at all, though, not after how easily he'd taken her in. However, she didn't think he could fake the parchment-pale of his complexion, the way his black pupils nearly swallowed the espresso irises or the way he breathed in what she would consider panicked gasps in anyone else.

"That day in my lab. It was planned."

"I needed to meet you. You are not a social person."

"So Yurkovich Tanner donated five million dollars to my department for research. That's an expensive introduc-

tion." Though nothing in comparison to what the Yurkovich fortune stood to lose if she had made her claim on the
Tanner shares in the company.

"It also ensured you were predisposed to look on me
favorably."

"Your idea, or the king's?"

"Does it matter?"

"No."

"You've read the will."

"Oxana told you."

"I saw you go into the personal archives library on the
video monitor feedback."

"Oh."

"I spent two hours watching the tapes, trying to find
you."

"We used the secret passages."

"Yes. You only showed up for brief periods on the video
monitors and there were too many extra people in the
palace to track you with the infrared body counter and
placement."

"Poor you."

"Cha…" Her name choked off and he stepped forward,
stumbling, though she knew the stone floor was smooth
with no hindrances.

"You never needed your glasses." For anything.

He stopped a couple of feet from her. "I told you that."

"But I thought you needed them as an emotional crutch."

"I do not use crutches."

"No. A man without emotions doesn't need crutches
for them, does he?"

"I am human, damn it, not a puppet. I have emotions."

"I bet it was the king's idea to approach me looking like
a corporate geek to match my science-nerd personality."

"He believed I would be too intimidating in my usual way."

"That man, the corporate shark, he's part of you."

"Yes."

"But he's not all of you."

"I thought he was."

"Until when?" she pushed.

"Until I met you."

"You don't mean that."

"I've never meant anything more."

"You lied to me."

"I am ruthless when it comes to protecting my country and those I love."

"I noticed."

"There is little hope that will change."

"No. It's part of your nature. You would have made a very good Cossack."

"We still have the elite in our army. As tradition dictates, I spent two years training with them before going to university."

"Wasn't that Prince Maksim's job?"

"He wasn't the oldest son to the king."

"But he is heir to the throne."

"Yes."

"Does that bother you?"

"No. I hate politics."

"I hate being deceived."

"I will not do it again."

"Can you really promise that, with your ruthless nature?"

"Yes."

"Why?"

"I don't understand."

"I think you do."

If anything, his face paled further. "Don't, Chanel."

"Don't what? Make you admit your vulnerabilities. If you have any, that is."

"I do."

"I'm not stupid by any stretch, you know. Legalese may not be science speak, but I understand it well enough."

"Yes?"

"Yes. Bartholomew Tanner's will is unambiguous. My marriage to you negated all claim I, or any of my children, had to Yurkovich Tanner."

Demyan nodded.

"The prenuptial didn't need to spell that out at all."

"No."

"You had that paragraph added as a kind of warning to me, didn't you?"

He shrugged.

"You also made sure I would be taken care of financially despite the fact that legally I would have no way of pursuing any monetary interests in the future."

"You are my wife. I wanted you provided for."

"I bet the king just loved the terms of the prenup."

"He agreed to them."

She was sure there was a story there, but right now she wasn't interested in hearing it. "You came after me with the intention of securing Volyarussian economic stability, no matter the cost."

"Yes." The word sounded torn out of him.

"You could have just asked me to sign the shares over and I would have done it. Especially after reading my grandfather's diaries."

"His diaries?"

"He spelled out his intention of leaving the shares to the people of Volyarus, but at first he was still holding out hope your great-uncle would marry my great-grandmother, then he got his hopes set on the next generation. He died before he could try to make that alliance happen."

"I am aware."

"What you didn't know was that he'd written my great-grandmother and told her that he planned to leave his interest in Yurkovich Tanner to the Volyarussian people. I never would have tried to undermine his clear wishes."

"Your stepfather would not be so sanguine. He might well have convinced your mother to bring suit on her deceased husband's behalf."

"A suit that wouldn't have gone anywhere without my cooperation, and I wouldn't have given it."

"We did not know that."

"You had to have realized, as you got to know me."

"Once I commit to a purpose, I do not change my direction on a whim or the hope of a different outcome."

"Maybe you decided you *wanted* to marry me." It was hard to say the words, to put it out there like that, but this man was about as in touch with his emotions as the puppet he was so adamant he was not.

"I did want to marry you."

"Why?"

He stared at her, his expression so open she wanted to cry. Because it showed so much that he so clearly didn't know how to express verbally. One thing was really obvious. This man did not know what to do with his emotions.

"We are very compatible."

"Are we?"

"You know we are."

"You're a prince. I'm a scientist."

"Those are our titles, not who we are at the core."

"Okay, then you're ruthless and I'm insecure. We're both emotionally repressed."

"But you are more secure about yourself with me."

"And you are less ruthless with me?" she asked, already knowing the answer.

Looking back on it, she saw that the prenuptial agreement was practically a love letter from Demyan.

The uncertainty in his expression was heartbreaking. "Yes?"

She couldn't hold back from touching him any longer. She stepped right into his personal space and he wrapped his arms around her like it was the most natural thing in the world to do.

"Yes, Demyan. *Yes.*" His ruthlessness wasn't always a bad thing, but she brought out the best in him, too.

Now, if she could just get him to realize what that meant.

"You turn me on like no other woman ever has." He spoke as if that fact confused him. "I don't like being without you. Not even for a couple of days. It makes it hard to focus."

"I'm glad to hear that. I feel the same way."

"I miss you," he stressed. "Every hour we are apart. Even when I am working."

No matter how this thing between them had started, it had caught Demyan in the whirlwind of emotion right along with her. Which was the conclusion she'd finally come to after a lot of pain-filled soul-searching and examination of every memory from the moment they'd met.

"It hurt finding out about the will and your reason for marrying me from your sperm donor."

Pain twisted Demyan's features. "I am sorry." He reached up to wipe along the tear streaks on one cheek. "You cried."

"At first, all I could think was that you'd tricked me into loving you when you felt nothing for me at all. That you probably planned on getting rid of me as soon as the ink was dry on the marriage certificate."

"No!" He kissed her, the connection between their mouths infused with a desperation stronger than anything she'd ever felt from him.

It was a magnified version of the feelings that emanated off him at night when making love since their arrival in Volyarus.

She did nothing to stop the kiss for a long time, needing this connection as badly as he so clearly did.

But eventually, she broke her mouth away. "Were you going to tell me?"

"Maybe someday. I do not know. I did not want to."

"You were afraid."

"I am never afraid."

"Not usually, but the idea of losing me scared you."

"Have I lost you?" His arms tightened around her even as he asked the question.

"No."

"No?" he asked, his voice breaking so the word sounded as if it had two syllables.

"Definitely not. Yet."

His big body went absolutely rigid. "Yet?"

"It all depends on your answer to a question."

He stared down at her.

"You never break your promises, right?" She let her body mold completely to his, trying to give him strength.

That's what people who loved each other did—they lent their strength when it was needed.

"Right."

"Tell me you love me."

The tension emanating off him increased exponentially.

"Your mom told me what she made you promise her."

Demyan's expression was haunted.

"You promised not to say you love me unless you really mean it," Chanel reminded him. "You can say it now, Demyan. I will treasure your love forever, too."

"But…"

"You love me."

"I do?"

"That stuff you were saying earlier, about missing me, being afraid to lose me, even the way you changed the pre-nuptial agreement, it all means one thing."

"It does?" Comprehension and acceptance dawned over his features, making him smile with heartbreaking happiness. "It does. I love you, Chanel, more than my life as a prince. More than anything."

More tears filled her eyes, but these didn't burn or hurt her heart. "I love you, too."

"I mean it."

"I know."

"No, I mean…we don't have to live with the whole royalty thing. I know it's not the life you want. I can abdicate my role."

It wasn't an empty promise and it would not come without significant cost to this amazing man. Especially after finally acknowledging his true role as son of Oxana and Fedir, but Demyan was entirely sincere in his offer.

"No. I love you, Demyan. Ruthless prince. Corporate king and shark. All of you."

"I love you for all that you are, too, Chanel, and that includes the woman who has never aspired to be a socialite."

"I'm not going to be one now, either."

"My uncle…father is not going to know what to do with you."

"He'll probably call me princess just to annoy me."

Demyan laughed, the sound freer and filled with more joy than she'd ever heard from him. "You may well be right."

"So long as you call me love."

"*Koxána moja,*" he said, calling her his love in Ukrainian. "Always and forever. You are the very heart that beats inside my chest."

And then he took her back to the rooms they would share whenever staying at the palace for the years to come and made tender, night-long love to her, using those words and so many others to tell Chanel that this man truly loved her and always would.

Later she snuggled into his body and yawned as she said, "I guess it's a good thing you've got a sneaky, underhanded side."

"Is it?"

"Yep."

"Why?"

"We never would have gotten together otherwise. You snuck past all my barriers."

"It is only fair, since you destroyed mine."

Two broken people who had not even realized they were broken had been made whole by love.

Yes, Chanel thought, that was exactly right and fair.

"Love you, Demyan."

"I love you."

"Always."

"For the rest of our lives."

"And beyond." Eternity would not end a love so strong.

"And beyond."

EPILOGUE

OXANA CUDDLED HER latest grandchild. The tiny infant was only three days old, but he was so alert that the queen could not help smiling into soft gray eyes so like his mother's.

Little Damon was her fourth grandchild and she had no doubts he would bring her every bit as much joy as the other three she'd been gifted by her sons and their wives.

The oldest, Mikael, was five and the only child Gillian and Maksim had conceived. Their youngest was adopted, a beautiful little girl who had both her besotted parents wrapped around her dainty little fingers.

Demyan and Chanel's oldest had turned two, four months before the birth of her little brother. Both children were cosseted and adored by parents who showed a decided ruthlessness when it came to putting their family first.

Oxana could not be more pleased. She'd given up a lifetime of love and found little personal happiness in order to give her sons the best chance at a better life. One would be king, the other would continue to oversee their business interests, but both were blissfully happy.

And Oxana thought that a more-than-fair compensation for the sacrifices she'd made. After all, she had her grandchildren around her now. They called her Nana, not Your Majesty, and didn't hesitate to muss her designer couture with messy fingers.

How incredibly blessed she was, but her sons had received the true gift beyond measure.

A lifetime love with women who not only knew but accepted both men for who and what they were.

Fedir often didn't know what to make of his independent-minded daughters by marriage, but he loved being a grandfather and already had grand plans for the children.

Oxana didn't tell him, but she had plans, too, and she knew exactly what each grandchild needed for the future. Love.

Just as she had done her best to make sure both her sons realized their loves, she would do whatever it took to ensure each of her grandchildren knew true love, as well.

Fedir could plan all the machinations he wanted, but in the end? Love would triumph.

Just as it had for her children.

* * * * *

HER SHAMEFUL SECRET

SUSANNA CARR

To Carly Byrne and Lucy Gilmour with thanks
for their insights and generous support.

CHAPTER ONE

ISABELLA WILLIAMS heard the throaty growl of an expensive sports car and lifted her head like a hunted animal scenting danger. The sudden move made her head spin. She took a step back, gripping the serving tray as she fought for her balance.

The sound of the car faded before she turned to see it. Isabella exhaled shakily, her bunched muscles relaxing. She swiped her hand against her clammy forehead, hating how her imagination ran wild. Her mind was playing tricks on her. One sports car drove past her and she immediately thought of him.

It was ridiculous to think that Antonio Rossi was in this part of Rome, or even searching for her. She rolled her eyes in self-disgust. She'd only shared a bed with him for a few glorious months in the spring. The guy would have long forgotten her. He was every woman's secret fantasy and Isabella was certain that she had been replaced the moment she left his bed.

The thought pricked at Isabella and she blinked away the tears that stung in the backs of her eyes. Glancing at the clock, she calculated how many more hours she had left on her shift. Too many. All she wanted to do was crawl back into bed, burrow under the threadbare covers and keep the world at bay. But she couldn't afford to take a day off. She needed every euro to survive.

"Isabella, you have customers waiting," her boss barked at her.

She simply nodded, too tired to give her usual sarcastic response, and headed toward one of the small tables on the sidewalk café. She would get through this day just like every other day. One foot in front of the other. One minute at a time.

It felt like she had waded through sludge by the time she got to the tiny table where the couple waited. They didn't seem to mind her slow pace. The man gently, almost reverently, kissed the woman's lips. Envy pierced through Isabella's stupor. She bit down on her lip to hold back a whimper as she remembered what it felt like to be adored and desired.

Isabella's shoulders slumped as the bittersweet memories poured over her. She couldn't recapture that kind of love. She would never be the center of Antonio's attention again, and he would no longer be her entire world. She missed his possessive kisses and the raw hunger they'd shared. But, much as she missed him, he would never take her back. Not when he discovered the truth.

Her knees threatened to buckle under the weight of her regret. She gritted her teeth and harnessed the last of her self-control. Those wildly romantic days were over, she reminded herself fiercely. It was best not to think of them.

"Are you ready to order?" she asked hoarsely in Italian. Her grasp of the language wasn't that great, despite her taking a few classes in college. Her struggle to communicate made it even more difficult to get through a day.

Once she'd had big dreams of becoming fluent in Italian, transforming herself into a sophisticated and glamorous woman and taking the city of Rome by storm. She'd wanted to find adventure, beauty and love. For a brief moment she'd had it all in her grasp, but she'd allowed it to slip through her fingers.

Now she worked all day in this dump and had no money. People either ignored her or viewed her as trash. So much for her transformation. She could have gotten that treatment back home. At least then she would know what was being said behind her back. She lived in a room above the café that didn't have running water or a lock on the door. All she had was the weight of the world on her shoulders and a deep need to survive.

As she took down the order and walked back to the kitchen Isabella realized that she was in danger of getting stuck here. She needed to work harder, faster and smarter if she wanted to return to America in the next few months. Now more than ever she needed to surround herself with the familiar. Find a place where she could keep her head down, work hard and complete her college degree. After all this time yearning for excitement, she now longed to find a safe haven.

But she didn't think she could keep this up, working long hours and barely getting by. And it was only going to get harder. The thought made her want to drop to the floor in a heap and cry.

Isabella leaned against the kitchen wall. One day she'd get out of this nightmare. She weakly closed her eyes, ignoring her boss's reprimand to hurry. Soon she'd have enough money to fly back to America. She'd start over and maybe get it right the next time. If there was one thing she could rely on it was learning from her mistakes.

Antonio Rossi surveyed the small sidewalk café. After searching all weekend he was going to face the woman who had almost destroyed him and his family. He strode to an empty table and sat down, his lethal grace concealing the anticipation of battle that was racing through his veins. This time he wasn't going to fall for Isabella's big blue eyes and innocent beauty. He would be in command.

He leaned back, his legs sprawled under the tiny table. Sliding dark sunglasses on his nose, Antonio looked at the paint-chipped, rusted furniture. Of all the places he'd thought she would be, he mused as he glimpsed the ratted, faded awning, he hadn't pictured a dirty little café on the wrong side of Rome.

Why was Isabella living in this filth and poverty? It didn't make sense. He had opened his world to her. She had lived in his penthouse apartment and shared his bed. She had had his servants to take care of her.

And she'd thrown it all away when she'd slept with his brother.

The knowledge still ate away at him. He had provided Isabella with everything, but it hadn't been enough. No matter how much he'd given, how hard he'd worked, he hadn't been able to compare with his brother. It had always been that way.

Still, he had been blindsided by Giovanni's drunken confession six months ago. Had responded by casting

Isabella and Giovanni out of his life. It had been swift and vicious, but they had deserved much worse.

Isabella stepped into his view. Tension gripped Antonio, and he braced himself for the emotional impact as he watched her precariously balance two cappuccinos on a serving tray. He had prepared himself for it, but seeing her was like a punch to his gut as she walked past him.

She wore a thin black T-shirt, a skimpy denim skirt and scuffed black flats, but she still had the power to draw his attention. His gaze lingered on her bare legs. He remembered how they'd felt wrapped around his hips as he drove into her welcoming body.

Antonio exhaled slowly and purged the image from his mind. He would not be distracted by her sexual allure or her innocent face. He had made the mistake of lowering his guard with her. He had trusted Isabella and got close to her. That wouldn't happen again.

Antonio grimly watched her serve the couple, noticing that she looked different. The last time he'd seen her, she had been asleep in his bed, flushed and naked, her long blonde hair fanning like a halo across the white silk pillow.

Isabella now looked pale and sickly. Her hair fell in a limp ponytail. The curves that had used to make him forget his next thought had diminished. She was bony and frail.

She looked terrible. A cruel smile flickered on the edge of his mouth. Antonio hoped she'd been to hell and back. He was prepared to take her there again.

He'd once believed she was sweet and innocent, but it had all been a lie. Her blushes and slow smiles had disarmed him and he had been convinced that she wanted

only him. But her open affection had been a smoke-
screen.

It turned out that Isabella was a master of the mind
game and outplayed the most conniving women in his
world, who would lie, cheat and bed-hop to get closer
to Gio, heir to the Rossi fortune. Isabella had seduced
Antonio with her angelic beauty. Made him believe that
he was her first choice. Her only choice. But all that
time she had been working her magic on Giovanni.

Isabella turned away from the table and headed towards him. Her head was bent as she grabbed her notepad and pen. Tension coiled inside him, ready to spring.
He sat unnaturally still, refusing to make any sudden
moves that would alert her to impending danger.

"Are you ready to order?" she asked uninterestedly.

Her hoarse voice was nothing like the husky whisper he remembered.

"Hello, Bella."

No, no, no!

She looked up sharply and her cloudy eyes cleared
as she focused on Antonio. He was here. In front of her.
Waiting for her to make the next move, even though
they both knew it was useless.

Run. The word screamed through her brain.

Isabella slowly blinked. Maybe she was hallucinat-
ing. She hadn't been herself lately. There was no way
Antonio Rossi, billionaire, member of the social elite,
would be sitting in this café.

But her imagination couldn't conjure the electric current coursing through her body from his nearness. Or
the panic that stole her breath. Her heart gave a brutal
leap before it plummeted.

Does he know? Is that why he's here?

She couldn't stop staring at him like a deer caught in the headlights. Antonio wore a black pinstripe suit, the ruthlessly tailored lines emphasizing his broad shoulders and lean, muscular body. The hand-made shirt and silk tie offered a veneer of civility, but they couldn't mask his animal magnetism. He was the most sensual man she had ever known, and the most powerful.

Antonio Rossi was also the most callous person she'd met.

Isabella took short, choppy breaths, but she was suffocating with dread. She couldn't gauge his next move or his next thought. She only knew that it was going to be devastating.

She had been an idiot to get involved with him. He was the kind of man her mother had often warned her about. Antonio would see a woman like her only as a plaything and then discard her when something better came along. Isabella knew all this but she had still been drawn to him like a moth to a flame. Even now she felt the pull and she couldn't stop staring at him.

His eyes were hidden behind the sunglasses, but the angles and lines of his savagely masculine face were just as sharp and aggressive as she remembered. Antonio wasn't beautiful, but his dark, striking looks made women of all ages eager for another glimpse of him.

Run. And don't look back.

"Antonio?" Her voice was high and reedy. "What are you doing here?"

"I've come for you."

She shivered. She'd never thought she would see him again or hear those words. But it was too late. She couldn't go back. She wouldn't let herself think that it was possible. "Why?"

"Why?" Antonio leaned back in his chair and arrogantly studied her appearance.

Her skin tingled as she felt his lazy gaze sliding over her tired body and cheap clothes. Her pulse tripped before galloping at maximum speed. *How much did he know?*

She couldn't tell because his sunglasses hid his eyes. Was he here because he missed the sex? What they had shared had been hot, raw and primitive. It had made her wild, irresponsible and addicted to him. When they were together nothing else had mattered. And if she were smart she would keep her distance before she fell under his spell again.

Her muscles were locked, her feet were still, but her heart pounded hard against her ribs. She should tell him to leave and then get as far away as she could, but instead she was letting him take a good, long look at her.

"You need to leave. Now." She forced the words out. She needed to be harsh. In the end it would be kinder this way.

"Bella..." he warned in a low growl.

Only Antonio called her that. She'd used to love hearing him say it with a hint of a smile when he greeted her, or in awe as she brought him satisfaction with her mouth. Now, hearing him say it again, this time in anger, it brought a pang in her heart.

"I have nothing to say to you," she said in a rush.

His face hardened with displeasure. Antonio whipped off his dark sunglasses and glared at her. "How about offering your condolences?"

Her chest tightened, squeezing her lungs until she

found it difficult to breathe. His dark brown eyes ensnared her. She wanted to look away, but couldn't. She had never seen such fury or pain. It wouldn't take much to unleash it. If she moved he would pounce.

"I only just heard about Giovanni's car accident. I'm sorry for your loss."

Antonio's eyes narrowed and she could swear his anger quivered in the air.

"Such a display of grief for an ex-lover," he said in a raspy low tone. "It must have been a nasty break-up. What happened? Cheated on him, too?"

He didn't know. She breathed a little easier. "I did not have an affair with Giovanni," she said, holding her notepad and pen against her chest as if they could shield her from Antonio's wrath. She took a cautious step back.

"Bella, one more move…"

"*Signorina,*" the man from the other table interrupted, "you forgot the—"

"One moment," Bella pleaded to the customer as she took the opportunity to shuffle away from Antonio. "I'll be right back."

She tried to march into the kitchen just as she felt Antonio's large hand fall on her shoulder. She still recognized his touch, she thought as she squeezed her eyes shut, fighting off the self-recrimination and longing swirling inside her.

Antonio whirled her around until she faced him. If he hadn't been holding her so tight she'd have collapsed. She felt so sick. So tired. Of worrying. Of barely surviving.

Isabella tilted her head back to look him in the eye. She had forgotten how powerfully tall he was. His height and strength had used to make her feel safe and protected. Now it made her feel extremely vulnerable.

"I've been looking for you," Antonio said. His voice was soft and dangerous. He lowered his head until he blocked out the rest of the world. "You were surprisingly difficult to find."

Isabella's stomach twisted with fear. Antonio placed both hands on her shoulders, his fingers digging into her like talons. He surrounded her. She felt caged. Trapped.

"What's going on here?" Her boss's harsh voice sounded close. "Isabella, what have you done?"

"I'll take care of it," she promised the older man without taking her eyes off Antonio. One touch, one look and she was his. It had always been that way.

The world started to spin and she swallowed roughly. She was mentally and physically exhausted. She wasn't at the top of her game when she needed to be the most. Why did Antonio have to reappear in her life when she was so fragile?

"I don't know why you bothered." Isabella took a quick glimpse and saw her boss next to the stove, saw his undisguised interest in the rich customer in his café. "You still think I was having an affair with Giovanni when I was with you."

Antonio's eyes darkened and his harsh features tightened with anger. "Oh, I *know* you were."

He hadn't forgiven his brother. Or her. He never would. Isabella swallowed hard, tapping into the last of her strength. She felt wobbly and weak, but the fight hadn't quite left her.

She just wished Antonio would take his hands off her. Her skin stung with awareness as tension whipped between them like a lash. She couldn't think straight when he touched her. She'd never been able to.

"I know you were his mistress," he drawled softly. "Why else would he leave you something in his will?"

Isabella cringed. That couldn't be good. She had thought Giovanni was her friend, letting her stay with him and helping her out. He hadn't revealed his true nature until it was too late. "Go away, Antonio. You don't know anything."

"I'm not leaving without you. You have to sign some documents in the law office as soon as possible."

Panic bloomed inside her. She wasn't going anywhere with Antonio. Isabella tried to show no expression, but she knew she'd failed when she saw the glint of dark satisfaction in Antonio's eyes. He wanted to make her uncomfortable. He wanted to see her suffer.

"Tell your family that you couldn't find me." She took a step away from Antonio and was relieved when he let go. "Give the money away to charity."

Antonio eyed her with disbelief. "You don't know how much it is."

"It doesn't matter." She could use the money, but she didn't trust this gift from Giovanni. There would be a price to pay if she accepted.

"Isabella!" her boss yelled. "Get the food on the table before it gets cold."

She turned abruptly and her head spun. She reached for the wall but her fingers gripped Antonio's strong arm. She battled desperately for her balance. She couldn't show weakness—or any other symptoms. She sensed Antonio's stare and held back a groan.

"You're ill?" he asked sharply.

"I didn't get much sleep last night," she replied in a rough voice.

She refused to look at him, not wanting him to see just how weak she truly felt. She could tell that he was assessing her and that made her worry. Antonio was smart and he'd made a fortune on intuitive connections. It wouldn't take him much longer to figure out what was wrong with her. She had to get away before he discovered the truth.

"Isabella!" her boss barked out.

"Let me serve this," Isabella told Antonio as she grabbed the tray of food. "Then we won't be interrupted again."

She didn't wait for his answer as she hurried out to the sidewalk. She served the food quickly, almost spilling it. She recovered just in time, murmuring her profuse apologies, but her mind was on possible escape routes. Isabella moved slightly until she was in a blind spot from the kitchen. This was her last chance to make a run for it.

Isabella placed the serving tray on one of the empty tables. She kept her casual pace until she turned the corner. Then she ran as fast as she could down the alley to the back stairs.

As her feet slapped against the pavement her lungs felt like they were going to explode—but she couldn't stop. Time was of the essence. Isabella reached the stairs and climbed them, two steps at a time. She tripped and bruised her knee. For a moment her world tilted, but she got back up and kept going.

Her legs burned and shook, but she pushed herself to go faster. Antonio would now have realized that she'd escaped. Any minute he'd start looking for her.

She reached the door to her room, but didn't stop to take a breath. She felt nauseous and her body ached. It didn't matter. She needed to get far away and then she would rest.

Swinging the door open, Isabella saw her backpack on the top of her lumpy mattress. She stepped into the small room and lunged for it. As she grasped the shoulder strap she heard the door bang shut.

Isabella turned around and the room moved. She saw Antonio resting against the door. He didn't look surprised or out of breath. From the glimmering rage in his dark eyes, she thought he had probably been waiting there for her the moment she stepped out of the kitchen.

"I'm disappointed, Bella," he said in a dangerously soft tone. "You're becoming so predictable."

"I—I…" She blinked as dark spots gathered along the edges of her eyes. She felt light-headed, but her arms and legs were unusually heavy. She couldn't move.

He stepped away from the door and approached her. "I don't have time for your games. You're coming with me *now*."

"I…" She needed to move. Run. Shamelessly lie.

But just as Antonio reached for her her head lolled back and she fainted, collapsing at his feet.

CHAPTER TWO

"BELLA!" Antonio sprung into action and caught her as her backpack fell onto the wooden floor with a thud. He lifted her and couldn't help noticing how light and delicate she was. *Fragile*. The word whispered in his mind like a warning.

She slumped against his arm and he held on tight as alarm pulsed through his veins. He swept the wisps of hair from her face. Her eyes were closed and her complexion was very pale. He laid her carefully on the mattress. Crouching down next to her, Antonio took a quick survey of the tiny room. The beige paint was peeling off the walls in chunks and a faint scent of rotting garbage wafted through the small open window. There was nothing else. No sink or refrigerator so he could get her water. There was hardly enough space for the mattress. How could she live like this? Why was she living here when she had a life and a future in America?

"Bella?" He tapped her cheek with his fingers. Her skin was soft and cold.

Isabella frowned and pursed her lips. She murmured something but it was incomprehensible. She didn't open her eyes.

Antonio started to get suspicious. His first instinct

had been to take care of Isabella. *Some things never change,* he thought bitterly. But what if this was an act? Did she hope that he would back off? Not a chance.

"Isabella," he called out sharply.

"Go away," she said drowsily. She turned to her side and curled her legs close to her chest.

"No." He grabbed her shoulder and gave her a shake.

"I'm serious." She squeezed her eyes shut and weakly tried to push his hand away. "Leave me alone."

He wished he could. He wished he had left her alone when he'd first seen her. It had been early March. The sun had been shining but there had been a chill in the air as he'd left his office. He had just pocketed his cell phone when he'd seen a young woman standing a few feet away on the sidewalk.

Antonio had done a double-take and halted.

"Is everything all right, sir?" his assistant had asked.

No. His world had taken a sudden tilt as he'd stared at the blonde, dressed simply in a fitted leather jacket, skintight jeans and knee-high boots. The violent kick of attraction had made him take a staggering step back.

He knew many beautiful young women, but there had been something different about this one. He had wanted to accept her silent challenge. It could have been her don't-mess-with-me stance or the jaunty tilt of her black fedora. Maybe it had been the bright red scarf draped around her neck that hinted at attitude. Whatever it was, he had found it irresistible.

"Sir?" his assistant had prompted.

Antonio had barely heard him. His attention had been on the blonde as she'd turned a map upside down, clearly hopeless at navigating. Then suddenly she'd shrugged her shoulders and stuffed the map carelessly into her backpack. Antonio had watched as the blonde had started walking away as if she was ready for whatever adventure she faced.

Her beauty and vitality had intrigued him, and her bold spirit had captured his imagination. He'd known he had to meet this woman or regret missing the opportunity.

"Cancel my meeting," he had said to his stunned assistant.

Following an elemental instinct he had not wanted to question, Antonio had ignored the chauffeured car waiting for him and followed the blonde.

His pulse had quickened as he'd watched the swing of her long blonde hair and the sway of her hips. She'd looked over her shoulder, and as their gazes connected he had seen the flare of attraction in her blue eyes. Instead of looking away she had turned and approached him.

"*Mi scusi*," she had said, her voice strong and clear as she'd met his gaze boldly. "Do you speak English?"

"Of course," he had said, noticing she was American. There had been no light of recognition in her eyes—just lust. She'd had no idea who he was.

"Great. I'm looking for the Piazza del Popolo," she had said, her attention clearly drawn to his mouth. She had absently swiped the tip of her tongue along her bottom lip.

Antonio had clenched his jaw. He had wanted to know how her lips tasted, but it had been too soon, too fast. The last thing he'd wanted to do was scare her off. "It's not far," he had replied gruffly as attraction pulsed between them. "I can show you where it is."

He had been fascinated as he'd watched her cheeks

turn pink. She hadn't tried to hide her interest, but she'd been fighting an internal struggle. He had seen the rise and fall of her chest and the eagerness in her expression. She had been tempted to explore whatever was happening between them.

"Wouldn't it be out of your way?"

"Not at all," he had lied. His voice had softened as his chest had tightened with growing excitement. "I happen to be going in that direction."

"What luck!" Her broad smile had indicated that she didn't believe him. She could have said she was going to Venice and he would have given the same answer. "By the way, I'm Isabella."

He had taken Bella to bed that night. There had been no games, no pretense. There had also been no indication that this American student on Spring Break would twist him in so many knots that he would never be the same again. She hadn't been very experienced, but a generous and affectionate lover.

Giovanni had thought so, too.

The reminder burned like acid, eating away at him.

Antonio stood up and shoved his clenched fists in his pockets. "You told me you weren't sick."

"I'm not sick," she countered faintly.

The Isabella he knew was full of life and ready to take on the world. This Isabella looked like a strong gust of wind would knock her over. "You need to see a doctor."

Isabella suddenly opened her eyes wide. She blinked a few times and darted a quick look at him before keeping her gaze on the floor. She rose, resting awkwardly on her elbow and pushing the wayward hair out of her face. "I've seen a doctor. I'm not sick. Just exhausted. All I need is to eat and sleep properly."

Antonio cast her a look of disbelief. "I would ask for a second opinion."

"I don't need one. Now, go away," she ordered with the flutter of her hand.

"I'm not leaving here without you."

"You have to," she urged as she held her head in her hands. "Tell everyone that you couldn't find me. Tell them that I'm back home."

It was tempting. He wanted to leave and not look back. Purge her from his memories. Do anything that would erase Isabella from his world. But he knew that was impossible.

"Sorry. I'm not like you. I choose to tell the truth whenever possible."

She lifted her head to glare at him. "I never lied to you. I never—"

He turned away and checked his watch. "I don't have time to rehash the past."

"Rehash?" Isabella's voice rose angrily. "When did we discuss it the first time around? I thought we were happy. We had been together for weeks and going strong. We had made love throughout the night. The next morning your security woke me up to kick me out. My bag was packed and you wouldn't take my call. You didn't tell me why you did that, and you never gave me a chance to talk about it!"

Antonio leaned against the wall by the door. The room felt like it was getting smaller. "I wasn't in the mood to hear your excuses. I'm even less inclined to now."

"There was nothing to excuse," Isabella argued as she rose slowly.

Her movements were wobbly and awkward. Antonio folded his arms so he wouldn't reach out and help her. He already regretted holding her close. He didn't like how much effort it had taken to pull away. His fingertips still stung from where he had touched her face.

Isabella looked him in the eye and jutted out her chin. "I did not have an affair."

He held up his hand. "Enough! I will not discuss it."

"Typical," she said with a sigh. "You don't like to discuss anything. Especially if it's personal. No matter how hard I tried, you wouldn't share how you felt. The only time I knew exactly what you were thinking was when we were in bed."

An intimate and very inconvenient image bloomed in his mind. Of Isabella, naked in his bed, eagerly following his explicit demands. When they'd been alone together he had held nothing back. He had demonstrated how much he wanted Isabella and how much her touch had meant to him. There had been many times when it hadn't been certain who was in command.

A muscle bunched in his jaw and ferocious energy swirled around him. "We are leaving," he announced in a gravelly tone. Antonio thrust the door open and waited for Isabella.

"No," she said firmly. "I'm not signing any papers. I don't want Giovanni's money."

"I'm sure you earned it." He didn't want her to know what was at stake here. All he wanted was to end this errand as soon as possible. By whatever means necessary. Antonio walked over to her.

Isabella's eyes widened. "Don't you dare touch me!"

"How times have changed," he said silkily as he wrapped his hand around her wrist. He ignored her racing pulse under his fingers as he picked up her backpack. "I remember when you begged for my touch."

Isabella tried futilely to pull out of his grasp. "I thought you didn't want to talk about the past? Let go of me."

"I will when we get to my car." If it was still where he had parked it. Trust Bella to find the most dangerous neighborhood to live in.

"I'm not going anywhere with you!" Isabella declared as she tried to grab onto the doorframe—but she couldn't hold on.

"Think again." He headed for the stairs, dragging her behind him.

"Pushy and selfish," she muttered. "It must be a Rossi trait. You are just like your brother."

Antonio stilled as the accusation lashed at him. He slowly turned and faced Isabella. He saw the wariness in her eyes as she backed away. She didn't get far as his grip tightened around her wrist. "*Don't.*"

Isabella's gaze fell to her feet. "All I meant—"

"I don't care what you meant." Her words had clawed open a wound he had valiantly tried to ignore. Were he and Gio interchangeable in Isabella's mind? How often had she thought of his brother when she'd kissed *him*? Had she responded the same way in Gio's bed?

His thoughts turned darker, piercing his soul. Antonio didn't say anything as he took a step closer to Isabella, backing her against the wall. Why had she chosen Gio over him? Everyone else he knew made that choice, but why Isabella? He had thought she was different. Was it because Gio had been the handsome and charismatic one? Had his brother fulfilled her deepest, darkest fantasies? Or had she actually fallen in love with his brother?

"Antonio?" she whispered with uncertainty.

He stared at Isabella. Her angelic beauty hid a devious nature. Her bold spirit and breathtaking innocence had led him straight to a hell that he might never escape. He blinked slowly as he battled the darkness enveloping him. He wouldn't let this woman destroy him again.

Antonio released her wrist as if her touch burned. He took a deliberate step back but met her eyes with a steady gaze. "Don't compare me with my brother. *Ever.*"

Isabella couldn't move as she stared into his brown eyes. Her heart twisted and her breath snagged in her throat. Antonio was always so careful not to show his thoughts and emotions, but now they were laid bare before her. The man was in torment.

But just as quickly as he'd exposed his pain his eyes were shuttered. When he opened them again he was back in control, while *her* emotions were in a jumbled mess.

Antonio turned away from her and Isabella sagged against the wall. She slowly exhaled as her heart pounded in her ears. She felt shaky, her limbs twitching as she watched Antonio take the stairs.

"I'm sorry."

Her words were just a whisper but she saw Antonio's rigid stance as he silently deflected her apology.

She hadn't meant to compare Antonio to his brother. They had very different personalities. It was impossible to confuse the two. Giovanni had been a charmer, with movie star looks, always the life of the party. He'd been entertaining—but not fascinating like Antonio.

The moment she had met Antonio she'd known he was out of her league. She didn't have the sophistication or sexual knowledge to hold on to him. It hadn't mattered. She'd only wanted to be with him. Just once.

Isabella remembered when they had first met and he had offered to show her Piazza del Popolo. The sight of him had jolted her as if she had woken from a deep slumber. Her heart had started to race when she saw him.

She knew she had projected an image of being bold and strong. Tough. It had all been an act. It had been her way of protecting herself as she went through the world alone. But the way the man had been looking at her—she had felt brazen. She had wanted to hold on to that feeling.

"I'm Antonio," he had said, and offered his hand.

She had hesitated at the sight of his expensive cufflinks. It had only been then that she'd noticed he wore a designer suit. His silk tie had probably cost more than her round-trip ticket to Italy. She didn't know anyone who had that kind of money.

Be careful of the rich ones. Her mother words had drifted in her head. *They only want one thing from women like us.*

Isabella had smiled. She had decided that it was okay because she was after the same thing.

She had reached for Antonio's hand and felt a sharp tingle as her skin had glided against his. She hadn't been able to hide her gasp of surprise. When she had tried to pull away Antonio had wrapped his long, strong fingers around her hand.

Instead of making her feel trapped, his touch had pierced through the gray numbness that had settled in her when she had nursed her mother through her final illness. Her breath had locked in her throat as he'd raised her hand to his mouth.

The earthy colors of Rome had deepened and the sun had turned golden. The blaring sound of traffic had faded as Antonio had brushed his lips against her knuckles. She had known that this man would be the highlight of her vacation. She hadn't expected to fall in love—and into his bed—with such wild abandon.

She hadn't expected that she would never be the same again.

Isabella jerked her mind to the present as she saw Antonio disappear from the stairwell with her backpack. Everything she owned—her passport, her money—was in there.

"Wait!" she called out, and hurriedly followed him. She rounded the building and saw Antonio striding down the block. Isabella ran after him. "Antonio, stop!"

He walked to his sports car—a menacing-looking machine that was as black as night. He punched a button on his keyring and the small trunk popped open. Isabella watched in horror as he tossed her backpack in and slammed it shut.

"Give me back my bag," she said as she reached the car.

"You'll get it after we visit the lawyers."

"You don't understand, Antonio. I have to work." She gestured at the café on the other end of the block.

"Who cares?" He walked to the driver's side. "This is more important."

Spoken like a man who had never had to scrape by

or go hungry. "I'm already going to get in trouble for taking an unscheduled break."

"Unscheduled break? You made a run for it and you weren't planning to return."

"I can't afford to lose this job." She rubbed her hand over her forehead as she tried to maintain her composure. "If I get fired I lose my room."

He glanced up at the broken rusted window of her room. "It won't be that big of a loss."

Isabella put her hands on her hips. "Maybe not to you, but this job is the only thing that is keeping me from becoming homeless!"

Antonio's eyes narrowed. "Is this about money?"

"What?" She stared at him across the car.

"Of course it is."

"It's about my *livelihood*," she corrected him through clenched teeth. Antonio wouldn't understand about that, having been born into wealth and status. She needed her job because she had no other form of support or resources. Why couldn't he see that? "Listen, let's make a compromise. I will go to the lawyers with you once I finish my shift at the café."

Antonio took another look at his watch. "That's unacceptable."

"Seriously? How is that unacceptable? You asked for a favor from me and I just agreed to do it."

"We both know you are prolonging the inevitable and will try to avoid it. Although I find it very curious that you aren't asking how much money you will get. Unless, of course, you already know."

"There's nothing curious about it," she said as she folded her arms protectively around her. "The only thing I know is that any money will come with strings attached. I don't want anything—especially if it means dealing with you or your family."

Antonio chose to ignore her comment. "I'm not willing to wait around and watch over you until your shift ends."

"Do you even know how to compromise?" she asked, tossing her hands up in frustration. Of course he didn't. The world bowed down to him. Just as she had done, once upon a time.

"This is what I know," he said as he slipped on his sunglasses. "The will was read three days ago. The contents will soon become public."

Isabella frowned. "What are you talking about?"

He opened the door and sat down in the driver's seat. "It won't take long before the paparazzi find you."

She jerked her head back in surprise. "Paparazzi? What would they want with me?"

"You're kidding, right? The woman who slept with the Rossi brothers has wound up with a fortune."

She stared at him with wide eyes. "There is no need to make it sound so salacious."

"I'm just telling it like it is," he said impatiently. "Now, get in."

Isabella hesitated. Giovanni had left her a fortune? That couldn't be right. Antonio must be exaggerating. If only she *could* accept the money. But even if she did it would take ages to go through the legal and financial systems and get the cash she so desperately needed.

What would happen to her after she'd signed the documents? She had no home, no money and no protection. She had been working for months to raise the money to get back to California and she didn't think she would make enough before the paparazzi found her. Could she ask Antonio for help?

She bit her lip as she weighed the pros and cons. *Could* she ask him? Was she willing to stoop that low? Antonio could easily afford the price of a plane ticket, probably had the cash in his wallet, but it felt wrong.

Antonio leaned back in his seat. "What do you want?"

She took a deep breath. "I need a plane ticket to Los Angeles. For tonight."

He nodded sharply. "What else?"

She was already regretting her request. She didn't want anything from Antonio. His presence reminded her of the poor choices she made because she'd been in love. She had fought for him, for them, and he had discarded her without a second thought. As much as it pained her to think about it, her mother had been right. She hated it when that happened.

"That's it."

He tipped his sunglasses and studied her face. "I don't believe you."

"That doesn't surprise me," she replied. "But I mean it. I don't want anything else."

"That will change soon," he said as he started the engine.

"Maybe I didn't make myself clear. I shall consider this a loan," she said as the car purred to life. "I'll pay you back once I get settled."

"It's not necessary."

"It is," she insisted. "It wouldn't be right to take your money."

"I don't care about the money." Antonio said. "Get in the car."

Isabella hesitated. Was that wise? The man hated her. He thought she'd betrayed him. Then again, he probably wanted her out of Italy and out of his life as soon as possible. She had nothing to worry about.

"Bella…" Antonio's tone warned of his growing impatience.

Isabella opened the door and sat down before she changed her mind. "Don't expect me to stay long," she said as she reached for the seatbelt. "I'll sign the papers and then I'm gone."

And if she were lucky she would never see Antonio again.

CHAPTER THREE

"THIS is a law office?" Isabella asked as she studied the old building. "I haven't seen one like this before."

Antonio glanced up and saw that the façade was pale, almost pink-gold. He noticed the faded mosaics next to the arched windows and pillars. It was strange that he'd never really looked at the building before.

"Where did you think I would take you?"

"You don't want me to answer that," she muttered.

They entered the dark and musty building. It was unnaturally quiet and the only sound was their footsteps as they climbed the stairs. The silence Antonio shared with Isabella felt strange but he was grateful for it. He didn't need to think about the easy conversations they'd once had that would last throughout the night. He didn't want to remember how he'd used to call her up during the day just to hear her voice. He wanted the barrier of silence. Needed it.

The receptionist took one look at Isabella and sniffed with disapproval. Antonio glared at the dour woman, letting her know that he wouldn't tolerate that kind of behavior. The woman bent her head from the silent reprimand and icily escorted them to the conference room.

When the door opened Antonio saw his mother, sitting regally next to the ornate rosewood table. Dressed severely in black, Maria Rossi was as elegant and private as always. She was trying to hide her distress, but he instantly saw it in her face.

"Mother, why are you here?" Antonio asked. "Your presence isn't required."

His mother's expression darkened when she saw Isabella at her side. "Is this the woman?"

"This is Isabella Williams," Antonio said with a hint of warning.

He reluctantly introduced Isabella to his mother. He had hoped to prevent these two women from meeting. With one wintry glance Maria made it clear what she thought of Isabella. She knew this blonde beauty was the reason her sons had been estranged.

Antonio's first instinct was to protect Isabella from the slight. But that didn't make sense. She was in the wrong and should suffer the consequences. She had created a scandal when she'd started living with Giovanni. The paparazzi had gone into a feeding frenzy, and had Antonio borne the brunt of the gossip. But he still couldn't stand by and watch Isabella receive this treatment.

Most socialites he knew would have wilted under his mother's apparent disgust. To his surprise, Isabella tilted her head proudly. She wasn't going to back down or hang her head in shame. She stood before this doyenne of high society in her cheap clothes, with her tarnished name, and held her gaze unflinchingly.

His mother was the first to break eye contact. She

turned to him. "I can't bear to be in the same room with her."

Isabella showed no expression as she watched Maria Rossi leave the room and closed the door with a flourish.

"I apologize for my mother's behavior," Antonio said, fighting back anger. "I'll see that it doesn't happen again."

"No need," Isabella crossed her arms and walked to the large window. "I know you feel the same way."

Antonio watched her as she stared at the view of the Pantheon. He suspected she wasn't really looking at anything. It was as if she was in another time, another place, trapped in a memory.

If only he could do the same. His mind was always racing, predicting problems and creating solutions. He required an outlet for his inexhaustible energy and found it in his work. The money and power that came along with it wasn't important. Antonio needed the challenge, to push himself to the razor's edge.

There had been one time when he hadn't felt that drive, and that had been when he was with Isabella. When they'd been together nothing else had existed. Isabella Williams had been his escape. And eventually his downfall.

"What did you tell your mother about me?" Isabella grimaced as the question sprang from her lips. She hadn't meant to ask, but it was obvious that her reputation had preceded her. Isabella knew she shouldn't care but it bothered her.

There was something about Antonio's mother that intimidated her. The woman was beautifully groomed, from her coiffed hair to her pedicured feet, but she also had an aura of power. No one would treat Maria Rossi with anything less than respect. Isabella had felt grubby next to her.

"We never discussed you," he said stiffly.

She wouldn't be surprised if that were true. Antonio rarely discussed his family. Everything she knew about his mother and his late father had come from Giovanni. And he'd probably been just as private about his love life with his family.

Isabella turned and approached Antonio. "But she knows you and I were once together?"

"Not from me."

"Giovanni?" No wonder his mother hated her.

"My mother was prying into the reason why her sons weren't on speaking terms again." Antonio crossed his arms and looked away. "I'm sure Gio concocted some story that made him look like the innocent victim."

"Again?" Her tired brain caught onto that word. "You and Giovanni had been estranged before?"

Antonio's jaw clenched. "Yes."

She felt the weight of guilt lift a little. All this time she'd thought she had ruined the strong bond between brothers. "But how could that be?" she asked as she remembered Giovanni and Antonio together. They'd had a tendency to use the same expressions, finish each other's sentences. "You two were close."

Antonio shrugged. "Gio had been trying to make amends and was on his best behavior. It was one of the few times we got along."

"Why did you accept him back into your life?" That didn't seem like something Antonio would do. You screwed up once and you were banished from Antonio's life. You didn't get another chance.

"I thought he had changed." He sighed. "I wanted him to change."

She saw the grief in his expression. She wanted to reach out and bring him comfort, but she knew Antonio would not appreciate the gesture. "How old were you when you first stopped talking to each other?"

His harsh features tightened. "I don't want to discuss it."

"Why not?"

"I answered your questions, now it's my turn."

Isabella jerked her head back. She saw the intensity in his eyes, the determined set of his jaw. Was he really trying to deflect her questions or had this all been a technique to draw her closer? Make her think he was opening up to her so she would feel obligated to do the same?

Isabella braced her shoulders. "I didn't agree to that."

"Why did Gio include you in his will?"

"I have no idea. I didn't ask him to." But she suspected she knew the answer. Giovanni had been playing games and now she was going to lose everything.

"The lawyers say that Gio changed his will a month ago."

Isabella paled. That could not be a coincidence. "S-so?"

Antonio tilted his head to one side as he studied her face. "You know why. No one else does. No one knows why he gave you millions."

"M-millions?" she whispered. "That doesn't make any sense."

"And half the shares in Rossi Industries."

"What?" The shock reverberated through her body.

"He gave you half my birthright," Antonio said in a growl.

She clapped her hand over her mouth. *Oh, Giovanni. What have you done? Why did you do this?*

"I lost part of my birthright once before," his said, his voice a harsh whisper. "I have no intention of losing it again."

Isabella frowned. She felt like she was missing crucial information. "What are you talking about?"

Antonio didn't hear her. "Why did Gio give all this to *you*? Why not the woman he was dating? Why not a woman who meant something to him? Why *you*?"

"Antonio…" She braced her legs and held her clenched hands at her sides. She didn't have the nerve to tell him. She didn't want to face the consequences.

"Was it so I would be required to work with the woman who had cheated on me?"

Had Giovanni done this out of spite? For his own perverse pleasure? It was possible…

"Or did you seduce it out of him? I admit you're good in bed—but *that* good?"

Isabella felt the heat in her cheeks. If only she could run away. The moment she uttered the next words everything would change. Everything would be lost.

"It's because I'm p-pregnant."

He stared at her in shock. Isabella hunched her shoulders, preparing for the world to fall around her as struggled to get the words out.

She nervously licked her lips before she added, "And Giovanni *is* the father."

Antonio staggered back as if he had been punched. His body went numb and his mind whirled. His world tilted and he swayed. He wanted to grab hold of something so he wasn't brought to his knees, but that meant reaching out to Isabella. The one woman who still had the power to hurt him.

"You…"

Isabella was having his brother's baby. Gio had known and hadn't told him. The pain radiated through his body.

"But I didn't have an affair with him. I swear."

An affair. A fling. Sex. It was all the same.

Antonio held up his hand. Rage billowed through him, crimson, hot and bitter. "You're pregnant," he said, as if he was in a daze. "How many months?"

She held her hands in front of her stomach. "I'm just past the first trimester."

"Three months?" he muttered as the fury seized his throat.

"Antonio, you have to believe me," she pleaded. "I only slept with him one time."

He fought back the red mist that threatened to overtake him. "*Only?* Is a one-night stand supposed to make me feel better?" he asked in a low, biting tone. Was he supposed to believe that when she had lived with Giovanni for *weeks*?

Isabella's face tightened with anger. "How many women have you slept with since we broke up?"

"That's not the issue. Those women were not the *reason* we broke up." He would not allow Isabella to distract him. "I kicked you out because you were sleeping with my brother. Now you're telling me you're carrying his child."

"It happened the night I heard on the news that you

were going to marry someone else." Isabella spoke haltingly, as if the memory still tormented her.

"And that's your excuse?" He stared at her. He didn't know if she was feeding him lies or if she was planning to thrust another knife in his back.

"No. I'm trying to explain." She covered her face with her hands. "I was emotional and I drank far too much. I had been like that for weeks. I was self-destructive and I made a lot of poor choices during that time. I'm not proud of what I did."

But she had done it. Would she have told him about Giovanni if she wasn't pregnant, or would she have taken her secret to the grave?

"Do you wind up in the nearest bed whenever you drink?"

She slowly lowered her hands. "I'm not sure what happened that night."

"How convenient."

She glared at him. "All I know is that I was an emotional mess. You had kicked me out, you didn't want to have anything to do with me, and then I heard you were planning a future with another woman."

"And what better way to get back at me than by sleeping with my brother?" He'd used to think Isabella was sweet and innocent, but she had hidden a vengeful streak. The people closest to him had warned him about Isabella, but he hadn't listened. He'd thought he knew everything about her. But it turned out he didn't know her at all.

"I didn't know about your history with Giovanni." Isabella stood rigid in front of him, her clenched fists at her sides. "I didn't know you had discarded me like a piece of trash because you thought I'd had an affair with your brother."

"And look at what you did," Antonio said. The red mist was creeping in and he was feeling dangerous. Out of control like never before. Antonio shoved his shaky hands in his pockets.

"Giovanni planned this!" she blurted out. "He took advantage of me."

"I'm sure he got you into bed in record time." Bile rose from his stomach and he wanted to be violently ill.

She thrust out her chin. "I'm not like that," she said in a trembling voice.

"Yes, you are," he said with a sneer. "You were with *me*."

Isabella eyes widened as if she'd been hit. "You throw that back in my face?" she asked in a shocked whisper. "What we had was different. It was special. It was—"

"Part of your routine," he finished coldly. "Only Gio got you pregnant. Was that planned or an unexpected bonus? Is that why he kicked you out?"

"He didn't kick me out. I left the next morning," she told him, her voice wobbling with emotion. "I didn't feel safe there anymore. I ran as fast as I could."

Antonio frowned and he crossed his arms. Her explanation niggled at him. Something didn't add up. "Then how did he know about the baby?"

"I told him when I found out. That was a month ago."

And his brother had changed his will a month ago. "What did Gio say?"

"Not much." Isabella looked away abruptly.

"Isabella," he warned in a firm tone, "tell me."

Her shoulders sagged in defeat and her expression

turned grim. "He laughed," she answered. "He said, 'Antonio will never touch you now!' and he laughed like a madman."

Antonio took a step back. He shouldn't be surprised, but he was. He hadn't fully appreciated the depth of his brother's hatred.

"And he was right." She gestured at him, the simple movement indicating her disappointment. "He knew exactly how you'd react if you found out the truth."

"That's why you ran away at the café?" Isabella had been afraid of how he would react. And she was smart, because right now he wanted to lash out. He wanted to smash and destroy everything around him. "You are not the woman I thought you were."

"That's not true," she spat angrily. "You just want to hear bad things about me. It's easier for you because you're looking for my faults."

Easier? He felt like he had been ripped apart. He was never going to be the same again.

She gulped in a ragged breath. "I want you to know that I didn't cheat on you."

"How can I know that? How can I believe you weren't sleeping with my brother from the first day you met him?"

"I have no way of proving it. Why can't you—?"

A polite knock on the double doors interrupted them. Isabella jumped back and pressed her lips together as a withered old man with snowy white hair in a black three-piece suit entered the room.

Antonio tried to rein in his emotions as he tersely introduced the lawyer to Isabella. The older man invited her into his office and she silently followed. As she passed Antonio he grabbed Isabella's wrist, forcing her to stop.

"This discussion isn't over," he said.

"Yes, it is," she said coldly as she pulled away from his grasp. "I don't have to explain myself to you. You have no rights over me *or* my child."

Isabella walked through the door and the lawyer followed. Antonio stared at the closed door, his body rigid as an idea formed.

"Not yet," Antonio murmured. "But I once I do there will be hell to pay."

CHAPTER FOUR

"I'M GOING to be a grandmother." Maria Rossi sighed and clasped her hands together. "Gio's child. Oh, I hope it will look just like him."

"I'm glad to see you're taking this well," Antonio muttered as he'd paced the floor of the conference room. He should have left his mother in the waiting room but he had to tell her that their situation had changed. Their strategy had been blown apart by Isabella's bombshell.

"I admit Gio had no business putting her in the will." His mother's voice was thick with annoyance. "Giving money and power to *that* woman."

"He did it to cut me out."

"No, Gio wouldn't do that to you. He wouldn't," she insisted as he made a face. "That woman bewitched him. He wasn't thinking straight. I can understand making provision for the child—but all that money?" Maria shuddered delicately. "We don't know if it's even his."

"We'll find out." But Antonio's instincts told him that the baby *was* Gio's. His brother wouldn't have pulled this stunt unless he had been absolutely sure. Gio wanted his child to inherit and gave Isabella the power over the money and shares until the child comes of age.

"Gio told me himself that that Jezebel seduced

him," his mother continued. "You both should have known better. I don't know what either of you saw in the woman."

He could easily make a list of things he had seen in Isabella, but it would scandalize his mother. Antonio raked his hand through his hair. "I don't want to hear it."

"There's only one way a girl like her can land a rich man. She has to get pregnant."

Antonio slammed his hand against the mahogany table so hard that Maria jumped. "That's enough." It also wasn't true. Isabella had had *him* wrapped around her little finger without an unplanned pregnancy.

"Temper, temper," Maria said as she patted her chignon. "If you plan to get full control of the Rossi fortune you need to show some patience."

Antonio walked to the window and leaned against the pane. "I have one or two plans," he admitted. He wasn't happy about either of them. Both required him to get very close to the woman who betrayed him.

"How many months along is she?"

He had been reluctant to ask for details, but at the same time his mind was filled with questions. "She says she's at least three months pregnant. I kicked her out the last week of May, so I know the baby isn't mine. She left Gio on the first of July and that fits the timeframe."

"You need to do something."

"I know. It leaves me two options. I can seduce her into giving up her inheritance and leaving the country for good."

But history had proved that he didn't have an infinite amount of sexual power over her. Isabella had left his bed to go into Gio's. He wasn't sure if he could seduce Isabella knowing she was carrying his brother's child.

"No," his mother said firmly. "That child is the only thing I have left of Gio. I want it to be part of my life."

Antonio inhaled sharply as jagged pain burned through him. His mother had had no problem banning *him* from her life when he had needed her the most. But then she'd still had Gio around.

"What is the second option?" she asked.

"Marry her and adopt the child as my own. That way I would have full control over the Rossi fortune."

He had never thought about becoming a father. As the second son, he'd felt no pressure to sire an heir. Now he might be required to accept Gio's child as his own. That baby would be a constant reminder of betrayal.

"That would be perfect," his mother said. "We wouldn't have to give up anything."

Just his freedom, Antonio thought he looked out of the window and gazed at the Pantheon. *And his peace of mind*. If there had been any other way he wouldn't have gone looking for Isabella. Now he might have to bind himself to the cheating vixen for the rest of his life.

"I really don't think this is a good idea," Isabella said as she entered Antonio's penthouse apartment. She heard the door close behind her and flinched when she heard it lock.

"I agree," Antonio said, "but the paparazzi have already found out about your windfall and my home is the safest place. Anyway, it's only for one night."

Isabella scoffed. As if that meant anything. She had slept with Antonio within hours of meeting him. But she wasn't going to tumble into his bed again, she reminded herself. He didn't want her anymore. He had someone else in his life.

But, to her shame, she knew that fact wouldn't stop her from falling into his arms. Despite everything—despite the way he'd discarded her and cast her out of his life—she still longed for Antonio's touch.

Isabella rubbed her bare arms as she stepped into the drawing room. She looked around and noticed that not much had changed. In fact the only thing different about the apartment was her. She was no longer the carefree and impetuous girl who'd seen the beauty in this room but not the power behind it. Back then she had put her dreams on hold for the man she loved. These days she had to play it safe. She would hold back instead of brazenly going forward. She had to protect herself and her baby's future.

She frowned when she noticed how quiet the apartment was. No music. No easy conversation. No laughter. The room was modern and dramatic. The sleek contemporary furniture and bold artwork were at odds with the panoramic view of Rome's ancient ruins. Isabella had always thought the apartment suited Antonio, a self-made man who bridged innovation and tradition. He'd conquered the business world with cutthroat strategy, but there was a dark sensuality about him that he contained ruthlessly. Yet *she* had seen it. In the artwork he was drawn to, in his movement, in his eyes.

She knew Antonio wanted a showdown, and he had brought her here because he wanted it on his territory. This place held wild memories. Did he think it would distract her? Or would he use their past as a way to seduce the truth out of her?

"The housekeeper has made up the guestroom for you," he said as he walked across the room.

"Thank you." She wished the housekeeper were here.

She didn't want to be alone with Antonio. She didn't trust him. She didn't trust herself.

She watched him as he strode to a table that held drinks. She tried to look away, but she couldn't. His striking features were so harsh and aggressive. Her hands tingled as she remembered brushing her fingertips along his slanted cheekbones and angular jaw. He radiated masculine power and raw sensuality. He had discarded the suit jacket that had cloaked his lean, muscular build. She dragged her gaze away so she wouldn't stare at his broad shoulders or sculpted chest.

"Would you like a drink?" he asked as he grabbed a decanter from the table. He froze and stared at the crystal in his hands. "I forgot. You can't drink alcohol."

"It's not just because I'm pregnant." She returned her attention to the window and looked out onto the night sky. "I don't drink anymore."

She heard Antonio pause in pouring a glass of whiskey. "Why is that?"

When she had stayed with Giovanni she had gotten caught up in his party circuit. She'd drunk to dull the pain. To forget. She hadn't realized she was out of control until she woke up in Giovanni's bed. "I overindulged one night and swore I wouldn't drink again."

"That often happened when you socialized with Gio and his friends."

"Yes, I found that out." She couldn't hide the bitterness in her voice.

"You couldn't keep up with his wild ways?" he asked as he took a sip of his drink.

Isabella breathed deeply and leaned against the cold glass. She had to control her temper. Had to keep her wits about her. She knew Antonio was going to interrogate her. "I thought you didn't want to talk about this?"

"I don't."

She believed that. He didn't want to know, but he had to find out. The curiosity was killing him. "Did you think for a minute that Giovanni might have lied to you?" Isabella asked. "That I might have been faithful to you?"

He stilled. "Yes," he said slowly.

The surprised her. Antonio didn't second-guess himself. "When was that?" she asked, watching him down his drink in one swallow.

"The day after you left." He curled his lip and set his glass down. "I considered the possibility that I made a mistake."

Isabella pulled away from the window. "And?"

"I made some enquiries." His expression darkened and he braced his hands on the table. "Only to discover that you had rolled out of my bed and into my brother's."

Isabella closed her eyes as she heard the raw pain in Antonio's voice. "It wasn't like that," she whispered.

"Right." His voice was low and biting as he glared at her. "You had already been in his bed before you left mine."

Isabella rubbed her forehead as tension pulsed underneath her skin. "I went to Giovanni because you had thrown me out. I had nowhere to go."

Antonio snorted with derision. "Hardly. You were right where you wanted to be."

She shook her head. "I wanted to be with you."

"Until you met my brother." Antonio walked over to where she stood. "You used your relationship with me so you could get closer to Gio and his money."

"I have never been interested in that!" Isabella said. She was surprised that he would think that of her, and she was also hurt that he didn't really know her at all.

"I thought I knew you." Antonio rested his arm against the window.

"You knew everything." But either he hadn't listened or he didn't care to remember. "Unlike you, I didn't hold anything back."

"Is this another stab at how I don't communicate?" He leaned forward, towering over her. "I disagree. We talked all the time."

She flattened her hand against her chest. "I did the talking. You didn't share anything. I didn't know about your hopes and fears. Your family life. You told me nothing."

"We're talking now," he said softly. "Tell me, how long were you sleeping with my brother when we were sharing a bed?"

"I was always satisfied in your bed. I didn't need to look elsewhere."

Isabella bit her lip, knowing she shouldn't have spoken so boldly. She saw the sensual heat flare in Antonio's eyes. Her skin tingled in response as a kaleidoscope of images swirled in her head. Tension curled around her. It was dangerous to bring up those memories. Isabella nervously cleared her throat.

"If that was true, why did you go to my brother in the first place?" he asked. "Why didn't you go back to California?"

Isabella sighed. She had asked herself that many times in the past three months. "I should have gone back home, but I thought we could get back together. I hoped it was a rough patch we could work through."

Antonio's eyes widened with disbelief. "Work through the fact that you were sleeping with my brother?"

"I didn't know you thought that I had!" she said in a raised voice. "How could I? You didn't share your suspicions with anyone. I didn't know anything. I only found out about Giovanni's lies three months ago."

Antonio's eyes narrowed as he watched Isabella's face. Impatience scratched at him. "Why did you think I dumped you?" he asked as he tugged his silk tie loose.

"I thought you had found someone else. When your security kicked me out, I tried to get in touch with you," she said coolly. Her eyes were blank, her composure restored. "You were blocking my calls. I went to your office and couldn't even get through the door."

He had cut her out of his life ruthlessly. He wouldn't deny that. It had been the only way he could get through the day. The nights had been the worst. He hadn't thought a man could crave a woman so strongly until Isabella had gone out of his life.

Isabella shrugged. "So I called Giovanni."

"You had his number?" Antonio gritted his teeth. He knew he was being possessive, but he didn't like the idea of Isabella having had *any* man's phone number.

"I told him what had happened and he invited me to his place." Isabella looked down and whispered, "I thought he was my friend."

"You two got along very well whenever I was around."

"Giovanni got along with everyone. But I wasn't interested in him," she said. "The only thing we had in common was you. When we talked, it was always about you."

"Why does that send a chill down my spine?"

Her mouth tightened into a straight line as she struggled with her temper. "I didn't know what your relationship was like. And when I accepted his invitation to stay I thought it would only be a day or two before you came to your senses. I kept trying to contact you but you blocked me in every way."

If she hadn't been living with his brother he would have crawled back and grovelled. But she had shown her true colors too early.

"Then, about the third day I stayed at Giovanni's, he told me that you had cut him out of his life because he'd taken sides."

"I cut him out of my life because he slept with *you*."

"Like I said," she bit out through clenched teeth, "I had no idea you thought that. I felt incredibly guilty for causing a rift between two brothers."

"Which you decided to fix by staying with him?" he asked, poking holes in her story. "How would that repair anything?"

"Giovanni told me it would all blow over and I believed him." She shook her head at her obvious mistake. "And, like a fool, I kept trying to contact you. He convinced me that I wasn't going to get you back by crying myself to sleep every night. He suggested I go out, act like I was having a good time, and remind you of what you were missing."

She'd done that very well. It had been difficult for him, coming back to this apartment every evening and knowing she wouldn't be there. Knowing she was in another man's bed. "You went out with Gio every night."

She nodded and slumped against the window.

"There were pictures of you and Gio in the papers. Every day." She had looked happy, relaxed and very sexy.

"I wasn't trying to make you jealous," she insisted. "Since I couldn't see or talk to you, it was my way of reminding you that I was still around."

"Clinging to his arm?" he added sharply.

Isabella scowled at him. "I did no such thing."

Antonio remembered how she'd used to cling to *him*. She'd curled up against him whether they were walking along the street, sitting on the sofa, or making love. It had been as though she couldn't get close enough. And he had welcomed the warmth and affection.

"In those tiny dresses."

Isabella blushed. She looked away and turned until her back pressed against the window. "That was probably a bad idea."

"Dresses that Gio bought you." They had been short, tight and revealing. The kind of dresses a man gave his mistress. "When you wouldn't accept any gift from me."

"I didn't have anything acceptable to wear to those events," she mumbled as she flattened her hands against the glass pane.

"And I didn't take you anywhere but to bed?"

She looked up sharply. "That's not true! We had so much fun exploring the city. I got to see Rome through your eyes."

"Obviously that wasn't enough." *He* wasn't enough, no matter what he had done and what he had given. "But you made up for lost time by attending every nightclub."

"I wasn't interested in those parties. Or those people. I preferred the places we went to alone."

He'd like to believe that. When he had learned she

was an art history student he had gone out of his way to take her to see private art collections and participate in specially guided tours. He had ignored all invitations to dinner parties and exclusive events because he hadn't wanted to share Isabella.

He'd thought she had felt the same. Isabella had never complained, or asked to go dancing. Isabella had never felt a need to dress up or entertain. The only other person who'd spent any time with them was his brother.

"If any of this is true, what made you leave Gio?"

She pressed her lips together. "I discovered that Giovanni was not my friend. He pounced when I was at my most vulnerable."

Antonio waited, but she didn't reveal any more details. "You'll have to do better than that."

Isabella exhaled slowly. "And then I found out about the lies he had spread. I was not unfaithful to you, and I don't know why you would have believed him. You should have confronted me," Isabella said, her voice wavering with emotion. "You should have told me about your suspicions."

He should have, but he knew what would have happened. He would have accepted her version because he'd wanted to believe her. He had wanted to be with her at any cost. Even now her story seemed plausible, even though she was carrying his brother's baby.

"But you cast me out." She gestured to the front door with a flutter of her hand. "You had your security staff do your dirty work. I would never have thought you'd take the coward's way out."

He had been cold and ruthless, but it had been an act of self-preservation. Isabella would have wrapped her magic around him, distracted him from the truth and made him believe anything.

Like she was doing now.

Right now he wanted to lean into Isabella. Sink into her soft, warm curves. Erase the past and drag her back to his bed. He was fighting her lure, but it was a losing battle. Her power over his senses, his mind, was humbling.

"How am I the coward?" he asked. "You ran away when you saw me."

"Why do you seem so surprised? I knew that seeing you again would destroy everything I've done so far to recover."

Her actions had caused her downfall, not his. "And that's why it's imperative that you return to America?" he asked. "Why do you need to leave immediately?"

"I want to go home and start over again." Her mournful voice pulled at him. "I want to forget Italy and everything that happened here."

Her words tore at him. Isabella had been the most important part of his life. Everything had fallen by the wayside when they were together. He had treated her like a queen and put her needs first, but it hadn't been enough for her.

Now she wanted to forget all that. She would move on while he stayed behind, haunted by memories wherever he went.

"I want to forget you."

He flinched as if he had been stabbed. No, he wouldn't let that happen. They'd shared heaven together and now they would share hell. He wasn't going to be the only one in torment. He would not carry the burden alone.

"I won't let you," he said. He stood in front of her, trapping her against the window. "I'm going to make you remember what we had and you will regret everything you did to destroy it."

CHAPTER FIVE

ANTONIO'S kiss was hot, hard and possessive. Isabella felt the kick of exhilaration before it rushed through her bloodstream. Her skin heated as she softened against him.

The flare in his dark eyes had been her only warning before his mouth claimed hers. At first she didn't fight it. She'd never thought she'd get the chance again, and his kiss was just as magical as she remembered.

Raw emotions crashed through her as she responded to his rough, hard mouth. He tasted of sensual, masculine power and a secret part of her wanted to surrender. Her heart pounded against her chest. Her flesh prickled with anticipation.

Isabella knew she needed to pull away. She had to stop this madness before she passed the point of no return. Had to break the spell. She had to find a way to keep her distance from Antonio.

Following her most primal instinct, Isabella sank her teeth into his bottom lip.

Antonio reared back. The red mark on his mouth should have made her feel guilty, but it gave her a dark satisfaction seeing her brand on him. She felt the angry puff of his breath and risked a look at his eyes.

An unholy glow leapt in them, and his face was taut with lust. Excitement lit through her body. She had unleashed something wickedly sensual she didn't think she could control.

Antonio crushed her against him, his strong arms caging her. She gasped as her breasts pressed hard against his chest. He plowed his hands into her hair, pushing the rubber band free before tangling his fingers into the long tresses. There was no escape, she realized as he kissed her.

Antonio easily broke through her resistance as his tongue plunged into her mouth. She had physically ached from the loss of this passion. This was what she wanted back in her life, whatever the consequences.

Isabella surrendered and sagged against Antonio. She grabbed onto his shoulders, needing to hold something solid as her world spun crazily. Her hands skimmed his back and she clutched his shirt, bunching the fine linen in her fists.

Antonio's growl of triumph vibrated deep in his chest. The sound tugged deep inside her as she rolled her hips restlessly against him.

Isabella skimmed her hands over his broad chest, shoving his tie to one side. Her fingers fumbled with urgency against his strong neck before she speared her fingers through his thick hair. She ground her mouth against his, craving another taste of him.

Antonio groaned with pleasure as he delved his tongue past her lips. Her skin tingled with anticipation as she drew him in deeper. He dominated and conquered her mouth, leaving her breathless.

He leaned in and trapped her firmly against the window with his body. Isabella wanted to feel his hands all over her, wanted him to pleasure her as only he could. She rubbed her hips against his thick arousal, teasing him until his fingers clamped down on her waist. Antonio held her still, the strength and size of his hands sending a thrill down her spine.

Tearing his mouth away from hers, Antonio muttered something in Italian against her cheek that she didn't catch. He slanted his mouth against her throat and laved her heated skin with the tip of his tongue. Isabella fisted his hair and tilted her head back, offering him free rein.

As he caressed her neck with his lips Antonio brushed his fingertips against the hem of her T-shirt. Her breath caught in her throat as he glided his hands along her ribcage. Isabella pressed her hands flat on the window behind her, arching her spine, brazenly offering herself to Antonio as he grazed his fingers along the underside of her breasts.

Isabella swallowed hard as impatient need swirled inside her. Her legs trembled, her heart raced and desire clawed through her. She felt a hint of feminine pride as she watched his chest rise and fall rapidly as he fought for restraint. She knew then that he too felt the relentless compulsion, but he was trying to control it.

Isabella didn't want him to hold back. She needed Antonio to act on the wild desire that pulsated between them. She had to relive this feeling one more time.

She reached for Antonio's necktie and pulled it free. The silk hadn't landed on the floor before she tore at his shirt buttons, her fingers scrabbling with haste. She parted the fine linen, exposing Antonio's golden-brown chest. Clutching the shirt with both hands, Isabella dragged him closer, until the hard, aching tips of her breasts rubbed against the coarse black hair on his chest.

Isabella moaned as her nipples tightened against the soft cotton of her T-shirt. She wanted to feel his skin on her. Isabella shoved Antonio's shirt off his powerful shoulders, desperate to feel more of him. She wanted all of him.

"Say my name," he said roughly as he dragged her shirt up.

"Anto—" Isabella frowned, momentarily confused, until it dawned on her why he'd made that request. Did he believe she was thinking of Giovanni? She gasped against his mouth as hurt ricocheted inside her. Flattening her hands against his hard chest, she tried to push him away. "How dare you?" she said in a whisper.

"Your eyes were closed," he mocked. "And you weren't saying anything. I wanted to make sure you knew which brother you were kissing."

Her palms stung with the need to slap him hard. She had surrendered to Antonio against her better judgment, but he'd seen it as another way to insult her. She shook with anger as she curled her hands into fists. "Get away from me."

Antonio ignored her command and grabbed her wrists. She tried to break his hold but he easily raised her hands high above her head. He held her captive and she was at his mercy.

He leaned against her until his body was flush with hers. As much as she tried to fight it her body softened, welcoming him closer. His heat, his scent clouded her mind. The fierce pounding of her heart matched his.

"Were you thinking of him when you kissed me?" he asked in a drawl.

"No!" How could he think that? Couldn't he tell that all she wanted—all she had ever wanted—was him? She rocked against Antonio in an attempt to break free.

He captured her earlobe between his teeth. Isabella stilled as the nip sent a shower of sensation through her veins.

"Does he kiss like me?" he whispered in her ear. "Do we taste the same?"

Fury and lust whipped through her body. "You are disgusting." But most of all she was disgusted with herself. How could she respond to his touch so immediately while he said those hurtful words?

"Did you think of me when he was deep inside you?"

"Stop it!"

Antonio rested his forehead against hers. "I want to erase his claim on you," he confessed in a harsh whisper. "I want to take you to bed and make you forget Gio."

"I am not going to bed with you." She wanted to. Oh, how she wanted to drag him to his bed and make love all night long. But her heart would never recover. Isabella knew he would kick her out in the morning. The hurt, the pain of his rejection, would overshadow any pleasure he'd given her.

He didn't reply. Instead he dipped his head and trailed a row of soft kisses along the line of her clenched jaw. Isabella shut her eyes, her anticipation escalating as intense sensations billowed through her.

"I mean it, *Antonio*," she said, emphasizing his name. "I will not sleep with a man who thinks so little of me."

She felt his mouth curve into a smile. "Bella, we both know that's not true."

He was right, and his certainty was humiliating.

Antonio knew the power he held over her. One touch, one kiss and she wouldn't deny him. She would make love to him anywhere, at any time. And she had.

Antonio met her gaze, his dark eyes blurred with desire. "I only have to say the word and you would surrender completely."

Her skin flushed hotly. The only thing that kept her glaring right back at him was the reminder that there had been times when *he* had surrendered. When she had tapped into his fantasies. Once she'd had this power over *him*.

Antonio claimed her mouth with his. Just when she thought she couldn't take it anymore Antonio captured her tongue and drew on it hard. She moaned as she felt the pull go deep into her pelvis. Pleasure spilt through her.

"So responsive," he murmured against her mouth. "You must have learned a lot in my brother's bed."

She turned her head sharply and avoided his mouth. If only she could avoid his words. She couldn't protect herself from his anger. From his accusations. He wanted to get close enough so she could share his pain, but she suspected he was getting caught in his own trap. And, even though he treated her like the enemy, she still clung to him.

"I could take you right here against this window, but I can't be sure whose name you'll cry out."

Isabella flinched. She desperately wanted to retaliate. Make wild comparisons between Antonio and his brother. Call out Giovanni's name. She wanted to hurt him so badly he would never recover.

But she wouldn't. His torment was hers. She was still

in love with Antonio and had already caused him so much pain. She couldn't forgive herself for that.

"Are you done with this little demonstration?" she asked brokenly as she fought back the tears. "I'm tired and I want to go to bed. *Alone*."

"You don't have to worry about that, Bella." Antonio slowly let go of her hands and took a step back. "What we had was good, but I've never been interested in my brother's cast-offs."

That burned. Isabella bolted away from him. Her movements were awkward and shaky as she walked across the room and grabbed her backpack. She wanted to keep walking. Out the door. Out of Antonio's life.

Let him think the worst of her. It didn't matter anymore. They had no future together. She had already wasted so much time trying to get him back. What they'd had was a dream, and the beauty and magic were fading every minute she tried to hold onto it.

"Leave and I'll drag you back in here," Antonio warned. "You are carrying the Rossi heir."

How could he be like this? So ruthless and hard after the kiss they'd just shared? And why couldn't she be just as unemotional?

She whirled around and glared at Antonio. His shirt was unbuttoned, his hair mussed, but he still had a commanding presence. He was in control while she felt like she was being tossed from one crashing wave after another.

"I was in love with you," she announced bitterly.

Antonio didn't show any sign of surprise. That rankled. He knew how she'd felt. He had always known. And it didn't make a difference.

"I was so deeply and so foolishly in love," she said. "It was the reason that I put my future on hold."

"I never asked you to do that."

"I changed the course of my life to be with you," she said as she walked across the length of the room to the doorway, avoiding Antonio. "And right at this moment I regret it."

His eyes glittered with anger. "You regret getting caught. You didn't expect Gio to tell me the truth."

"I regret *you*," she retaliated. She wasn't sure if it was true. Her emotions were running high. Frustration billowed through her chest. "You were the biggest mistake of my life. But don't worry, Antonio. I learn from my mistakes and I never repeat them."

CHAPTER SIX

MORNINGS were the worst.

Isabella groaned as she sat on the bathroom floor, her bare legs sprawled on the cold linoleum. She had to get up and get dressed. She wished she could sit here until her stomach settled, but she didn't have the luxury of time.

How was she going to get through this pregnancy? Hell, how was she going to get through this morning?

Another question slipped into her mind and she couldn't push it away fast enough.

How was she going to be a mother?

A heavy ache settled in her chest. She was scared of going through this alone. She wasn't ready to be a parent. A single mom. Isabella had always assumed she would be a mother one day. Far, far in the future. But in the meantime she'd had other plans. A few goals she'd wanted to accomplish. She had promised her mother.

Isabella weakly closed her eyes. If her mother were alive, she would be devastated by the news. Before Jody Williams had become ill she had done everything possible to give her daughter the opportunities she hadn't had. Isabella remembered the litany of advice and warnings. *Finish college before you have a child... Never rely on a man... Protect yourself...*

At the time Isabella had thought her mother had a bitter view of the world, but her negativity was understandable. Jody's dreams had been cut short when she'd become a teen mother. Everyone had turned her back on her. The first one to walk away had been the father of her child. *Stay away from the rich ones*, her mother had said frequently. *They have so many choices that they don't know how to commit.*

Isabella wiped a tear from the corner of her eye. She had been so certain that nothing could sidetrack her from her dreams. No man would stand in her way.

She had been so arrogant. So naïve. But she couldn't dwell on that anymore. Now she needed to protect herself and her child. She would be as strong and resilient as her mother had been for her.

She slowly stood, her legs shaky and weak. Her stomach churned and she tried desperately to ignore it. Clutching the rim of the sink, Isabella turned on the faucet and rinsed her mouth out with water. She splashed her face and glanced up in the mirror.

Her hair, which had once been her glory, fell limp against her shoulders. She was pale, her eyes dull and her lips colorless. She saw the strain tightening her features. She was a mess. It would take hours to make her appearance presentable. Normal. Even longer until she felt that way.

The morning sickness was worse today, Isabella decided as she reached for a towel. Was it from the lack of sleep? The stress? Why did it have to be today, when she needed to be strong as she faced Antonio and demanded her plane ticket? She couldn't show any weakness around him.

"Bella?"

Panic radiated from her chest to her arms and legs when she heard the authoritative knock on her bedroom door. *No!* He couldn't come in here. He couldn't see her like this. Bella propelled herself forward just as Antonio entered her bedroom.

She slammed the bathroom door closed but it was already too late. He had seen her. He had stopped in mid-step at the sight of her in a T-shirt and panties. She could only hope her skimpy sleepwear had distracted him from the dark circles under her eyes and the greenish cast of her complexion.

"Why are you hiding in the bathroom?" he demanded.

"I'm not dressed," she said.

"I'm well aware of that." His voice was close and she knew he stood on the other side of the door. "But I've seen you in a lot less. Come out."

"No." She rested her head against the door and fought the urge to slump to the floor. Her body was punishing her for the sudden movement and the jolt of panic.

"Is this because of last night?"

"Maybe." She took a few shallow breaths but her stomach still threatened to revolt.

"I told you, I'm not interested in my brother's castoffs," he taunted.

"Yes," she said, and swallowed hard, "you really proved that last night."

Antonio sighed and she pictured him raking his hair with his hand. "We need to meet with the doctor in an hour."

"That isn't necessary," she insisted. "I've been to a doctor recently and everything is fine."

"You may be okay with that but I want a second opinion. Why wouldn't you want to visit one of Italy's top obstetricians?"

Isabella's shoulders sagged in defeat. When Antonio explained it like that, she really didn't have a reason to decline. "I'll be ready soon." *If she was lucky.*

"You still need to eat breakfast."

The idea made her gag, which she tried to cover up with a loud cough. "No, thanks. I'm not hungry."

"Then eat dry toast. Or have a cappuccino."

She grimaced as she pictured the milky drink. Oh, God. She was going to be sick again.

"Bella?" He turned the doorknob.

"Fine," she said in a high, urgent voice. She didn't care how it sounded. The less she argued, the faster he would leave.

She fought against the nausea, her skin going hot and cold, as she listened to Antonio's familiar footsteps. When he closed the bedroom door she ran to the toilet and vomited.

That had been too close, she decided as she lay on the floor. If Antonio had known she had been sick he wouldn't have left her alone. While she wouldn't mind having someone take care of her, Antonio would have seen how weak she felt. She couldn't allow that.

She was no longer his lover and was now a hindrance. An inconvenient obstacle. She was the reason he wouldn't inherit what was rightfully his. Isabella couldn't forget that. If she showed a chink in her armor, if she revealed any vulnerability, Antonio would take advantage. It was his nature.

She had to get out of here.

And I will once I've visited the doctor, Isabella thought as she turned on the shower. She would demand a plane ticket and deal with any paperwork through the lawyers. She couldn't be around Antonio anymore. Especially after last night. Because if he didn't suspect already Antonio would soon realize that *he* was her only weakness. And he would use that information ruthlessly to get what he wanted.

Weak and shaky, it took her much longer to get ready than she'd anticipated. She pulled her damp hair back in a tight ponytail and dressed simply in a gray T-shirt, jeans and her scuffed-up flats. Looking in the mirror, she wondered how she'd ever gained Antonio's attention. She wasn't beautiful or sexy. There was nothing special about how she looked. She had nothing to offer someone as rich and worldly as Antonio.

Maybe he'd slept with her because she was different from the women he normally had in his life. She was earthy compared to those glamorous creatures. Isabella grabbed her backpack and strode across the bedroom. Or maybe it was because she'd made it known that she found him desirable. That was more likely. Isabella swung open the door and jumped back when she saw Antonio standing in front of her.

"Here—eat this." He offered a piece of dry toast.

Isabella reared her head back. The bread did nothing to whet her appetite. "I was heading for the dining room."

"Where you would have found an excuse not to eat breakfast," he predicted. "I know you don't believe me, but you will feel better after you've eaten."

Once she would have found comfort in the fact that

Antonio knew her so well. Now it made her feel vulnerable. She snatched the toast from his hand, deciding she needed to pick her battles. She didn't want to argue with him when she needed to get her plane ticket.

She looked at the toast with hesitation and then glanced up at Antonio when she noticed he wasn't walking away. "Are you just going to stand there and watch me eat?"

"It's the only way I'll know you've been fed."

Isabella frowned. Why did he care? "I can take care of myself."

"I've already caught you once when you fainted," he reminded her as he crossed his arms as if ready for battle. "I don't want to make it a habit."

"It won't be," she said as she leaned against the wall and nibbled on the toast. She hated being an inconvenience. Or, worse, an obligation. She always toughed it out on her own, took care of her problems alone, and promptly repaid any favor or debt. She didn't accept charity and she wasn't going to start now.

"Can you give me the address of the doctor's office?" she asked Antonio, avoiding his intent gaze as she took another bite of toast.

"No need. I'm coming with you."

She almost choked on the bread. "Why? It's a simple examination and a blood test. You don't need to be there."

"Why do you hate the idea so much?" he asked, and his gaze narrowed on her face. "Do you have something to hide?"

"No, but I don't need to be watched like a hawk." She wanted to handle this alone. Antonio would immediately take over and she knew she would lose the power struggle.

"We'll need to do a DNA test to prove paternity," he explained.

"I'll sign a release form and the lab will send you the results," she promised as she finished the last of the toast. "Or are you afraid I might tamper with the procedure?"

"Are you always this suspicious when someone tries to help you?" he asked as he arched an eyebrow.

"Yes." Because no one offered help unless there was an agenda. The last time she'd accepted assistance she had become a pawn in Giovanni's games.

Antonio took a step forward. "Then you need to work on that, because from now on I'm going to be with you every step of the way."

She should take that as a threat, but she felt her body soften and warm at the promise. "We both know that's the last thing you want to do," she muttered.

"You are carrying the Rossi heir." He gestured at her stomach. "This is my concern as much as yours."

Isabella automatically wrapped her arms around her belly. "You can't possibly want to have anything to do with me or my child. You think this baby is proof that I cheated on you."

"I wouldn't blame a child for his parents' sins."

Isabella stilled as Antonio's words stung. She took a deep breath. "I'm not willing to test that out."

Antonio flattened his hands against the wall as a dark, unpredictable energy swirled around him. "Do you think that I'm the kind of man who would mistreat a child?" he asked in a low, biting tone.

Her instincts said no. She knew Antonio would use

all his power and resources to protect a child. But this was Giovanni's baby. She didn't know much about the history between the brothers, but she knew it was filled with pain and betrayal. Could Antonio separate his feelings for Giovanni from the feelings he had for the baby?

"I don't know," she admitted, tilting her head up to meet his angry gaze. "I've never seen you around kids."

"I haven't seen *you* around children, either," he said as he leaned in, "but I know enough about you to know that you would be a good mother. I don't need a blood test to know that this child is family."

Family. She really wanted her child to grow up with a sense of belonging and surrounded by unconditional love. Her mother had given her those things, but there had been times when she had wanted acceptance from the family that had shunned her. There had been times when Isabella had wondered what was wrong with her that her relatives should withhold their love and approval.

"I take care of my family," Antonio said, his voice strong and clear, "and I will take care of this child."

Isabella blinked slowly as she listened to his vow. Why was he claiming this child? She hadn't expected that. But then why would she? Her own father hadn't claimed *her.* Giovanni had only claimed his baby because he could use the information to hurt Antonio. What did Antonio expect to get from all this? What was his end game? Whatever it was, she didn't think she could afford the price.

"My baby doesn't need your financial support," she declared huskily, and tried to move away. Antonio settled his hand against her shoulder and she stopped.

"It's not just money," he explained. "Your child will

one day head the Rossi empire. He will be part of this world. He needs me to guide him through it," Antonio said as he removed his hand from her shoulder. "Unless you think you're up for the challenge?"

Isabella felt her skin flush. She was an outsider while Antonio's family ruled high society. "Who says my child will want this world?"

"That should be his decision, not yours. Your child will need to be groomed from the beginning. He will need to attend the best schools, train—"

"I can provide that now. I am *not* a disadvantage to my baby," she insisted, hating how her voice shook.

She was surprised when Antonio hooked his finger under her chin and guided her face up so she could look into his eyes. "Your baby is already lucky to have you as a mother," he assured her softly. "You are very nurturing and affectionate."

Maybe too much so. During their affair she hadn't held back on her embraces and caresses. She'd always been touching Antonio. Holding on. Clinging. It had led him to think that she was like that with everyone.

"But you don't think I can give this child the sort of life that befits a Rossi heir?" she said.

Antonio dropped his hand and took a step back. "That's where I can help."

It was too good to be true. There must be some strings attached to his offer. An expectation of good behavior or a short expiration date.

"For how long? Until it's no longer in your interest? When you start a family of your own?" With that fiancée of his. The thought of the other woman made Isabella want to crumple up in pain. She'd seen pictures of the sophisticated lady. She was beautiful, from a prominent Italian family. She would be an asset to Antonio while Isabella had been a liability.

"I am committed to being in this child's life. From this moment on. Whenever I am needed I'll be there."

"Antonio, you don't know the first thing about commitment."

"How can you say that? I have always met my obligations. I have a duty to—"

She raised her hand to stop him. "I am *not* your obligation and you have *no* duty to my child," she said fiercely. "I am solely responsible for my baby and I don't want your help."

He gave an arrogant shrug. "Too bad because you already have it."

"Your type of help will be more like interference and influence." She stopped as she thought of her words yesterday. *You have no rights over me or my child.* That was what this was all about. Isabella closed her eyes as anger washed over her. Oh, she was so stupid for not realizing it sooner. "You want to control the power and the money Giovanni gave to me."

"No," he said through clenched teeth.

"Are you worried that I would squander the family fortune? Or that I will abuse my power?" She shook her head. "Don't worry. I didn't ask for this kind of responsibility. I don't even want it. But I'm doing it to protect my child's interests."

"If you don't want the responsibility I can help you with that. If the tests prove that this child is Giovanni's I'll pay you a lump sum in exchange for your interest in the Rossi empire. You will have millions more dollars at your fingertips instantly and you won't have to make any business decisions."

Isabella noticed he'd come up with the alternative quickly. It was almost as if he'd been waiting to present it. "And you won't have to deal with me or my baby," she pointed out sweetly.

Antonio's nostrils flared as he reined in his temper. "My commitment to you and the baby would remain the same."

"It's a tempting offer," she said with exaggerated politeness, "but I'll have to think about it."

Isabella turned away as she battled conflicting emotions. She'd known Antonio had an ulterior motive, but she was filled with disappointment because she was right.

She knew better than to accept Antonio's help. He'd said he was fully committed, but what he really meant was that he would be committed until he could get full control of the Rossi money. The minute he got what he wanted Antonio would discard her from his life with the same ruthlessness as before.

"Committed? Yeah, right."

"What was that?" Antonio was right behind her. She felt his heat and his towering strength.

Isabella knew she should let it go, but the anger was building up inside her. She slowly turned around, wondering if this was the smartest move, and confronted Antonio. "I think your definition of commitment is different from mine. You couldn't commit to me, but now you'll pledge a lifetime of commitment to a child?"

Antonio clenched his teeth and a muscle bunched in his jaw. "You question my ability to commit when *you* are the one who cheated?" His harsh voice was almost a whisper.

"I didn't cheat," she said with a weary sigh. "Not

that it matters. If Giovanni hadn't come up with that story I'm sure you would have found another reason to dump me."

Antonio's eyes darkened as tension crackled around them. "That's not true."

"It is. Men like you don't *do* relationships." She had been warned, but she hadn't listened. She'd thought what she'd had with Antonio had been different. Special. That it would beat the odds.

"Men like me?"

"You have money, power and so many choices." And she'd had nothing to offer to make him want to stay. "Why make a commitment when something new and exciting, something better, is just around the corner?"

Antonio grabbed her wrist and pulled her close. "I wanted you and only you."

She believed him. But she also believed the feeling had been temporary. "And how does your fiancée feel about that?" Isabella asked as she pulled from his grasp.

"So that is where all this is coming from?" Antonio exhaled sharply and rubbed his hand over his face. "Let me assure you, Bella, I do *not* have a fiancée."

"Isn't that just a technicality?" she asked as she rubbed her wrist, hating how her pulse skipped and her skin tingled from his touch. "You haven't put a ring on her finger yet, but there is an agreement."

"I was engaged, but that was before I met you."

He had been engaged? Maybe he did know how to commit, but just not to her. "To the woman they mentioned in the news? Aida?"

Antonio nodded. "Her parents were good friends with mine. It was to be an arranged marriage."

Isabella's mouth parted in surprise. "Why would you

do something like that?" Antonio was the most sexual man she knew. Passionate. He would have suffered in a paper marriage.

"We came from the same world, had the same interests, and the marriage would have been advantageous for both families. Aida would have made a good wife."

Aida clearly offered everything she could not. Isabella tried not to think about that. "If it was such a good match, why aren't you married?"

He rubbed the back of his neck and looked away. "Before we announced our engagement Aida decided she couldn't bear the idea of getting married to me when she had fallen in love with Gio."

"Oh." Isabella's eyes widened. "Is *that* why you and your brother were estranged?"

Antonio shook his head. "Gio never knew, thank God. He had no interest in Aida. She might as well have been invisible to him."

Isabella wondered if this was why Antonio was so quick to assume she'd used him to get to Giovanni. His own fiancée had rejected him for his brother. It would have been hard to get over that, arranged marriage or not. "I'm sorry."

"Why? I wasn't in love with Aida, but I would have taken my wedding vows seriously. I know how to make a commitment and how to honor it." He took a step back and glanced at his watch. "That's all you need to know."

"No, it's not," she said with exasperation. Typical of Antonio. If he felt he'd revealed too much, or if it veered into uncomfortable territory, he shut the conversation down immediately.

"Then let me be clear," he said in a clipped tone. "It doesn't matter whether you accept your inheritance or let me buy you out. This is still Gio's baby and I'm still going to be part of this child's life. Get used to it."

He was in hell.

The white walls of the doctor's office were closing in on him. His hands were cold, his chest clenched and he wanted to walk away. Instead he stood by the door, arms folded, as the amplified sounds of an infant's heartbeat filled the examination room.

He watched Isabella as she listened. Her face softened and she pressed her lips together as she listened to her baby. The child might have been unplanned, but Isabella had already bonded with this child and wanted it fiercely.

The ultrasound technician invited him to come closer. Antonio declined with a shake of his head and didn't move. He felt like he shouldn't be there, that he was intruding on a very private moment. He'd promised to look after Isabella and her child, but that didn't erase the fact that he was standing in for his brother. *Again.*

And Isabella had made it clear she didn't want him around. Her instincts were right on target. He *was* doing all this to gain control of her. She wasn't going to give up her fortune—that had been a long shot. Which meant marriage. He could make her fall in love with him, but that wouldn't be enough. He needed to demonstrate that he could accept the baby as his own.

"Everything looks fine and your baby has a strong heartbeat," the lab tech said as she got up from her chair. "You can get dressed now and go to the lab to get your blood taken."

"How long will it take to get the results?" Antonio asked.

"I'll ask them to hurry," the woman said as she approached him, "but it can take up to a week."

A week was too long. He wasn't thinking only about the legal aspects of confirming Gio's heir. Having Isabella in his life, in his home, was already placing a strain on his self-control. She had only been under his roof for a few minutes when he had pounced.

He thanked the technician, ignoring the flirty promise that lay beneath her fluttering eyelashes. He closed the door firmly behind her and turned around when he heard Isabella's deep sigh.

"This is why I wanted to come alone to this doctor's appointment."

"Why?" Antonio asked as he watched Isabella sit up and swing her bare legs over the edge of the examination table. "What did I do?"

"She was paying more attention to you than the screen."

"You're exaggerating," he said. Her comment surprised him. Isabella wasn't the jealous type, but then he had never given her reason to worry. His adoration had been painfully obvious.

Isabella hopped down from the table and her paper gown rustled loudly. "I'm going to get dressed."

Antonio retrieved his phone from his jacket and leaned against the door. He scrolled through a few messages before he glanced up again. Isabella was tapping her bare feet impatiently and had her hands on her hips.

"I'd like some privacy."

He raised an eyebrow. This from the woman who had once given him a striptease so erotic that his body still clenched from the memory of it? "You can't be serious."

She glared at him. "Will you at least turn your back?"

"No." He pocketed his phone and crossed his arms. He should probably be a gentleman and allow her to get ready in private, but he didn't like being relegated to the status of an acquaintance. A stranger. They had once been lovers and he didn't want her to forget it.

"Fine. Hold this while I dress." She thrust the ultrasound printout in his hand.

He automatically looked down at the black and white image of Isabella's baby.

Gio's baby.

His fingers pinched the edge of the picture.

Antonio braced himself for searing pain as he stared at the image. But all he felt was curiosity and regret. He wished Isabella were carrying *his* child.

What kind of father would Gio have been? Antonio wondered. Would he have been a disciplinarian, like their father, or would he have been an absent parent? He didn't think Gio would have offered stability or comfort. His brother had been famous for his playboy lifestyle and wouldn't have changed his ways to accommodate a baby.

Antonio, on the other hand, was already prepared to make changes for this child. He frowned at the picture, noticing how small and innocent the baby appeared. He could offer the child a stable environment. Protection. But love? *That* he didn't know.

"Is something wrong?" Isabella asked softly.

Antonio realized he had been staring at the picture all this time. "I think it's a girl," he said gruffly.

"I haven't asked about the sex of the baby," Isabella said. She turned around and walked to the chair that held her clothes. "All I care about is the baby's health."

Antonio glanced at the paper gown that fell onto the

floor. A kick of anticipation heated his blood. His gaze trailed from Isabella's bare feet to her slender legs. He wanted to let his eyes roam, to memorize every line and bend of her body, but that would be dangerous. Antonio knew once he did that he wouldn't be able to keep his hands off Isabella.

"Was your assistant able to find a plane ticket for me?" she asked as she stepped into her panties. The cheap cotton didn't detract from the gentle curve of her hips, and his hands stung with the need to drag it down her thighs.

"Plane ticket?" he asked in a daze. He remembered the warmth and softness of her skin. The way she'd nestled perfectly against him when they slept.

"To Los Angeles," she said as she hooked thin bra straps over her shoulders. "That was the deal."

He watched the muscles in her back move sinuously as she hooked her bra. Her fingers fumbled on the last hook and Antonio stood very still as desire whipped through his body. He wasn't going to offer any assistance. He would not brush her hands away and let his fingers graze her skin as he unhooked the bra and peeled it off...

Antonio cleared his throat. "That was before I knew you were carrying the Rossi heir."

She glanced over her shoulder. "A deal is a deal, Antonio."

He could argue, point out that she had withheld important information. Instead he watched, fixated, as Isabella bent from the waist. Her long blonde hair swayed along her shoulders as she shimmied into her jeans.

"Wait until the results are back?" he suggested. It

wasn't a great idea. For his own preservation it would be better if Isabella was far away.

"There is no need," Isabella said as she hastily put on her shirt. "I know what the results are going to say."

"But you don't know what you plan to do. If you want to support your interest in the Rossi fortune then *you* need to learn the business, too. That means staying here."

"And you're going to teach me? Is that right?" she asked as she straightened the hem of her shirt. "And eventually my child. That way you can wield influence even if you *don't* have all the power."

He gritted his teeth. "Your child needs to grow up here in Rome. She needs to understand where she comes from and who her family is. Then she will know what to do when she takes charge of the family business."

"Heritage?" Isabella paused in slipping her foot into her shoe. "She needs to know her heritage?"

Antonio was surprised by the longing in Isabella's voice. "She can only do that around her remaining family," he added. He needed to keep a close eye on Isabella. The last thing he needed was another man in the picture. Antonio's stomach twisted violently at the thought.

"It's a good point." Isabella said, her gaze on her feet. It was obvious that she was having second thoughts. "I need to think about this."

"Think about it here in Rome," he urged.

She nodded slowly. "I'll stay until the test results are ready."

"Good." Antonio felt a hint of relief. He had a week to seduce her. Considering their history, she would capitulate sooner than that.

Isabella reached for the sonogram printout. "Once

we're done here I'll move into a hotel. I don't have the money right now, but maybe I can work something out with the lawyers dealing with the will."

Hotel? He couldn't let that happen. "I have no problem with you staying in my apartment."

"I don't want to take advantage of your hospitality," she replied. "I think I've already overstayed my welcome."

"Not at all. In fact I won't be in Rome for the rest of the week. I have business to attend to in Paris," Antonio lied.

Isabella bit her bottom lip. "I don't know…"

"Stay. I insist." His strategy would only work if she remained in his home and in his control. "It will put my mind at ease knowing that you are cared for while I'm gone."

"Okay, thank you," she said with a grateful smile. "By the time you come back I'm sure I'll have made my decision."

And Antonio was determined to do everything in his power to have the decision work in his favor.

CHAPTER SEVEN

FIVE days later Isabella sat in Maria Rossi's grand home just outside Rome. She perched on the edge of a sofa and silently accepted a fine china teacup. She winced when the cup rattled on the saucer.

Do not drop it. The tea set looked like it had cost more than her entire college tuition fees. The rug beneath her feet had to be obscenely expensive. It didn't take any expertise in antiques to know that everything in the room was priceless. She needed to keep her hands in her lap and refrain from making any sudden movements.

She and Antonio's mother made an odd tea party. Maria wore a silk dress and pearls, while Isabella wore dime-store denim and cotton. Her skin prickled as she remembered the disapproving look from the butler when she had arrived. She fought the urge to tug at her skirt, which was several inches above her bare knees.

Isabella wasn't sure what the protocol was for tea, so she waited for the older woman to drink from her own cup, then took a polite sip from her tea and carefully set the cup and saucer down gently on the table in front of her.

"It was kind of you to invite me to your house, Mrs.

Rossi," Isabella said, hoping to get through this quickly. "I'm wondering what the occasion is."

"Please, call me Maria."

The woman must want something if she was trying to be friendly, and Isabella felt a stab of guilt. She didn't know anything about Maria Rossi. It was possible that she was a kind soul who only turned into a lioness when she felt her family was being threatened. It was highly unlikely, but anything was possible.

"It must be important," Isabella continued. "I know you aren't entertaining while you're in mourning."

"This isn't entertaining," Maria corrected her. "You're practically family."

She was glad she wasn't holding the china cup when Maria said that. Unsure how to respond, Isabella smiled tightly and glanced around the room. Her eyes bulged when she recognized a painting from one of her art history classes.

Her fingers tightened and she pushed her elbows in closer to her body. She'd never seen a home like this, even when she'd used to clean houses with her mother. It made her uncomfortable. Nervous.

"I understand you took a DNA test to establish paternity?" Maria said.

Isabella slowly returned her attention to Antonio's mother. "Just a formality." She was sensitive about the fact that she had been made to take the blood test. She wasn't a slut who didn't know the father of her baby.

"Have you received the results?"

Please. Isabella narrowed her eyes at Maria. She'd got the call this morning and an hour later had been summoned to the Rossi family estate. That was no coincidence. Maria had probably known the results before she had. "Yes, I have."

"And?" Maria prompted as she took another sip of tea.

Isabella took a deep breath, knowing that Maria was going to be a part of her life once she gave the answer whether she liked it or not. "Giovanni is the father."

To her surprise Maria's eyes dulled and a sad smile flickered across her lips. "It's a shame he will never be able to see his child," she said softly.

Isabella tried to remember that this woman was grieving for her son. Maria had been rude and hurtful to her, but she was suffering. Isabella remembered how it had felt when her mother had died, and tried to find some compassion.

At least Maria had Antonio, Isabella reminded herself. She wouldn't feel lost and alone. Unlike her, Maria had other family to rely on.

Maria regained her composure and took another fortifying sip of her tea. "Anything else?" she asked briskly.

Isabella wasn't sure what she was asking. Did Maria know something she didn't?

Isabella shrugged. "Antonio thinks it's a girl."

"I'm only going by the ultrasound." Antonio said as he entered the room.

Isabella heart lurched when she heard Antonio's deep voice. She whirled around and saw him striding toward her. He was a commanding figure, his confidence and energy crackling into the stifling atmosphere. Although he was dressed casually, in faded jeans and a long-sleeved shirt, Antonio looked like he ruled the world.

She didn't know why she had such a fierce reaction

from seeing him again. It had only been five days. It wasn't as if she'd been out of contact with him. She had spoken to him daily on the phone while he was gone. He had also sent links throughout each day to websites about pregnancy and maternal health. Only this morning she had discovered he had been in contact with the doctor's office, asking advice about her debilitating morning sickness.

This was a side to Antonio she hadn't expected, Isabella realised as she watched Antonio greet his mother with brief kiss on the cheek. He was her fantasy lover and a fascinating man—but thoughtful and protective…?

She saw Antonio pause as a shadow passed along his face. Isabella immediately knew he had caught a glimpse of Giovanni's photo next to Maria's chair.

He was being a picture of strength and power for the sake of his mother and the employees who depended on him, but she knew he was hiding his own suffering. Giovanni had been his brother. Isabella wanted to offer him comfort, but he was too proud for that. She would lighten his burden if she could, but Antonio wasn't someone who shared his thoughts or his pain.

Oh, damn. Isabella closed her eyes weakly as the truth hit her. She was still in love with Antonio. She had never stopped loving him. For months she had wished for reconciliation, with the loss of what she'd had with Antonio almost driving her mad. She'd tried to be practical, tried to move on, but she couldn't extinguish that whisper of hope.

Rubbing her aching head, Isabella wondered if she'd ever learn. This was why she needed to keep her distance. She wasn't going to start up again with Antonio.

It didn't matter how much they wanted each other or how much she loved him. Nothing would change the fact that he still believed she had been unfaithful.

"What are you doing here?" Isabella blurted out.

Antonio faced her, his gaze warming as it traveled from her face to her bare legs and back to her eyes. "I was going to ask you the same."

"I invited her to tea," Maria explained. "She told me the blood test results are in and Gio is the father."

Isabella saw a stealthy look pass between mother and son. She didn't know what it meant. Had they seriously questioned the paternity of her child?

"And," Maria continued, "I was hoping to know what her plans are now."

The two looked at her expectantly and Isabella felt her nervousness spike. She knew they weren't going to like her decision, but she had to be strong.

"I'm leaving Rome. Today," she added. She had to leave before Antonio discovered her weak points. Had to get out before he talked about family and heritage. Before he made seductive promises he had no way of keeping.

She sensed Maria's disappointment. She tried not to look directly at Antonio. She couldn't determine his reaction. Was he surprised? Did he know how much she had wrestled with this decision? Had he been hoping she would stay?

Maria frowned. "But…"

Isabella raised her hand to hold off any arguments. "I plan to visit Rome frequently. I want my child to know his or her family. But it's best for me to return to Los Angeles and finish my degree."

Maria tilted her head to look at Antonio. "Talk to

her," she said in Italian. "Take her into the gardens and convince her to stay in Rome."

Isabella lowered her head and kept her gaze on her hands. Did Maria think she didn't understand *any* Italian? How did she think she had been able to live in Rome all these months? She pressed her lips before she corrected the older woman. She knew some Italian, but not enough to speak fluently.

Isabella's pulse quickened as Antonio approached her. She glanced up and her heart did a slow tumble when she saw his weary face. She didn't think she'd ever seen him like this. She wanted to smooth away the lines and hold him tight.

"Bella, let's discuss your travel arrangements," he said in English. "Would you like to join me in the gardens?"

Isabella nodded and rose from her seat. She quietly followed him to a door that led out to the magnificent garden. It was as large as a public park, artfully designed with statues and fountains. The lush green lawn was beautifully maintained, and contrasted against the crimson and gold leaves on the large, solid trees.

She shouldn't be doing this, Isabella thought as she walked alongside Antonio. She was obediently following him just to *be* with him. Her chest tightened as she realized this was the last time they would be alone together. Instead of getting closer, she needed to start creating distance.

"You don't need to pretend, Antonio," she said. "I understood what your mother told you."

"I know," he said with a hint of a smile. "But I didn't want to have this conversation in front of her."

"There's nothing to talk about. I thought about staying here in Rome, so my child would know his family and his heritage, but I think it's best for me to return to Los Angeles and finish my college degree."

"You can always finish your degree here."

She shook her head. "My Italian isn't good enough."

"Those are obstacles we can easily overcome. Tell me what you need and I'll make it happen."

Isabella stared at the pale stonework under her feet. No one had offered that kind of support for her while she'd pursued her education. She had done it all on her own. She was proud of her accomplishments, but she'd love to share her future ups and downs with Antonio. Have someone at her side during the journey.

But she couldn't rely on him. If she accepted his help he would expect something in return. Something like allegiance and obedience when it came to matters concerning the Rossi fortune.

"I appreciate the offer," she said woodenly. "I really do. But—"

"What is the real reason you're leaving Rome?" he interrupted. "It's not because you want to continue your education. The academic year has already started and you can't re-enrol for another couple of months. So what is the urgency?"

"Once I make a decision I act immediately."

"No, that's not it." He dismissed her answer with the flick of his hand. "You're leaving because of me."

"You are so—" She stopped herself. What did it matter if he knew how she felt? "Okay, fine. *Yes*, Antonio. It's best for me to leave Rome because of *you*. You think I cheated on you. I gave you no reason to be jealous, and there is no evidence that I cheated, but you're determined to believe the worst about me."

He took a deep breath. "I regret letting Giovanni get between us."

Isabella stopped walking and closed her eyes as old pain washed over her. "But you believed him. You *still* believe him."

Antonio took a step closer. "If I could do it all over again I would do it differently," he said softly. "I should have confronted you. I should have told you about the history between Gio and me. I regret allowing his accusations to ruin what we had."

Isabella noticed he no longer called it Gio's *confession*. She wondered if she was investing too much significance in Antonio's word choice. She opened her eyes and turned to him. "Do you believe me? That I was faithful?"

She saw the struggle in his eyes before he answered. "I want to," he answered slowly. "I'm trying to believe it."

But he couldn't. Disappointment welled up inside her. "Why can't you? What is it about me that makes it so hard to believe?"

He shook his head and tossed his hands up in frustration. "I don't know."

Isabella pressed her lips together as she considered a few possibilities. "Is it because I wasn't a virgin when I met you?"

"No!" Antonio looked surprised by the suggestion.

She squinted as she watched his face. "Or because we fell into bed the day we met?"

"No…"

She heard the moment's hesitation. "Don't you *dare*." She pressed her finger against his chest. "Don't tarnish that memory."

"I'm not," he insisted. "You are bold and passionate. Adventurous and trusting. I'd like to think you were only that way with me."

"I have never fallen that hard or that fast for anyone," Isabella said fiercely, and immediately dropped her hand. She took a step back and pursed her lips. She felt exposed and uncertain, but Antonio needed to hear this. He had to understand just how important he was to her. "And I never will again."

His eyes darkened. "Because you regret it?"

"No," she said, realizing he had gotten it all wrong. "Because the next time it won't be *you*."

Antonio stilled. He didn't speak or move. He stared at her with quiet intensity.

"You know what?" she said, feeling foolish as a blush crept up her cheeks. "It doesn't matter anymore. For one reason or another you can't believe that I was faithful. Tonight I'm out of here and I will be just a memory."

Her words jerked him out of his stupor. "About that…"

She didn't like the sound of that. "About what?"

"Bella…" he said softly.

"No." He wasn't going to give her the ticket. She shook her head and sliced her hands in the air in case she wasn't getting her point across. "No, no, *no*. You promised."

He bent his head and shoved his hands in his pockets. "I'm aware of that."

She pressed her hands against her head as frustration billowed through her. "I need to get back to where I belong. To be in familiar and comfortable surroundings. I have some big changes ahead of me and I need to be ready."

"I understand. I think it's the nesting instinct. But that shouldn't occur until around the fifth month of pregnancy."

Isabella forgot what she'd been going to say next. She stared at Antonio as if he was speaking a different language. "What are you talking about?"

"It's in this book I'm reading about pregnancy and labor."

"You're reading a book about *pregnancy*?" His admission astounded her. She hadn't expected him to have an interest. When they had visited the obstetrician it had looked as if Antonio had wanted to be anywhere but in that examination room. "If you understand why I need to leave, then why are you asking me to stay?"

Antonio swallowed, opened his mouth and stopped. He clenched his jaw and looked away.

Isabella watched with growing concern. She had never seen him hesitant.

"Antonio?" Isabella prompted. "What is it?"

"Gio left a mess." The words came out in a rush. "It's a nightmare."

"Okay." What did that have to do with her? Did it have something to do with the will? Wouldn't the lawyers inform her if so?

He squeezed his eyes shut and raked his hand through his hair. "Never mind. Forget I said anything."

She watched Antonio walk away abruptly, his shoulders stooped as if he was carrying the weight of the world. He was a dark, solitary figure among the bright colors of the garden.

He wasn't *really* alone, she told herself.

But who was there for him?

He was grieving for his brother, but he couldn't show

it while he took care of everyone else. His mother was leaning on him and no one was offering support while he had to move into his brother's role. He'd almost swallowed his pride and asked her to stay.

But why? Why *her*? Was it because there was no one else? He didn't trust her. He still suspected the worst of her. She was not the ideal candidate to stay by his side.

Damn. She wanted to stomp her foot. Why did he have to do this to her? Now? She was so close to leaving. She was almost home.

It wasn't like he'd asked her to bed. He was simply asking for support, right? She could do that. She wanted to do that.

"Antonio, just ask," she called out.

He stopped but didn't turn around. "I understand if you can't," he replied stiffly. "We didn't part on good terms."

Maybe that was why her resolve was weakening. Isabella reached his side and placed her hand on his arm. She couldn't recapture what they'd had, but she could change the ending of their relationship.

"What do you need?"

"You."

Her heart lurched to a stop and then pounded violently. Was he asking for something more than emotional support? Why did she feel that kick of excitement? Almost a week ago she'd told him she wouldn't sleep with a man who didn't trust her. But he wasn't asking to sleep in her bed. He was putting his trust in her hands as he asked for her help.

Isabella nervously swiped her tongue along her bottom lip. "Could you be more specific?"

"I need you at my side," Antonio admitted. He looked

down at her, his eyes stormy and troubled. "Just for a few days while I deal with some competitors. They are circling Rossi Industries hoping to find a weakness. It would help if we looked like a united front. Once that's accomplished then I'll send you home."

Antonio could handle his enemies without her at his side. Isabella suspected this was not really about business or about his mother's request. He was reaching out in his own way. He was taking a risk, knowing she had every right to reject him.

"Do you still want me to stay at your apartment?" she asked calmly as her mind raced. Had Antonio figured out that *he* was her weakness? That, despite her better judgment, she couldn't stay away?

He frowned as though he'd made it obvious. "Yes."

"And I stay in the guestroom?" She didn't know why she'd said that. She didn't want to be there.

"Yes, of course."

She saw that glint in his eye. He had no intention of having her stay in the guestroom. He wanted comfort and support in the most basic form. Antonio wanted a few hours to forget—a few nights where he could lose himself.

And she wanted it, too. She knew his trust in her was fragile, that his motivations had nothing to do with love. She was willing to risk it all if it meant having another night with the man she couldn't stop loving. If he propositioned her, would she reject him? She didn't know.

But she was tired of playing it safe. And she didn't want this affair to have ended when he'd kicked her out of his bed. This time she would walk out when she was ready.

"Sure, Antonio," she said calmly as her heart started to race. "I can stay for three more days. But that's all I can promise."

CHAPTER EIGHT

ISABELLA was relieved when she and Antonio left the Rossi estate a short time later. Once they'd told Antonio's mother that she was extending her stay for a few more days Maria had sent them on their way with barely disguised haste. It was as if Maria had got the result she desired and wanted Isabella gone.

Antonio guided her to his black sports car with a large hand at the small of her back. Her skin tingled from the gentle touch. She knew he didn't mean anything by the gesture, that it was something he did automatically, but she liked it. It made her feel like he was looking after her.

Once Antonio had helped her into his low-slung car, he slid into the driver's seat and checked his watch. "There is a party that I have to attend."

Disappointment filled her. She knew what that meant. When they'd been together Antonio had rarely accepted invitations to a party or event, but there had been times when it was required. He would dress up in a suit or tuxedo, looking so devastatingly handsome that it almost hurt to look at him, and then he would go alone and she would stay at home and wait for him.

In the past Isabella had told herself that she was glad

she hadn't had to go to those parties. She wouldn't know anyone, struggled with the language, and wouldn't feel comfortable in extravagantly luxurious settings. But there had been times when she'd wondered *why* Antonio didn't include her. Was she not good enough to be seen with a Rossi? Had he only wanted her for sex?

She wasn't his lover anymore, but the old insecurities were still there, along with her desire to be with him. She hadn't seen him for days and now he was going out for the night. Only this time she didn't have a claim on him. She wasn't sure she ever had.

But she wasn't going to make the same mistake this time. She was in the city of Rome. There was beauty and excitement all around her. She wasn't going to stay at home in hopes that Antonio would return earlier than planned. She had wasted too much time waiting for him and putting her life on hold. Isabella wanted to make the most of her time in this vibrant city.

"Okay," she said, and she stared straight ahead at the Rome skyline, her gaze focused on the famous dome of St. Peter's Basilica. "I might be home late tonight too."

Antonio started the ignition and paused. "Where are you going?"

Isabella had no idea, but she was sure there were many choices. Maybe she would go to the Piazza di Spagna. She didn't care so long as she wasn't home alone. "I've always wanted to experience Rome at night," she said. "I never really got the chance."

"You were out every night with Gio," he muttered darkly as he sped the car down the wide lane that was flanked by big trees.

"I'm not talking about nightclubs. When you've seen

one, you've seen them all," she said. "I want to explore the city and see a different side of it."

"Can't you postpone that till tomorrow?" Antonio asked as they passed the intimidating iron gates that barred ordinary people from the Rossi world. "I promise I will make it worth the wait and show you Rome under the stars. Tonight I want you to come with me to the party."

"You do? Why?" What had prompted the invitation? Was it because he knew she wasn't going to stay at home and he wanted to keep an eye on her? "I've never gone to a social event with you before."

She knew why. It simply wouldn't have *done* for her to be at his side. He was sophisticated, powerful, part of prestigious family. She, on the other hand, had had no money, no connections, and hadn't known the secret handshakes of high society. She had been a disadvantage. A liability.

"I wanted you all to myself," he confessed. "I know it was selfish but I didn't care."

Isabella jerked her head and stared at Antonio. *That* was why he'd kept her from his world? "I thought it was because you were embarrassed by me."

"Why would you think that? Hell, I would have shown you off, but that would have encouraged an invasion of our privacy. I didn't want anyone intruding on us. But I went too far. It was only this week that I realized how isolated you must have been. That was not my intention."

"I see," she said softly. Why hadn't he told her that earlier? But then, why didn't she insisted that he take her along? Because she had been afraid of making demands. She hadn't felt secure in her relationship with Antonio and hadn't wanted to start a battle.

"Would you *like* to go to this party with me?" Antonio asked as he shifted gears. "I think you'll enjoy it."

She didn't know why he was making the effort now, when she was leaving in a couple of days. Was it an apology or did he really want her to accompany him? She admitted that she was curious about Antonio's life. What was he like when he was around friends and acquaintances? Antonio didn't need to grab the spotlight like his brother, but he wouldn't stay in the shadows, either.

Isabella wanted to accept his invitation, but one thing was holding her back. "I don't have anything to wear. And my hair…" She threaded her fingers along the ends of her hair, certain it was a tumbled mess. She didn't usually style her hair, but she needed to go all out if she wanted to make a good impression.

"You don't need to change," Antonio assured her. "It's a casual party."

"We may have different definitions of *casual*." She remembered Giovanni's circle of friends. *Casual* had meant preparing all day at the spa and wearing outfits that cost the same as a car.

Antonio cast her an appreciative look that made her blush. "Trust me, Bellà. You'll fit right in."

Isabella couldn't believe what she was seeing. She couldn't pull her gaze away from Antonio as he leapt into the air. His strong arms were reaching, stretching as he dove for the soccer ball. Isabella's stomach clenched and her skin felt flushed at the sight of his vigor and masculinity. Just when Isabella thought he would grab it, the ball zoomed past him and Antonio tumbled to the ground, rolled and shot to his feet.

A group of young boys cheered as the ball hit the net.

Unbelievable, Isabella thought. She'd never thought Antonio could be having fun at a child's birthday party. He should look out of place among the colorful balloons, party hats and streamers. Instead the children gravitated toward him, eager for his attention. He gave it freely and didn't refuse when several boys asked him to play.

"I have told Antonio a thousand times that he shouldn't let Dino win," said Dino's mother, Fia, as she stood beside Isabella, bouncing baby Giulia on her hip. "But at least he makes my son work for it."

"Maybe soccer isn't Antonio's sport."

"Ha!" Fia said as she tried to give a pacifier to her grumpy baby. "He was one of the best athletes in school. Football, swimming, skiing. He could do it all. He needed a sport for every season to expend his energy."

"I had no idea." She should have known. Antonio was lean and muscular and moved with enviable grace.

"Really?" Fia gave up on the pacifier and shifted baby Giulia onto her other hip. "How long have you known him?"

"A few months." But she hadn't known that he loved sports. There were no trophies or sports equipment in his home. He didn't tell stories about his adventures or his triumphs. Was it really a passion of his or did his abilities come to him so easily that he didn't think much about it? "How about you?"

"My husband has known him since their schooldays, and they've been together through the good times and bad." Fia raised her voice over Giulia's tired cry. "That's why Antonio is Dino's godfather."

Isabella watched Antonio ruffle Dino's hair. His affection for the boy was apparent. "He takes that role seriously."

Fia nodded. "We couldn't have asked for anyone better."

"I've never seen him around children," she murmured as she watched Antonio approach her. Her heart began to beat fast. "He's completely different."

"Not different," Fia said. "More like he's…"

"Unguarded?"

"Exactly." Fia patted Giulia's back but the baby continued to fuss. "I think it's the little one's bedtime."

"Here—let me hold her," Antonio said, and reached out for the baby.

Isabella couldn't hide her surprise as he cradled Giulia in his arms. The baby stopped fussing and stared at Antonio with wide eyes as he spoke softly to her.

"How did you do that?" Isabella asked. She couldn't soothe a baby that quickly even after years of babysitting.

Antonio smiled. "I have this effect on all women."

Fia laughed and lapsed into Italian. She spoke fast and Isabella struggled to keep up with the conversation. Eventually she allowed her gaze to fall on the baby, who was now falling asleep in Antonio's arms.

He was good with children and he liked being around them. How had she not known about this side of Antonio? Before she would have described him as sexy, powerful and remote. But today, as she watched him around his friends and their children, she knew there were many sides of him she had yet to discover. She needed to dig deeper to understand him.

When they left the party it was late at night and the

birthday boy had been asleep for hours. Isabella had enjoyed visiting Antonio's friends. She could tell they were curious about her but they'd made her feel welcome.

She'd noticed how open and relaxed he was with his friends. He was much more formal with his mother, and had been watchful and cautious with his brother. If she wanted to understand Antonio she needed to know the source of the strain between him and his relatives.

But Isabella was hesitant to ask. She bit her bottom lip as Antonio drove back to his apartment in comfortable silence. She didn't want to ruin a perfect evening, but she didn't have a lot of opportunity to find out before she left Rome.

"Antonio, why did you have such a difficult relationship with your brother?"

Antonio frowned, and she felt the mood shift in the small confines of the car. "It's not something I like to talk about."

"I know, but I feel like I'm missing a huge piece of the puzzle." If she had known their history she could have avoided so much heartache. But some instinct warned her that Antonio would have kicked her out sooner or later even without his brother's interference. "What happened between you two?"

Antonio felt Isabella looking at him, curious and expectant. He knew he owed it to her. It wasn't just about him and his brother. Isabella had been affected, too.

"My brother and I were close when we were young," he said, looking straight ahead as he drove through the busy streets. A smile tugged at the corner of his mouth as he remembered how much fun he'd once had with his brother. "My parents didn't have any more children so it was just the two of us. I often heard us described as the heir and the spare."

"Ouch. That's not very nice. Did they said that to *you*?"

He didn't care about the label anymore, but he found Isabella's indignation a comfort. "The servants or guests would say it when they didn't think I understood. Or when they thought I was out of earshot."

"Still, that's not something anyone should say about a child. It's something he'd carry with him. Either he tries to live up to it or fight against it. It would have the power to define him."

"I knew there was some truth to it," he admitted. "My parents loved me, and I was cared for, but Gio was the center of attention. There were times when I felt envious and resentful, but as I got older I realized I was the lucky one."

"Lucky? How can you say that?" she asked. "Your parents played favorites."

Antonio glanced at Isabella. She was curled up against the passenger side door with her arms crossed. If she was trying to keep her distance she was failing miserably. Isabella was already taking sides in his story.

"I was lucky because I wasn't pressured to perform better. My parents had high expectations for both of us, but I was lazy and unfocussed. Everyone knew that Gio was smarter, faster and better than me," he said matter-of-factly.

"That's not true," Isabella said.

"It was at the time," he said, frowning as he noticed how Isabella leapt to his defense. She'd used to do that when she read an unflattering news item about him, even when she didn't have all the facts. "Or it could have been my family's mindset. He was firstborn. He was the heir. Of course he was the best at everything."

"That is *so* unfair," she muttered. "I don't know how you could have stood it."

"Don't worry, it didn't last long," Antonio said. He glanced at Isabella as the streetlights flickered through the window. She looked upset for the child he'd used to be. "I hit my stride in my late teens."

"Uh-oh," she said. "You shook up the status quo?"

He nodded. "We started getting competitive. Gio needed a challenge, but he never thought I would eclipse him. I was tired of hearing, 'If only you were more like your brother…' I wanted someone to say that to Gio. And they did, but not in the way I wanted."

Isabella leaned closer. He caught a faint hint of her scent.

"What happened?"

Antonio shifted uncomfortably in his seat. "One day my father told us that he thought the Rossi empire was going to the wrong brother."

Isabella's gasp echoed in the car. "Why would he say that?"

"I think he said it to make Gio work harder. It made *me* work harder. I openly gloated, but I was secretly horrified." He hated how he had felt. How he had acted. Antonio closed his eyes, wishing he could forget the devastation in Gio's face. "For once I wasn't the other brother. The spare. And I wasn't going to have that taken away from me."

Isabella scooted closer. "But being the heir was part of Giovanni's identity?"

He nodded. "My father unintentionally created a

chasm between Gio and me. Our competition wasn't so friendly anymore. Gio saw me as a threat."

She reached over and placed her hand on his arm. "Did he hurt you?"

"No, there wasn't any physical fighting. And we were a team when we needed to be. But I learned to keep my thoughts private. I could never show what I wanted or what was important to me. Otherwise Gio would go after it."

"Like what?" Isabella asked.

He shrugged. "It was little things at first. I saved up and bought a motorcycle, but I didn't have it for more than a week before Gio stole it one night and wrecked it. Stuff like that."

"I don't consider that as *little* stuff," Isabella said. "He destroyed your property. It was vandalism. It was *wrong*. Why didn't your parents intervene?"

"At first they just believed that boys would be boys. Then they decided that it was a phase we would grow out of."

"It sounds like they just didn't want to take sides. Or deal with it," she said, and gave a sympathetic squeeze on his arm.

"Probably." He wanted to cover her hand with his and enjoy the feel of her. "Then it started to escalate. Sometimes I felt I was being paranoid. I had no proof he was behind the sabotage and the thefts, but I had my suspicions. And then we were in the running for the same honor at university. I knew he was going to pull something, but I didn't think he would get me expelled."

"He got you kicked out?" Isabella's voice trembled with outrage. "That's horrible. How did he do that?"

"He told the dean at the university that I was cheating and he manufactured evidence." His voice was calm and controlled, but cold anger weighed heavily against him as he remembered the injustice. No one had believed him. And to add insult to injury Gio had been commended for making the difficult decision to reveal the deceit of his own brother.

"Couldn't you have proved otherwise?" Isabella asked. "What about your parents? Didn't they defend you?"

He shrugged his shoulders, hiding the hurt. "My mother believed I was set up, but not by Gio." She had refused to hear a bad word about her firstborn, and Antonio still felt the sting of betrayal.

"And your father?"

The sting intensified. "He believed that I was cheating and that I had shamed the family," he said quietly. It was hard to get the words out. "I was disinherited."

"You were punished and Giovanni got away with it? Did you retaliate?"

"I wanted to, but my friends talked me out of it. They told me I was lucky to get out of that poisonous atmosphere and I needed to move on or it would destroy me. I knew they were right but I was still bitter."

"Something tells me that's an understatement," Isabella said. "Now I understand what drives you to work so hard."

It did have something to do with his success. He had something to prove. "Eventually my father welcomed me back into the family." He smiled as he remembered the awkward reconciliation. "After I made my first million. My father was very proud of what I had achieved without his help."

"And Giovanni never confessed?"

"No." He didn't know if Gio had kept silent because he'd wanted to enjoy the spoils of war or if he'd been afraid of what their disciplinarian father would have done if the truth came out. "I didn't speak to Gio for years. Not until I saw him at my father's funeral almost two years ago. He asked for forgiveness. It was sincere and genuine."

That was what his instincts had told him, but now he wondered if he had gotten it wrong. Maybe he'd wanted to believe Gio and have his brother back.

Isabella pulled her hand away from him. "And were you able to forgive?"

"Not forgive so much as move on," he admitted. "Gio should have felt secure. I didn't think we were in competition anymore. But for some reason I didn't trust that the treaty would last."

"He was your competitor for longer than he was your friend?"

Antonio nodded. That was why he'd he still been cautious around his brother. "I knew I had to keep my guard up. But I made a mistake." He paused, unsure if he wanted to reveal this to Isabella. "I couldn't hide how I felt about *you*." He felt Isabella's tension.

"So you think Giovanni went after me and I wasn't able to resist his charms? That's why you were so quick to believe him?"

"It fit his pattern. He went after something, or in this case someone, who was important to me."

Isabella leaned back in her seat. "Why didn't you tell me about this? You could have shared your concerns."

"I didn't think I had to." He had trusted Isabella, but he'd seen how close she'd become with Gio. He'd thought that Isabella wouldn't choose his brother over him. That she wasn't capable of crossing that line. But Gio's charm had been too seductive for her.

"It would have helped knowing that I was a target," Isabella said. "Or maybe you wanted to test me?"

"Why would I do that?" he asked, suddenly weary.

"Did you ever consider that your brother knew he could sabotage our relationship with just a lie? All he had to do was raise suspicion." She tossed her hands in the air. "He knew you wouldn't open up and talk about it. That your suspicion would fester until finally you couldn't trust me anymore."

"That's not what happened," Antonio said as anger curled inside him. Why was he telling her any of this? He should have kept quiet.

Isabella crossed her arms. "Your brother's ploy worked better than he could have imagined."

Antonio gritted his teeth. "You're giving Gio far more credit than he deserves."

"Giovanni played on the weakness in our relationship," she pointed out. "He was around enough to see what we couldn't. He knew you wouldn't talk about what was on your mind, and he knew I would do anything to get you back."

Isabella's words pricked at him. There was some truth in them. Hadn't he learned anything from the past?

"You kept making the same mistakes with your brother," Isabella accused. "But don't worry, Antonio. I've learned *my* lesson. We weren't meant to be together. I'm not fighting for us anymore."

Her words were like a punch to his chest. He wanted to say something sarcastic. Something biting. But it would only reveal how much he felt the loss. Instead Antonio stared straight ahead and pressed his foot harder on the gas pedal. Isabella might not like it when he went quiet, but he had learned that silence was his best shield.

CHAPTER NINE

ISABELLA lay in bed wide awake and restless. Her bed-sheet was tangled around her legs from her tossing and turning. The silence in Antonio's apartment made her tense. She stared at the ceiling, wondering if she had made the right decision to come back here. Lately she'd made the wrong choices. Like Giovanni.

When she had slept with Antonio's brother she had been drunk and deeply hurt. She blamed the alcohol, Giovanni—and herself. She didn't remember a lot about that night, but she knew she had made the choice. She could have stopped it anytime.

But she hadn't. Because she had been acting out. She had lost Antonio, allowed her dream to slip through her fingers, and she hadn't known why. She had tried to blunt the pain with drinking and partying. She'd sought comfort where she shouldn't have.

She couldn't change the past, but Isabella knew she wouldn't make those choices again. Next time she would recognize the warning signs of her own behavior. She'd have to; her baby was relying on her.

Isabella rubbed a protective hand over her stomach and heard a noise in the hallway. She lifted her head from the pillow and looked at the door. Her pulse skipped a beat when she saw a shadow underneath the door.

Antonio. He was coming to her. *Finally.*

She exhaled slowly as she stared at the strip of light underneath the door. She had been getting mixed signals from Antonio. He had refrained from touching her but she had felt his heated gaze. He had been the perfect gentleman but she sensed his self-control was barely contained.

Her restraint had been shaky, too. She wanted to be with him, but would it send her into a tailspin like last time? Did she want to be with him because she felt alone and scared of her future? Or did she want a do-over and nothing more?

Isabella watched the door as her heart pounded in her ears. Her chest was tight with anticipation. When she heard him mutter something softly in Italian and walk away, she bit her lip to prevent herself from calling out.

Antonio might want to relive the memories, but he obviously didn't think it was worth the risk. He still didn't trust her. Isabella sank back onto her pillow, disappointed.

She didn't trust her decision-making. What if she had invited him into her bed? Would it have taken her down the same path and brought the same outcome? Would she have regretted it?

No. She would regret not giving herself another chance.

"Antonio?"

Antonio felt his shoulders bunch when he heard Isabella's soft voice. He had tried to banish all thoughts of her by working, but his legendary focus was absent tonight. He needed to lose himself in reports and e-mails. It had almost worked. He hadn't heard Isabella enter his study. He didn't have a chance to put up his guard.

He glanced up from his laptop computer. His chest tightened when he saw her at the doorway. Her long blonde hair was tumbled, her face free of make-up. She wore only a white T-shirt and panties.

Isabella was a tantalizing mix of innocence and sin. Antonio clenched the edge of his desk, his fingers whitening as he struggled for control. The shirt barely skimmed the tops of her thighs. The thin cotton couldn't hide the shape of her breasts or the dark pink of her nipples. He didn't know why she bothered wearing it. It would take only a second to tear it off her body.

Don't do it. The words reverberated in Antonio's head as his gaze focused on her long, bare legs. His study was in the farthest corner of her apartment from the guestroom. It was his sanctuary and no one disturbed him when he was working. Antonio had thought he would be safe from temptation tonight. He hadn't thought she would seek him out.

"Yes?" he said, his voice hoarse.

She looped her long hair over her ear. "It's late."

It *was* late. Too late to stop what he had put into motion. When he'd asked her to stay for a few more days he had been looking for more than a shoulder to lean on. He needed Isabella to return to his side—and also to his bed. But when she had asked about the guestroom, he'd known she wasn't ready for them to become lovers again. After the way he'd treated her, the things he'd said, he couldn't blame her.

But it didn't stop him from hoping. Planning. Strategizing. He shouldn't consider getting her back. He should send Isabella away once and for all so he could focus on his responsibilities. Now that his brother had died Antonio needed to fix the mess Gio made of the family's fortune.

Yet all he could think about was Isabella.

"You shouldn't be working," she said as she leaned against the doorframe. The movement caused her T-shirt to hike up, offering him a glimpse of her tiny white panties.

He pulled his gaze away but it didn't stop the desire heating his blood. Antonio cleared his throat and pulled at the collar of his shirt. "I have a lot to do."

"Do you need any help?" Isabella offered.

He imagined Isabella assisting him. Leaning over his shoulder as her T-shirt gaped. Sitting primly on the edge of his desk, her legs brushing against him as she inadvertently offered a glimpse of white silk. Antonio swallowed back a groan as his imagination went wild. Isabella would be more distraction than help.

Distraction. That was putting it mildly. As he silently declined Isabella's offer with a shake of his head Antonio realized that Isabella had become an obsession. Thoughts of her interrupted his daily life. She invaded his dreams. He was addicted to her touch to the point that nothing else mattered.

This woman had destroyed him once. Yes, she had sent him soaring to the heavens, but she had also sent him crashing into hell. And he was willing to risk going through all that again if it meant one more night together.

What was it about this woman that made him so reckless? Was it how she had fit so perfectly in his arms? Was it her soft curves or the warmth of her smile?

No, it was more about how she had brightened his day. Just her presence had transformed his mausoleum of an apartment into a home.

But was that enough to make him forget that this woman had been unfaithful to him? That she'd cheated on him with his brother?

That reminder should have burned like acid, erasing any desire for her. He waited for dark emotions to wrap around him like a heavy cloak. But they didn't this time. He felt conflicted because he wasn't sure if she *had* cheated on him.

What is it about me that makes it so hard to believe?

"Excuse me?" Isabella frowned and pushed away from the doorframe.

Damn. He hadn't realized he had spoken out loud. "I was thinking about what you asked earlier. Why I have a difficult time believing you."

"You never gave me an answer." She crossed her arms and the cotton strained against her full breasts.

Antonio's mouth went dry. "I don't think I have one," he answered gruffly.

"You never asked me about my sexual past, but maybe that's because you didn't think you would like the answer."

He'd never asked because he didn't like the idea of her with another man. He had struggled with the unfamiliar possessiveness. Had he been willing to believe she was unfaithful because she was so incredibly sensual and eager? Had he assumed she was like that in bed with any man?

"I kind of have a reputation back home—but I didn't earn it," she said. "A lot of guys brag that I slept with them, but it isn't true."

It seemed Isabella was *always* struggling with her reputation. She was beautiful and sexy, and she wasn't cautious. The girls in her youth must have been jealous, but he also suspected that a few teenage boys had misread her friendly smile and bold attitude.

"I want you to know that I only had three boyfriends before I met you. And there was never any overlapping between. I also think you should know that I never had a one-night stand. I don't jump into bed with just anyone."

Three? That was it? Antonio was deeply grateful she didn't ask how many sexual partners *he* had had. He wasn't surprised that she had fallen into his bed the first day they'd met. They'd had an instantaneous connection and it had been so powerful she'd done something she wouldn't normally do.

"That day we met was special. Perfect," he said in a husky voice. "Too perfect."

"Too perfect?" She raised her eyebrows. "Is there such a thing?"

"Yes, because I always knew something that perfect couldn't last." He had often thought that Isabella had broken down his barriers, but now he realized that wasn't true. She had knocked some of them down, but he hadn't been as unguarded as he'd thought.

"It was supposed to be a fling," Isabella said. "It lasted longer than it should have because… Well, I held on longer than I should have." She looked away as she blushed. "I didn't mean to do that. I pushed too hard and I clung on tight when I should have let go."

"No, that's not true." When she'd pushed, he'd known she cared. When she had deferred her college education, he hadn't taken it for granted. He wasn't used to his loved ones choosing him first. It had felt strange and temporary. As if somehow he would mess it up and her loyalty would be taken away from him. That was why he had always been on his guard. "Maybe you should have pushed harder."

Isabella couldn't hide her surprise. "Are you kidding me?"

Antonio wasn't sure how to explain why he'd acted the way he had. He wasn't comfortable exposing this side of him. "We had a whirlwind affair. Everything was fast and furious."

"What's wrong with that?" she asked with a smile.

"I tried to shove a lifetime of memories into a few months, knowing it couldn't last." He frowned as he thought about what he had just said. "*Expecting* it wouldn't last."

"I don't understand," Isabella said, her smile fading. "*Why* couldn't it last? Did you *expect* me to cheat on you?"

"No, not exactly. I expected that it wouldn't take much for you to leave my side," he said. "I had nothing to hold you. You didn't want my money or enjoy high society. The sex was amazing, but I didn't think it was enough to keep you in my bed. For all I knew it was always like that for you."

"I was interested in *you*, Antonio," Isabella said. She looked stunned, with wide eyes and parted lips. "You were my world. I thought it was obvious. I would never have chosen your brother over you."

"But I didn't know that." He sighed and rubbed his face with his hands. Isabella had been faithful. He, however, hadn't shown any faith in her. "You were right: all Gio needed to do was plant a kernel of suspicion. I took care of the rest."

"Because you don't think anyone can be loyal to you. I understand that now." She rested her shoulder against the doorframe and sighed. "I wish I had known that a long time ago. I should have seen it."

"But you *were* loyal," he insisted. "You always took my side when you read the news or when my brother tried to rile me up. I noticed, but I didn't trust it. It was too good to be true. Even after all I did you didn't give up on me. You stayed here. You kept fighting for us."

But he had refused to see it that way. When she had remained in Rome with Gio he'd thought it was evidence of her infidelity. He had twisted her actions into proof that she'd betrayed him.

"Yeah," Isabella muttered, "that wasn't one of my better ideas."

Antonio barely heard her as he accepted he had been wrong. He'd allowed his insecurities to poison something beautiful. His actions sickened him. Isabella hadn't destroyed him. *He* had destroyed everything. He was his own worst enemy.

"I'm sorry, Isabella." His throat felt tight, but he had to get the words out. "What I put you through was unforgivable. None of this was your fault. I'm to blame."

She stared at him in surprise. It was obvious she'd never expected an apology and that shamed him even more.

Isabella nervously darted her tongue along her lips. "It's not *unforgivable*."

"I don't deserve your forgiveness. Your kindness," he said slowly. "Even now, after all I've said and done, after I promised you a ticket back to Los Angeles, you're still here. Simply because I asked."

"Well…" She nervously pressed her hand against her

chest and cleared her throat. "My motivations aren't *that* pure."

Antonio heard the sensual promise in her voice and his heartbeat began to gallop. His gaze slowly traveled from her eyes to her feet. "So I gather."

Isabella didn't know what she was doing. No, that wasn't quite true. She had plans to seduce Antonio. She had done it dozens of time before without second-guessing herself. But this time she wasn't sure. Would he reject her out of guilt? Bed her and then have a change of heart once the sun came up? He'd asked for forgiveness, but would he cruelly kick her out of his bed again?

His reaction could be even worse. What would Antonio think of her if she propositioned him? She had told him the truth about her sexual past, but did he believe her? Her brazen act could blow up in her face. He could twist it around and believe that her passionate nature couldn't be contained. That she wanted a man—any man. He might even believe that she'd seduced Giovanni in the same manner.

That thought made her want to run back to the safety of her room. But she didn't want to play it safe anymore. She didn't want to stand on the sidelines and wait for permission. She wanted to live again. Love. Be with Antonio once more.

She took a step forward. Her legs shook, but there was no way she could hide it. Isabella knew she should have worn something different. She wished she had sexy lingerie or something more feminine. She shouldn't attempt to seduce someone as sophisticated as Antonio wearing an oversized T-shirt. In the past it hadn't mattered what she wore, but then she had been confident of the outcome. This time she needed all the help she could get.

She shouldn't even attempt this, she decided as she took another step forward, but she knew she hadn't been bold since the moment Antonio had kicked her out of his bed. She had lost everything that was important to her and become too afraid to make a move. Those days were over. She wanted to be her old self again.

Antonio closed his laptop computer, his eyes never leaving hers. He rose from his chair and walked around his desk. He was silent and his movements were deliberate, reminding her of a hunter circling his prey.

Isabella's stomach clenched as her gaze traveled down the length of him. Antonio Rossi was effortlessly sexy. His shirt accentuated his broad shoulders and muscular arms. She shivered as she remembered what it was like to be held in his embrace.

She had always felt safe and secure when she was in his arms. She could go wild with lust and still know Antonio would take care of her. He would take to the heights of ecstasy and hold her when she felt like she would shatter into pieces. And then he would curl her against his chest and hold her all night long.

Desire, thick and overpowering, coiled tight in her belly as her gaze traveled from his flat stomach to the dark jeans that emphasized his powerful legs. She noticed his bare feet and her mouth twitched into a small smile. She always liked it when he was casual and barefoot. It didn't make him any less intimidating. Instead it stripped away another layer of civility and gave her a glimpse of the earthy man underneath.

Isabella slowly raised her gaze back to his face. Her skin went hot when she saw the lust in his dark eyes.

She didn't have to worry whether or not her seduction was going to work. He was going to take her to bed before she could make a move. He was going to make love to her. Hard, fast and wild.

She could barely catch her breath as the excitement pressed against her chest. Antonio would make love to every inch of her. She shook with anticipation and her knees threatened to collapse.

The baby.

Isabella lowered her gaze, shielding her thoughts from Antonio. What would he think about the gradual changes in her body? Her breasts already seemed larger and more sensitive. Her belly wasn't as flat as it used to be. And what if she woke up in his bed and had morning sickness? That would permanently ruin the mood.

Maybe she was taking too much of a risk. She should back down. Accept that what they had was truly over. Run away. Go back to her room and lock the door.

Isabella hated that idea. Her feet refused to move. She didn't want to give up Antonio. It was time to reclaim him and the woman she'd used to be. It was time to be bold and grab her dreams before they got away from her.

She wanted this. She raised her lashes and looked directly in his eyes. She wanted Antonio. She would regret not having this one last time with him. She couldn't get back what they'd used to have, but she could end this relationship with a happy memory.

"I need to know something first," Isabella said in a rush as emotions swirled around her so fast that she could barely speak. What she was about to ask could ruin the moment, but she needed to know. "Do you trust me?"

"Yes."

He didn't hesitate or embellish. She saw the certainty in his eyes. One little word and he had given her something she'd never thought she'd have again. He trusted her.

That was all she needed to know.

CHAPTER TEN

ISABELLA had longed for Antonio for months. His touch had haunted her and she knew she would never have the same experience with another man. She trembled before him, eager to touch him again—but what if they couldn't recapture the magic? What if everything that has happened between them cast a dark shadow and she could never reach that pinnacle of beauty and love again?

Their gazes clashed and Isabella felt the anticipation stirring deep inside her. From the look in his eyes, Antonio had no qualms. He knew what he wanted and he wasn't going to wait anymore.

Isabella's gasp was muffled as he claimed her mouth with his. He demanded entry and she kissed him hungrily, matching his aggression. She couldn't fight her shameful response to his forceful nature.

He bunched her cotton T-shirt in his hands. Isabella wanted him to wrench it from her body. Tear it off. She felt the tremor in his fingers as he peeled the shirt over her breasts and shoulders. When he pulled it over her head and tossed it on the floor Isabella knew he was trying to slow down. Hold back. He didn't want to scare her with the intensity he felt. Didn't he realize that she felt the same?

Antonio gathered her close against him. She sighed when he wrapped his arms around her. His shirt rasped her tight nipples and she moaned against his mouth. His hands slid down her body as he roughly caressed her curves. He impatiently shoved her panties down her legs. When she kicked them aside, he grabbed her waist and pressed her against his erection.

Isabella felt her desire heat and thicken as it flared low in her pelvis. She knew this was going to be fast and furious. She already felt out of control. Her world tilted and she grabbed onto Antonio's shirt.

She felt Antonio lower her onto the floor. Their kisses grew untamed. She pulled him closer as he knelt between her legs. Isabella felt surrounded by Antonio as she inhaled his scent and felt masculine heat coming off him in waves. All she could see and feel was him, but it wasn't enough. She needed him closer. She needed him deep inside her.

Isabella jerked her mouth away, her lips swollen, her lungs burning for air. She grabbed the back of his head, clutching at his dark, thick hair as he licked trail down her neck.

His hands were everywhere and she offered no resistance. He knew what she liked. Antonio remembered her pleasure points, teasing and stroking her until she didn't think she could take it anymore. Antonio's touch was merciless as he wrung out every bit of pleasure.

Her defenses were crumbling. She couldn't wait, and the forbidden thrill chased through her blood. She wanted to see Antonio in his conquering glory. She wanted him to claim her heart and soul.

As Antonio drew her nipple deep in his mouth he boldly cupped her mound with his hand. She bucked against his possessive touch, moaning as Antonio dipped his fingers into her moist heat.

Isabella stretched her arms on the floor in surrender. She was his for the taking. He gently massaged her sex, teasing her as he kissed along her hipbone. She bucked her hips restlessly. She thought she was going to go out of her mind with wanting.

"More." Her breaths came out in short pants. She wanted it all, and she wanted it right now, because she didn't think she'd get another chance.

Antonio didn't respond, but she knew he wouldn't deny her. She could ask for anything and he'd give it to her. He always fulfilled her deepest needs. He parted her legs wider with a forceful hand and lowered his mouth against her sex. Isabella cried out in ecstasy at the first flick of his tongue.

His touch was just as addictive as she remembered. Antonio swiftly took her to the edge and then held back. She begged for his touch, pleaded for satisfaction as he took her pleasure to another level. Just when she thought her mind would shatter, Antonio granted her the sexual release she craved. He ruthlessly drove her over the edge and a white-hot climax consumed her.

She was shaking with the aftershocks when she heard the rustle of his clothes and felt the tip of his penis pressing against the entrance to her core. Isabella groaned when he gave a savage thrust. She tilted her hips to accommodate his heavy thickness and curled her fingers into his shoulders, digging her nails into his shirt.

Antonio withdrew almost completely. Isabella cried out as her core clenched. She then saw the look on

Antonio's face. His features were blunted with lust and his eyes glittered with need.

"I can never get enough of you," he growled as he plunged into her.

His thrusts were long and measured. It was testament to his willpower. But as Isabella went wild underneath him his relentless rhythm broke free. He grabbed her hips, his fingers digging into her skin, and sank deep into her heat. He tensed and shuddered as she let out a hoarse cry of triumph.

He collapsed onto her. Isabella wrapped her arms around him as his choppy breath warmed the crook of her neck. Antonio didn't say anything as they tried to catch their breath. She felt small tremors rocking her heated body as Antonio raised his head.

"Don't fall asleep on me now, Bella." He looked down at her face, his eyes gleaming with sensual promise as he picked her up and carried her out of the room. "The night has just begun.

Isabella gasped and her eyes widened as she escaped from a bad dream. She jackknifed into a sitting position and looked around, ready to escape. Her heart was racing. She was shivering but her skin felt hot and sweaty.

It took her a few moments before she recognized her surroundings. It was turning dawn. In Rome, she noticed as she glanced through the window. She was in Antonio's bedroom. Not Giovanni's.

She was with Antonio. Isabella studied him in the shadowy room as he lay sleeping. He was sprawled across the bed, naked and glorious. She wasn't reliving that horrible moment three months ago. It was just a bad dream mixed with a bad memory.

Isabella instinctively reached for Antonio to rouse him. She needed to be in his strong arms. There she would feel safe and secure. Her fingers slowly curled against his shoulders and she stopped herself.

What was she thinking? She couldn't tell Antonio about her bad dream. She couldn't discuss Giovanni. Not while they were sharing a bed. Not when they just had made love. Antonio would think she was comparing him with his brother.

Isabella pressed her hand against her head. She felt a little dizzy from moving so fast. She lowered herself carefully, gently resting her head on the pillow, and faced Antonio.

When would she stop having these dreams? Isabella cautiously closed her eyes, hoping she didn't fall into a troubled sleep again. She had heard that pregnant women often had strange dreams and nightmares. Something about worry and hormones colliding. Isabella really hoped that wasn't the case. She didn't think she could take another six months of this.

Isabella stilled when Antonio shifted. His arm draped over her side and he nestled her against his chest. She pressed her lips together as she resisted temptation to melt against him. As Antonio cradled her his large hand spanned her abdomen.

Her breath caught in her lungs as the protective gesture nearly undid her. Even in his sleep he was fulfilling his promise. He would look after this baby. Emotions stung her eyes and clogged her throat. She didn't move and she kept her eyes closed.

Had he noticed the changes in her body? She didn't think he had. Throughout the night he had shown his appreciation for her body. He had been fascinated and had paid particular attention to her breasts. Isabella blushed at the erotic memories. From what she remembered, he'd made no mention of any changes.

She waited for Antonio to move his hand. Nothing happened. He continued to sleep soundly as she rested her head against his bare chest. His warm breath wafted over her skin and his broad chest rubbed against her back. Isabella slowly exhaled, but the tension didn't leave her body.

Isabella reached for Antonio's hand and carefully removed it from her stomach. She couldn't let him get this close. She couldn't get used to this. She had already taken too many risks. All for the sake of being with Antonio one more time.

It had been worth it, but she couldn't indulge in this kind of recklessness. The child was reality and Antonio was fantasy. She needed to remember that.

She didn't want to hide anything from Antonio, but she had to protect herself. She wasn't going to look for emotional support from him only to feel the sharp sting of rejection. It was only a matter of time before Antonio would move on and find a suitable woman. A society wife. She needed to rely on *her* strength and not his when that happened.

Isabella squeezed her eyes shut as tears burned. She took a choppy breath and slowly turned around, her back facing Antonio. She wanted to talk through her fears about being pregnant and share her dreams for her child. But she couldn't. She had to go through this alone.

She needed to start making plans. Although she had only promised a few days, Isabella knew she was taking a step back. If she weren't careful she would promise a few more days, and then a few weeks. She wouldn't find the strength to break away. She'd be clinging onto this relationship again.

It was time to create some distance. Isabella slowly moved from Antonio's embrace. She suddenly felt cold. She wanted to return to Antonio's bed and curl up against him.

It was tempting. Isabella wavered for a moment, and was about to lie back down when she felt a wave of nausea. It was a sign of morning sickness she couldn't ignore. Pressing her hand against her mouth, Isabella hurried back to her room.

Antonio stretched his tired muscles as a satisfied growl rumbled in his chest. He finally had Isabella back in his bed. All was right with the world, he thought with a lazy smile. He reached for Isabella, wanting to hold her against him and enjoy the feel of her warm skin against his.

His hand touched the bedsheet. Antonio blinked and opened his eyes. Isabella wasn't there. The pillow still held an indentation, but the wrinkled sheets were cool. She had slipped out of his bed hours ago.

What the hell was going on here? Antonio jumped out of bed, his feet hitting the floor as he strode to the door. Isabella had never left him while he slept. If she didn't wake him up with the sweetest kisses and caresses, he was the one to wake *her*, in the most wickedly erotic ways. He was getting hard just remembering.

He reached the guestroom in record time and opened the door without knocking. Isabella was curled up in her bed, sound asleep. "Bella?"

She raised her head with a start. Her hair was still damp from a shower and a bathtowel was wrapped around her. "Oh, I lay down and fell asleep again," she said groggily. "What time is it?"

"Why are you sleeping here?" he asked as he towered over her. "Why did you leave my bed?"

"Uh, because I wanted to get some rest." Her eyes widened as her gaze traveled down his naked body. He saw the flare of desire in her eyes and couldn't hide his response.

But it didn't change a very important fact. She'd had sex with him and then she had left. That wasn't like Isabella. She'd used to burrow as close as she could and cling to him throughout the night. Now she couldn't get away fast enough. "Bella, do you see me as a one-night stand?"

"Um…" She shoved her tangled hair from her face.

"You just wanted one more time before you left? Needed to scratch an itch and nothing more?" He wouldn't allow it. When they'd been together it had been wild and mind-blowing because there had been no games or limits. Just pure sensation and emotion.

"What if it was?" she asked with a hint of defiance.

He was no one-night stand or meaningless fling. Antonio wanted to be the most important person in her life. He was used to being second choice, but not with her. He wanted their past and their future to be inextricably linked. He was prepared to bind her to him in any way possible.

"Then I will change your mind," he said, and he flipped the bedsheet over and crawled into her bed.

CHAPTER ELEVEN

ISABELLA tightly held the edges of the towel as she scooted to the edge of the mattress. "Antonio, don't pretend that this is anything more than what it is."

He slid his hands underneath her and pulled her close to him. She wanted to push him away but that would mean losing the towel.

"Why did you leave our bed?" he asked.

His tone was firm and it held a dangerous edge that made her hot.

"Your bed," she corrected him. They didn't share anything. Not anymore. It would be good to remember that.

"*Our* bed."

No, it had never been theirs. It was his bed, his apartment, his world. She was a temporary guest. She didn't belong here and probably never had.

"Really? Our bed?" she asked. She struggled to hold her towel in place as he placed a kiss against her collarbone. She felt his smile against her quickened pulse. "How many women have slept there since I've been gone?"

He lifted his head and held her gaze. "Don't even

try," he warned softly. "I know you want to create a barrier between us. I won't let you."

Isabella gritted her teeth. He had no right. She needed to place a short expiration date on this relationship. If she could even call it that. This time she couldn't get caught up in a whirlwind affair. She needed a stable environment for her baby.

She would love to think that they could try again and their affair would last longer. But who was she kidding? Would he want her when she was heavy with child? How long would it be before he needed to marry and have children of his own? She didn't fit any of the requirements he had for a wife and there was no getting around that.

"I left because it's not our bed anymore," she said. "We are no longer a couple."

"We have a connection that can't be broken." He threaded his hands through her hair and spread it across her pillow.

She winced when his fingers got tangled in her hair. "That doesn't make us a couple."

Antonio smoothed his fingertips along the side of her face before cupping her jaw with his strong hand. He tilted her face so she couldn't look away from his serious gaze. "Why do you think I asked you to stay?"

"For the sex." She knew that was the truth. He couldn't argue with that.

"And that's all?" he asked lightly as his hand drifted down her throat to her chest.

Her skin tingled from his touch and she was having difficulty remembering what they were talking about. She should get out of this bed and into some clothes, but she couldn't move. She didn't want to.

"When we're together you have the ability to shut out the world," she said. They both did. Time stood still when they were making love. "You want to do that because you're dealing with a family crisis. That's why you want me around. So you can take me to your bed and lose yourself."

"I want to make love to you," he admitted. His fingers dipped behind her towel.

Isabella's chest rose and fell as she felt his fingers graze her breasts.

"But I also want more from you."

She swiped her tongue along her bottom lip "More?"

"I need you at my side," he confessed in a low, husky voice. "When you're there, I feel like I can conquer the world."

Isabella wanted to believe she had that kind of influence in Antonio's life, but she knew it wasn't true. She was an ordinary girl with no special skills or powers. "You don't rely on anyone, Antonio."

"It may not look like it, but I do," he said as he gently tugged the towel from her slackened grasp. "It meant a lot to me when I could wake up and see you in my bed. When you shared how you felt and what you thought. When you changed the course of your life to be with me."

"That was then." She couldn't make those sacrifices again.

"But you're still looking after me," he pointed out as he parted the towel and revealed her body to him. Her nipples puckered and his eyes darkened with pleasure. "You delayed your trip back to Los Angeles to be with me. You had no trouble sharing your feelings and thoughts, even though I might disagree. But when I woke up you weren't in my bed."

He hadn't noticed. He didn't realize that she was having trouble sharing her fears and dreams. She wasn't going to tell him. This time she was holding back. She wasn't giving him everything because she didn't want to get hurt again.

"Your bed?" she teased, determined to distract him from the truth. Let him think she was the same as before. It was only for a few days. "I thought it was *our* bed."

Antonio wrapped his hands around her wrists and lifted her arms above her head. She twisted her body in protest, her skin tingling as she thrust out her chest.

"Stay next time," he ordered softly.

"I can't promise you that." She wanted to bite her tongue. She should have just agreed. He wasn't going to let this go until he got his way.

"There was a time when you never wanted to leave my bed," Antonio said as he dipped his head and took her tight nipple in his mouth.

Pleasure, white-hot and blinding, crackled through her body. "Antonio!" she exclaimed. She tried to pull away, but he held onto her wrists. She arched against him, trying to get closer.

When he turned his attention to her other breast his touch was just as ruthless as he took her almost to the height of ecstasy. Just when she thought she would shatter he pulled back, denying her release.

"Please, Antonio," she said in between gasps as hot pleasure pressed just under her skin. "Let go of me. I want to touch you."

Antonio raised his head and she saw the glitter in

his eyes. He bestowed upon her a hard, almost brutal kiss before he let go her wrists. She greedily clasped her hands on the back of his head and pressed his mouth on her breast.

He teased her nipple with the edge of his teeth and grabbed her hips. Her fractured sigh echoed in the quiet room as he urgently caressed her body.

Antonio pulled away and gazed down at her. His features were carved and taut with desire. "So beautiful," he murmured as though he were mesmerized.

He surged forward, capturing her mouth with his, and gently parted her legs with his hands. Antonio pressed his hand against the apex of her thighs and growled his appreciation. She was so aroused that she couldn't hide it even if she wanted to.

Antonio plunged his tongue into her mouth and caressed her swollen clitoris. Isabella rocked against his hand as she chased the pleasure coiling low in her pelvis. The sensations were so exquisite that it almost hurt.

"Now, Antonio," she said against his mouth. "Take me now."

She reached for him, but Antonio ignored her hands. His face was grim as he grasped her waist. He lifted her hips slightly and nestled his erection at the juncture of her thighs.

Isabella felt the rounded tip of his penis prodding against her. She wrapped her legs around his waist and held on tight. She took a deep breath just as he slowly penetrated her.

Isabella closed her eyes and bit her bottom lip as he stretched and filled her to the hilt. Antonio paused and she felt his muscles twitch as he fought for self-control. His fingers trembled as they dug into her hips.

Antonio retreated and gave a deep thrust. Her pulse skipped a beat and her breath hitched in her throat as pleasure tightened inside her, ready to spring wildly and explode. He bucked against her and sensations showered through her like fireworks.

Antonio withdrew slightly before driving into her wet heat. Isabella gasped and dug her nails in his shoulders. One more deep thrust and she knew she would climax hard. She would need Antonio to hold her tight as she splintered into pieces.

He gave a shallow thrust.

"More," she whispered urgently. But Antonio didn't move. He held her tightly, his muscles shuddering as his restraint started to slip.

She opened her eyes and his gaze ensnared hers. The stark need in the dark depths was raw and elemental. More powerful than she'd ever seen.

"First," he said in a gravelly voice, "tell me why you won't share my bed."

Her eyelashes fluttered as she tried to hide her eyes. Why wouldn't he let the matter drop? Why did he find it so significant? "What did you say?" she asked as she frantically tried to come up with a believable excuse.

"I can take you against the window." He rocked against her tauntingly, reminding her of the pleasures he could give her. "Or on the floor. But you won't stay in my bed?"

She shook her head, refusing to meet his eyes that willed her to answer. Need pulsed inside her. "It's not important."

"I disagree. I think it's very important." Determination rang clearly in his raspy voice.

"Please, Antonio." She desperately bucked her hips, hoping his willpower would give away. "Don't stop."

Tension rolled through him, but Antonio didn't move. "That's up to you."

"I don't have a reason," she said on a sob. She was shaking and her body burned for satisfaction. He couldn't be this cruel.

"It's because you don't trust me like you used to." He reached down to where they were intimately joined and pressed his thumb on her clitoris. She shuddered, gasping for air as white-hot pleasure streaked through her. "I'm not going to kick you out of my bed again. I promise."

"You can't give me that kind of guarantee," she said between gasps. Was that why she'd had the bad dream? Because he had kicked her out of bed once before and knew he could do it again? She couldn't think straight, was tempted to tell him anything he wanted to know. Her body demanded release.

"Bella," his voice was thick and uneven. "Promise me—"

"Yes! Yes!" she cried out recklessly. "I'll share your bed."

She was rewarded with a series of deep, plunging thrusts. Her body accepted each stroke with unrestrained hunger. She writhed against Antonio, her movements frantic. His unforgiving rhythm made her delirious. Her breath snagged in her chest and a hush blanketed her mind as a violent climax lashed through her.

Her core clenched and squeezed Antonio. His muscles rippled with a hard tremor and his thrusts were suddenly wild and untamed. Antonio tilted his head back, his eyes shut, the tendons of his neck straining, as he unwillingly surrendered to the demands of his body. His hoarse cry tore at her heart and he gave one final, powerful thrust before tumbling on top of her.

As she clung to Antonio, Isabella tiredly stroked his sweat-slickened back. She didn't know if she'd made the right decision. She'd always thought that she learned from her mistakes, but she was right back where she had started. Only this time she wasn't so naïve. Not that it would help. She was still hopelessly in love with Antonio.

If only she had more willpower. She shouldn't have made that promise.

She didn't protest when Antonio rolled on his back and gathered her in his arms. She relaxed as she listened to his strong heartbeat. It felt right being with him. She should enjoy it while it lasted. What could possibly happen in two more days?

"The other bed is so much better," he said.

Was he wondering if she would follow through on the promise she'd made in the heat of the moment? "I agree. Much more room."

"You should move your things into the master bedroom," he said as he stroked her back with his strong fingers. "No point in keeping them here."

He wasn't giving her any room to retreat and hide. Antonio was making it clear that they were going to resume where they'd left off.

"I'm only going to be here for two more days. It's not worth the effort."

His fingers went still against her spine. "Two days?"

No, no, no. She recognized his tone but was not ready

to renegotiate. "Antonio, I'm not staying here any longer. We agreed."

Antonio rolled over and braced his arms on either side of her. His abdomen rested lightly against hers as he settled his hips between her thighs. He surrounded her, and she hated how her body softened and yielded to his.

"About that…" he drawled.

CHAPTER TWELVE

ANTONIO entered his apartment and heard Isabella's laughter coming from another room. He imagined the way she would toss back her head and her blonde hair would cascade over her shoulder. She put her whole body into it. It was always a beautiful sight and he couldn't get enough of it. He did everything he could to keep her laughing.

He paused at the threshold and allowed the joy of his home to wash over him after a stressful day. The music that blared from Isabella's MP3 player was fun, vibrant and very American. It should be at odds with his apartment's décor, but he liked it. It reminded him of Isabella.

Antonio closed the heavy front door and heard Isabella's footsteps. She rounded the corner with her usual exuberant style and Antonio stilled at the sight of her. Her hair was pulled back into a high ponytail and she wore one of his sweaters. It was too big, but the colour brought out the blue in her eyes. The sleeves were folded up and the hem went to her knees. It also concealed her curves. He liked seeing her in his clothes and in his home, but he wanted to see more of her. *All* of her.

His gaze traveled down and he gave an appreciative

whistle when he saw her legs encased in form-fitting black leggings. "I see you went shopping."

"I did," Isabella said as she draped her arms over his shoulders and leaned into him.

His hand automatically rested on the small of her back and he drew her close. He took a moment to savor her softness and warmth as she kissed him.

Antonio deepened the kiss and she matched his eagerness. They hadn't seen each other all day and all he wanted to do was take her to bed, shut out the world and reacquaint himself with Isabella's body.

But he couldn't do that anymore, Antonio reminded himself and reluctantly pulled away. He'd promised he wouldn't be selfish and isolate Isabella. He had been good on his word for the past month. Antonio had introduced her to his friends and important business associates. It had been a pleasant surprise to discover that not only was Isabella a natural hostess, but that she had already become close with his friends.

"What did you do today?" Antonio asked as he smoothed his hand along the curve of her hip.

"Fia came over for lunch and she took me to some great shops. I needed a couple of things to replace my old clothes. What do you think?" She raised her arms and spun around.

Antonio saw how his sweater draped over her stomach. His heart skipped a beat as he noticed the small bump.

Giovanni's baby.

He had dreaded this moment because he'd been unable to predict how he would respond. Isabella was now noticeably pregnant with his brother's child.

"Well?" Isabella asked warily.

He took a step forward and placed his palm gently over her stomach. His large hand rested perfectly against the baby bump. "You look beautiful."

She blushed and dipped her head. "Are you sure?"

Her shyness surprised him. It wasn't like her. He suddenly understood Isabella's concern. Did she think she would be less attractive to him? Or that the baby would be a constant reminder of her one night with his brother?

He didn't know how to reassure her. The baby wouldn't come between them. It would bind them closer together. Antonio was about to remove his hand but Isabella placed hers over his fingers. He held her gaze but she didn't say anything.

She didn't have to. At this moment nothing else existed. They were sharing this journey as parents together.

"I can't wait to meet this baby," he confessed. "She's going to look just like you."

"That would be unfortunate if 'she' turns out to be a boy."

Antonio watched her smile and his heart did a slow tumble. He loved Isabella. Deeply, madly and irrevocably. He wanted to be with her forever—and not because of the baby or the terms of Gio's will. He wanted to share every moment with her, starting now.

Antonio must have had an intense look. Isabella frowned and took a step back. "I shouldn't have stolen your sweater, but it's so soft and cozy."

"What's mine is yours," Antonio said, and he meant it.

Isabella's eyelashes flickered with uncertainty. Was

she uncomfortable because she didn't think she had anything to give *him*?

Then she was wrong. Isabella had made his apartment a home once again. The music, color and laughter seemed brighter this time around. His life had been stagnant and bitter after she had gone. Lonely. Now he felt surrounded by her love.

Isabella chuckled nervously and pulled at the collar of the sweater. "That's very generous of you, but I'll start with the sweater."

"You need to think bigger," he encouraged. "It's time to make some changes around here."

He looked around the apartment and saw the small additions Isabella had made. The big bouquet of yellow and orange flowers made him think of her bold personality. A small picture frame held a photo of the two of them when they'd visited the Trevi Fountain late one night. A bright red throw was casually draped on a chair and he imagined Isabella there moments ago, curled up and waiting for him.

He also noticed something else. This apartment wasn't ready for a child. "We need to baby-proof this place. And turn the guestroom into a nursery. Don't worry about the cost," he said when he saw Isabella's eyes widen. "Only the best for this baby."

Isabella knew her mouth was hanging open as she stared at Antonio. Had he just said the word *nursery*?

"You...you want to do what?"

"We haven't done anything to prepare for the baby," Antonio said as he curled his arm around her shoulder.

"There's no need to worry about that," she said as she

looked around the room. She couldn't imagine a child growing up here. *Her* child. "I've got plenty of time."

Antonio's hand tensed at her choice of pronoun. "The baby arrives in four months."

"No, that's not right. The due date is in late March."

"Right. Four months," he repeated patiently. "It's already November."

Oh, my God. Isabella went rigid as she recalled the date. How had that happened? She had been staying at Antonio's for more than a month. She'd only been supposed to stay for a few days and then Antonio had suggested she extend it for a weekend. And then another week. After a while she'd stopped asking about the plane ticket. But she couldn't believe over a month had already passed.

She was enjoying her stay with Antonio. It was better than anything she had hoped for. In some ways she felt their relationship was much stronger than when she'd first met him. She knew him better and had had a glimpse of his world. She also believed that he would be there for her when she needed him.

But it was time for her to go. What had started out as a vacation fling had derailed her from her goals. And, as much as she hated to think about it, she was keeping Antonio from what he needed. One day he would have to find a suitable wife.

"Antonio, I would enjoy tackling that project, but I'm not going to stay here for much longer. In fact, I think I should leave by the end of the week."

"I don't understand," Antonio said with a fierce frown. "I thought you were happy here?"

"I am," she quickly assured him. "These have been the happiest days of my life. But I've taken a huge detour from my future plans and it's time for me to return home."

"Is this about returning to college?" he asked. "Because you don't need a degree. I can take care you and the baby. I want to."

But she didn't want to be a kept woman. She needed to stand on her own two feet and take full responsibility for her child. "I made a promise to my mom. And, actually, it was also a promise to myself. I have to do this."

Antonio sighed. "I can't talk you out of it, can I?"

He could. That was part of the problem. She hugged him tightly and rested her head against his shoulder. "I'm going to miss you."

"I want you to visit Rome during your next Spring Break."

"I can't travel that late in my pregnancy." And she was worried that if she returned to Rome she would be reminded of everything she'd given up and wouldn't finish her college education.

"Then I will visit Los Angeles and be there for the birth," he promised.

"Sure." But she wouldn't hold him to his promise. He led a busy life that offered a great deal more than she could. She wasn't naïve. Long-distance relationships didn't work with someone like Antonio. Once she left Rome she would be out of sight and out of mind.

"I mean it, Bella. Whenever you need me, I'll be there."

CHAPTER THIRTEEN

TODAY was her last day with Antonio.

It hadn't quite sunk in, Isabella thought as she lay in bed watching the sunrise over Rome. She wanted to create some lasting memories. She wanted to remember Antonio's passion and heat. She needed to touch and taste him one last time. It was her wish to end the relationship on a kiss and then she could say goodbye.

Isabella reached out and cupped Antonio's jaw. The dark stubble was rough against her soft palm. She stroked the sharp angles and hard planes of his face, remembering the lines fanning his eyes when he smiled and the grooves bracketing his mouth when he frowned. She was going to miss his scowls as much as his sexy, slow smiles.

She lowered her head and brushed her lips against his. Isabella didn't know how she was going to live without Antonio's kisses again. Whenever he claimed her mouth with gentle seduction, or with hot, pulsing need, it was like an electric current snaked through her veins. She felt wildly alive each time Antonio touched her.

Isabella lips grazed Antonio's mouth again and she felt his body shift. "Bella..." he said in a sleepy growl.

Her breath hitched in her throat as a bittersweet ache filled her chest. She loved the way he said her name. It was a mix of masculine satisfaction and adoration. She hoped that it would always be that way when he thought of her.

Isabella trailed her hand down the thick column of his neck and memorized the strong lines and bronze skin. She gave a start when Antonio draped his arm around her waist and his fingers spanned her side. She felt the possessiveness in his touch through her T-shirt.

She glanced up at his face and her gaze collided with his. The sleep faded from his eyes and he studied her face with serious intent.

Isabella lowered her lashes, veiling her eyes from him. She didn't want him to read her thoughts. Her sadness.

Her hand stilled against his chest as Antonio bunched her T-shirt in his fist. "Why," he asked softly, "do you hide underneath this when you know I want you naked in bed?"

She smiled at the teasing quality in his voice. "I wear it so you will have the pleasure of taking it off me." That was partly true. What she didn't add was that she wore an oversized T-shirt to conceal her baby bump.

"No, you do it because you want to tease me." He let go of the cotton and tucked both his hands under his head. "This time I want *you* to take it off."

A wicked curl of excitement unfurled low in her pelvis. Antonio didn't simply want her to strip for him. He wanted her to express how she was feeling—or rather how he made her feel.

Isabella knelt beside Antonio on the mattress, her gaze never leaving his. She reached for the hem of her shirt. Her fingers flexed against the cotton. Today she wouldn't hold back.

She slowly raised the shirt, sensuously rolling her hips and arching her spine as anticipation sizzled in her veins. She felt Antonio's hot gaze on her skin. It made her feel scandalous and beautiful. She wasn't worried about her pregnant belly. Isabella thrust her breasts out and stretched as she freed herself of the shirt.

Antonio didn't move but watched in intense silence as she tossed the shirt onto the floor. She was naked before him. Instead of feeling shy, she felt gloriously alive.

Heat suffused her skin as she caressed her collarbone and shoulders. He was unnaturally still as he watched her. His harsh features and radiating tension were subtle responses. She didn't want that. She wanted to shatter that self-control once and for all.

Isabella massaged the tips of her breasts just like Antonio would. She bit her lip and moaned as her nipples stung. Antonio's chest rose and fell as he watched her hands trail down her body. Isabella felt like a harem girl pleasing her master. She felt powerful but submissive. Daring yet obedient. She wanted to give Antonio his fantasy, but at the same time she wanted to make him beg.

She skimmed her fingers along her pelvic bone. Just when she was about to cup her sex with her hand she changed her mind. She grasped Antonio's hard erection that angled toward his flat stomach. Antonio gasped, his hips vaulting off the mattress as she curled his fingers around his thickness.

Isabella pumped her hand with slow deliberation. She watched Antonio's eyes squeeze shut as his mouth slackened. His big hands clenched the pillow under his head. She was fascinated as she watched pleasure and agony chase across his face.

She bent down and wrapped her lips around the tip of his penis. Antonio's jagged breath was the sweetest sound to her ears. She sighed with delight as his large hands knotted in her hair. His fingers twisted with every swirl of her tongue and the deep draw of her mouth.

Isabella felt the tremors storm through his hard body and heard his uneven breath. He was so close to surrendering to her. She felt his hands dig into her shoulders as he urgently dragged her up his body.

She gave a cry of complaint. As much as she wanted to lie with him naked, she was determined to give him everything he desired. She wished she was bold enough to show him, tell him how she felt.

Driven by an urgency that scared her, Isabella pressed her mouth against Antonio's ear. Her heart was pounding against her ribcage and her nerves tingled just under her skin.

"I love you," she whispered.

Antonio didn't move. Isabella's heart lurched and plummeted. At that moment she felt more exposed than when she had stripped off her clothes. She was glad she'd had the courage to finally tell Antonio, and she refused to regret her impulsive words, but she didn't dare look at him.

She flinched when he cradled her jaw with unsteady hands. She kept her gaze lowered, not willing to see if there was rejection or indifference in his eyes. She was unprepared when Antonio covered her mouth with his. The kiss was raw and untamed. Isabella felt weak as the heat rushed in her blood.

Antonio's hands were everywhere, drawing her

closer, molding her body against his. She wanted to melt into him. She wanted to be a part of him forever.

When he anchored his heavy leg against hers Isabella knew Antonio was about to take all control away from her. She was tempted to be swept away one last time, but today she wanted to focus all her love and attention on Antonio.

Isabella moved swiftly and escaped Antonio's embrace. Before he could protest or pin her down she straddled his hips. His hands fell on her waist, his fingers digging into her skin as she slowly sank down on his erection.

She closed her eyes as Antonio's groan echoed around her. Hot pleasure bloomed inside her, pressing heavily until she thought every inch of her skin would blister. She tentatively rolled her hips and was immediately rewarded with a deep thrust from Antonio.

He gained a firmer hold on her hips and lifted her slightly before he bucked hard against her. White-hot sensations rippled through her center, zooming to the top of her head and the soles of her feet.

She rocked her hips faster, compelled to follow an elemental rhythm. She couldn't get enough of Antonio writhing underneath her. She felt like she was harnessing his power and making it hers. No, she realized as she swiped her hair from her eyes. She was making Antonio hers.

He sat up and her eyes were level with his. Antonio guided her hips to counter each savage thrust. She placed her hands on his jaw and kissed his mouth.

"I love you so much, Antonio," she said against his lips.

His fingers bit into her skin as he ground his mouth

against hers. She matched his raw passion with every kiss, every touch and roll of her hips. The need clawed inside her, stripping her control to ribbons. She arched her spine and tilted her head back just as a ferocious climax screamed through her. Her body clenched, her mind went blank and her skin went hot and cold. Antonio burrowed his face against her breasts, his stubble rasping against her as he let out a hoarse cry of triumph.

Time stood still for Isabella. She wanted to hold on to this moment but it was already slipping away. She clung to Antonio as he guided her back onto the mattress. She curled up next to him and pressed her face against his sweat-slicked chest. She inhaled his scent and closed her eyes.

This was how she wanted to end their affair. No tears, no drama. This was how she needed to say good-bye.

But she had to say it one more time, even if Antonio's breathing indicated he was falling back to sleep. She had to do it now because she wouldn't get another chance.

Isabella looked up at Antonio. His eyes were closed and his features were softened in sleep. "I love you, Antonio," she whispered. "I will always love you."

Hours later, Isabella stood on Antonio's balcony which overlooked Rome. The November breeze was crisp but she didn't go back inside. Her mood was quiet and reflective as she waited for Antonio to finish his phone call and leave his study. She knew he was a busy and important man, but she resented how his business intruded. She didn't want to share Antonio's time and attention while they were leaving for the airport.

Isabella glanced down at her clothes, wishing she had something sleek and sophisticated to wear. Something glamorous that he'd always remember instead of her usual jeans and T-shirt. The sweater did nothing to add to her appearance. It was black, bulky, and it hid her baby bump.

She absently rubbed her belly, excited and nervous about her growing baby. The changes in her body were a physical reminder that it was time to move on. She had been greedy and stayed longer than she should. She didn't want to outstay her welcome and ruin these memories.

"Bella, you must be freezing," Antonio said as he stepped onto the balcony. "What are you doing out here?"

"I just wanted one more look," she said. To her horror, she felt her eyes water and her throat constrict with emotion.

Isabella ducked her head and reached for her backpack. She tried to focus on something else and keep her hands busy. She checked once again that she had her passport, ticket and money. As she was about to put them away something caught her notice.

"Antonio?" Isabella frowned as she read the printout in her hand. She straightened to her full height and looked at him. She tried not to think how masculine and powerful he looked in his dark suit and tie. "Is this a first-class ticket?"

"Yes," he answered abstractedly as he looped a wayward strand of her hair behind her ear. His fingertips brushed her throat and lingered.

Isabella took a step away as dread settled in her stomach. That had to have cost thousands of dollars.

Money she didn't have yet. Money she'd need for her baby. "You shouldn't have done that," she admonished in a hushed tone.

He shrugged and reached for her free hand, slid his fingers between hers. "You wouldn't accept my private plane," he reminded her as his thumb caressed her skin.

"I can't accept it, Antonio." It was going to take a long time before she would have the money from Giovanni's will. There were strict rules about how she could spend the money. She could use it to raise her baby but not repay a personal debt. "It's going to take me forever to pay off this ticket."

"I don't want you to repay me." He raised her hand to his mouth and pressed his lips against her knuckles.

She sighed and rested her head against his shoulder. It was tempting to accept his offer. She was going to be a poor student for a while. She needed all the help she could get. But she'd made a deal and she wanted to honor it. "It's too expensive."

His hand tightened against hers. Isabella flinched and lifted her head to look at him. His expression was closed and she couldn't tell what he was thinking.

"Then don't use it," he said.

Isabella blinked and gave him a small smile. "And do what instead? Swim my way back to Los Angeles?" she asked lightly.

She felt the nervous energy simmering in Antonio as he braced his shoulders. "You could stay."

She stared at Antonio's profile. He wasn't looking at her but she saw the ruddy streaks against his cheekbones and the tension in his jaw. If she didn't know any better she'd think he was feeling shy.

Stay? Hope blossomed through her body. She tried

to tamp down her growing excitement. She could have misunderstood his offer, but was he offering something more than affair? More than a duty to her and her child?

"Here? With you?" she clarified, her breath lodging in her throat.

"Yes." He risked a glance in her direction. "If that's what you want."

Antonio appeared vulnerable. His muscles were stiff and his dark eyes were hooded. He was reaching out, uncertain of her answer. He knew she loved him, but he wasn't sure if she would make the same sacrifices again.

She shouldn't. She had put her life on hold to be with him and then, when he had dumped her, she'd had nothing. Working in that café, with no money or opportunities, she'd sworn she would not put herself in that situation again. She would protect herself and not rely on any man. Especially not Antonio, who had the power to destroy her.

So why was she even considering his offer? Hadn't she learned anything? But this time it was different. This was not a vacation fling or an affair. Or was it?

Her chest squeezed with dismay. He had asked her to stay—something she'd needed to hear after he'd kicked her out all those months ago—but he hadn't said that he loved her. He wasn't offering anything more.

Isabella felt tears burn her eyes. "I want to," she said in a raspy voice. "But I can't."

Antonio closed his eyes briefly. His throat tightened as he swallowed. "Why not?"

She pressed her hand against his cheek. Oh, how she wished she didn't have to reject him. It hurt her just as much as it hurt him. "It's complicated."

He placed his hand on hers, trapping her against

him as he opened his eyes and held her gaze. "It's actually very simple. I want to be with you. You want to be with me."

Was that enough? It hadn't been enough last time. And this time she had a baby to consider. She needed more. She needed to know that he was going to be with her no matter what.

"You shouldn't make big changes when you're still in mourning," Isabella decided. She had learned that after her mother's death. Antonio had had a complicated relationship with his brother and needed time to come to terms with Giovanni's death.

"You think I'm doing this out of grief?" His eyes glittered with annoyance. "Do you believe that because I no longer have my brother I feel alone in the world?"

"Well, yes. It's possible." Isabella hoped it wasn't. She wanted to believe that the bond they shared was deep and powerful, but knew his feelings might only be temporary. She wasn't going to stay only to discover that Antonio had made this choice because he was bereaved.

"I'm not trying to fill a void," he said, his voice low and rough. "If anything I've realized how I want to spend the rest of my life. I want to spend it with you."

Isabella froze. Had he really said that or was she hearing what she wanted to hear? She was almost too scared to move. "What are you saying?"

"I love you, Isabella." He turned his head and pressed his mouth against the palm of her hand. "I want to be with you. Always."

Isabella inhaled a jagged breath. *He loved her.* She wanted to fling herself into his arms but something was holding her back. She was scared to trust his words. Scared to find out that her idea of love wasn't his.

"This is moving too fast." She snatched her hand away from him and clenched her fists, her pulse skipping erratically. "I…I need to think about this."

Antonio moved closer. His harsh features were sharp and there was a predatory gleam in his eyes. He didn't like her answer and was determined to make her yield. "What's there to think about? Why do you need to think about it in Los Angeles instead of here with me?"

"I…. It's just that…"

There was an apologetic knock on the balcony door. Isabella whirled around and saw the housekeeper standing in the doorway. She was wringing her hands in her starched apron.

"I'm sorry to interrupt," Martina said, trying not to make eye contact, "but your mother is here, sir."

Antonio closed his eyes and took a deep breath. He didn't hide the displeasure on his face as he held his temper firmly in check.

"Why is your mother here?" Isabella said. She couldn't imagine that Maria wanted to see her off to the airport. She had not spoken to Maria since the day she had been invited for tea.

"I don't know," he said as he reluctantly moved away. "I'll be right back."

She didn't say anything as she watched him leave. Antonio loved her and wanted her to stay. But as what? His girlfriend? His mistress? His wife?

And would he love her child?

She tried to imagine Antonio as a father.

He would be loving and affectionate. She knew that deep in her bones. He would be firm but gentle. He wouldn't make the same mistakes as his own parents. He would encourage and support his child no matter what challenges they faced. Antonio would give his child unconditional love, but would he give it to *her*?

Her opinion was swift. Yes, he would love her child. She didn't know why she was even questioning it. Antonio was already a part of her baby's life. He'd been there every step of the way.

Isabella felt as if a weight had been lifted off her. She was willing to take the risk and tell Antonio that she'd stay. She knew they could be a family. She didn't need to hear a marriage proposal. She wanted one, but she didn't need it to make her decision. Antonio loved her and cared about her baby. He proved it every day.

They could have a wonderful future together, Isabella thought as she grabbed her backpack and strode across the balcony. She was prepared to live and love boldly, without a safety net.

Isabella stepped into the apartment but didn't see Antonio or his mother. She heard voices coming from the study and hesitated. She didn't really want to see Maria Rossi. The woman intimidated her. But she was Antonio's mother and the grandmother of her child. Isabella gritted her teeth and threw back her shoulders before marching over to the study.

"Why is she leaving?" Isabella heard Maria ask in Italian. "You were supposed to convince her to stay."

"She hasn't left yet," Antonio replied. "And she can always come back."

"Yes, yes, yes. She *says* she'll visit so the child can know his heritage and his family, but there's no guarantee."

Isabella frowned as she listened by the study door.

Did Maria still think she would prevent her from knowing her grandchild? That she had no intention of keeping in contact?

Isabella was about to step into the study, but froze mid-step when she heard Maria's next words.

"You were supposed to marry her and adopt the baby so we can gain full control of the Rossi shares." Maria's tone was sharp. "What happened?"

Isabella went cold. Antonio had said he wanted her. That he wanted to look after the baby. That he loved her. Her stomach made a sickening twist. It had all been lies.

"I *will* marry Isabella," Antonio told his mother.

His confident tone scraped at Isabella. There was no question that she would have accepted his proposal. Hell, she would have jumped at the offer with pathetic eagerness. She loved him and had been about to give up everything again to be with him.

"And adopt the baby?" Maria asked.

Isabella gasped as pain ricocheted in her chest. She clasped her shaky hand against her mouth. How could Antonio have devised such a diabolical plan? And how could she have fallen for it so easily?

She should have known he wasn't going to accept Giovanni's baby into his heart. This was why he'd said he wanted to take care of them and show full support. So down the line he could win full custody of Gio's child.

Isabella pressed her hand against the wall as her knees threatened to buckle. It would have worked. If she had married Antonio she would have wanted him to adopt the baby. She would have encouraged it!

And he would have stolen her child away from her. The cold-hearted bastard.

Isabella thrust out her chin and took a deep breath. She wasn't going to let that happen. She didn't care that Maria intimidated her or that Antonio wielded enormous power. She would protect her child from the Rossi family.

Isabella stepped into the study, prepared for battle.

CHAPTER FOURTEEN

WHEN Antonio saw Isabella enter the study a sense of dread shrouded him and weighed heavily on his shoulders. Isabella's complexion was pale and her posture was rigid. Her hands were clenched at her sides but it was her eyes that gave her away. She looked wounded. He knew she'd heard his damning words.

Antonio prided himself on his quick thinking. He was usually a man of action. Yet at this moment he couldn't move. His mind went blank as blinding panic flared inside him. There was no way he could recover from this.

His mother frowned as she watched his expression transform from annoyance to caution. She turned to the door and saw Isabella. Maria immediately pasted on a polite smile and acted as if nothing had been said. After years of gossiping and backbiting with her social circle Maria Rossi wasn't flustered. She was in her element. The only sign that she was taken by surprise was the way she fiddled with her pearl necklace.

"Isabella," his mother greeted her in English. "I wanted to see you before you left for America. I hope you will return soon."

"I have no intention of coming back," Isabella replied in Italian, "I am not giving you the opportunity to steal my child."

Maria flinched and her face went a mottled red. Her movements were choppy as she turned his attention to Antonio. "You told me she didn't speak Italian," she hissed.

"I said no such thing," Antonio replied, his gaze firmly on Isabella's trembling jaw. "Gio probably gave you that impression but he was wrong."

Unfortunately for him. How could he convince Isabella that he had abandoned his plans? Would she believe that now he really wanted to marry her and adopt her child? No. She would never trust his motivations. He didn't blame her.

"Isabella—" his mother began, but faltered to a stop as Isabella glared at her.

"Mother, I think it would be best if you left. Bella and I need to talk."

Maria looked uncertain as she glanced at Isabella and then back at him. She was very aware of Isabella's unpredictable anger quivering in the air.

"I don't think that would be wise."

Antonio sighed softly. Of all the times his mother chose now to give him support. She knew she'd made a big mistake, and he appreciated her need to back him up, but he didn't need her here. This was between him and Isabella. "Please?"

Maria's shoulders sagged in defeat. She grabbed her purse from his desk, patted her chignon to make sure every hair was in place, and gave Isabella a wide berth as she walked out of the study.

Antonio held Isabella's furious gaze but they didn't exchange a word. The moment they heard his mother leave the apartment and shut the door Isabella took an angry step forward.

"Was *anything* we shared true?" Her tone was low and fierce. "Or was it all a lie?"

Antonio saw the pain and the rage in her eyes. He wanted to wrap his arms around her, hold her close and take the hurt from her. He knew how she felt. He had wrestled with that very question when he'd thought she had cheated on him. It ate away at him to the point where he didn't think he would be whole again.

"You still believe I cheated on you," she said, her eyes narrowing into slits. "You told me you believed me so I would get closer to you."

"No, I believe you." She had been innocent, and he had renewed this affair under false pretenses. She would never forgive him and he had to live with the fact that he'd ruined their second chance for happiness.

"I don't think so. You will say anything to get what you want. You'd even go so far as to marry me if it means getting control of the family fortune. Why, you'd even say you love me when you can't stand the sight of me."

"That's not true." Antonio moved and stood in front of her. "I do love you. You don't have to question that. I have proved it every day since we got back together."

"No, you've proved that you're a very good actor. You've pretended to look after me when what you were really doing was looking after your own interests." Her hand shook with fury as she pointed accusingly at him. "You said you wanted to give me everything, but once you'd got what you wanted you would have taken it all away."

Antonio reared back as if he'd been hit. How could

she say that? Did she think him that low? "I would never do that and you know it."

"I thought I knew you, but obviously I don't." She shook her head in disgust. "I was thrilled when you finally opened up to me, but that was part of the plan, wasn't it? Were the stories even true?"

"Of course they were." Her accusations stung. He had shared those memories knowing he could trust them to Isabella. "I told you things I haven't told anyone else."

She wasn't listening. "But the *pièce de resistance* of your plan was pure genius," she declared with the sweep of her hand. "Proving that you could be a good father to my child. Only it was all a show."

"No, it wasn't," he said through clenched teeth.

"You even got your friends involved so that you could demonstrate how good you are with children. And I fell for it!"

"That's not true," he insisted. "I didn't fake anything with my friends. I adore those kids and you have no right to question that."

She thrust out her chin. "And *you* had no right seducing me," she said in a growl, her eyes flashing with ferocious anger. "Making me believe that you wanted a second chance. I knew you wanted to control my child's inheritance but I didn't think you'd try to take my child as well."

"That was not my intention." Antonio said coldly. He needed his words to pierce through her tumultuous emotions. "I would never separate you from your child."

"I heard what your mother said."

"Yes, my mother said it. Not me."

"Then what *was* your plan?" she asked, placing her fists on her hips. "I know you had one. You set it in motion when you found me at that café. Why would you come looking for me when you could have had someone else do the job?"

Antonio couldn't deny it. Isabella knew him well. That hadn't been a disadvantage in the past. She'd known his good and bad sides and still fallen in love with him. He had destroyed that love once before but this was different. There was no hope after this.

He wanted to lie. He should lie if he wanted to save what they had together. But he couldn't. It was time he owned up to his plan. Isabella deserved to know the truth and understand what he was capable of doing.

"I didn't know why Gio named you in the will. I thought it was to remind me of what he could steal away from me—you *and* my birthright. I wasn't going to let that happen and I planned to take back the power he'd given you."

She crossed her arms and glared at him. "I've already figured that out. What did you plan to do?"

Antonio looked away guiltily. Maybe it was best if he didn't tell her *everything*.

"Oh, my God," Isabella whispered and dropped her hands to her sides. "You were going to seduce me so I would give up my child's claim to the Rossi fortune."

Isabella took a cautious step back as she realized Antonio's plan. *That* was why he'd wanted more than a one-night stand. *That* was why he had been insistent on sharing his bed. It wasn't because he found her irresistible. He had been manufacturing emotional intimacy before he moved in for the kill.

She blanched as she remembered how open and trusting she had been in Antonio's arms. "Giovanni said you wouldn't touch me once you found out I was pregnant with his child," she said in a broken whisper. "I thought that was true until you kissed me...." She had thought Antonio couldn't help himself despite everything that happened between them.

"I always wanted you," he confessed. "Even when I thought you were sleeping with my brother. I can't stop wanting you."

His raw tone revealed how much he loved *and* hated the power she had over him. She knew the feeling. Antonio was her weakness, her vice. Only he'd used it against her.

"I knew early on that you weren't going to accept any financial settlement," Antonio said. "I *didn't* have sex with you to regain power over the family fortune. I made love to you because I wanted to be with you."

Despite the anger and pain pouring through her, Isabella wanted to believe him. And that scared her. She wanted desperately to believe that their relationship was as straightforward as it had been in the beginning. It hurt even to think about how beautifully simple their love affair had been.

Pain seeped into her bones. Her limbs felt heavy and she wanted to lean against the nearest wall before sliding down to the floor. She refrained from wrapping her arms around her middle or curling into a protective ball. She would not show any weakness or tears in front of this man. He would use her feelings to his advantage, just as he'd used her attraction and seduced her back into his bed.

"So," she said, her voice rough as her throat tightened, "you had to go with a Plan B. You needed to marry me. That would have been very difficult for you.

Antonio Rossi making a commitment? Especially to a nobody."

"I have never thought of you as a nobody."

"No, you saw me as the woman pregnant with the Rossi heir. That's the only reason you'd consider marrying me. You certainly weren't thinking that when we were together the first time."

Antonio shoved his hand in her dark, thick hair. "I admit that my reason for restarting our affair wasn't honest, but that changed. *I* changed."

Isabella snorted. "How convenient."

He grabbed her arms and forced her to face him. She met his gaze head-on. She wasn't afraid. She wasn't going to back down. Nothing he said or did could make her feel any worse.

"I want a future with you, Bella. When you came back into my life I knew that I couldn't let you go. It isn't about the money or the baby. It's about *us*."

Isabella slowly raised her hands and flattened them on his solid chest. She felt the strong beat of his heart. Antonio was telling her everything she needed to hear. Just like he had week after week. And somehow she was supposed to believe that the lies had become the truth?

Isabella pushed him away and he reluctantly let go of her arms.

"You have to believe me," Antonio said. "I don't know how to prove it to you. How can I show you how much I love you?"

"You can't." It was over. She couldn't make it work by clinging on to him, on to the promise of this relationship. Isabella turned around and headed for the door. She had to get out of here before she found a reason not to.

"I'm not going to let you walk out of my life again," he warned her.

"Yes, you are," she said hoarsely as emotion clawed at her throat. She didn't dare face him. "Last time you dumped me. This time I'm making a run for it."

She felt Antonio follow her. Isabella wanted to hurry and hide. She had to get out before her resolve weakened. Before she allowed herself to believe anything he said. She grabbed her backpack and swung it over her shoulders. Ducking her head and keeping her eyes straight ahead, she reached the front door in record time.

"We are a part of each other's lives," Antonio said. "You can't shut me out."

"Antonio, soon you will be a distant memory. Ancient history." She wrenched the door open. "A cautionary tale I'll share with my daughter."

"You're forgetting something."

Antonio's harsh voice was right behind her. She felt him tower over her, inhaled his scent that invaded her senses.

"We share power over the Rossi empire. That means we'll have to work together. We will be in constant contact."

Isabella's hand flexed on the doorknob. What he said was true. Antonio would be part of her life from now on. She would need to deal with him on a daily basis. She would have to watch from the sidelines as he got on with his life while she was once again picking up the pieces.

"I'll give you power of attorney, or whatever they call it," she said impulsively. "You can make all the decisions without having to discuss it with me."

"That's not how it works and it's not what I want."

Antonio cupped his hand over her shoulders and turned her around. "You can't throw me out of your life that easily."

Why not? He'd done it to her and he would have done it again. "I don't want to have anything to with you or the Rossi business."

"Too bad. I'm going to be with you every step of the way whether you like it or not. You're angry with me now—"

"Angry? Try furious. Try homicidal."

"But soon you will realize that everything we shared was true. That I wasn't pretending and that I am committed to you and the baby."

"I can't take that chance." She had taken too many risks only to have them blow up in her face. She couldn't trust Antonio at his word only to have him try to take her child away.

There was only one way she could protect her baby and her future. Her heart started to pound and she felt her skin flush. The idea was crazy, and she should think it through, but it was the only way she would get Antonio out of her life for good.

"I'm giving up my child's claim to the Rossi fortune," she said in a rush. "I don't want the shares or anything. It's all yours."

Antonio's eyes widened and his hands tightened on her shoulders. "Are you crazy? What are you talking about?"

She pulled away from him. "When I get back to Los Angeles I will have a lawyer draw up the paperwork. All the money, all the shares—everything will belong to you."

"You can't do this."

"Yes, I can," she said defiantly. The more she thought about it, the more she knew it was the right decision. This was the only way she'd be free.

"You can't give away a fortune. What about your child? It should belong to him. This is part of who he is."

It didn't have to be. "I don't want him to know anything about his heritage or his family. I need to protect him from becoming someone like Giovanni or you."

Antonio's eyes flashed with anger. "Bella, I won't let you do this. You're making a big mistake."

"Why are you fighting me, Antonio?" she asked as she crossed the threshold. "You're getting everything you want without making any sacrifice."

"Not everything," he told her. "I want *you*."

"Don't worry, Antonio," she said as she walked away. "I'm sure the feeling is temporary."

CHAPTER FIFTEEN

Four months later

Isabella gripped onto the wall railing and paused. She was shaky and she felt sweat bead on her forehead. She had tried to do too much, determined to heal quickly after the Caesarean. After all, she was going home alone with her baby girl in a couple of hours. She needed to be able to move.

Glancing around the busy maternity ward, she saw that her room was at the end of the hall. Isabella was tempted to give up and ask for a wheelchair, but she wasn't a quitter. She had become a fighter. There'd been plenty of days when she'd survived on grit alone.

After she had returned to California she'd ignored the desire to curl up in a ball and cry. She'd had to get on with her life and take care of her baby. It had not been easy, but she now had a tiny apartment, a few friends, and a job at an art gallery. Soon she would return to college and complete her art history degree.

Now if only she could erase Antonio from her mind… If she could stop dreaming about him, that would be great. Those dreams reminded her of what she had lost, what she would never have again. One day she would be rid of the empty hollowness inside her, but until then she needed to stop thinking about the past and focus on the future.

When she stepped into her room Isabella swore she would never take walking for granted again. All she wanted to do was get back into bed and rest. Intent on putting one foot in front of the other, she didn't realize she had a visitor.

"Bella."

Only one person called her that. Isabella glanced up, the movement so sharp and sudden that she almost lost her balance. She flattened her hand on the wall when she saw Antonio standing by the window.

Her heart did a slow and painful flip as she greedily took in the sight of him. She must be imagining things. Isabella blinked but the vision of Antonio didn't go away. He looked exactly as he had when she'd left him. Powerful, harsh and incredibly sexy. His scowl and the tailored business suit made him even more intimidating.

Isabella knew she looked a mess, with her limp hair and voluminous hospital gown. "What are you doing here?" she asked weakly.

"I'm here for you."

Damn, those words still sent a shiver of excitement down her spine. Antonio was always going to have this effect on her. It wasn't fair. She didn't need this in her life. She didn't need *him*.

"You need to leave." She wished she could leave, but she knew she wouldn't get far. Gathering all the strength she could muster, Isabella pushed one foot in front of the other. She needed to get to the bed before she collapsed.

Antonio frowned as he saw her awkward gait and

was suddenly at her side. "Let me help you," he offered as he gently placed a hand on her back.

She would have shrugged him off if she'd trusted her balance a little more. "I can do it myself. I need the practice," she insisted.

Antonio dropped his hand but walked with her to the bed. The journey was slow and painful, and she knew Antonio was tempted to pick her up and carry her. She increased her speed, finding it easier to walk having someone nearby. Antonio might have betrayed her, but she knew he wouldn't let her fall.

Once she'd sat on the bed Isabella gave a sigh of relief. She lay down, wincing and hissing a breath between her clenched teeth. Antonio didn't say anything as he pulled the blanket over her and tucked her in.

She didn't want his kindness. She might read too much into the gesture. "Now tell me why you're here," Isabella said as she sank into her pillow.

"I saw your daughter," Antonio said, his voice low and husky. "She's beautiful."

Antonio had already seen Chiara? She stiffened as the need to protect her child crashed through her like violent wave. She hadn't been prepared for that. She hadn't thought Antonio would be interested.

"She looks like her father."

He nodded. "Yes, she does. But I also see a lot of you in her."

She glanced at his face, but Antonio showed no sign of resentment. He had simply stated a matter of fact. It was as if Chiara's parentage didn't bother him. How was that possible? Was she seeing what she wanted to see?

Isabella closed her eyes. "Antonio, I'm really not up for visitors."

"You haven't been for four months," he said in a growl.

She wouldn't apologize for that. The first time he'd called her Isabella had recognized the number and hadn't picked up. She had spent the rest of the day alternating between tears and stone-cold anger. But she'd also known that she wanted to talk to Antonio, hold on to that connection. And that had scared her. How could she move on if she still felt like that?

"I've been busy," she said. "My life has gone through a lot of transitions."

"I tried to contact you."

"Yeah, I know." She had blocked his calls and texts, deleted his e-mails without opening them, and trashed the flower bouquets that had appeared on her desk at work. Anything related to her child's inheritance had been directed to her lawyer, whom she could barely afford. She had to avoid anything that reminded her of Antonio.

She'd wanted to give him full power over the Rossi shares, but he had refused to accept it. He still acted as if he needed her approval over every decision. Isabella wasn't sure why he was trying to include her in everything. He didn't need to keep in contact with her. He no longer had to pretend that he could love her and her child.

Disappointment coiled tightly in her chest. So, if he had everything he wanted, why was he here? Today of all days? She didn't want to talk to Antonio about her baby.

"I don't have the money yet to pay you back for the ticket," she said in a rush. "We'll have to make a payment plan. It'll take a while because—"

"I don't want your money. That ticket was a gift," he interrupted, annoyed. "I'm here because I heard you were in labor. Unfortunately I didn't get here in time. If I had I would have found you better accommodations."

She opened her eyes and looked around the room. It was clean, simple and private. It was better than she had hoped. What more could she possibly want? "This is fine. I won't be here for much longer. They are sending me home in a couple of hours."

Outrage flickered in his dark eyes. "That is unacceptable. You can barely walk. I will speak to the doctors immediately."

"Wait a second." She weakly lifted her hand as she realized what he had said a few moments ago. "How did you know I was in labor? Are you having me watched?"

"Of course. I was worried about you. I remember that room you had over the café when I found you." He suppressed his shudder of distaste. "I didn't want that to happen again."

"I don't like being watched or followed," she told him. "I can take care of myself. I don't need your help."

"Then why did you put me down as emergency contact on your medical forms? Why did you make me the guardian to Chiara if anything happened to you?"

Isabella cringed. She had wrestled with that choice. She could have named a friend, but in the end she'd wanted Antonio to look after Chiara. "You know about that?"

"I do." Triumph flared in his eyes. "You know deep down that I would take care of you and the baby. That I would treat your daughter as my own."

She felt the heat crawl up her neck. "You shouldn't

read anything into those decisions. I was required to give a name."

"And you chose mine. Because you know I want to be here. That I want to help."

He said that now, but how long would it last? "No, you don't want to help. Not unless you get something in return. I can't figure out your ulterior motive, but I know you have one."

Antonio sighed. "I regret that. At the time I made promises that I wasn't planning to keep."

"Just as I expected."

He shoved his hand through his hair. "But that changed once we were back together. I started to believe that this was our second chance. I wasn't thinking about gaining control as much as I was thinking about recapturing what we'd once shared."

"And when did that change of heart happen?" Isabella asked, her voice filled with skepticism.

"When you handed me the sonogram." Antonio said, his voice fading as he recalled that moment. "I looked at it and I didn't see the baby as an obstacle or a sign of betrayal. I saw this small, innocent child that was part of *you*. And I knew I wanted to go on this journey with you."

Isabella stared at him as the sincerity in his voice tugged at her. She wanted to believe him, but what if this was another act? How could she trust her instincts when he had played her so well before?

Antonio cleared his throat and awkwardly rubbed the back of his neck. "Once I found where you had gone I tried to reach out. I wanted to talk to you."

"You were very persistent."

Antonio reached out and covered her hand with his.

"I now know how you must have felt when I kicked you out. I was desperate and out of control. No matter how hard I tried, you wouldn't talk to me."

"I still don't want to talk to you." As much as she wanted to hold onto his hand, she purposely removed her fingers from his grasp.

"I understand, but I should have been here. You shouldn't have gone through this alone."

"I wasn't alone. I have friends." Friends who would adore her and her baby, no matter what her shortcomings were.

"Yes, I know," he said, the corner of his mouth slanting up in a smile. "They gathered around you in a protective circle. My security team could take a few lessons from them."

"Considering our history," Isabella said gently, "it's better if I don't accept your help."

"No, it's not." Antonio leaned over Isabella, bracing his arms on the bedrails. "If you don't want me by your side then I'll help you behind the scenes. I want to give you every opportunity to finish your college degree. I will support your dreams and goals. I'm not asking for your permission, Bella. I'm doing this because I want to."

Isabella fought back the hope that pressed against her chest. "And Chiara?"

"I want to take you and Chiara back to Rome," Antonio replied.

She frowned. "Why would you do that?"

"So we can be a family." Antonio leaned in closer. "These months have been hell, knowing that I've lost you again."

Family. There was that word again. It was as if he

knew her weakness and understood her deepest desire. "You can't just walk in here and expect me to change my life again so we can have another affair. My situation has changed. I have a child I need to think about."

"I said a family." Antonio's gaze held her immobile. "I want us to get married."

Married?

"You don't need to marry me," she said, her eyes wide and her heart starting to pound. "I offered you full control of the Rossi shares."

"I love you."

His sincerity tugged at her heart.

"And I know you love me."

"I… I…" She couldn't deny it. She loved Antonio and wanted to be with him—but love wasn't enough.

"Marry me, Bella." He rested his forehead against hers. "I want to be with you and Chiara. Always."

She slowly exhaled and looked away. There had to be another reason. An ulterior motive. Why would he want her as his wife if she didn't meet any of his requirements?

"No," she whispered.

Antonio froze. "Excuse me?"

"I'm sorry, Antonio. I can't marry you."

Antonio drew back. Isabella had said no. *No.* The word sliced through him like a knife. He gripped the bedrail as hurt bled through him. Had he ruined what they'd shared? Was it beyond repair?

He wouldn't accept that. They loved each other and they would get through this. He needed Isabella. His life was dark and empty without her and he didn't want to go through another day apart from her.

He should have come for her earlier. Antonio bowed his head with regret. He had stayed in Rome to fix the financial mess his brother had left. Not only had Gio been deeply in debt, but the Rossi family fortune was at stake. If Antonio hadn't stepped in Chiara would have inherited nothing.

And he had also stayed in Rome to make some changes in his life. He'd scaled back on his work significantly so his focus could be on his family life. He'd also found a house that would be perfect for raising children. Now that he had suffered twice from being separated from Isabella, he didn't want to miss out on another moment.

But Isabella didn't see it that way. She didn't want him to be a part of her life.

A horrible thought occurred to him. His stomach twisted with dread as he asked, "Do you want to be with me?"

"Yes," Isabella said. She wiped the tears from her eyes and sniffled. "But it's not possible."

"Of course it is," he insisted as relief poured through him. "We are free to get married. I don't want anyone but you. I know you haven't dated anyone since you were with me. There is no one holding us back."

"I don't trust you," she said. "You say everything I want to hear, but you did that before and it was all lies."

He took a step back as hurt seeped into him. "It wasn't all lies."

"You showed interest and concern because you wanted control of the money. What do you want from me now?"

"I wasn't faking it."

"Why are you still around?" Isabella asked. "I tried

to transfer my interest in the Rossi empire but you won't sign the paperwork. Just take it. You'd have full control with my blessing."

"I don't want your blessing," he said in a growl. "I want you and the baby."

"That doesn't make sense. I would not make you a good wife. I don't have the right background, the right—"

"You *are* good for me," he insisted. "You're generous and affectionate. You're bold and adventurous. You nurture and protect the ones you love. You love ferociously and you are deeply loyal."

"There's nothing special about that."

"You have no idea how rare that is." He crossed his arms and began to pace the room. "I know what it's like to grow up in a family and feel like an outsider. I'm not going to let that happen to Chiara. She won't have to earn my love or my affection. She already has it."

"How can she have it?" she threw back at him angrily. "You think I was being unfaithful to you when she was conceived."

"I did at first. I can't deny it." He rubbed his hands over his face. "It destroyed me. But that was when I thought you had cheated on me. I don't care that she's Giovanni's daughter or even that she's a Rossi. She is *your* child and I want to raise her with you."

"That doesn't change anything," she said slowly, as if she'd been taken by surprise. "I won't marry you."

"I won't stop asking," he said as he stalked back to the bed, unable to hide his frustration. "I am bound to you whether or not we're married."

"And if I keep refusing?"

"That won't change how I feel. You walked away

from me but I kept my commitment to you. I will make sure you and the baby are getting the best care," he confessed. "I will always take care of you and Chiara even if we don't marry. Never question that."

He didn't know how he could prove his love for her and Chiara. He had demonstrated it when they had been together, but those actions had been tainted with his original plan. If Isabella returned to him she'd been taking a great leap of faith.

"I'm asking you to trust me," he said as he took her hand again. This time she didn't pull away. "I will show you, Bella. You once gave everything to make our relationship work and I have the same commitment to you and Chiara."

"You say that now…"

"I will prove it every day," he vowed. "Starting today. I'm taking you to my hotel and I will look after you and the baby."

She pressed her lips together as she considered his offer. "I'm not sure about this," she said nervously.

It wasn't quite a yes, but she hadn't said no. Antonio smiled triumphantly.

"I'm still not marrying you," Isabella warned him.

"You will," he said as he raised her hand to his lips. "When you trust me. You will."

EPILOGUE

ISABELLA stirred awake and instinctively reached for Antonio. Her fingers brushed against the warm, crumpled bedsheet. She frowned and slowly opened her eyes, her gaze focusing on her hand. The diamonds on her wedding ring caught the faint light and sparkled in the shadowy bedroom.

Propping herself on her elbow, Isabella squinted at the bedside clock and saw that it was a little after three in the morning. She glanced around the large room. The curtains were still pulled back and she saw the Rome skyline glittering in the distance.

"Antonio?" she called out softly, her voice husky with sleep.

She rose from the bed when she didn't receive an answer. Grabbing her discarded nightgown that was lying on the floor in a pool of satin, Isabella slid it over her body. The hem skimmed her thighs.

She tiptoed barefoot out of the bedroom and paused at the threshold when she heard faint whispering. It sounded like Antonio's voice, and it came from the direction of the nursery. Isabella felt a flicker of worry. Had Chiara cried out and she hadn't heard it?

Isabella reached the door to the nursery and peered

inside. She saw Antonio, wearing a dark pair of pajama bottoms slung low on his lean hips. The sight of him gently cradling her fussy baby in his arms made her breath hitch in her throat.

Antonio should look out of place in the pink and green nursery. He was too sexy, his looks too darkly erotic, to sit in a rocking chair. He was known for his power and ruthlessness, but one year-old Chiara had already wrapped him around her tiny finger.

"Chiara, listen to your papa," Antonio said in a hushed, mesmerizing tone to the infant snuggled against his bare muscular chest. "We had an agreement. You are to sleep when the moon is out."

Isabella leaned against the doorframe as she watched her husband and her child. They had an agreement? She bit back a smile. How frequently did Antonio and Chiara have these late-night heart-to-hearts?

It shouldn't surprise her. From the moment she and Chiara had left the hospital Antonio had gotten into the habit of long talks with her daughter. He would encourage Chiara to reach for a toy, he would read the newspaper to her as if it was a children's fairytale, and he would soothe her when she cried loudly during her bath.

"A Rossi always honors his word," he murmured as he stroked the baby's back.

Chiara sighed and her tiny body relaxed against Antonio's chest.

"Remember," Antonio said softly as he laid the baby in her crib, "you get your mama's undivided attention during the day while I'm at work. I get your mama at night."

"Did you ever think," Isabella whispered as she walked into the nursery, "that Chiara gets up in the middle of the night so she can have *your* undivided attention?"

"Then she's a smart girl." He tucked a light blanket around the infant.

Isabella was enamored of the depth of patience and tenderness Antonio demonstrated. He always had words of praise and optimism, whether Chiara had an accomplishment or a setback. She knew Antonio would be a great father.

Antonio turned and Isabella could see his exaggerated scowl in the faint moonlight. "That nightgown looks familiar. Didn't I strip it off you earlier tonight?"

"You did," Isabella said with a smile as sexual excitement bubbled inside her. "I thought I should wear something special for our wedding night, but you ripped it right off me."

"And now you've put it back on?" His voice was low and playful. "You should be punished."

"You need to catch me first." She hurried out the door and got all the way to the hallway before she felt Antonio's arm wrap around her waist. Isabella bit back a squeal as he flattened her spine against his chest.

"I've got you," he said triumphantly against her ear as he pushed the straps of her nightgown past her shoulders. "And I'm not letting go."

She sensed a deeper meaning in his words. The nightgown slid past her hips and onto the floor. She turned and looped her arms around his broad shoulders, the tips of her breasts grazing his chest. "I'm not letting go, either. You can count on that."

* * * * *

THE DARK SIDE
OF DESIRE

JULIA JAMES

CHAPTER ONE

LEON MARANZ lifted a glass of champagne from the server standing just inside the entrance to the large, crowded first floor salon of the exclusive Regent's Park apartment that he'd just been shown into by one of the household staff and surveyed the scene before him. It was the type of social gathering he was very familiar with. A cocktail party in one of London's premier residences, ITS guests, however disparate, unified by one common factor.

Wealth.

A great deal of it.

A casual flick of Leon's opaque eyes could tell him that, simply by seeing the unbroken sea of designer outfits the women were wearing, let alone the glint of precious gems at their throats, ears and wrists. The women uniformly had a look about them of pampered, sleek felines, and the men were also uniformly alike in their projection of self-assurance and self-worth in the eyes of the world.

Leon's mouth tightened infinitesimally. That projection was not always a guarantee of the solidity of the worth behind it. Probingly, his dark eyes lanced through the throng, seeking its target. Alistair Lassiter's back was turned to the entrance of the salon, but Leon recognised him instantly. Recognised, too, what he wanted to see. Probably invisible to the rest of the guests, but not to him: a discernible tension in his stance. For a moment longer he held his gaze. Then, his assessing surveillance done, he lifted his glass of champagne to his mouth. But even as he did so he stilled.

A woman was looking at him.

She was nowhere near Alistair Lassiter, but Leon could see her at the periphery of his vision. Every finely tuned antenna told him she was levelling a stare at him that had an intensity about it that demonstrated she had no idea he was aware of her scrutiny. But Leon had been on the receiving end of female interest for close on two decades—even long before he had made the fortune which he knew, cynically, was high prime attraction for women these days. Far and away more attractive to them than the six-foot frame and strong, saturnine looks that had been his appeal when young and impoverished. Years of enjoying all that beautiful females had to offer meant he knew when a woman was looking at him.

And this one was most definitely looking at him.

He took a mouthful of champagne, turning his head slightly as he did so, to move the woman into the central frame of his vision.

She was in the English style, with a fine-boned face, oval, contoured with a delicate, narrow nose and wide, clear eyes. Her chestnut hair was drawn off her face into a chignon that would have looked severe on any woman less beautiful, just as her indigo raw silk cocktail dress would have looked plain on a woman with a less than perfect body. But this woman's body was indeed perfect: slender waist, gently rounded hips and, Leon could see, despite the modest décolletage, generous breasts. The bracelet sleeves of her cocktail frock showed the length of her forearms, and her elegant hands were cupping a glass of mineral water. The hem of her dress skimmed a little way above knee length, displaying long, slender legs lengthened by high heels.

The total impact was, despite the severity of her style—or perhaps because of it—stunning, making every other woman present appear overdressed and flawed. Leon felt anticipation fizz through him. Against all his expectations, the evening ahead was clearly not going to be only about business after all…

He narrowed his eyes and let his gaze rest on her, acknowledging what she made him feel. The flare of desire…

His gaze swept back up to her face, intercepting her scrutiny, ready to make eye contact and register his interest in her, to start to move towards her.

And immediately the shutters came down over her face.

It was like a mask forming over her features. An icy mask that froze her expression.

Froze him out. Blanked him completely. She was looking straight through him as if he were not there, as if he did not exist…as if he were not even the barest part of her universe.

Abruptly, she moved away, turning her back on him. Emotion spiked through him—one he had not felt for a long, long time. For one more moment his gaze continued to hold. Then he moved purposefully forward into the throng.

Flavia forced a polite smile to her lips, as if paying attention to whatever it was that was being discussed. She had more on her mind than making polite conversation to her father's guests here tonight. A lot more.

She didn't want to be here, in her father's opulent Regent's Park apartment. The hypocrisy of it nauseated her—playing the pampered daughter of a lavishly indulgent millionaire when both she and her father knew that that was bitterly far from the truth.

What did she care for this stupid cocktail party? For standing around looking expensively ornamental in this over-decorated apartment, designed only to impress and show off her father's wealth? It was awash with glass and chrome and the ostentatious, tasteless extravagance of gold fittings and showy furniture, conspicuous statement pieces, and she could never feel anything but a total alien here.

She wanted to be home! Home in the heart of rural Dorset, deep in the countryside. Home in the grey-stoned Georgian house that she loved so much, with its square frontage and sash windows, filled with furniture that had aged with the house where she had grown up, roaming the fields and the woods all around, cycling the narrow hedged lanes, rambling far and wide—but always, always, coming home. Home to the grandparents she'd adored, who had raised her after the tragically early death of her mother, to be enveloped in their loving arms.

But Harford Hall was a world away from her father's glitteringly deluxe apartment and she was *not* free to flee, however much she longed to do so.

She shifted her weight from one unfamiliar high heel to the other, sipping at her mineral water and trying to pay attention to the conversation. She had no idea who the couple speaking to her were, but presumably the husband was some kind of businessman who was useful to her father, for her father, Flavia knew, only ever invited people who could be beneficial to him. That was the way he divided up the population of the world—people he could use, and people he could toss aside. She, his daughter, counted as both.

For most of her life it had been the latter—someone to be tossed aside. Ignored and discarded. The way he'd done her mother. Oh, he'd gone to the trouble of marrying her, once she'd found herself pregnant. But that had only, Flavia now knew, been because her grandparents had gifted him a substantial sum of money. Ostensibly it had been to start their married life together, but in reality, Flavia was grimly aware, it had been a bribe and an inducement to marry their pregnant daughter.

Her father had done well out of her mother financially, and the money he'd got had helped provide the capital he had needed to build his business empire. What he had not needed was a wife and child, and barely six months after Flavia had been born her father had packed them both off back to Dorset and taken up with another woman. A wealthy divorcee, as it happened. She had not lasted long, however. Once she'd provided more investment capital he'd moved on yet again.

It was a pattern he'd continued to repeat as he progressively amassed his business fortune. A cynical light glinted sourly in Flavia's eyes. Although these days the women were getting younger and younger, and her father was the one providing the money they wanted to keep themselves looking alluring for him. Her father had got used to having the best, and his wealth had provided it lavishly.

She glanced around. This Regent's Park apartment was worth at least a few million pounds, given its premier location and the glittering lavishness of its décor. It was only one of his properties, however. There was also a house in Surrey's stockbroker belt, an apartment in Paris in one of the best *arrondissements*, a villa in Marbella's Puerto Banus, and another on the beachfront on Barbados.

Flavia had been to none of them, and wouldn't have wanted to. Nor did she want to be here. But three years ago her now-widowed grandmother had needed a hip replacement operation, and her father had been ruthlessly blunt.

'The old bat can have her operation privately, but the money for it will be a loan—and you'll repay it by turning up when I want you to chat and smile graciously at my guests. Everyone will say how charming and delightful and well-bred you are, and anyone who thought I was too nouveau bloody riche to swallow will think again!'

She'd longed to tell him to get lost, but how could she have done when the National Health Service waiting list had been so long, and her grandmother, not only in severe pain had also been frustrated by her growing incapacity. And her increasing poverty. Harford Hall, the greystone Georgian house Flavia had been brought up in, was a money pit, like all large, old houses, and maintenance and repairs swallowed her widowed grandmother's dwindling income from stocks and shares. There were no spare thousands left over to pay for a private operation.

So, despite her deep reluctance to be indebted to her father, Flavia had succumbed to his offer, and now, three years later, she was still paying him off in the way he had demanded.

Summoned to London to play the complaisant daughter, dressed to the nines, and chit-chatting, exchanging social nothings with people she couldn't care less about but whom her father either wanted to impress or wanted to do lucrative business with. She was playing a role just as much as if she had been an actress on a stage. A role she hated for its falseness and hypocrisy, with her father treating her in public as if she were the apple of his eye, doting and devoted, when the truth was completely different.

Now, though, it was even more of an ordeal than ever. Since her hip operation, though successful, her grandmother had started to deteriorate mentally, and for the last two years her dementia had been remorselessly worsening. It meant that leaving her even for a few days, as she was doing now, made Flavia even more anxious about her. Although one of her grandmother's carers, who came in regularly to help relieve Flavia for an hour or two so that she could drive into the local market town to get the shopping and other essentials done, was staying with her, it didn't stop the anxiety nagging at her. But her father had been particularly insistent she come up to London this week.

'No bloody excuses!' he'd fumed. 'I don't give a toss about the old bat. You get yourself on the next train. I've got people coming over tomorrow evening, and it's got to look good!'

Flavia had frowned—and not just at the summons. There had been an edge to her father's voice that was new. A note of strain. Cynically, Flavia had put it down to discord between her father and his latest girlfriend, Anita, whom Flavia could see across the room, wearing a fortune around her neck. She was a demanding mistress, and maybe her avarice was beginning to grate.

The impression of her father being under new tension had

been intensified when Flavia had arrived at the apartment. He'd been shorter with her than ever, and clearly preoccupied.

But not so much that he had not gripped her elbow as the guests started to arrive.

'I've got someone particularly important turning up to-night, and I want you to keep him smiling—got it?' Her father's cold eyes had flickered over her. 'You *should* be able to hold his interest—he likes his women, and he likes them to be lookers. And that's one thing you're good for! But lose all the damn barbed wire around you—why the hell you can't be more approachable, I don't know!'

It was a familiar accusation, and one that Flavia always ignored. She was polite, she was civil, and she was sociable to her father's guests, whoever they were—but never more than that. There were limits to how much of a hypocrite she would be…

'Approachable like Anita?' Flavia had suggested sweetly, knowing how much her father hated his girlfriend's predilection for openly flirting with other men.

Annoyance had flared in his face, but he'd snapped back, 'Women like her get results! They know how to make up to a man and get what they want. *You* don't make the slightest effort. Well, tonight you'd better. Like I said, it's important.'

The edge had been back in his voice, and Flavia had wondered at it. Not that it took too much wondering. Obviously one of this evening's guests was to be someone her father intended to do some highly lucrative deal with, and when money was at stake, increasing his wealth, her father, she thought cynically, put the highest priority on it. And if that meant wanting his own daughter to smarm over some fat, ageing businessmen, it didn't bother him in the least.

Filled with distaste at her father's unsavoury tactics, Flavia had pulled away from him and gone forward to greet the first arrivals, a polite but remote smile on her face. She knew she came across as stand-offish, but there was no way she was going to ape the likes of Anita, and pout her lips and flutter her eyelashes at the influential businessmen her father wanted her to charm!

She glanced unenthusiastically over the chattering guests, and as she did so, she stilled. Something had caught her attention. Correction—some*one* had caught her attention…

He must have just arrived, for he was standing by the double doors that led out into the wide entrance hall of the huge apartment, a glass of champagne in his hand. He was looking into the crowded room, his eyes resting on someone she couldn't see from this angle. She found she was glad of it, because what she wanted to do, she realised with some dim part of her mind, was look at him.

He drew her eye, drew her focus—made it impossible for her to look away. Impossible…

Impressions stormed in her mind.

Tall—broad-shouldered—dark-haired—strong features starkly defined.

He made her want to stare, and that sent a hollowing arrow through her, stilling the breath in her throat.

There was an air about him as he stood there, one hand thrust into his trouser pocket, the other holding his champagne glass, looking tall and lean and very, *very* assured.

He was a rich man. She could see that easily. Not just because of his bespoke suit and clearly expensively cut sable hair, but because of the aura he projected, the air of supreme control.

A man to draw eyes.

Especially female eyes.

And she could see why—helplessly acknowledged the effortless power of his frame, the strongly defined features that comprised a blade of a nose, a planed jawline, a wide, mobile mouth and, above all, the dark, opaque, hooded eyes that were resting, focussed and targeted, on whoever it was he was looking at.

Who is he?

The question formed itself in her head, though the moment it did so she tried to erase it. What did it matter who he was? There were any number of people at her father's parties, and one more or less made no difference. But even as she thought it she knew it was not true. Not for this man. This man was different...

She swallowed, freeing the breath that had been stuck in her throat, and as she did she realized with a start that her pulse had quickened. Realised, too, with more than a start, with a hollowing, knifing dawning, that somehow—and she didn't know how, couldn't know how—the man's gaze had shifted, pulled away from whoever it was in the room he'd been looking at and he was now looking at *her*...

Right at her.

Instantly, instinctively, she veiled her eyes, shutting him out of her vision as if he were some kind of threatening presence—disturbing and disruptive—making herself invisible to him.

Tautly, she returned her gaze to the people she was with, and haltingly resumed her conversation. But her mind was in tumult, and when, some indeterminate time later, she heard her father's voice directed at her, she welcomed the interruption to her mental consternation.

'Flavia, my darling, over here a moment!' he called in the doting, caressing voice he always used to her in public.

Dutifully she made her way towards him, trying to put out of her head the image engraved on her retinas of the darkly disturbing man who had so riveted her. She could feel agitation increasing her heart-rate.

As she approached her father the shifting pattern of guests moved, showing that there was someone standing beside him. Her agitation spiked erratically and her eyes flared involuntarily.

It was the man who had drawn her eye—more than her eye—a moment ago. Numbly, she walked up to her father, who was smiling with a benign air. 'Darling.' Her father's hand reached for her arm and closed over it. 'I'd like to introduce you—'

Flavia let herself be pulled forward. Her mouth had gone dry again. She could hear her father saying something, but it was like a buzz in her ears. All she could focus on was the man standing with her father. The same tall, broad-shouldered, confident-stanced man she'd seen in the doorway.

'Leon Maranz. And this is my daughter, Flavia.'

Her father's voice was affectionate and indulgent, but Flavia didn't care. All she could do right now was gather her composure, which had no reason—*no reason*, she echoed vehemently—to go all to pieces like this.

With palpable effort she made herself speak, forcing herself to say what was socially required. 'How do you do, Mr Maranz?' she said. Her tone was clipped, distant. Her acknowledging glance at him was the merest flicker, the barest minimum that social courtesy demanded.

She wanted urgently to take a step back, to move away, keep her distance. Up close like this, the impression he'd made on her that she'd found so disturbing even from halfway across the room was a hundred times stronger. Just as before she took in height, easily topping six feet, and shoulders sheathed, like the rest of his lean body, with the material of a bespoke handmade suit that, like the pristine white shirt he wore, stretched across a torso that was honed and taut. He might scream 'filthy rich', but fat cat he was not…

More like a sleek-coated jaguar…

That strange, disturbing, subliminal shiver seemed to go through her again as the thought passed across the surface of her mind.

'Ms Lassiter…'

The voice acknowledging her clipped greeting was deep, almost a drawl. There was an accent to it, but not an identifiable one. She didn't need a foreign name, or a foreign accent, to know that the last thing this lean, powerful, disturbing man was British. The natural olive hue of his tanned skin, the sloe-darkness of his eyes, the sable of his hair and the strong, striking features all told her that—had told her so right from the moment she'd set eyes on him.

Her eyes flickered over him again, trying not to see him, trying to shut him out. She saw something glint briefly, swiftly gone, in his dark, black-lashed eyes—something that exacerbated the strange shiver that was still going through her.

She fought for control. *Self*-control. This was ridiculous! Absurd to be so affected by a complete stranger—some rich, foreign business acquaintance of her father that she neither knew nor cared about, nor had any reason at all to be so… so…*reactive* to!

Her spine stiffened and she could feel the motion drawing her body slightly away from Leon Maranz's powerful orbit. Withdrawing a fraction—an essential fraction. Again, just for a barest moment, she thought she saw that dark glint in his eyes come again, and vanish.

She took a breath, instinctively knowing she was being less than courteous but feeling an almost atavistic urge to get away from the impact he was having on her. She gave the barest nod of acknowledgement to his return of her greeting, then turned her head towards her father. The relief of being able to look away was palpable.

'I must check with the caterers,' she announced. 'Do excuse me.'

She could see her father's face darken, knew she was being borderline rude, but she couldn't help it. Every instinct was telling her to go—get away—right away from the man she'd just been introduced to.

Her glance flickered back to him, as brief as she could make it. His expression was empty, closed. She knew she was being impolite, but she didn't care. Couldn't afford to allow herself to care about her rudeness, her glaringly obvious reluctance to engage in any kind of social exchange with him.

'Mr Maranz.' Again the barest nod towards him, and then

she turned on her heel trying not to hurry, as she found herself wanting to do, to wave to the doors leading into the dining room, where a sumptuous buffet had been laid out by the hired caterers.

As she gained the sanctuary of the other room she felt her tension immediately ease. But not her heart-rate. That, she realised, was still elevated.

Why? Why was she reacting like this to that man?

She'd met any number of rich, foreign businessmen at her father's social gatherings—so why was this one playing havoc with her nerves?

Because none of them had ever looked the way this one did!

None of them had had those dark, saturnine looks. None of them had had that packed, powerful frame. None of them had had that air about them that spoke not just of wealth but a lot more...

But what *was* that more...?

As she made herself walk the length of the buffet, pretending to inspect it, absently lifting a silver fork here and there to occupy herself, she knew exactly what that 'more' was. Whatever name you gave it, he had it—in spades.

She took an inward breath. It didn't matter what he had, or that he had it, she told herself resolutely. And it certainly didn't matter that she'd taken one look at him and felt its impact the way she had. Leon Maranz might be the most compellingly attractive man in the universe—it was nothing to her! *Could* be nothing to her.

Her face tightened grimly. She would never, *never* have anything to do with anyone she'd met through her father! Oh, he'd been keen enough on the idea of her socialising in that way—had actively encouraged it, despite her gritty resistance to any further manipulation by him for his own ends. Leon Maranz was part of her father's world—and that meant she wanted nothing to do with him, whatever the impact he had on her!

Her expression changed. Bleakly she stared at the picture hanging on the wall above the buffet table. There was another overpowering reason why it was pointless for her to react in any way at all to Leon Maranz. Even if he'd been nothing to do with her father she *still* couldn't have anything to do with him.

She wasn't free to have anything to do with *any* man.

Sadness pierced her. Her life was not her own now—it was dedicated to her grandmother, dedicated to caring for her in this the twilight of her life. It was her grandmother who needed her, and after all her grandmother had done in raising her, caring for her and loving her, devoting her life to her, she would never, never abandon her!

Flavia's eyes shadowed. Day by day the dementia was increasing, taking away more and more of the grandmother she loved so much, and whilst it broke her heart to see her declining, it was even worse to think of what must inevitably one day happen. But until that time came she would look after her grandmother—whatever it took. Including, she knew, dancing to her father's tune like this.

Other than these brief, unwelcome periods away from home, she would confine her life entirely to the needs of her grandmother, stay constantly at her side. She would do nothing that wasn't in her grandmother's best interests. And if that meant denying herself the kind of life that she might have been leading as an independent solo woman of twenty-five—well, she would accept that.

So it really didn't matter a jot that her father's guest had had such a powerful impact on her—it was completely irrelevant! Leon Maranz was nothing to do with her, *could* be nothing to her, and would stay that way.

She gave a little shake of her head. For heaven's sake—just because he'd had an impact on her, obviously it didn't mean she'd had an impact on *him*. OK, so he'd seen her looking at him when he'd been standing near the doorway, but so what? With looks like his, a magnetically brooding presence like his, every other women here would have done the same—were doubtless doing it right now! All she had to do was get a grip, stop reacting to him in this ridiculous way, and avoid him for the rest of the evening. Simple.

'Tell me, are you always so short with your guests?'

She spun round, dismay and shock etched in her face.

Leon Maranz was standing not a metre away from her in the empty room. His expression, she could see instantly, was forbidding. Equally instantly every resolution she'd just made about getting a grip on her composure and not reacting to him utterly vanished. She could feel herself go into urgent self-protective, defensive mode. She stiffened.

'I beg your pardon?'

The words might be polite, might theoretically mean what they were saying, but her tone implied utterly the opposite. It was as freezing and as clipped as if she was cutting the words out of the air with a pair of the sharpest scissors.

His expression hardened at the icy tone. 'You should,' he said. 'What reason did you have for snubbing me when your father introduced me?'

'I didn't snub you!' She spoke shortly, aware with part of her mind that she was once again bordering on rudeness, even though she didn't mean to be. But her nerves were on edge—yet again. His presence seemed to generate such an overpowering reaction in her she couldn't cope well with it.

He raised a sardonic eyebrow. 'What do you do when you *do* snub someone, then?' There was a taunt in his voice, but beneath the taunt was another note. Something she could recognise because she knew there was justification for it.

Anger.

For a moment, just the briefest moment, she almost made a decision to do what she knew she must—apologise. Mollify him with a soft word. Defuse the situation. But even as she made that resolve, she made the fatal mistake of meeting his eyes.

And in them was an expression that she'd have recognised even if she'd been blind.

She'd have felt it on her skin—felt it in the sudden heat of her blood, the quickening of her pulse. Felt the wash of his eyes, the open message in them. Felt the breathless congestion in her chest.

He was looking her over…signalling his sexual interest in her…making it plain…

For one long, disastrous moment she was helpless, out of control, taking the full force of what was being directed at her. She could feel the hot, tumid breathlessness in her lungs, the flare of heat in her veins, and then—even worse—the betraying flush of her skin. A tautening all through her body, as if a flame were licking over her…

She couldn't move. Couldn't break away from the eyes holding hers.

Then slowly, deliberately, he smiled. Lines indented around his mouth, emphasising the strong blade of his nose, the sensual twist of his lips. Long lashes swept briefly down over his sloe-dark eyes.

'Shall we start again, Ms Lassiter?' he murmured, and the deep, faintly accented voice was rich with satisfaction.

And she knew why—because he now knew *exactly* the reason she'd been so short with him. Had found a reason for it that brought that sensual smile to his lips. The smile that was playing havoc with her resolve to be immune to him, to have nothing whatsoever to do with him!

For one endless moment her mind hung in the balance. All she had to do was smile back. Let the stiffness of her spine soften…let the rejection in her eyes dissolve. Accept her reaction to him…accept what he was so clearly offering her. The opportunity to share what was flaring between them so powerfully, so enticingly, to explore with him a new, sensual world that she had never before encountered but which was now drawing her like an enticing flame…

No!

It was impossible! Unthinkable. Leon Maranz moved in a world she didn't want to have anything to do with. The slick, shallow, glossy, money-obsessed world her father inhabited, which was nothing to do with the reality of *her* life—a reality that had no room in it for any priority other than her grandmother. A life that could have no place for Leon Maranz or anything he offered.

No place!

Which meant it was time to stop this now. Right now.

Before it's too late...

The disturbing words whispered in her head, and she knew she had to cut them out—decisively and sharply. Stop what must not start.

'I don't think so, Mr Maranz.'

Her voice was like a scalpel, severing the air between them. Severing the opportunity to negate the rudeness she knew he did not deserve, but which she was driven to deliver from a sense of urgent, primitive self-preservation.

Because if she didn't—if she allowed him to get through to her, to smile at her...smile *with* her...get past her defences—then what would happen?

What would happen if she let him 'start again'?

The question rang inside her head, demanding an answer. An answer she refused to give. Not now—not when the adrenaline was pumping in her veins and dominating her mind, urging her to do the only sensible, safe thing even if it meant being rude. She needed to minimise her exposure to this man by any means possible.

She gave a small smile, tight and insincere—dismissive. 'Do please excuse me...'

She walked off, unbearable tension in her back, knowing with a cold burning in her body that she had behaved inexcusably rudely, but knowing she had had to do so. Because the alternative—the one that she'd thrust out of her head urgently, ruthlessly—was unthinkable.

Quite, quite unthinkable.

Behind her, as he watched her threading her way back into the crowded, opulent reception room, Leon Maranz stood, his face tight.

Anger was spiking in him. Yet again she'd blanked him! Cut him dead. Then walked off as if he didn't exist!

His eyes, watching her stalk back into the main reception room, darkened to black slits. Emotion seethed in him as she disappeared from view. Her rudeness was breathtaking! Unbelievable!

Who the hell does she think she is to do that to me? To hand that out to me? Talk to me in that way?

Once again he felt that old, suffocating, burning sensation in his chest that he'd used to feel long years ago. He had thought it would never strike him again. Yet at Flavia Lassiter's curt dismissiveness it had reared up in familiar, ugly fashion. Bringing with it memories he didn't want. Memories he'd left far, far behind.

He fought it back, mastering the destructive, dark emotion, refusing to let it poison his mind. It was unnecessary to evoke it now—that burning sense of being looked down on, looked through, that had evoked his burst of anger at her. No, her rude rebuff of him was not for *that* reason. He forced control over his wayward reaction to her cutting rejection, subduing it. In its place he reached for an alternative—an explanation for her rudeness, her dismissal of him, that was far more palatable to him. One he could seize on.

Every masculine instinct told him there *was* another, quite different reason for her behaviour. One he should welcome, not resent. Her glacial attitude might have attempted to freeze him out, but all it had done was reinforce a quite different interpretation.

It was only a mask. A mask she had adopted in an attempt—however futile!—to conceal from him her true reaction to him. A reaction he had seen flare betrayingly in her eyes as he had smiled at her. It had told him exactly what he'd wanted to know, confirmed what he had felt with every masculine instinct, with all his years of experience in feminine response—a reaction that mirrored his to her.

Desire.

A simple, brief word, but it was the one he wanted—the only one he wanted. Nothing else. Because desire was the only emotion he wanted to associate with Flavia Lassiter. Everything else about her could be put aside as unnecessary for what he wanted. And pointless—and destructive.

The anger that had spiked in him as she'd stalked away ebbed away completely, the bunched tension in his muscles relaxing. There was no need for either anger or tension. No need at all. He was sure of it. Flavia Lassiter could be as dismissive of him as she liked, but it was only a mask—a futile attempt to deny what it was useless for her to deny. The fact that everything about her told him she was as responsive to him as he was to her.

Tension eased from his shoulders. His features lightened. He strolled back into the main reception room, a strategy forming rapidly in his mind. For now he would let her be. It was clear to him she was fighting his impact on her, and that she was resisting facing up to it. OK, it *was* sudden. He allowed that. And for a woman like her, clearly used to being in strict control of herself, adept at presenting an outwardly composed and indifferent front, that was understandable. For the moment, then, she could stay safely behind the crystalline shield she was holding him at bay with. When the time was right he would shatter it completely. And get from her exactly what he knew with complete certainty now he definitely wanted...

As did she...

It was just a matter of time before she accepted it. That was all. A slight smile started to play around Leon's mouth. The prospect of persuading her was very, very enjoyable.

CHAPTER TWO

How Flavia got through the rest of the evening she didn't know. It seemed to go on for ever. She kept a perpetual eye open for Leon Maranz, and was grateful he seemed to be keeping himself away from her. She could see her father with him and Anita sometimes—clearly more than happy to be so—but more often than that he was surrounded by any number of other guests. Especially female ones, she noticed without surprise and with a distinct tightening of her mouth. She avoided her father as well, because the last thing she wanted was to have him grill her on why she'd been so short to his favoured guest.

Her avoidance continued even when the endless party finally wound down, the guests all left, and her father and Anita headed off to a nightclub. Whether or not Leon Maranz had gone with them she didn't know, and refused to care. She could feel only relief that he had gone, and that the ordeal of the evening was finally over.

The moment she could, Flavia disappeared into her bedroom. For the first time since her gaze had lighted on Leon Maranz that evening she started to feel the tension ebb out of her. Safe at last, she thought with relief.

But as she stood under the shower some minutes later she had cause to question that assumption. Leon Maranz might be out of the apartment but he was not out of her head. Far from it...

The water pouring over her naked body was not helping—running down her torso, between the valley of her breasts, down her flanks, her limbs... It was a sensuous experience that she was all too aware was the last thing she should be experiencing when trying to put out of her head the image of the man who had caught her attention, impacted upon her as no other man had.

As she massaged shower gel into her skin, its warm soapy suds laving her body, she could feel her breasts reacting, see in her mind's eye those dark hooded eyes resting on her as if he were viewing her naked body...

No!

It was insane to let her mind conjure such things! Leon Maranz wasn't going to see her again, let alone see her naked body, for heaven's sake! Time to put him totally out of her mind.

With a sharp movement she switched the shower dial to cool and doused herself in chilly water, then snapped the flow off completely. Stepping out of the stall, she grabbed a bath-towel and rubbed herself dry with brisk, no-nonsense vigour. It was completely irrelevant that Leon Maranz had had the effect on her that he had! It was an effect every woman there had shared, so she was hardly unique. And even if—*if*, she instructed herself ruthlessly—he had made it clear in that brief, fraught exchange by the buffet that he was eyeing her up, that only made it *more* imperative that she put him completely out of her head!

Nothing can come of this and nothing is going to. That is that. End of.

She dropped her towel, donned her nightdress, and climbed into bed. Then she reached for her mobile. Time to check with Mrs Stephens on how her grandmother had been this evening.

Familiar anxiety stabbed in her mind, displacing her troubling thoughts about Leon Maranz and his disturbing impact on her with even more troubled thoughts. The constant worry she felt about her grandmother surfaced again through the layers of her ridiculous obsessing about a man who meant absolutely nothing to her, whom she'd only seen for a few hours, and exchanged only a few words with.

Angry with herself for the way she'd reacted that evening, when there were real worries and concerns for her to focus on about the one person she loved in this world, she settled herself into bed and phoned home. It was late, she knew, but Mrs Stephens would be awake, and these days her grandmother could be awake for hours into the night sometimes. It was one of the things that made it so wearing to care for her, Flavia admitted, labour of love though it was for her.

When she spoke to the carer Flavia was relieved to hear that her grandmother was quite soporific, and seemed not to have realised her granddaughter was not in the house. It was a blessing, Flavia knew, because it would have made these visits to London at her father's behest even less endurable knowing that her grandmother was at home, fretting for her.

What did cause her grandmother unbearable distress, though, was being away from home herself. Flavia had discovered that when, some six months ago, her grandmother had had a fall and had had to spend a week in hospital being checked over and monitored. It had been dreadful to see how agitated and disturbed her grandmother had become, trying to get out of the hospital bed, her mental state anguished, tearful. Several times she'd been found wandering around the ward incoherent, visibly searching for something, distressed and flailing around.

Yet the moment she'd come back home to Harford the agitation had left her completely and she'd reverted to the much calmer, happier, and more contented person that her form of dementia allowed her to be. From then on Flavia had known that above all her grandmother had to remain in the familiar, reassuring surroundings where she had lived for over fifty years, since coming to Harford as a young bride. Whatever the dimness in her mind, she seemed to know that she was at home, and presumably it felt safe and familiar to her there, wandering happily around, or just sitting quietly, gazing out over the gardens she had once loved to tend.

Flavia gave a sad smile. It still pained her to see her beloved grandmother so mentally and physically frail, but she knew that at the end of a long life her grandmother was starting to take her leave of it. Just when that would happen no one could say, except that it was coming ever closer. Flavia was determined that, come what may, if it was at all medically possible her grandmother would die in her own home, with her granddaughter at her side.

Her gaze grew distant as she stared blankly at the far wall opposite the bed. Just what she would do once her grandmother died was still uncertain, but she knew she would do her very best to hang on to Harford. She loved it far too much to let it go. Her plan was to run it as an upmarket holiday let, though it would require modernising for the bathrooms and kitchen, plus general refurbishment—all of which would require some kind of upfront financing, on top of coping with the inevitable death duties. One thing was certain, though— her father wouldn't offer her a penny to help.

Not that she would take it. It was bad enough owing him for her grandmother's hip operation, let alone anything else. Her father, she thought bitterly, was *not* a good man to be in hock to… Who knew how he might wield such power over her head?

She reached out to turn off the bedside light. There was no point thinking about anything other than her current concerns. Her grandmother's needs were her priority, and that was that. There was no room in her life for anything else.

Any*one* else.…

Yet as she slowly sank into slumber echoes seemed to be hazing in her memory—a deep, drawling voice, a strong-featured face, dark, unreadable eyes…holding hers…

Leon Maranz poured himself a brandy, swirling it absently in his hand. His face was shuttered.

He was alone in his apartment, though he might easily have had companionship. He knew enough women in London who would have rushed to his side at the merest hint of a request for their company. Even at Lassiter's cocktail party he could have had his pick had he wanted to. Including—he gave an acid smile devoid of humour—Lassiter's current *inamorata*, who had shown her interest and looked openly disappointed when he'd declined her pressing suggestion that he accompany them to a nightclub.

What would she have done, he thought cynically, had he decided to amuse himself by inviting her back here? Would she have played the affronted female and gone rushing back to her ageing lover's side? Or would the temptation to gain a lover much, much richer than Lassiter—and so much closer to her in age have overcome whatever scruples she had left in life? And what would Lassiter himself have done? Tolerated the man he so badly wanted to do business with bedding his own mistress? His cynicism deepened.

Not that he would have put either of the pair to such a test. Anita's bleached-blonde, over-made-up looks had no allure for him—nor the voluptuous figure so blatantly on display. When it came to women his tastes were far more selective compared to the likes of Lassiter.

An image flickered in his mind's eye as he slowly swirled the brandy in its glass. Flavia Lassiter was cut from a quite different cloth than her father's overdone mistress.

Contemplatively Leon let his mind delineate her figure, her fine-boned features that were of such exceptional quality. The very fact that she did not flaunt her beauty had only served to draw his eye to her the more. Did she not realise that? Did she not see that hers was a rare beauty that could not be concealed, could not be repressed or denied? Leon's dark eyes glinted as he raised his brandy glass to his nose, savouring the heady bouquet. She could not repress or deny what she had betrayed when she'd met his gaze, what had been evident to him—blazingly so—in the flare of her pupils, the slight but revealing parting of her lips. She had responded to him just as he to her. That had told him everything he needed to know...

His expression hardened. The curt disdain she had handed out, dismissing him, burned like a brand in his mind. Had it indeed been nothing more than an attempt to deny her response to his interest in her—for reasons he could not fathom? Since he did not intend that denial to persist he could afford to ignore it. An expression entered his eyes that had not been there for many, many years. Or had it been the result of something quite different? Something he had not encountered for a long time, but which could still slide like a knife through the synapses of his memory.

Like clips from an old movie, memories shaded through his mind, taking him far, far away from where he was now. To a world...a universe away from where he was standing in this five-star hotel suite, wearing a hand-tailored suit costing thousands, enjoying the finest vintage brandy and everything else that his wealth could give him effortlessly, in as much abundance as he wanted.

His life had not always been like that...

It was the cold he could remember. The bitter, biting cold of Europe in winter. Icy wind cutting through the thin material of his shabby clothes. The crowded, anonymous streets of the city where he was just one more homeless, desperate denizen, pushed aside, ignored, resented.

Making his way slowly and painfully in that harsh, bleak world, grabbing what jobs he could, however menial, however hard, however badly paid—jobs that the citizens of the country he had come to did not want to do, that were beneath them, but not beneath the desperate immigrants and refugees grateful to get them.

He had become used to being looked down on, looked through as if he did not exist, as if those looking through him didn't *want* him to exist. He had got used to it—but he had never, even in his poorest days, swallowed it easily. It had made him angry, had driven him ever onwards, helping to fire and fuel his determination to make something of himself, to ensure that one day no one would look through him, no one would think him invisible.

Yet even now, it seemed, his hand tightening unconsciously around the brandy glass, when he moved in a stratospheric world with ease and assurance, that anger, the cause of which was long, long gone, still possessed some power over him...

Why? That was the question that circled in his mind now, as he stood in his luxurious hotel suite, savouring the vintage brandy, enjoying the bountiful fruits of his hard work, his determination and drive. Why should that anger still come? Why should it have a power over him?

And who was *she* to have the ability to revive that anger? Who was she, that upper-crust daughter of Alistair Lassiter, to look through him as if he were as invisible as the impoverished immigrant he had once been? Someone to serve drinks, clear tables, to wait hand and foot on wealthy women like her? Who was she to blank him, snub him, consign him to the ranks of those whose existence was barely acknowledged?

He could feel his anger stab like the fiery heat of the brandy in his throat. Then, forcing himself to lessen his grip on the glass, he inhaled deeply, taking back control of his emotions, subduing that bite of anger. The anger was unnecessary. Because surely, he argued, his first explanation of Flavia Lassiter's coldness was the correct one—she was fighting her own response to him, and it was *that* that had made her avoid meeting his eyes, made her so curt towards him. That was the explanation he must adhere to. For reasons he as yet found unfathomable, but would not for very much longer, she was trying to hold him at bay.

A cynical glint gleamed in his eye. Alistair Lassiter would be overjoyed by his interest in his daughter. He would see it, Leon thought cynically, as an opportune way of keeping him close—something Lassiter was extremely keen to do.

The cynical glint deepened. Right now Maranz Finance was Lassiter's best hope of saving his sinking, profligate business empire from complete collapse…

CHAPTER THREE

FLAVIA was sitting, tight-lipped, in the back of her father's limo. Her face was set. On the other side of her father, Anita leant forward.

'You look *so* good, sweetie, with your hair down and some red lippy,' she informed Flavia, sounding pleased with herself. 'It really jazzes up that dress.' As her false eyelashes swept up and down over Flavia, they cast a critical eye over the gown the younger woman was wearing. 'Great style—just a shame about the draggy colour.'

Flavia's expression changed minutely. She'd been despatched with Anita that afternoon by her father to buy herself 'something glamorous for a change' as he'd snapped at her, looking the worse for wear after his late night, his eyes bloodshot and his face puffy.

Flavia had objected, but her father had been adamant.

'We're going to a flash charity bash tonight, and just for a damn change I don't want you dressing like a nun!'

Knowing Anita's predilection for bling, Flavia had been on her guard, and when the other woman had picked out a clingy scarlet number she'd at least succeeded in swapping it for a pale aqua version at the counter, while Anita had been trying on the ruched and sequinned purple gown she was poured into now. Discovering the colour swap when Flavia had emerged from a bedroom before setting off had so annoyed Anita, however, that she'd managed to unpin Flavia's tightly knotted chignon and flash her own bright red lipstick over her mouth just as Alistair Lassiter was hurrying them out of the apartment to the waiting limo.

He was visibly on edge, Flavia could tell—but then she was as well. The moment they arrived at the Park Lane hotel where the charity event was being held she would dive into the Ladies' and wipe Anita's vivid lipstick off her, and repin her hair.

But her intentions were foiled. As they made their way into the hotel Anita's hand fastened around her wrist. 'Don't even *think* about it!' she breathed, and her hand remained clamped where it was.

Stiffly, feeling self-conscious enough as it was in the bias-cut gown, let alone with her hair loose and heaven only knew how much garish lipstick, Flavia had no option but to let herself be swept forward into the banqueting hall. They were, as her father had complained, running late, and everyone except a few other latecomers like themselves had already taken their seats at the appointed tables.

Threading her way towards their table, flanked by her father and Anita, Flavia could only determine a sea of people and hear a wave of chatter and the clink of glasses and rustle of gowns. Her father was greeting people here and there, and Anita was waving conspicuously at people she knew, too, while Flavia looked neither to left or right. When they reached their table, with their three places waiting for them, she slipped into the seat on her father's right hand side with a sense of relief.

The relief lasted less than a second.

'Ms Lassiter...'

The deep, accented voice on her right made her head whip round.

Leon Maranz was seated beside her.

Emotion sliced through her. Shock and dismay were uppermost. But beneath both another emotion stabbed. Instantly she fought to subdue it, but the physical impact was too great, and she could feel that treacherous quickening of her blood. Feel, even more powerfully, the urge to get to her feet and bolt.

Why—why was she reacting like this to the man? It was absurd to be so...so...

So...what, exactly? She flailed around in her mind, trying to find the word she needed. Trying to blank out the way she was reacting. Trying to wipe the dismay and shock from her face. Trying to gather her composure and force herself to do what she had to do—which was simply to nod civilly, politely, courteously and nothing more than that. Nothing at all.

'Mr...Maranz, isn't it?' She hesitated over his name, as if she had difficulty recalling it. Then she made a show of flicking open her linen napkin and spreading it over her knees. She was grateful, for once, for her father's presence, as he leant across her.

'Ah—Leon. Good to see you!' he said effusively. 'I'm so pleased you accepted my invitation to be my guest here tonight.'

At Flavia's side Leon Maranz's eyes glittered darkly, and he found himself reconsidering his decision to attend the function as Lassiter's guest. Despite his attraction to Flavia Lassiter, *should* he have come this evening? Yes, she had made an immediate impact on him the moment he'd set eyes on her, but was it truly a good idea to pursue his interest in her? The glitter in his eyes intensified. Especially since it meant he would have to spend time in Alistair Lassiter's over-attentive company this evening.

Even if he did decide to invest in his business, socialising with the man was not necessary—unless, of course, it was a means to an end in respect of his daughter...

On that note, it was clear from her frosty reception of his greeting that she was still very much on her guard with him. Was it truly worth his time and effort to thaw that freezing demeanour? Yet even as he considered it he knew, with a little stab of emotion, that seeing her again had in no way lessened his response to her. Indeed, it had been accentuated...

He had had time only for a moment's appreciation, but that had been enough to confirm that the sinuous gown she was wearing, baring shoulders over which the shimmering fall of her loosened hair was cascading, not to mention the sensuous, vivid scarlet of her mouth, were a stunning enhancement of the beauty he'd seen last night. Tonight, he thought appreciatively, there was no question of her seeking to subdue her beauty with the severity of her dress or sedate maquillage. The effect was—stunning.

Decision raced through him. Yes, Flavia Lassiter, despite her father, was well worth pursuing.

As for her father—well, he would put up with him as best he could this evening, and for the moment reserve judgement on whether he would supply the bail-out that Lassiter was so desperately in need of.

Leon's mouth pressed to a thin line. What kind of fool was Alistair Lassiter to have got himself into such an irretrievable mess? The global recession should have made him cautious, but instead Lassiter had taken unwarrantable risks—too many of them—and his spending had been lavish. Now he was teetering on the brink of complete collapse. Now he was going to have to rely on a turnaround specialist like Maranz Finance to rescue him.

Leon's eyes were veiled. *Would* he bail out Lassiter? How much real value was there left in the company? And was it worth the trouble to secure it? Lassiter was walking on thin ice. Far too many of his assets, as Leon knew perfectly well from his own investigations, were paper-thin and his debt was punitive. For all the surface gloss he still reflected, Alistair Lassiter had precious little beneath. Even the Regent's Park apartment was mortgaged up to the hilt, and his other personal properties had already been sold off.

While he decided whether to bail out Lassiter he would further his interest in his daughter. He levelled his veiled gaze on her as she reached for a bottle of sparkling water and poured some into her glass. Waiters were already circling with white wine, but she'd covered her glass with her palm, giving her head a slight shake. Did she eschew all alcohol? Leon wondered.

'You don't drink wine?' he enquired.

She seemed to start at his words, and her head jerked around.

'Very seldom,' she answered, her voice clipped. She made to turn her head away again, as if that were all she were going to say on the subject.

'Empty calories?' Leon's voice was bland.

'Yes.'

She lifted her glass of water, aware of how stiffly she had spoken. But then her spine was as stiff as a poker right now. Why on earth had her father not told her he'd invited Leon Maranz this evening? The answer was obvious, of course. He hadn't wanted her to know because he hadn't wanted her to be warned beforehand. And now here she was, trapped between them, wearing a dress she didn't want to be wearing, with her hair hanging down her back and her mouth covered in vivid lipstick.

She raised her napkin and made a show of dabbing her lips after drinking, covertly attempting to dab off some of the sticky red layer. Beside her she was aware—ultra-aware—of Leon Maranz's eyes on her.

How on earth am I going to get through the evening?

The question was uppermost in her mind. Closely followed by its companion.

Why am I being like this?

She had met plenty of men her father wanted her to take an interest in for his sake, but she had never freaked out like this before! She had always managed to be indifferent, without being so ridiculously tongue-tied and affected. So why was she being like this with this man?

But then, she acknowledged, with a hollow sensation inside her, no one her father had tried to set her up with before had been anything like Leon Maranz.

No one could be...

The words formed in her mind, shaping themselves. No one could possibly have the kind of impact he had. It hadn't lessened in the slightest in the twenty-four hours since she had first experienced it. Instead it had intensified. She could feel it like a kind of forcefield. She was far, far too close to him for a start—hyper-aware of him only a few inches away from her at the table, knowing she only had to tilt her head slightly to see him, instead of straining forward, apparently finding the floral arrangement in the middle of the table absolutely fascinating.

But she could still sense him there sitting beside her, his powerful frame set off by the tuxedo, see from the corner of her eye his large, tanned hand reaching for his wine. Nor was sight the only sense he impinged upon. The deep, accented drawl of his voice was resonating in her head as well. And there was another sense, too, more subtle, yet there all the same. His raw, male scent assaulted her, overlaid by the slightest hint of something citrus, musky, in his aftershave.

She tried to blank it out but it was impossible. Just as blanking out his presence beside her was impossible, however doggedly she stared ahead and toyed with her water. The only mercy was that, thankfully, he seemed to have accepted her reluctance to engage in any conversation with him, however trivial, and had turned his attention to the woman on the other side of him. Flavia could hear her light tinkle of laughter, though what they were talking about she neither knew nor cared.

'Leon! I must have your opinion!'

Anita's piercing voice cut across her, demanding his attention. Flavia could have slapped her for it.

He turned towards her again, away from the woman on his right.

'On what?' he replied. His voice seemed reserved.

Anita flapped a heavily beringed hand. 'Don't you think

Flavia looks so much better with her hair loose rather than pinned up the way it was last night?'

Like two burning brands Flavia felt her cheeks flare. Anger and mortification warred within her. She wanted to snap viciously at Anita, but Leon Maranz was replying.

'Very…uninhibited,' he drawled, and Flavia could feel, like a physical touch, his eyes working over her.

The brands in her cheeks burnt fiercer.

'You see?' Anita's voice was triumphant. 'I told you, Flavia. You could look a knock-out if you tried more! I tell you, darling,' she said, 'if you can persuade Leon Maranz to admire you, you've got it made!' She gave a gush of laughter as insincere as it was overdone.

Flavia's expression iced over.

It remained like ice for the whole of the eternally long meal—it was the only way she could get through it.

She was given some mercy—Anita laid off her, and Leon Maranz, when he wasn't talking to the woman on his right, or to the other guests across the table who seemed keen to engage his attention, talked to her father. Or rather, she realised, her father talked to Leon Maranz. The edginess he'd displayed earlier seemed to have vanished, and now he was in effusive mode, she could tell, mingling loud bonhomie with an eager attentiveness that told Flavia that, whatever potential use Leon Maranz was to him, it was considerable.

Was it reciprocated? she wondered as she steadily ate through the courses, despite a complete lack of appetite. Eating was easier than talking. So was being aware of what her father was doing.

But on what Leon Maranz was doing she was far less clear. There was no evidence of reciprocation, no evidence of anything except the fact that Leon Maranz seemed to prefer her father to do the talking. His laconic answers only seemed to drive her father onward. He was getting more and more exuberant—or, a sudden thought struck her, should that be more and more desperate?

She glanced sideways at her father. He'd loosened his bow tie slightly and his cheeks were reddening, his eyes becoming pouchy. His glass was frequently refilled, and Flavia wondered how much he'd had to drink. Distaste flickered in her face. Thank God she was going back home tomorrow. She couldn't wait to get away from her father, away from the shallow, money-obsessed life he lived. However worthy the cause of this evening's function, she didn't want to be here in this vast ornate banqueting room, with the scent of wine and flowers and expensive perfume everywhere, the glint of jewellery on the women and the sleek, fat-cat look of the men.

She wanted to be at home, at Harford, deep in her beloved countryside. Back with her grandmother in the quiet, familiar world so very dear to her…so very precious…

But for now all she could do was tough it out—get through the evening however long it seemed.

After an interminable length of time the meal and the fund-raising presentations from the charity directors finally drew to a close, with coffeepots and *petits-fours* and an array of liqueurs being placed on the tables. At the far end of the huge room on a little stage a band had formed, and was starting to strike up.

Flavia closed her eyes, trying to shut it all out. She wanted out of here. Now. But it wasn't going to happen. She knew that. And she also knew, with a heaviness that was tangible, that Anita and her father were going to head off to the dance floor, and she would be left with Leon Maranz. Unless—dear God, *please*, she found herself praying—he went off with someone else. But the woman on his other side had got up to dance as well, with her partner, and with a hollowing sensation Flavia realised that she was now sitting next to Leon Maranz with empty seats on either side of them.

Stiffly she reached for the coffeepot.

'Allow me.'

His hand was before her, lifting the heavy pot as though it weighed nothing and pouring coffee into her empty cup.

'Cream?' The drawling voice was solicitous.

She gave a minute shake of her head.

'Of course—more empty calories,' he murmured.

She shot him a look. It was a mistake.

A mistake, a mistake, a *mistake*.

He lounged back in his chair, one hand cupping a brandy glass. There was an air of relaxation about him, and yet there was something else that told Flavia at some alien, atavistic, visceral level of her being that he was not relaxed at all. That he was merely giving the impression of being relaxed.

It was in his eyes. They were heavy-lidded, yet she could see that they were resting on her with an expression that was not in the least somnolent.

For a second, almost overpoweringly, she wanted to get to her feet and run—run far and fast, right out of the building. But she couldn't. It was impossible. She couldn't do something so obviously, outrageously socially unacceptable.

She could head for the Ladies' Room, though.

She seized on the notion with relief. That would be OK—in fact it would be ideal, because then she could pin her hair up and make sure any trace of Anita's lipstick was gone.

She steeled herself to stand up, but before her stiffened limbs could move Leon Maranz pushed back his chair and surveyed her. His eyes moved back to hers, holding them effortlessly, and in the space of time it took to lock eyes with him she became paralysed, unable to move, breathe, to do anything at all except read in his dark obsidian eyes the unmistakable glint of an unmissable message.

Desire.

It was as flagrant as his audacity in letting his long-lashed eyes rest on her like a physical caress.

Tangible. Intimate…

She thrust up from her chair, stood up, every muscle taut like a wire under impossible tension. She had to go—right now.

'Do please excuse me. I really must…'

Her voice was high and clipped and breathless. Thoughts seared through her mind.

I can't cope with this! It's too flagrant, too overpowering, and it's all far, far too impossible! Impossible to have anything to do with a man from my father's world! Impossible to have anything to do with any man when my overwhelming responsibility is for my grandmother. So it doesn't matter—doesn't matter a jot what this ridiculous reaction to him is, I can't let it go anywhere, and I have to stop it in its tracks now. Right now!

But he wasn't to be evaded. Instead he matched her gesture, getting to his feet in a lithe, effortless movement, towering over her. Too close—much too close. She stepped back, trying not to bump into the empty chair beside her.

'You know…' he said, and his voice was a deep, dark drawl that set her nerve-endings vibrating at some weird, subliminal frequency. His eyes did not relinquish hers, did not allow her to tear her gaze away from his. 'I don't think I *do* excuse you, Ms Lassiter. Not two nights in a row.' The dark glint in his eye was shot through with something that upped that strange subliminal frequency. 'This time I think I will just do—*this*.'

He moved so fast she did not see it coming. His hand fastened around her wrist. Not tightly, not gripping it, but encircling it…imprisoning it.

He looked down at her, even taller somehow, his shoulders broader, his eyes darker.

'I'd like to dance with you,' he said.

He drew her hand into the crook of his arm so that her hand splayed involuntarily on the dark sleeve of his tuxedo jacket, her nails white against the smooth black cloth. She wanted to jerk free, tear herself away, but he was looking down at her still, a taunting smile playing on his lips.

'You don't want to make a scene, do you, Ms Lassiter?' he said, and a saturnine eyebrow quirked. The dark eyes were glinting. Mocking.

Emotion flashed in her eyes. For a wild and impossible moment, she wanted to do exactly what he'd said she could not—tug her hand free of its imprisonment, push away from him, storm off in a swirl of skirts and leave him standing there.

But there were too many people around. This was a formal function, with people who knew him, knew her father, knew who *she* was. Too many eyes were coming their way. Heads were turning at other tables set too close by.

He saw her dilemma, mocked it, and started to draw her away, towards the dance floor beyond. He could feel the stiffness of her body, the anger in the set of her shoulders. Well, he had anger of his own. Anger because she had spent the entire meal as if he did not exist, blanking him out, doing her best to ignore him, refusing to see him, talk to him. Refusing to do anything except the one thing she could not refuse.

She could not refuse to react to him.

Satisfaction—shot with grimness—spiked through him. That was the one thing she could not do. She could not hide her body's response to him. A response that shimmered from her just from his presence at her side, despite the tense straining of her body away from his.

They reached the dance floor. She resisted him every step of the way, but was helpless to do anything about it lest she break that unspoken code of her class—never make a scene, never draw attention to yourself, never break the rules of social engagement. And he would use that code ruthlessly for his own advantage—to get what he wanted. To draw her to him.

'Shall we?'

The taunt was in his low voice even as he turned her towards him, slipping a hand around her waist. His other hand clasped hers and he started to move her into the dance.

Helpless, Flavia could do nothing—nothing at all—to stop him.

Inside her breast, emotions stormed.

It was like being in torment—a torment that was lacerating every nerve-ending in her body. Everything about her body seemed to be registering physical sensation at double—triple—the intensity. She could feel his hand at her waist as if it were a brand, her hand clasped in his as if it were encased in steel. Steel sheathed in smoothest velvet.

And he was too close to her! Far, far too close! He was holding her, guiding her, turning her into the movements of the dance so that his body was counterpoised to hers, and hers was encircling his. Around and around they moved to the lush rhythm of the music, weaving through the press of other dancers. He was bending her pliantly into the dance, though her body felt as stiff as wood, and she could feel every muscle in her body seeking to strain away from him. It was as if he was endlessly drawing her towards him and she was endlessly resisting him, yet pinioned at her waist by the heat and pressure of his hand against her spine, the velvet steel of his hand around hers.

He was holding her captive.

And there was nothing she could do about it! Unless she broke free by force, tore herself away from him and stormed from the dance floor. And she couldn't do that. Couldn't because it would make a fuss, make a scene, draw eyes to her…

Couldn't because she didn't want to…

For a second—one fatal moment as the knowledge knifed through her brain like the edge of a sword, cleaving through her consciousness—she felt the tension in her body dissolve. Felt her body become pliant, supple.

And he felt it, too. She knew that he felt it, too, by the sudden flaring of his eyes to which she had suddenly lifted hers instead of what she was supposed to be doing, which was to stare rigidly, stonily over his shoulder.

Shock was in her gaze, and then that too dissolved, and she could feel the weight of her body shift as his hand at her waist seemed to deepen its support of her suddenly relaxed body. His fingers splayed out and she could feel each one fanning across her back, the thin silky material of her dress no barrier at all. And now his dark eyes held hers as she gazed helplessly across at him, feeling the warmth of his hand at her back, the warmth of his clasp on her other hand.

'You see...?'

His voice was low and intimate—disturbingly intimate, below the level of the music and the conversation all around them. There was a smile—knowing, satisfied—playing at his mouth as he spoke to her. He knew what she was doing, what she was feeling, how her body was reacting to his, how the rest of the world was disappearing, how there was nothing left except themselves, turning slowly together in each other's arms.

Each other's embrace.

Like a string jerking tight she strained away again, tensing all the lines of her body, maximising the distance between them, stiff and rigid once more. Her eyes cut away, gazed unseeingly out over the room; her lips compressed, hardening the contours of her face.

The music stopped, and she felt the tension racking her body lessen. Relief filled her that her torment was over. Impulsively she tugged her hand free, stepping away from him, not caring if the gesture was too abrupt for social usage. She couldn't afford to care.

'Do please excuse me.' Her voice was clipped and she would not look at him. Would not do anything except escape from the dance floor.

She threaded her way as rapidly as she could towards the doors that led out to the foyer, where she knew the powder room was. The ballroom was a blur, her only focus on gaining the haven of the Ladies'. Inside, she collapsed down on a velvet-covered stool in the vanity section of the spacious facilities.

Her reflection dismayed her.

Even in demure aqua, the bias cut of the dress did its work—far too well! It sheathed her body with glistening watered silk, its narrow straps showing too much bare shoulder and arm and—for her—too much décolletage, modest though it was by Anita's sultry standards.

But Anita's damage was worse than the style of the dress. Letting down her hair had completely changed the image she habitually presented to the world. Instead of a neat, confining chignon, her loosened hair formed a long, slinky coil down her bare back, its unfastened tresses softening her face. As for the slash of scarlet lipstick Anita had applied—even after several hours and Flavia's liberal use of her napkin over dinner—her lips still looked flushed and beestung.

Full and inviting…

She stared, transfixed. Oh, God—was that what Leon Maranz had been seeing all evening? All through dinner? And now—much worse—after that dreadful, disastrous dance her face had a hectic flush to it. Her pupils were distended, her breathing far too rapid.

This wasn't her! It wasn't! It *wasn't*! What had happened to her? Where had she gone, that restrained, composed female she strove to be when she was summoned to her father's side? Because one thing was glaringly, appallingly clear: she wasn't here any more. She wasn't sitting on this velvet stool, staring wide-eyed at the reflection gazing back at her. It was a different woman—a completely different woman! Alien and strange.

Sensual…

The word formed in her head and she instantly tried to shake it out, as she would a burr on her sleeve. But it wouldn't go. It would only wind itself sinuously around her consciousness, whispering its poison in her ear.

Sensual…

Instantly she rejected the word. It didn't matter. It didn't matter a jot what Leon Maranz could make her feel! She was not going to have anything to do with him! He belonged to the world of her father—a world in which making ever more money was the most important thing, and spending it as flashily and extravagantly as possible the next most important thing. A shallow, empty, superficial world! She belonged somewhere quite different. In the country, at home at Harford, with her grandmother who loved her so much, needed her so much...

Nothing could alter that,

So it was definitely time to put a stop to whatever Leon Maranz had in mind! A complete full stop. Time to send him a quite different message from the one she'd so disastrously given him by dancing with him.

Squaring her shoulders, she scooped up her hair, twisting it fiercely around her fingers until it was pinioned against the nape of her neck. Then, helping herself to some of the complementary hairgrips laid on for guests at the vanity unit, she ruthlessly pinned it into place. A tissue scrubbed repeatedly over her lips dealt with the remnants of Anita's wretched scarlet lipstick.

She got to her feet. Lifted her chin. She had the rest of the evening to get through somehow, but get through it she would—she must. She would refuse point-blank to dance with Leon Maranz again—refuse to do anything other than offer him the barest civility.

She stared at herself. With her hair up, her lips pale once more, she looked almost her normal self. Only the faint, betraying flush of the skin on her cheeks told of her discomfiture.

Unconsciously she felt the unseen pressure of his hand at her waist, hers on his shoulder. For one lingering moment she could *feel* Leon Maranz's touch...

Then, with a sharp little rasp in her throat, she got to her feet and walked out of the powder room.

CHAPTER FOUR

LEON levered his broad shoulders away from the wall that he'd been propping up while Flavia Lassiter hid from him in the Ladies' Room. Now, finally, she had emerged, as he'd known she would have to eventually, and was walking briskly forward. She'd managed to put her hair up again, and the last remnants of the stunning lipstick that had turned her mouth into a tempting curve had disappeared, but nothing could hide the sinuous beauty of her body in the elegant, figure-skimming evening dress.

As he straightened she saw him, and stopped dead. Colour flared in her cheeks and her eyes flashed. Satisfaction knifed through Leon. She could play the chilly ice-maiden all she liked, but she could not hide that physical, visceral response to him. The one she revealed every time he broke through her guard—every time she stopped holding him at bay the way she was so rigidly trying to do.

'There you are,' he said smoothly, reaching for her arm and tucking it into his with a proprietorial air.

Flavia clenched her teeth. How had he done it? How had he gone and helped himself to her like that? Yet again, just as before, she had the choice of either going along with him or tugging away and making a fool of herself in doing so in front of other people. Stiffly, she let him lead her back into the ballroom, back towards their table. Her hopes that her father and Anita—anyone at all!—might be there, were dashed. The table was deserted.

Courteously, Leon Maranz relinquished her in order to pull out her chair, and stiffly Flavia lowered herself onto it. Dear God, would this evening never end? Surely her father and Anita would get off the damn dance floor and come back? Even the sight of her father fawning over Leon Maranz and Anita flirting with him would be preferable to having to sit here like a sour lemon beside him, while he beckoned to one of the passing waiters to serve fresh coffee and refill his brandy glass.

Then he relaxed back in his chair, hooking one arm over the back and crossing one long leg over the other, and turned his face towards her. Long lashes dipped down over his glinting eyes.

'Your father's girlfriend was wrong,' he informed her. 'You look as beautiful with your hair up as down. But then—' his eyes washed over her consideringly, as if he were scrutinising an Old Master '—you are, of course, quite exceptional. As you must know.' He reached for his brandy glass and swirled the contents slowly. Even more slowly, almost contemplatively, he said, his tone inviting, 'But I am sure there is a great deal more to you than your exceptional beauty. Tell me about yourself. What do you do when you are not gracing events like this evening's? Do you have a career?' he enquired.

His gaze levelled on her and she looked away. She did not want to talk about her grandmother, or her life in Dorset. It was completely separate from these unwelcome sojourns in London with her father. Besides, caring for a grandmother with dementia and single-handedly looking after an eight-bedroom house and its gardens was hardly a career.

'No,' she said baldly.

Leon frowned slightly. For all her chilly reserve, Flavia Lassiter had not struck him as unintelligent, and it was unusual these days for a woman like her to have no life of her own. Most society women made a pretence, at least, of having an occupation of sorts—even if it were little more than a stab at something they considered light and easy, such as interior design. Many, of course, were high-powered businesswomen and career professionals in their own right.

'No?' he echoed.

'No,' Flavia repeated, looking back at him coolly. Let him think what he would of her. She hardly cared, after all. After this evening she would have nothing more to do with him.

Leon's frown deepened. 'You are content, then, merely to be your father's pampered daughter?' he posed.

Flavia could feel her face freezing at the implication.

'Evidently,' she clipped out.

Leon studied her expression. She hadn't liked the imputation, but then, he mused, perhaps few men had actually put it to her that living off her indulgent father's wealth at her age was not something that could be admired. A thought flickered across his mind. If Flavia Lassiter was indeed entirely reliant on her father's wealth for her comfortable lifestyle— her gown, however lacking in 'bling', was clearly a designer number, for instance, and those were definitely high-carat diamonds in her earlobes and in the slender bracelet snaking around her wrist—how would she cope if that wealth were to evaporate? He knew all too well that if he—or another turn-around expert—did not rescue her father it was the very likely outcome of Lassiter's disastrously fragile financial situation.

Does she know how close to the wind her father is? he speculated. If she truly were a pampered princess then it was unlikely she did. Females like that did not trouble themselves over the source of their funding. They took it for granted that the largesse would not stop. Besides… His eyes narrowed infinitesimally. Unlike Lassiter's mistress, she had made no effort to fawn on him. Just the reverse! Had she any realisation of just how essential he was to her father's continued affluence—and therefore her own—she would surely not be so chilly and rejecting of him!

But her frigid demeanour was because she was trying

to deny the effect he was having on her, he reminded himself. She was trying to resist him. That was why she was so determined to give him the cold shoulder. His dark eyes glinted briefly. Did she really not realise that her attitude would merely spur him on?

Her tension now was visible in the stiffness of her spine. Clearly she was wishing him to perdition—but in that he was not going to oblige her. He took a contemplative mouthful of his drink, enjoying the fine bouquet and fiery resonance of the vintage cognac.

'Perhaps you occupy yourself in charity work?' He trailed the suggestion in front of her.

His reward was a daggered glance. 'Of course,' she agreed. 'Attending essential functions like this one. Which as you can see—' her voice was viciously sweet '—I am *so* enjoying.'

Even as she spoke she knew she'd been unacceptably rude. But it was too late to take her unpleasantly sarcastic riposte back now. Too late, she thought with a hollow grip inside her, to do anything at all about Leon Maranz's disastrous, unwanted impact on her except hold him as far at bay as she possibly could! Even if that meant crossing every boundary of social courtesy.

A desperate thought crossed her haunted mind. Perhaps if she were sufficiently rude to him he'd at least back off and leave her alone. Go off and seek a more willing, complaisant woman—goodness knew there were enough of them here tonight! He could have his pick if he wanted. So why, *why* did he have to focus on *her*, for heaven's sake!

I can't cope with this! I can't cope with having this happening to me here, and now. He's part of my father's world, and I have every reason to reject that world—reject anything to do with it! I've got responsibilities and duties that are two hundred miles away which I cannot abandon even if I were to want to—which I don't. So I just don't want this—I don't want this man paying me attention, trying to pull me, trying to get me into bed. Because that, obviously, is what he wants...

Like a guillotine slicing down, she cut off her train of thought. It was far too dangerous. Emotion writhed in her. All she wanted to do was get to her feet and bolt—just get away from the man invading her presence, disquieting and disturbing her, making his impact felt so powerfully and overwhelmingly.

The sudden tightening of his expression showed her that he had not appreciated her sarcasm, and for a moment she felt an impulse to apologise to him. Then she hardened. Making him dislike her was as good a way as any to keep him at a distance. Besides, a resentful voice said in her head, she didn't *want* to be so affected by him. She didn't *want* to have this fluttery quickening of the pulse, this perpetual shimmer of awareness of him. She wanted to be immune to him, to be unaffected by him, completely indifferent to him.

This time tomorrow I'll be back at home—safe.

She made the thought hang in her head, clinging to it. All she had to do was get through the remainder of this wretched evening and she'd be done. Done with Leon Maranz for good!

She reached for her coffee cup and deliberately let her gaze wander out over the ballroom with an expression of boredom on her face.

Beside her, Leon felt his anger snap its jaws.

'Tell me,' he drawled, his voice like a blade, 'what makes you think you have a right to be rude to me?'

Flavia's head swivelled. Words jumbled fiercely in her brain—hot, angry words that she wanted to hurl at him! But she couldn't—couldn't say the words she was burning to throw at him.

What makes you think you can come on to me the way you are? What makes you think you can drag me out on to the dance floor and make me dance with you, invading my body space, making me react to you the way I did? What makes you think you can look at me the way you do—making it obvious...blindingly, searingly obvious...what you want?

But she couldn't hurl those words at him. Instead, all she

could do was glare at him stonily, her face tightening, and retreat behind her rigid, icy guard to keep him at bay. Resort again to the unforgivable rudeness that she knew, with a small, shaming part of her brain, that she was handing out to him.

'I don't think anything about you at all, Mr Maranz,' she said, forcing her voice to be cold. 'You're my father's guest, not mine, and I would far rather he did a host's duty by you instead of leaving the task to me.'

Involuntarily her eyes went past him to the dance floor, urgently trying to seek out her wretched father and Anita. Would they get off the floor and come back to their table?

Leon saw her searching gaze. Was that, maybe, what this was all about? Was Alistair Lassiter's idle, pampered daughter sulking because her father paid more attention to his mistress than to her?

He took a mouthful of brandy, studying Flavia's rigid face. 'Are you jealous of Anita?' he ventured.

Again Flavia's gaze snapped to him. *'What?'*

He gave a slight shrug. 'It would not be surprising. Daughters—especially those who are used to being Daddy's darling—are very often extremely possessive of their fathers, and resent them paying attention to any other female. Let alone one as young and glamorous as Anita.'

Flavia could only stare. 'You think I'm jealous of *Anita*?' She could not hide the disbelief in her voice.

'Why not?' Leon replied. 'Your father seems quite…smitten by her.'

Flavia could feel her face icing. 'Anita,' she bit out, 'is a gold-digging piece of work who wouldn't look twice at him if he weren't rich! Every bit of jewellery she's dripping with, every designer number in her vast collection, was paid for by *him*!'

There was scorn in her voice, and she didn't bother to hide it.

Leon's reply was hard. 'You are fortunate, then, that *you* only had to be born your father's daughter to enjoy his wealth.'

At least she had the grace to look discomfited, he saw. His gaze studied her face. Just what *was* Flavia Lassiter's character? On the plus side she seemed unimpressed by his wealth, disdaining to fawn on him, yet she enjoyed the fruits of Alistair Lassiter's largesse and admitted she made no attempt to earn any money for herself, or even busy herself with charity work, which so many women of her type did. And she was perfectly willing to be shamelessly rude to him—was that truly only because she was trying to deny what was so obviously flaring between them?

A dark thought shadowed his mind yet again. Or was it because she saw no necessity to be polite to him because he did not come from the well-bred world she moved in so effortlessly. Because he had started life half a world away in a South American shanty town and come penniless to this country, nothing more than yet another indigent immigrant—someone to look down on and resent, to look through as if he simply did not exist…?

Again he felt the familiar sting of anger inside him, fuelled by an old, old memory of a time when few had seen any need to show him politeness.

He thrust the reflection aside. He would not be haunted by it…by memories of his past…

There was a swirl of glittering purple skirts and Lassiter's mistress, closely followed by Lassiter himself, was approaching the table once more. Anita's face was animated as she hailed Leon.

'There you are! I wondered where you'd got to. *Do* come and dance! Alistair says he's too tired to go on.'

She pouted flirtatiously at Leon and moved to take his hand, but he raised it in negation, giving a slight but definite shake of his head.

'I never dance with another man's woman,' he said.

Anita's pout turned into a displeased moue. Leon could

immediately see she was peeved to be thought of as Lassiter's 'woman', but at the same time she clearly wanted to dance with Leon himself. He could understand why. Alistair Lassiter was not looking his best right now. His face was red and puffed, and there was a line of sweat around his collar. As he sat down heavily he looked his age, and he was running to fat.

Anita perched herself petulantly on the vacant chair next to Leon, then busied herself spending the next ten minutes making up to him shamelessly. Leon could see Lassiter— not liking it, but at the same time he was obviously not keen on objecting to it. Cynically, Leon found himself once again considering whether Lassiter would actually go so far in ingratiating himself with him by not objecting if he took matters even further with his mistress.

Or his daughter...

His eyes slid past Anita's over-made-up face to where Flavia Lassiter was still sitting stiffly, taking small, repetitive sips from her coffee cup, clearly in an attempt to avoid all further conversation. She was pretending she was occupied in staring out across the ballroom, though it was obvious she was paying her surroundings no attention at all.

Except to him. Flavia Lassiter, whatever his uncertainty or speculation as to her disdain for men of lowly foreign origins, was, Leon knew with complete assurance, radiating a totally female awareness of him on all frequencies—she was bristling with it. Once more a grim sense of satisfaction permeated him. She could snub him all she liked, claim whatever that she didn't think of him at all—but she was lying. Lying all the way down her beautiful slender body...

Making some anodyne reply to whatever it was Anita had just said to him, he turned full face to Flavia.

'If events such as this one tonight are not to your taste, what *do* you care to do with your evenings? Parties? Clubbing?' Deliberately he suggested two things that he'd bet she'd loathe.

He could see her start and stiffen visibly as he addressed

her. Presumably she'd thought he'd turned his unwanted attentions to Anita and she was off his unwelcome hook.

As if all too aware of his daughter's intransigence, Alistair Lassiter answered for her. 'Oh, Flavia's a real culture-vulture,' he effused heartily. 'Offer her a Shakespeare play and she's perfectly happy.'

Leon lifted an eyebrow. 'Indeed? And have you seen the current West End production of *Hamlet*?' He directed his question at Flavia.

'No.' The answer was forced from her.

'Then I would be delighted to take you,' came Leon's smooth reply.

'I don't like the lead actor,' Flavia riposted shortly.

'The National has *Twelfth Night* running,' countered Leon.

She looked straight at him. 'I've seen it too often,' she replied, sounding bored.

No way, no *way* was she going to get cornered into going to the theatre with Leon Maranz. Anyway, she reminded herself with relief, this time tomorrow she'd be back home in Dorset.

'The National's production is highly innovative,' Leon came back.

'I prefer traditional interpretations,' Flavia returned dismissively.

She knew she was being ungracious and rude, and hated herself for it, but she had to do whatever was necessary to get Leon Maranz's attention off her. It was like being caught in a searchlight, pinning her down, trying to disarm her to get past her guard, her desperate defences.

It was imperative that she hold him at bay. Now even more so. Her father's ingratiating suggestion about the theatre had sent alarm bells ringing yet again. He evidently wanted her to go out with the man, and the only reason he wanted that must be that he'd decided it would further his ambitions to do lucrative business with Leon Maranz.

I won't be used like that! I won't!

The rejection was vehement, adamant. She had never let

herself be set up by her father in such a way, and she wouldn't start now! Not even with a man she was so attracted to. *That* was why she had to cut Leon Maranz—even if it meant she had to resort to open rudeness the way she was doing. He wouldn't leave her alone, wouldn't accept that she was refusing to have anything to do with him, refusing to give an inch, a centimetre to him.

And if she didn't…

Like a traitor to her resolve, her gaze refocussed, for a fleeting moment, on his face. She could feel her pulse surge treacherously even as she hated herself for succumbing. Feel her eyes flare, her breath quicken.

Why this man?

That was the impossible question. The one she had no answer to. The one that confounded everything.

But it doesn't matter! The cry sounded in her head, silencing the question she could not—would not—answer. It didn't matter why this man? Because the only salient thing about him was that he was all bound up with her father and his endless attempts to use her to his own advantage. And because of that it didn't matter a damn what she thought of Leon Maranz, or what she might otherwise do about the way he looked at her, the way he got under her skin, the way he got past her guard, the way he made her feel. It just didn't matter!

And this evening didn't matter. And it didn't matter that she was being rude to him. It didn't matter that her father was clearly hopping mad at the way she was behaving, and that Anita was throwing dagger-looks at her. Or that Leon Maranz's eyes were resting on her as if he had just lifted a stone and seen something crawl out from underneath it

It just didn't matter…

For a moment sheer, raw misery filled her, intermingled with the self-contempt she could feel flushing through her for the way she was being right now—the way she had been ever since she had realised that it was *this* man her father wanted her to be nice to. He wanted her to accept his company, his attentions, his invitation to go the theatre with him.

Resentment spiked through her misery. Resentment at her father for putting her in this invidious position in the first place, for not giving a damn about her at all and never having done, for not caring about her mother, or her grandmother, or anyone else except himself and what he wanted. Resentment of Leon Maranz, who wanted to do business with a man like her father and who assumed she was nothing more than a pampered, workshy snobbish socialite!

And yet underlying all those layers of resentment was a deeper layer still—resignation. Resignation because with her grandmother to care for any relationship with anyone was impossible…just impossible…

Emotion twisted inside her, like wires around her throat.

'I *adore* the theatre!' Anita's breathless gush was a welcome invasion of her inner turmoil. 'And cabaret especially.' Her eyes widened as if she'd had a sudden idea. 'There's a really good new cabaret club opened recently—it's got rave reviews. How about if we all go on to it now?' She beamed.

'Great idea,' Alistair Lassiter enthused, getting heavily to his feet. 'I think we've done our bit here,' he said portentously, nodding at the charity signage.

Anita stood up eagerly. 'Brilliant!' she breathed, and radiated her fulsome smile at Leon.

Flavia's heart sank. *Oh, no.* To be dragged off to some wretched club—please, no!

But Leon Maranz was shaking his head. 'I've an early start tomorrow,' he said. 'I must be making a move.'

Thank God, Flavia found herself thinking fervently. But the next moment she realised she had been premature—disastrously premature.

'Well, in that case,' her father was saying, holding Anita closely at his side, 'I'd be very grateful if you could see my daughter home safely. You'd be all right with that? I'd worry about her otherwise.'

He spoke with his customary public doting fondness that made Flavia cringe at its falsity. And at the implications of what he'd just asked Leon Maranz to do.

She stood up hastily. 'I'm perfectly capable of getting a taxi,' she said tartly.

But Leon Maranz had got to his feet as well. 'I wouldn't dream of it,' he replied. His voice was smooth, emollient. 'Of course I'll see you home.'

Her father was rubbing his hands. 'Good, good,' he said. 'Well, then, if we're all ready for the off...?'

Stiffly, relieved the ordeal of the charity bash was finally over, but more than dreading the journey back to her father's apartment, Flavia walked briskly from the ballroom. Could she possibly manage to snaffle a taxi immediately outside the hotel and make her getaway?

But getting away from Leon Maranz when he was on the prowl proved impossible. Leon's chauffeur was already holding the door of his waiting car open for her, and she had no recourse but to climb in. Thankfully the interior was huge, and she squeezed herself against the far side of the wide seat, hastily drawing the seat belt over her and fastening it, lest Leon Maranz attempt the office himself. But he had simply thrown himself into the other side of the seat, fastened his own belt, and stretched his long legs out into the spacious well behind the glassed-in driver.

A moment later the limo was pulling out into the late night traffic of Park Lane. It would take a good fifteen to twenty minutes, at best, Flavia knew with sinking heart, to get to Regent's Park.

She wondered whether Leon Maranz was going to attempt any form of conversation with her, but to her relief he merely glanced at her, bestowed a brief, social smile upon her, then took out a mobile phone from his tuxedo and proceeded to make a series of phone calls. All were of a business nature, and Flavia allowed herself the respite of letting her head rest against the smooth, cool leather of the headrest and close her weary eyes.

She didn't want to look at him. Didn't want to see him, long legs stretched out, shirt moulding his broad chest, strong, compelling features animated, as he gave what appeared to be a series of terse instructions to those who were presumably his minions. No, she didn't want to look at him at all. Wanted to blank him out—write him out of her existence.

In a short while I'll be done with him and this whole impossible situation will finally be over! I'll never have to set eyes on him again!

She waited for relief to flood through her—because it must, obviously, at the thought of finally being shot of the man who had caused her nothing but nerve-racking jitteriness all the endlessly long evening.

But it didn't come.

Instead she felt her eyes flick open, her head turn sideways. Her gaze light on the man who had caused her so much torment.

Out of nowhere she felt her pulse jolt, her throat catch. Her eyes fastened to him, to his aquiline profile, to his features cast into stark relief by the street lights as they moved across his face with the car's motion. She wanted to gaze at him, not tear her eyes away. Just go on gazing at him. Drinking him in.

She was never going to see him again...

And suddenly—ridiculously, absurdly, insanely—she knew she didn't *want* never to see him again. Didn't want to know that for the rest of her life the most she would ever see of this man would be if she looked him up on the internet, or saw his photo in the pages of the financial news.

In this enclosed, contained space, with the anonymous driver invisible behind his smoked glass partition, the outer world beyond the tinted windows was shut out. The world that was full of resentment of her father and responsibility for her grandmother. It all seemed suddenly remote, distant. Instead, there was only the cocooning space of the car's interior, a world of its own, closed and intimate. Enclosing herself and the man sitting only a metre away from her, his presence so close it was like a physical pressure on her.

She caught the male scent of him—the faint aroma of brandy, of expensive lightly spiced aftershave. Saw the slight darkening of his jawline, the sable feathering of his hair, the profile of his long dark eyelashes. Everything about him was assailing her senses. She felt faint with it, her breath catching. She clung to the leather strap in the car's interior, her other hand crushing her clutch bag, her breath held in her lungs, and she could not tear her eyes away from him.

As if in slow motion, it seemed to her, he turned his head towards her. Looked back at her full-on, meeting her helpless gaze. Helplessly she saw him halt his call in mid-speech. In slow motion he seemed to cut his call, slide his phone back into his jacket pocket, keeping his attention totally, completely on her.

And she couldn't tear her eyes away—still couldn't. She could feel her eyes flaring, her focus dissolving. Her breath was frozen, and his gaze on her made her feel as she had never felt before...

And then he smiled.

Not a brief, impersonal one as he had before.

A slow, sensual smile.

Personal.

Intimate.

It was as if the whole world had slowed down. The car was at a traffic light and the low, powerful throb of the engine seemed to be vibrating all the way through her, accentuating the slow, heavy throb of her own heartbeat. She felt herself dissolving, melting, kept upright only by the physical power of his gaze levelled on her, holding her like a physical grip, refusing to relinquish her.

He was forcing her to acknowledge him—to acknowledge his power over her. The power of his desire for her...

Of hers for him...

Because that was what it was—she knew it, accepted it. Whatever she might think of this man, she knew that he affected her in a way no other man ever had. In a way that she'd had no idea she *could* be affected. She might resist it, resent it, reject it—but she could feel the potent force of it, feel her susceptibility, her vulnerability. Feel herself, her body, the blood in her veins, answering it. Feel it drawing her...

She sat motionless, her eyes fastened to his, as the low throb of the car's engine vibrated through her consciousness. She was there, in that captive space, the world beyond nothing but a dim blur of noise and discordant lights. All that existed was her—and the man now reaching out his hand, letting his fingers trail slowly down the curve of her cheek, a smile playing about his mouth.

And she let him. Let him smile at her knowingly, intimately. Let him reach for her, touch her. Let his fingers draw softly down the satin of her cheek. Felt a thousand nerve-endings sigh like velvet melting.

Let him curve his hand around the tender nape of her neck, the tips of his fingers shaping her skull. Let him murmur something...she knew not what. Because her gaze was held by his, liquid into liquid, and then his head was bending towards hers, he was taking her mouth with his.

She could not move. Not a muscle. Not a fibre of her being. Her entire being was in the sensation he was creating, the silk of his mouth laving hers.

Her eyes closed, helpless, as his kiss deepened. And she yielded to it—to him—for how could she do otherwise? How could she do anything but let this exquisite, sensuous touch go on and on and on? She arched towards him, yearning towards him, and the pressure of his fingers at her nape strengthened. She felt with a susurration of shock that his other hand was shaping her breast, splaying across it, and it was ripening to his touch, her nipple cresting against his palm. It was the most incredible feeling she had ever felt. Her mouth was opening to his, and all she wanted in all the world was to have him kiss her, to arch her body towards him and feel it fire with a pleasure so intense she gave a low, insensible moan in her throat.

'I've been waiting for this moment since the first I set eyes on you...'

His voice was low against her mouth. Husky, but with an intensity about it that penetrated through all the layers of her defences just as his touch, his possessing kiss, had penetrated.

For a long, endless moment his eyes entwined with hers, and she was helpless, utterly helpless, to do anything but let her gaze sink into his, let the slow, heavy slug of her heart resonate with his. His eyes held hers, his mouth grazed hers, his palm cupped her breast...

'Come back with me now—tonight—stay with me.'

The low husk of sensual desire was still in his voice, but there was another note, too...

Confidence. Assurance.

Assumption.

And suddenly her body was no longer boneless, pliant in his clasp. She pulled back, pulled away. He reached for her again, as if to reclaim her, but Flavia stiffened. In an instant she was the way she had been all evening.

And in the next instant she had reached for the door handle, acting instinctively, urgently. She had to get out! *Now!*

'Flavia!'

She heard her name, but she was gone. Pushing open the car door, standing momentarily on the road, then in the next instant registering that the vehicle in the lane beside her was a taxi with its 'For Hire' light showing. She yanked open the passenger door and tumbled inside just as the driver, taken by surprise, started forward when the lights changed to green.

'Regent's Park!' she bit out urgently, and collapsed back into the seat. Her heart was pounding, her head muzzy with shock. She closed her eyes.

Dear God, what had she let happen? How—*how* had she let it happen? How had Leon Maranz gone from ignoring her and making phone calls to making love to her...?

Kissing me like that—caressing me like that!

She glanced down at her torso. Mortification swept over her—her nipples were still crested, aroused. Compelling, undeniable witness to just what she had done—what she had let him do...

Her body seemed to be fizzing as if champagne were bubbling through it, as if it was still resonating from his kiss, his caress. It seared through her brain so she could still feel the impact of his touch.

I got out just in time—just in time!

It was a mantra that replayed itself for the rest of the night and was still there in the morning. Desperately she tried to find a reason for why Leon Maranz had been able to so precipitately sweep aside her defences the way he had—overwhelm her guard as effortlessly as if she had never raised it in the first place.

He took me by surprise. I didn't stand a chance!

Yes, that was it—that was how it had happened! She'd been holding him at bay all evening—holding down her hopeless reaction to him, her disastrous attraction to him—and it had been so hard to do, so hard to keep fighting it the whole time, with him doing his best to get past her guard, to thaw her frigid defences against him. And then out of nowhere, just as she'd thought him finally distracted by his business calls, she'd stupidly let herself gaze at him, and then he'd sensed her momentary lapse, realised her weakness...and made his move.

Swiftly, expertly, overwhelmingly...

Sweeping away all her resistance. Overpowering her defences as if they were made of cotton wool.

Hot, sensuous memory flooded through her synapses like a warm, seductive wave of sensation, as she replayed those moments in his arms, his mouth exploring hers, his palm shaping her breast...

No! No, she *must not* let herself remember, recall, replay...

Must shut that memory right down, lock it down so that she was no longer haunted by it.

That was what she told herself all that day, on the train journey down to Dorset. She had set her alarm early to get out of the apartment before her father and Anita surfaced, to get to the station and pile herself on to a morning train, to stare sightlessly out of the window as she passed the time *not* thinking, *not* remembering…

Only rationalising. Ruthlessly, remorselessly, rigorously.

I met a man. A man like I've never met before. And for some inexplicable and irrational reason he had an effect on me no other man has ever had. Which is ridiculous, because he's nothing like any man I've ever been out with! And it's impossible even to contemplate anything with him! He belongs to my father's world and I want nothing to do with it—and even if he didn't I still can't have anything at all to do with him, because my place is with my grandmother. I have an indelible responsibility for her, and nothing on earth can change that. Nothing.

And if he did sweep past my defences last night, then I must take that as even stronger evidence that I should and can and must have absolutely nothing more to do with him! Because he's made it clear—crystal clear!—that he'd sweep me off to bed as well!

Would she have gone with him?

That was the stark, unanswerable question that hung in her head. He had assumed she would—she'd heard it in his voice, heard that note of confidence, of assurance. Of course, since she'd melted in his arms in the back of his limo, she would melt all over him in bed straight away!

And you would have, too…

The whispering, treacherous thought wound into her brain and found an echo in her treacherous flesh…which quickened at the thought. Her pulse was insistent, a sensual, shimmering tremor quivering through her body. A vision leapt in her mind: herself entwined with him, laid upon a wide, waiting bed, and his dark sloe eyes burning into her as he possessed himself of her with mouth and hands and all his strong, lean body...

But it was a vision—only that. Nothing more. Not real, not actual—and it never could be, never would be.

She swallowed, forcing herself to focus on the passing landscape beyond the windows of the train. All around her the wide English countryside spread to the horizon. Fields and hedges and woods and little houses, all flashing past. She was going home. She was going back to her grandmother and *that* was her reality. Only that.

A man who could melt her with a single glance of his dark, dark eyes was *nothing* to do with her.

Nothing.

She went on staring sightlessly.

Inside her, a little pool of bleakness formed.

CHAPTER FIVE

LEON sat back impassively in the large leather chair in his London office. Alistair Lassiter was talking at him. He'd been talking at him for the last twenty minutes, and Leon had stopped listening after the first ten. He'd heard all he needed to know. The man was getting desperate. That much was screamingly obvious. Leon had been well aware of the financial precariousness of the Lassiter organisation, but now—whether he realised it or not, and Leon suspected he didn't—Alistair Lassiter had shown him that there were no white knights in the offing to save his sorry, extravagant skin.

All that was left for Leon to decide was whether he would do so.

But that wasn't what was currently occupying his mind.

It wasn't Alistair Lassiter's business affairs that were pre-occupying him. It was his daughter. Thoughts about her were going round and round in succession.

Talk about conflicted...

After their final barbed exchange at the charity function, with Flavia Lassiter doing her damnedest to make him think her rude and stuck up to the point where he was almost ready to wash his hands of her, he'd then completely reversed his decision while taking her home! She'd only had to look at him the way she had, so close to him in the dim, closeted privacy of the car. When she'd met his gaze full-on, drowning in his eyes, every reservation about her had been submerged in an overwhelming desire to do just what he had—sweep her into his arms and kiss her....

And it had been a disaster! Oh, not the kiss—that had been a sensual white-out!—but the timing couldn't have been worse.

I rushed her.

That was the accusation that was staring him in the face. He'd rushed her—and panicked her. And she'd bolted.

It was too much, too soon. She couldn't handle it, couldn't accept it—not so suddenly.

Her rudeness to him he could now see was obviously her attempt to fight their attraction to each other, which she just couldn't cope with—at least not yet. Hence her precipitate reaction to him when he'd kissed her. Self-accusation stabbed again. He'd indulged his own desires at her expense, and the result had been she'd bolted.

He took a steadying breath—OK, so he'd mishandled the situation, acted like an impulsive teenager instead of an experienced man who should have read the situation more adroitly, but that kiss had been proof to both of them of just how powerfully attracted they were to each other. She would find that kiss as impossible to forget as he did.

Resolution replaced his berating of himself. All he had to do now was consider the best way of taking the situation forward to the conclusion that was, he knew with every atom in his body, as inevitable as day following night. All he had to do was find the right way to woo her.

Leon's eyes refocussed on Lassiter, glinting in impatience—he would far rather be focussing on Lassiter's daughter, undoing the damage his kiss had done, not listening to her father extol the wonderful 'investment opportunity' of saving his company. A frown creased Leon's brow minutely. How would Flavia react if he decided *not* to bail out her father? Would she still want anything to do with him? A disquieting memory of their conversation last night about how she seemed content to accept her father's financial support wormed its way into her head. Impatiently, he thrust it aside. To many women of her background acting as a social hostess was occupation enough. It was the way they'd been brought up.

What will she do if her father goes under?

The question hovered in his head, uncomfortable and troubling.

With sudden decision he shifted in his seat and flexed his shoulders. He wasn't prepared to take the risk that Flavia Lassiter would want to have anything more to do with him at all if she knew he'd chosen to let her father go down the drain. So he'd bail out Lassiter—but on his own terms.

He held up a hand, interrupting Alistair Lassiter's self-justifying peroration.

'You've made your case. I'm interested. But there are conditions. I'll want equity, executive control, and my own finance man in place to authorise future spending. And you'll have to pull out of some of your African deals—the ones in Luranda—I don't do business with dictators, however much they lavish their country's foreign aid revenues and natural resources on me.'

Lassiter's face reddened. 'Equity? I was looking more at lines of credit—'

Leon shook his head. 'I always insist on equity,' he spelt out.

Lassiter promptly took another tack instead. 'You can't be serious about pulling out of Luranda? The profit margins are massive!'

'At the expense of the country's benighted people,' Leon retorted.

'Lurandans are notoriously lazy and feckless—like all too many in the Third World,' Lassiter blustered.

Leon levelled a cold gaze on him. 'Desperate and exploited,' he said.

'Yes, well…as long as they stay in the Third World and don't keep trying to get here and leech off us—' started Lassiter, then stopped abruptly.

'You were saying?' Leon queried. The coldness in his eyes was sending a message even Lassiter could read.

'Well, obviously the enterprising ones can make a go of things—just like you have.' Lassiter was back to blustering again.

'But those like me,' Leon pursued, 'would far prefer to be able to make a go of things in their *own* countries. Which is seldom possible when outside money is propping up their corrupt, exploitative and grossly economically inefficient government for its own benefit. Which is why,' he spelt out, 'Maranz Finance only ever makes investments in such countries direct at ground level, and retains control over them to ensure middlemen and government officials can't take the profit away from those who do the actual work.'

He got to his feet. He wasn't about to debate the issue. Those were the terms of his involvement, and if Alistair Lassiter didn't like them he could walk. But he wouldn't, Leon knew. He had no choice. There were no other white knights in the offing, and if Lassiter wanted to save his company and, more importantly for him, Leon thought cynically, his fortune, then he'd have to swallow his self-importance and accept the deal on the table.

However, there was no point rubbing the guy's nose in it—Lassiter might prove a pain to work with if he felt too put down by Leon. Maybe it was time to back off and lighten the atmosphere.

It was obvious that Lassiter liked to do business via socialising, and although Leon had had quite enough of *his* company, the reverse was true of his daughter. Knowing he was keen on his daughter would definitely sweeten the atmosphere.

'Now,' he said, his voice warming as he walked around the desk, 'with our business discussion out of the way, I wanted to thank you for a most enjoyable evening last night. However, I don't believe I have the phone number of your London apartment. I'd like to ask your daughter out to dinner tonight.'

A quiet dinner—a chance to make amends for his behaviour the night before, a chance to get to know Flavia properly, woo her properly. That was what he was after now.

He paused expectantly by Alistair Lassiter, who got to his feet. But to his surprise, instead of being immediately and eagerly forthcoming with the number, the man looked discomfited.

'Ah, yes, Flavia—of course,' the man floundered. 'Yes, yes—the thing is she's gone out of town—left this morning—prior engagement, so she told me.'

Leon stilled. 'She's not in London?'

'Er…as it happens, no,' corroborated Lassiter.

'When is she planning to return?' Leon asked.

His voice was even, unemotional. But inside his emotions were streaming through him. He'd thought, when she'd jumped ship into that taxi, it had only been the spur of the moment, that she'd just panicked, been overwhelmed by what had happened between them, and had needed some space to come to terms with it. But actually leaving town?

'And,' he went on, keeping his voice deliberately cool through the emotion spiking in him, 'where has she gone?'

'The thing is, I'm not really sure.' Lassiter attempted to sound nonchalant, and failed. 'You know these days they're so independent.'

'Any ideas?' Leon wasn't about to let him off the hook. 'Where do her friends live?'

'Oh—all over, really. I couldn't say. Could be anywhere.'

Leon decided to cut to the chase. 'OK, give me her mobile number and I'll find her myself.'

'Er—yes, of course. The thing is though…um…she may not answer it.'

'I'll take my chances,' said Leon implacably.

Wherever she'd run to, he would find her. He'd screwed up with her and he had to fix it.

He wanted her too much not to.

Far, far too much.

'Hello, Gran, darling.' Flavia leant over her grandmother's bed and kissed her cheek tenderly. She'd only just arrived from the station, but there was no point telling her grandmother that. It would not register. 'Mrs S says you've had a very good lunch,' she said encouragingly. 'Mashed potatoes, peas and plaice.'

Her grandmother looked at her uncertainly, and her thin fingers picked at the turned-down sheet across her torso. Pain shafted through Flavia. It hurt so much to see her once vibrant grandmother so frail, so lost in the mist of her own mind.

'Plaice is your favourite type of fish,' she said.

But her grandmother's gaze had drifted away, settling on some indeterminate point ahead of her. Flavia lifted her veined hand, and squeezed it gently, looking down at her grandmother, lying there in her double bed—the same bed she'd slept in for over fifty years, since coming to Harford as a young bride. Her heart contracted as she felt the pity of it all. Yet there was a kind of mercy in it, too, she knew. It had been the death of Flavia's grandfather that had first set her off on this journey into a darkening land. Had she lost the will to take part in life once the man she had lived with and loved for so long, had gone?

Flavia smiled sadly as she left the room. What would it be like to love a man so much that you no longer wanted to live once he was not at your side any more? To her it was unimaginable. She'd never been in love, fond though she'd been of former boyfriends. There had never been any great depth of feeling for them, and whilst she'd found them attractive there had never been anyone to arouse a storm of passion in her breast.

Of desire.

Her expression changed, and the memory she'd been banning since getting back home leapt vividly in her head. Instantly, helplessly, she was back in Leon Maranz's arms...

Passion and soft, sensual arousal that teased and laved and melted, so that the breath quickened, the pulse surged, and the body arched and yearned towards the source of it. His mouth warm on hers, pliant and tasting, taking hers with his, and heat starting to beat up through her body, like a dissolving glow...

No! With sheer effort, she dragged her mind away. It was madness to let herself remember. She had spent the whole train journey down to Dorset trying to shut it out, trying not to let it play over and over again in her mind like some impossible video loop she could not turn off.

But now, safely back at Harford, with her grandmother again—back in her real life, a cosmos away from her father's world and the darkly dangerous man who moved therein—surely she was safe from that disastrous memory? If she could just put it completely behind her, write it off as some appalling, unforgivable misjudgement, a lapse that she must never think of again.

This—here, now—was her real life.

As she walked downstairs, heading for the kitchen, she made herself look about her, see the safe, familiar walls enclosing her, the safe, familiar paintings, the safe, familiar furniture and décor, the same now as it had been all through her childhood. Her home, her grandmother's home—her safe place to be.

She went through into the large stone-flagged kitchen with its huge, ancient Aga and massive scrubbed wooden table centre stage, and repeated the reassuring litany of familiarity and safety. Everything here was as it had always been, and that was what she wanted.

She busied herself making her grandmother's supper—just something light: soup and scrambled eggs on toast and a mashed banana. She would eat the same, in her grandmother's bedroom, once she'd bade goodbye and thanks to the stalwart Mrs S, and paid her for her extra time. Then, when her grandmother had settled for the night and slipped over into sleep, she would settle down in the armchair by the table by the window, with a low-lit lamp for light, and read. The only sound would be that of her grandmother's gentle breaths and the occasional hooting of an owl outside, sweeping soundlessly over the gardens. Later she would make herself a cup of tea, read a little longer, then head for bed herself, leaving the door to the landing open so she would hear if her grandmother proved restless in the night.

It was a long-familiar routine. Just as the routines of the daytime were. Getting her grandmother up, helping her downstairs, settling her in the sunny drawing room while she got on with the housework, and then, after lunch, if the weather were clement, opening the French windows to the gardens and getting some gardening done while keeping an eye on her grandmother at the same time.

Sometimes the occasional visitor would come and pay a call on her grandmother, though the conversation was always with Flavia herself, and one of the district nurses or healthcare workers would make a daily phone call to check on things. Twice a week they would come and look after her grandmother while Flavia drove into the nearby market town to buy groceries and any other necessary shopping.

A familiar, routine way of life. Quiet, safe, and very dear to her.

Too safe, too quiet...?

The disquieting thought flickered through her synapses. Restlessly she pushed it aside. Yes, of course anyone might tell her that living quietly in the country as she did, looking after an elderly, frail grandparent, with nothing else in her life at all but that and housework and gardening, was no life for a woman in her twenties! But there was nothing she could do about it. Nothing she *wanted* to do about it.

Even as she formed the thought memory licked again, and

it was as if she could feel the pressure of his mouth on hers, feel the surging of her body, her breast straining against the sensuous palm of his hand shaping her. Involuntarily she felt her breasts tightening.

No! It was no good—no good at all letting herself think about that kiss, that embrace. It had been a terrible mistake, a disastrous weakening of her resolve, yielding to an impulse that was impossible—*impossible*! She'd gone through all the reasons why it had been impossible—what was the point of reiterating them? She was home now. Home and safe...

Gratitude filled her that she was safely back here again, where she loved to be, and where the only person in the world who loved her was. The *only* person she loved.

Her heart tightened. Seeing her grandmother again after a space of several days had brought home to her just how much frailer she was, how her body was steadily giving up the will to stay alive, how she was drifting ever deeper into the mists that were calling her.

How long would it be before she slipped away entirely? Body as well as mind? The doctor, on his regular visits to check her over, always said that it was impossible to know for sure, but Flavia knew that now it really could not be that long. Months, perhaps? If that? Or would she still be here this time next year?

Resolutely she put aside such pointless speculation. All that was important—essential—was that her grandmother would live out her days here, at Harford, with her beloved granddaughter, and that was that. Nothing could change that, and Flavia would allow nothing to endanger it.

Her thoughts moved on, becoming more troubled. Here in the familiar surroundings of Harford's comfortably old-fashioned kitchen, as she cracked eggs into a bowl and set the soup to heat, it was as if she had never been away. But she had—and this latest compulsory visit to London had been incredibly disturbing. She could use all the mental discipline she liked to try and shut out what had happened, but it could not shut out that it *had* happened. That she had encountered such a man as Leon Maranz—and that he had had such a devastating impact on her.

And she had fallen into his arms...

But I ran! I ran just in time! Got back here.

Apprehension webbed about her. What if she had to encounter him again, when her father next summoned her? If her father were going to do business with him she might well have to see him again.

I can't! I can't risk seeing him again—I just can't!

That disastrous, debilitating embrace in his limo had shown her just how terrifyingly vulnerable she was to the man. If she had to socialise with him again, and if he still wanted to amuse himself with her, would she find the strength to resist his advances?

Bitterly, she knew the truth.

It would be impossible.

Even now, two hundred miles away from him, she could feel his power dominating her memory if she for a single moment allowed him in. He would overwhelm her, invade her sanctuary here. And she couldn't allow it—she just couldn't! She could never allow herself to become involved with Leon Maranz—however much he drew her with his dark, disturbing sensuality.

Resolve filled her. There *was* a way to avoid it—a way to ensure that she never had to go into that world again, a way to ensure that her father had no power to summon her like a puppet whose strings he could jerk whenever she wanted. Her face shadowed. It was an option she had considered before and turned down. Harford was not hers, and nor were any of its contents. Yet she had power of attorney for her grandmother, so legally she was free to do what she wanted with her grandmother's possessions.

Up till now she had always refused to do anything other than sell the barest minimum to keep them both here at Harford. But to pay off the thousands of pounds of debt her father kept dangling over her head in order to ensure her compliance with his determination to use her when it suited him she would, she knew with a heavy heart, have to sell some of the more valuable antiques that were left, deeply reluctant though she was to do so.

The next morning, before she could change her mind, she phoned the auction house that was located in the county town, and arranged for one of their valuers to call that afternoon. When he came he identified several items—furniture and silver, and a landscape painting by a well-known Victorian watercolourist—that he expected to sell for the amount of money she would need to pay back her father, but it was still with that heavy heart that she committed them to the saleroom's next auction.

Guilt continued to pluck at her. But by early evening, however, she knew she had made the right decision. She had started to receive messages on the landline answer-machine from her father.

She'd been aware he'd been phoning and texting on her mobile, which she'd ignored, and now she did the same to the landline messages he left, irately ordering her to phone him back. The latest, however, which she heard as she came down from her grandmother's room in the early evening, stopped her in her tracks.

'Leon Maranz is trying to get in touch with you. He's complaining to me that you aren't returning his calls on your mobile. Damn well answer them, girl—he's not someone I want annoyed! What the *hell* do you think you're playing at? Just phone him back!'

Her father's angry voice was cut off, and Flavia was left staring at the handset in its cradle on the table by the front door. Cold flushed through her.

Then heat.

Then, jerkily, she snatched up the phone and hit the 'message delete' button.

But she could not delete the memory of what her father had said.

Leon Maranz was trying to get in touch with her.

Emotion spiked through her. It was dismay—of course it was dismay! How could it be anything else? This was exactly why she had fled London! Just as she'd dreaded, he'd taken that damn episode in his limo as some kind of encouragement! And now he wanted more.

Into her mind's eye leapt a vivid imprint of his strong, saturnine face, the dark, heavy-lidded eyes levelled at her. Their message crystal clear. As if she had lifted a floodgate memory poured into her head, and for one long, endless moment she was back in the limo, gazing helplessly at him as with the lean, casual power of a predator he moved in on her to take his fill of her...

She dropped the phone back in its cradle, realising her hand was shaking.

Whatever it took—*whatever* it took—she would never go back to London—never again put herself in the path of Leon Maranz. She would sell those antiques, pay back her father and never again be used and manipulated by him. Never again be trailed by him like alluring bait in front of the men he wanted to do business with.

Even if that man were Leon Maranz.

Especially if that man were Leon Maranz.

CHAPTER SIX

LEON dropped his phone on his desk and threw himself moodily back in his chair.

Were the hell *was* she? Flavia Lassiter had disappeared off the face of the earth. Her father had admitted he had no idea where she was, speculating only that she must be staying with friends, and her mobile was perpetually on voicemail, his texts unreturned. He glared stormily ahead of him across the vast expanse of his office.

Frustration bit at him. OK, so he'd been an idiot, pouncing on her like that, and he'd obviously spooked her big-time. But he was trying to make amends now. Yet how could he do that if she was running shy of him the way she was now?

Was there someone else in her life? If there were, all she had to do was tell him—not bolt and hide the way she had! The poisoning suspicion crawled into his head yet again. Or was it that Flavia Lassiter was not hiding from him because he'd scared her off, but because she had no intention of having anything to do with someone who was not from her own gilded background—who'd made his own painful way up from penury, a no-name immigrant without breeding or class…?

His eyes darkened as he felt once more the suspicion and resentment that her dismissive attitude had first spiked in him. Was that why Flavia Lassiter had gone to ground? Because she wanted nothing to do with a man like him, born and raised in a South American shanty town?

For a moment emotion swirled within him, dark and turbulent. Then, abruptly, he reached for the phone on his desk again. If Flavia Lassiter thought herself above the world he came from, well, he didn't—and he would remind himself of that right now. Remind himself that, for all the glittering riches of the world he lived in here in Europe—the one Flavia Lassiter had been born into and took for granted—back across the Atlantic, in the vast southern hemisphere, teemed millions just like him, living the way he'd once lived. Wanting only a chance, a hope, a stepping stone to a better life, a better future. And to get that future they would work every bit as hard as he had done—harder. All they needed was that first, vital step on their way.

Which was where *he* came in.

He punched through to his PA in the outer office. An impromptu visit would put his fixation with Flavia into perspective—remind him of his roots, of what his wealth had made possible. Values infinitely more essential than those the Lassiters held dear.

'Book me on a transatlantic flight this afternoon—first available carrier. I'll need all the *pro bono* project files updated, and have the local project managers on standby. Tell them to get their latest proposals ready for me to look over—and alert Maranz Microloans I'll want to see their books, plus take in some site visits.'

'What about your appointments today, Mr Maranz?' his PA enquired dutifully. 'Mr Lassiter has phoned twice this morning to check the deal's still on.'

Leon's mouth tightened. Lassiter was trying to hustle him, hoping to change the terms of the deal in his favour. It would be no bad thing to let him sweat for a while—show the man that his terms were non-negotiable.

'Tell him it's postponed,' he said tersely.

'Till when?'

'Till I get back to London—and, no, I don't know when that will be. Next week some time. Maybe later. I'll let you know.' He disconnected. He didn't want a discussion or a debate. He didn't want anything right now except to clear his London desk this morning and head far, far away.

A change of perspective was what he needed. It might help take his mind off the woman who was frustrating the hell out of him.

Flavia was in the garden, dead-heading one of the rows of hydrangeas just beyond the open French windows leading into the drawing room. Her grandmother was in an armchair by the window, a rug over her lap, looking out at her. There was no expression in her face, but her eyes went to Flavia from time to time, and Flavia would pause and chat to her, as if she could really take in what she was saying.

'There's a lot of new growth coming through,' she was saying cheerfully. 'I think I'm going to need to do some watering, too—it's been so dry today. Mind you, if it does stay dry I can get the lawn mown tomorrow. It's looking quite long already.'

She chattered on, determinedly cheerful—as much, she thought with a hollow feeling, to keep her own spirits up as in an attempt to do the same with her grandmother.

It was one thing to know with her head that she absolutely must not have anything more to do with Leon Maranz.

It was quite another thing to accept it.

This is my world, here.

She looked about her. It was a beautiful day, and Flavia could feel her spirits respond to the uplifting sight of Harford's extensive gardens. The lawn was framed by shrubberies, and fronted by a wide herbaceous border. It was a lot to keep up single-handedly, as Flavia did, but it was a labour of love.

Just as caring for her grandmother was a labour of love.

She glanced back, her smile deepening, but there was sadness in it, too, as she looked at her grandmother. She seemed so small and frail and vulnerable, sitting there so still in her chair. As if she were already living in another world.

But she was safe here—safe in the home she had known for over half a century—and this was where she would end her days, with her granddaughter at her side. Nothing would change Flavia's mind on that. If it meant putting her own life on hold—well, so be it. It was a gift she would gladly give her grandmother.

She stretched her shoulders and resumed her clipping, dropping the dried dead heads of the hydrangea into a willow basket. As she got stuck in to her task again she picked up the sound of a vehicle approaching by the front drive. Murmuring to her grandmother, she went in through the French windows and out into the front hall just as the doorbell rang. Opening it, she saw it was the postman.

'Special Delivery,' he said, holding out a pad for her to sign.

She did so, and took the large thick envelope wonderingly, bidding the postman goodbye and shutting the door. She stared at the envelope a moment. It had been franked, but there was a name on the frank she could not read. It was addressed to her—a typed label. Junk mail? Surely not, she reasoned, if it was a special delivery.

She started back to the drawing room, opening the envelope with her fingernail and extracting the contents. Thick folded paper—some kind of document beneath a letter. Frowning in puzzlement, she started reading.

It was from a firm of City solicitors—one she'd never heard of.

As she read, the blood started to congeal in her veins. With shaking hands she dropped the letter on the sofa and sank down beside it on wobbly legs, her eyes burning into the documents. Sickness filled her.

Then, abruptly, she leapt to her feet, seized up the letter, and plunged into the room her grandfather had used as his study. She picked up the phone. Her hands were shaking, the sickness like acid in her stomach, and she could hardly dial the number she knew she had to call.

Her father took her call—as if he were expecting it.

'So,' he said, 'I've finally got your attention, have I? About bloody time!'

Flavia's teeth were gritted. 'What the *hell* have you sent me?' she demanded.

Her father's voice sounded unmoved by her agitation. 'Isn't it clear enough? It's what it says it is—a loan agreement. Plus a note of the accumulated interest since the loan was made.'

'But *when*—when did this happen?' Flavia tried to keep the panic out of her voice and failed.

'It was after your grandad snuffed it. Your gran was worried about money—funeral expenses, legal fees, house repairs, utility bills, all sorts of things. She'd never had to cope with all that stuff. So...'

He paused, and there was an unholy note in his voice. Flavia could hear it, with a hollowing of her insides.

'I offered to help out. Tide her over, so to speak. 'Course, I had to make a bit of profit out of it, didn't I? So maybe the interest rate *was* a bit more than the bank would have charged. But then your gran wouldn't have wanted anyone to know she was borrowing money, would she? Bit *infra dig*, don't you know?' Her ruthlessly mimicked an upper-class accent. 'Whereas having your own son-in-law lend a hand—and some filthy lucre—was quite different!'

Flavia's jaw clenched. Yes, *different*, all right! Though the principle sum loaned had been high, the ruinous, outrageous rate of interest her poor bewildered grandmother had agreed to made the total repayments monstrous! She was still reeling, heaving with shock and sickness. She stared again at the solicitor's letter setting out the total amount currently owed. Dear God—this wasn't a question of selling a few antiques to raise a few thousand. This was ten, twenty times more! A fortune!

Her mind raced frantically. She *had* to pay that terrifying debt off! It was mounting daily, and it was hideous—hideous! But there was only one way to do it. Borrow money to pay it off.

She swallowed, her hand gripping the phone like a vice. 'I'll get it repaid,' she said grimly. 'I'll raise a mortgage on Harford and settle the debt that way!'

How she would pay the mortgage off was something she'd cope with later—right now the only priority was to stop her father's rip-off loan increasing even more, even faster.

Her father gave a laugh. It raised hairs on the back of her neck.

'You haven't got time. The next letter you get from me will be a foreclosure.'

'What?'

'Didn't you read the loan agreement? The loan is secured against Harford, and I can demand repayment at any time. Which means—' there was a fat, satisfied note in his voice that made Flavia want to scream '—I can force a sale whenever I want. Like…tomorrow.'

There was silence. Absolute silence. Flavia could not speak, could not think. Could only stand clutching the phone, swaying with shock, disbelief and horror.

Into the silence, her father spoke.

'It doesn't have to be this way, Flavia. It can be a whole lot easier. In fact—' a new note entered his voice, which made her flesh crawl '—it should be very enjoyable for you—that's what Anita says, and she knows about these things. She's very envious of you.'

Through her pounding heartbeat, Flavia spoke. 'What… what do you mean?'

Her father gave another laugh. Fat and satisfied.

'You've made a conquest,' he informed her. 'Leon Maranz has taken a shine to you—he's keen to get in touch. The only problem is—' Flavia could hear her father's voice ice with anger '—*you* are refusing to play ball!'

Colour flared out along Flavia's cheeks. 'I don't want anything to do with Leon Maranz!'

'Tough!' retorted her father. 'He wants you, and right now anything Leon Maranz wants and I can get him he gets.'

Flavia's chest heaved. 'If you think for a single moment that I—'

Her father cut her off. 'What I *think* is that you will pack your bags and take the first train to London tomorrow morning. And you *will* get in touch with Leon Maranz, and you *will* be very, very nice to him. *Do you understand me*?'

There was ice in Flavia's veins. Ice in her voice. 'What *exactly* do you mean by "nice"?'

Her answer was a coarse, impatient sound. 'Oh, for God's sake—do you want diagrams? You're not a nun—even if you try and dress like one! Though God knows it seems to have turned *him* on, so I guess I can be grateful for that. Maybe he's so spoilt by having stunners all over him that he wants a change? Who cares why? So long as it's you he wants, it's you, my girl, that he's going to get!'

She was gripping the phone so hard she thought it must shatter beneath her hands.

'You want,' she said slowly, each word forced from her, 'to pimp me out to a man you're doing business with?'

Her voice seemed to come from very far away. Horror, disgust and loathing were rising like vomit in her throat. Her father—her own father—was doing this to her...

How can he be this vile—how?

But it didn't matter how. She knew what he was—had known it all her life. Had known all her life that her father did not love her, cared absolutely nothing for her, saw her only as someone to be used...exploited.

Pimped.

Her father was speaking again, and she forced herself to listen. His voice sounded angry now.

'Let me spell out some home truths to you, my girl! This recession has played bloody havoc with me! Right now I need to keep Leon Maranz happy, any damn way he wants, because he's all that stands between me and being totally wiped out! Got it? He's a turnaround merchant—invests in hard-hit companies and pulls them through. Why the *hell* else do you think I'm all over the man? I wouldn't give him the time of day if I didn't need him! Some bloody foreigner lording it over me!'

Instinctively Flavia flinched at the offensive term.

'And you want to pimp me out to him—' scorn was acid in her voice '—just to save your skin.'

Her father gave a derisive, mocking laugh. 'Little Miss Pure and Virtuous? Is that it? Well, you can be as bloody pure and virtuous as you like when you and your senile old bat of a grandmother are out on the streets! Because I promise you—' his voice congealed the breath in her lungs as he spoke '—if you don't play ball and make sure Leon Maranz gets everything he wants from you, I'll rip Harford from you. It'll be on the market this week. So what's it to be? It's make your mind up time.'

Slowly, very slowly, Flavia looked at the documents lying on her grandfather's desk. Saw the zeroes blur, and then reform. Felt acid leach into her stomach, cold inch down her spine.

Slowly, very slowly, she gave him her answer.

The team of project directors seated around the table were setting out their next round of *pro bono* proposals for funding. Leon knew he should be paying more attention, but his mind was distracted. Focussed elsewhere.

It had been for days now. Focussed on the mobile phone in his jacket pocket. Whenever it rang he was aware of a distinct jolt of expectation and hope. Would it finally, this time, be Flavia Lassiter returning his calls?

But it never was.

He'd hoped that leaving London would stop him being constantly on the alert for her, but here he was on the point of heading back east across the Atlantic and he was just as frustrated by her silence as ever. He'd tried accepting that she just didn't want to know, tried putting her out of his mind, even tried looking out for another woman to take his mind off Flavia Lassiter.

But even the famed beauty of South American womanhood had failed to beguile him. The more he'd tried to be beguiled, the less he had been. The more he'd kept seeing Flavia in his mind's eye, feeling her lips beneath his in his memory, the pliant softness of her body in his embrace...

It was infuriating. It was exasperating. It was unnerving.

I'm becoming obsessed...

The unwelcome notion played in his head, disturbing and disquieting. He tried to rationalise it away, reminding himself that up till now he'd never had to face female rejection—that was why he was reacting so badly to Flavia doing it. But he could rationalise it all he wanted—what he couldn't do was expunge her from his memory or cease to want her.

They'd reached the end of the proposals, and he realised he must make the appropriate answers. Forcing his mind to focus on the subject in hand, he found himself simply giving blanket approval to everything. And why not? he reasoned impatiently. His team were first class, reliable and hardworking, with excellent judgement—it was why he'd picked them in the first place. So their proposals would be fine. He need not check them. Instead he would do what he'd been itching to do all through the meeting. Check his incoming texts.

Dismissing his team with a smile and an expression of appreciation and encouragement, he slid out his phone and hungrily skimmed down the messages.

As he reached the last one he stilled completely. Not a muscle moved in him. For a moment the brief text blurred in his vision, then cleared again.

Sorry I was out of range—FL.

That was all it said—but it was enough. More than enough. For one long moment he simply stared, as if the message might be a mirage. Then, tamping down the emotion that had sprung forcefully inside him, he texted back. A message just as simple—but all he needed to say.

Have dinner with me tomorrow night.

As he hit 'send', his nerves felt strung out like wires. Then, with a total sense of all tension snapping, he saw the brief two-letter reply that told him everything he'd been waiting so long to hear.

OK

It was all he wanted.

Everything he wanted.

Without further hesitation he set off for the airport. He could not be back in London soon enough…

CHAPTER SEVEN

FLAVIA sat on the bed in her bedroom in her father's Regent's Park apartment. Once again she had left her grandmother in the care of Mrs Stephens. Once again she had made the train journey back to London.

A journey that had always been an ordeal for her.

But never like this…

Her hands were clenched in her lap and she felt cold all through her body, despite the warmth of the evening.

She hated her father with all her being for what he was forcing her to do.

Because there was no way she could defy him. That was what was so appalling. She had been over and over and over it in her head, round and round and round. It had occupied her like a hideous monster. She had phoned her grandmother's solicitors the moment he had rung off but, as her father had sneeringly warned her, they knew nothing about the massive loan her grandmother had so rashly, dangerously accepted from her father. Any small hope that he might be bluffing—though really she had known from his air of triumph that he was not—had been swept away the next morning when, after a churning, sleepless night, a car had drawn up at Harford and a slick-looking estate agent from a non-local firm had emerged, primed to inspect the house and value it for 'immediate sale', as he'd oleaginously declared. He'd been closely followed by a courier who had delivered an ominous packet with the name of her father's city solicitor's name on it. Filled with dread she'd opened it, and there it was—a foreclosure notice.

For twenty-four hours Flavia had wrestled with the nightmare, taking all the documents in to the local solicitors in a hope against hope that there might be something flawed about them. But, as her father had told her, there was nothing they could do. Nothing at all. He could take Harford from her and her grandmother any time he wanted.

Any time at all...

Unless she did what he was demanding of her...

Anguish filled her. Not just because she was having to face up to just how monstrously selfish her father truly was, how utterly uncaring of her, but because of more than that.

Into her head came the image she was trying not to let in. The lean, disturbing face of Leon Maranz, who had had such a dangerous, powerful impact on her. An impact she had had to deny, reject. Her stomach hollowed. But now she was being forced to accept it after all.

Her hands twisted in her lap. She hated herself for what she was doing.

But she was going to do it anyway. She was going to go out to dinner with Leon Maranz, accept the situation—accept anything and everything he wanted of her.

She swallowed heavily, then, a moment later jumped. It was the internal phone. The concierge was calling up to tell her that her car had arrived. For a long moment she did not move. Then, slowly, very slowly, she stood up and left the apartment.

Walking on leaden feet.

Leon had chosen the restaurant with care. He wanted Flavia to like it—to feel comfortable there. It was the antithesis of anywhere Alistair Lassiter and his flashy girlfriend would choose. They would want somewhere fashionable, where people went to see and be seen. This place was totally different.

He glanced around with a sense of having chosen well. The restaurant was an eighteenth-century town house in Mayfair that prided itself on retaining and recreating as much of the ambience of that period as possible. All the furniture was antique, and the panelled walls were hung with old paintings and portraits. The original sash windows were draped with Georgian-style floor-length curtains. The original room layouts had been preserved, so even on the first floor there were only half a dozen tables—if that—giving the impression of discretion and privacy. This evening several tables were still unoccupied, and he hoped Flavia would not feel crowded or under observation. He wanted her to feel at ease.

Restlessly, he glanced around, anticipation flickering within him. He'd waited so long for this—and now, finally, it was about to start. He had checked with the driver of the car he'd sent for her—she would be here any minute…

And there she was! Pausing in the doorway. One of the restaurant staff was ushering her in, indicating his table to her with an unobtrusive murmur. For a moment she was completely still, but Leon did not mind. He was drinking her in.

Seeing her again, in the flesh and not just in his memory, was confirming everything that had drawn his eye from the first. That perfect bone structure, the clear eyes, the oval frame of her face, the long, slender throat and her beautiful, graceful figure—all was just as he remembered. Yes—she was exactly what he wanted.

His eyes worked over her assessingly, the slightest twist tugging at his mouth.

She was dressed with an even greater austerity of style than she had been that first evening at the cocktail party at her father's apartment. Not only was her hair tightly drawn back into a sleek chignon, and her make-up subtle to the point of being understated, but she was wearing a knee-length dress in dark grey, with a little stand-up collar and sleeves that reached almost to her elbows. All that brightened her was a single row of pearls, and pearl studs at her earlobes.

He got to his feet, and as if a switch had been turned on in her back she started to walk towards him. She looked very pale, but he thought that might be because of the low lighting from the wall sconces. As she took her place at their table, the candelabra to one side gave her pale flesh a warmer glow.

He sat down opposite her, letting his eyes rest on her in appreciation.

'You came,' he said.

She inclined her head, reaching for her linen napkin, which she flicked across her lap. The barest smile, the least that would pass muster in a social situation, fleeted across her mouth.

The mouth that opened to mine—that tasted of honey, and roses, and all the delights that she promised with that kiss...

His eyes flickered. Well, those delights would come now. It was impossible that they should not. Now she wanted them as much as he did. Her presence here was proof of that.

As he let her settle herself, let the waiter pour her water, proffer menus to them both and the wine list to himself, he contented himself with looking, not talking.

She was still not meeting his eyes, and for a moment there was a darkening glint in his. Then enlightenment dawned. It was obvious—the set of her shoulders, the ramrod-straightness of her back, the way she wouldn't look at him, the briefness of her smile not just to him but to the waiter as well. All showed one thing only.

She was nervous.

It was as clear as a bell. *That* was what was constraining her. Nerves. And she was nervous, Leon knew with every male instinct, because she was doing exactly what he wanted her to do—being ultra-aware of him.

Ultra-aware of the fact that *he* knew, and *she* knew, and they *both* knew that they had shared an embrace that meant she could never—not for a moment—go back to the way she had been before that embrace: pretending to him, to herself, that she was not responsive to him.

But she didn't know how to handle that—that was why she was sitting there so stiffly, so nervously. Well, she need not be nervous. This time he would not rush her, as he had so rashly before, overcome with wanting her. He would give her the time she needed to feel at ease with him.

To come with him on the journey he would take her on—deep, deep into the sensual heart of the passion that he knew with absolute certainty awaited them together.

But that was for later. Much later. For now, they were dining together. Getting to know each other. Starting their relationship.

He opened his menu and, slightly jerkily, she did likewise. He gave her time to peruse it, then made some passing observations and some suggestions. Stiltedly, she made her choice.

How she was going to manage to swallow, she didn't know. Tension was racking through her, tightening her throat, churning her stomach. She seemed to be frozen inside, and for that she was abjectedly grateful. It was though she were watching the world from inside a glacier—a glacier that was keeping her safe inside its icy depths. Numbing her with its cold.

If only, she thought desperately, it could numb her other senses! If only she didn't have to sit here looking at him, listening to him, hearing his voice—that dark, accented voice that seemed to resonate deep within her—her eyes trying to blank him out and failing utterly, totally.

The moment she'd walked into the room her eyes had gone to him instantly, as if drawn by some giant magnet. The image that had been burning on her retina since she'd flung herself out of his limo had leapt into life, imprinting itself on the flesh-and-blood man. Despite her frozen insides, she had felt her throat tighten as her body responded to him. And now, sitting so close to him, his presence was impinging on her so that she was ultra-aware of him. Of the strong, compelling features, the dark, expressive eyes, the breadth of his shoulders sheathed in the dark charcoal jacket, the sable hair that caught the light from the candelabra.

Deep within the frozen core of her body she could feel the layers of ice shift and fracture...

Hatred for what her father was making her do writhed within her. Her consciousness of the lie she was parading in front of Leon Maranz was like a snake in her mind—the lie of behaving as though she were here willingly, as if her hand had *not* been forced by her father in the most compelling way he could devise.

For a moment, as her eyes rested on the man opposite her, she felt a flaring impulse within her.

Tell him! Tell him the truth of why you are here with him tonight! Tell him what your father is threatening you with! You have no right to be here under such false pretences—no right to deceive him, pretend that you haven't been forced into this!

But she couldn't—didn't dare. Cold ran in her veins. What if she did tell Leon Maranz the truth about what her father was making her do and he was so angry that he then walked away from bailing out her father? Let her father go down the tubes.

The cold intensified. If that happened she knew with absolute certainty that her father would revenge himself on her by foreclosing on Harford. Punish her for not saving him.

So there was nothing she could do—nothing at all. She had to live out this lie. Do what her father ordered. Continue with this tormenting ordeal that was tearing her apart...

The wine had been poured and Leon was raising his glass 'To a new beginning for us.'

His voice was slightly husky, and Flavia could feel it resonate within her. Feel the pressure of his dark gaze on her. Her eyelashes dropped over her eyes, veiling them, as she took a tiny sip of her own wine.

Leon set down his glass. 'I wanted to thank you for accepting my invitation this evening,' he said, his voice low and measured.

Her fingers tightened around the stem of her glass. The lie of what she was doing—she had not accepted his invitation at all; she had been manipulated and forced into it by her father—screamed silently in her head. But there was nothing she could say—nothing.

'And I wanted to apologise to you. Apologise for the way I behaved when I was taking you home—and you felt you had to flee from me.'

There. He had said it. He'd known he'd have to—that it was the only way forward with her, to ease the strain between them. Now, though, two spots of colour flared in her cheeks, and he could see her expression blank completely. *Damn.* Maybe he shouldn't have said anything at all! Maybe that infamous English reserve meant that even his apologising was embarrassing to her!

Or maybe—the thought sliced into his mind like an acid-tipped stiletto—maybe the reason for her tension was quite different...

Like sharp stabs, words darted through his mind.

Maybe her tension is because she does not want to be here at all. What if she is here only because she now realises I am likely to bail out her father?

His expression darkened. Was that the bald, blunt truth of it? He could feel his thoughts running on unstoppably, ineluctably.

Because if that's so—if that's the only reason she's here, the only reason she's putting up with me—then...

Then *what*? That was what he had to decide. But even as he thought it he knew what the answer had to be.

Then there could be no future for them. None.

If she is not here because she wants to be—of her own volition, because she is as drawn to me as I to—then we end this right now! Whatever the strength of my desire for her, I will not succumb to it.

He could feel emotion roil within him as suspicion barbed him with poisonous darts. The ghosts of his past trailed their cold tendrils in his head. Who did she see as she sat there, the epitome of her class and her well-bred background, all pearl necklace and crystalline vowels? Did she see nobody but some jumped-up foreigner, utterly alien to her, distasteful and beneath her? Someone to look down on—look through—because, however much money he had, he could never be someone to keep company with, to be intimate with…?

Was *that* the kind of woman Flavia Lassiter was?

He watched her toy with her knife, straightening it minutely, then drop her hand to her lap to pick up her linen napkin, dabbing it momentarily to her lips, dropping it again to her lap, smoothing it out. Her gaze was fixed on it, on anything that wasn't him. Small, jerky, awkward movements, indicating glaringly how totally ill at ease she was.

Because she was embarrassed about desiring him or just embarrassed by his company?

The damnable thing was it was impossible to tell. Impossible to know what was going on inside her head. Was she essentially cut from the same cloth as her father, who had not troubled to hide his sense of superiority to those not from his privileged world? Did her outer beauty conceal an inner ugliness?

Or was there, as he so fervently hoped, more to her than that?

He *had* to find out.

Their waiter had approached, and was ready to set down their first course. Leon watched Flavia turn her head and smile at him as he carefully placed the plate in front of her, murmur thank you to him. That was a good sign, he realised. Not everyone bothered to acknowledge waiters. He felt reassurance go through him. Then it wavered again. It was easy for women like Flavia Lassiter to be gracious towards those who served them—it didn't mean they regarded them as their social equals.

He glanced at her plate as she lifted her fork to make a start.

'That looks very frugal,' he observed, referring to the scattered salad leaves and slivers of asparagus.

She gave a constrained flicker of a smile—the barest acceptable. 'I'm not very hungry,' she replied, focussing her gaze on her food, not Leon.

Leon's eyes washed over her. 'You are very slender,' he observed, meaning it as a compliment.

She didn't reply, only gave that brief, constrained flicker in response, and reached for her glass of mineral water. Her movements were still stiff and jerky. Leon cast about for another subject, as he started in on his own first course, an array of seafood.

'What do you think of the restaurant?' he enquired conversationally.

Flavia glanced around. 'It's very…good,' she said, having sought for an appropriate word, and only coming up with 'good'.

'I thought you might prefer somewhere like this to anywhere more flashy and crowded.'

The hesitant indentation of her lips in acknowledgement came again as she gathered some asparagus onto her fork. 'Oh, yes. Thank you. I do.'

Even to her own ears her voice sounded staccato and disjointed. She tried again, looking about her, knowing that she had to make an effort, that she owed him that, at least, however impossible—*totally* impossible!—her presence here was.

'I like the way it's been furnished, in eighteenth-century style,' she managed to say.

He must have sensed the unspoken approval in her voice, for she heard him say, as he took a mouthful of his wine, 'Do you like historic houses?'

Without thinking, she glanced across at him. 'Yes. I live in one.'

He frowned slightly. 'Your father's apartment is very modern, its style ultra-contemporary,' he said.

She looked at him. 'I don't live there,' she said.

Leon's expression changed. 'Your father didn't say—'

Flavia's face tightened. 'No, I doubt he did.' Her voice was clipped.

'So where *do* you live?' Leon was intrigued, realising just how little he knew about her. 'Do you have your own flat in London?'

'No.' The rejection of such an idea was audible in her voice.

'So where…?' He let the question trail.

Flavia bit her lip. The last thing she wanted to risk was Leon finding out about Harford. He might start asking questions about it she dared not answer.

'In the country,' she said shortly, keeping it deliberately vague. 'I don't like cities.'

He was looking at her curiously and she could see he was about to pursue the subject. She knew she must head him off instantly. It was dangerous ground—far, far too dangerous!

'How…how does eighteenth-century style in Britain compare with its equivalent in South America?' she asked, trying to find an anodyne topic, the kind of neutral small talk she made when at her father's social gatherings, to draw him away from her own situation. 'I've never been anywhere in Latin America, but the historic colonial style is very distinctive, and so attractive—both in the town houses and in the country *estancias*.'

Leon's voice, when he replied, was dry. 'Yes, indeed. For those few fortunate enough to live in such style. Unfortunately most of the population does not. It was not until I visited my country for the first time in a dozen years since I left for Europe that I was able to set foot in such a property—one that had been converted into a luxury hotel. Until then my only experience of accommodation in my native land was in a shanty town.'

Flavia stared. Frowned. 'A shanty town?' she echoed.

'A *favela*—though strictly speaking that is a Brazilian term.' He paused, looking at her openly astonished expression. Questioning it. 'I was raised in a city slum,' he said. 'I came to this country, penniless, at the age of fifteen.'

Flavia set down her fork. 'I had no idea,' she said.

Leon's frown deepened. Could it be true that she had no

idea of his background? There had been astonishment in her voice.

But not revulsion.

He could feel hope flare within him again. Were his doubts about her unnecessary? Let them be so...

'How did you manage to get here?' she asked. There was genuine enquiry in her voice, interlaced with her astonishment.

She wanted to know? Well, he would tell her. Tell her the grim, difficult story of his rise from penury to wealth. See how she reacted to it.

'I came with my uncle—he spent his life savings getting us here. He wanted a better future for me, his dead sister's son, than could ever have been possible at home.'

She was still staring at him. 'But how on *earth* did you manage to get from that to...to what you are now?'

There was a note of disbelief in her voice, as if she thought he must be exaggerating the poverty of his origins. But what there was *not*, Leon could tell—and the realisation surged through him—was any note of repugnance or revulsion at his lowly start in life.

'I worked,' he said simply. 'To anyone from the Third World Europe is a place of incredible opportunity to make good. So I worked non-stop. And, though it was hard, little by little I put money aside. My uncle, to my grief, became ill three years later and died, but by then I was on my way. I studied at evening college to understand the financing of business, and did any work going to increase my savings.'

He warmed to his theme, feeling memories leap in his head from a dozen years ago. 'What I spent them on was others like me, striving to make good. I chose very carefully, and if I thought they were serious and dedicated, and above all, hardworking, I loaned them the small amounts of money that they needed to buy inventory, rent premises, machinery, transport—to start their own businesses. I took a share in their profits—a fair one, no more as they prospered, and little by little I prospered, too. I increased my investments, my loans, nearly always amongst the immigrant community who understood—still understand—how much the West has in comparison with the Third World, how hard work can lift them out of poverty with an ease that is almost impossible in the Third World primarily because of the lack of credit, the mass poverty there. And that is why,' he finished, 'now that my investments are on a corporate scale, and my profits, too, I run an extensive financing programme in microloans and similar on-the-ground investment back in South America.'

There was a caustic note in his voice now, Flavia heard, listening with growing astonishment and attention as he went on. 'Some economists who are used to vast government-backed investments from the global banking community, and they might consider my efforts small fry. But—' his eyes narrowed, becoming piercing with his intense emotion '—they have never lived in those shanty towns, never realised that it is individuals who are poor—not populations. National prosperity is built from the ground up, family by family, and *that* is my focus. My goal. My mission in life.'

He fell silent at last, burningly conscious that he had done something he had never done before—bared his soul about what was most important in his work. She was gazing at him, lips parted. The expression in her eyes was different from any he had yet seen there.

And it filled him with an emotion he had never yet felt.

'I think it's extraordinary,' she said quietly. 'An extraordinary achievement.' She paused, picked up her fork again. 'No wonder you think me shallow and spoilt for not working.' Her voice was small, subdued, and she would not look at him.

Emotion was coursing through Leon. Not just because he had bared his soul, but because of how Flavia had reacted. Relief—more than relief—leapt in his breast.

She didn't know I was born poor—and she is not offended or contemptuous of it!

If there was any hint of contempt it was for herself.

He was swift to dissolve it.

'None of us is responsible for our background. Only for what we do, how we live our lives, the decisions we make,' he said.

It was meant to be a gentle remark, a soothing one. Yet before his eyes her face changed. The animation that had been there a moment ago as she'd spoken to him vanished. Tension leapt again, and it was as if a mask had shut down over her. Her eyes dropped and she swallowed, reaching for her wine glass.

She took a mouthful, feeling the need for it. His words burnt like a new brand on her skin. Consciousness of what she was doing here—why she was there, at whose bidding and for what purpose—scalded her. But there was nothing she could do—*nothing*! If she did not go along with what her father wanted he would turn her grandmother out of the house she loved, sell it from under her feet, without pity or compunction or remorse.

But if she'd felt bad before about what she was doing at her father's behest, now, having heard just what kind of man Leon Maranz truly was, she was excruciated.

I thought him just one more fat cat financier, born to some wealthy South American family, cocooned in money, caring only about the next profit-making deal to be made.

The truth was utterly different.

Involuntarily her eyes went to him again, seeing for the first time not the five-thousand-pound Savile Row suit, the silk tie, the gold watch snaking around his lean wrist—all the appurtenances of wealth and luxury. Seeing something quite different.

The young, impoverished, desperate immigrant, striving with all his determination, all his dedication and perseverance, to transform his destiny from what would have awaited him in his place of birth—the teeming, fetid *favela*—to one he had wrought for himself out of the opportunities he had been given in coming to Europe, to the rich Western world.

And not just for himself. Leon Maranz had not turned his back on his origins, not left his compatriots to rot, but had determined to use the wealth he'd made to help lift them out of the same poverty he'd once known. He'd have to have faith in them, offered them a chance just as he'd once had.

Emotions clashed within her. One, she knew, was a strong, bright glow—a shining sense of admiration for what Leon Maranz had achieved, was still achieving. An admiration that brought with it something else.

He's a man I need have no reservations about, no qualms— he's free from the venal, avaricious taint of my father, who built his fortune ruthlessly and without any compunction for anyone else. He's nothing like my father—for all his wealth— nothing like him at all!

Yet even as the realisation sent that glow through her it brought in its wake more bitter anguish. A burning, shaming consciousness of being her despised father's tool, being used by him for his own ends, forced into deceit, manipulation, lies, to safeguard what she held so dear.

It was unbearable—unbearable!

Her eyes dropped again, tension once more racking her body.

Across the table, Leon watched the transformation. He had almost broken through the web of constraint and nerves that had been so visibly possessing her since she had walked into the restaurant—almost! But now it had webbed around her again, and she was back to being as tense as a board...

For the rest of the evening he strove to break through again, to see once more that spark of contact, of communication with her. But it was gone. Extinguished. All he could achieve was a strained, awkward conversation, with him doing nearly all the talking, about one anodyne subject after another. Frustration bit in him. Just as she'd started to thaw towards him she'd frozen solid again. Yet something had changed between them, making his fears about her attitude towards him dissolve. And on that he could build—work. Work to rekindle that small but so-revealing spark of human warmth he had seen in her. Work to draw her out, draw her to him—win her to him.

And if that took time—well, so be it, then.

He accepted her halting conversation, making the evening as easy for her as he possibly could. And when the meal was over he thanked her for her company, evinced his pleasure at it, told her his car would take her back to her father's apartment and then asked if he might see her again.

Flavia stood on the pavement outside the restaurant. At the kerb the large black limo was hovering, its driver dutifully holding open the door for her. Leon was smiling down at her.

'Can I persuade you, if not to Shakespeare, then to something else at the theatre? Is there anything playing that might tempt you? Or perhaps,' he elaborated, wanting to give her not the least reason to turn down his seeing her again, 'you might prefer the opera, or a concert? Or what about an art exhibition?' he finished, wanting to give her as many options as he could in the fervent hope that something—anything!—might trigger her interest, be the key to break down her constraint.

But all he got was a low-pitched, awkward, 'I don't really mind… Whatever you would like…'

What I would like, thought Leon frustratedly, *is what you would like.* But all he said in response to her lukewarm reply was a measured, 'Well, I'll see what I can come up with, OK?' He delivered it with a smile he hoped was reassuring and complaisant. Then, in a slightly brisker tone, he said, 'Till tomorrow, then—will seven o'clock be all right for you?'

'Yes. Thank you. Thank you for this evening. Um—goodnight.'

She flickered her hesitant social smile at him and climbed into the car, murmuring a semi-audible thank you to the driver holding the door. Then she sank back into the deep leather of the interior.

Misery writhed within her. Seeing Leon Maranz again had been a torment of exquisite proportions! To sit opposite him, across that small table lit by candlelight, to want to do nothing more than drink in everything about him! But to be every single moment tormentingly conscious that she was there at her father's bidding, the tool of his machinations— pimped out to the man he wanted to save his riches for him...

Shame burnt along every nerve-ending, inflamed with anger at her father—anger at his threat to her frail, vulnerable grandmother; anger that he was prepared to use his own daughter to try and save his sorry skin; and anger, above all—the realisation came like a blow to the heart—that he was poisoning something that could have been so incredibly special to her.

For the first time in my life I have met someone like no one I have ever met before! Whatever it is about Leon Maranz, he can affect me as no one else ever has! For the first time, I have known what desire truly is...

But it had been poisoned by deceit. Polluted by her father's blackmail.

Making it impossible for her to be as she truly wanted to be with Leon. Making her frozen with the shame twisting inside her like wires of guilt. Holding him at bay because of the unspoken lie between them, the threat hanging over her head that she dared not tell him about yet which held her in unbreakable talons.

Misery welled dully within her as Leon's car drove her away. Back to the father she hated with all her being for what he was doing to her. Making a cruel mockery of her tormented, anguished feelings.

Alone on the pavement, Leon watched the car disappear into the London traffic. Frustration warred within him, against a steely determination. There must be a way of getting through to her! A way to persuade her to finally lower her guard against him and start to respond to him. He had seen a precious, essential glimpse of it as he'd told her of his background—but then she had clammed up again!

But at least, he reasoned, as he hailed a taxi to take him

back to his apartment, she'd agreed to see him again—and the very next night. He had till then to come up with something that might appeal to her—something that might help her relax a little towards him. But what? She'd sounded nothing more than polite about any of his suggestions.

His brow furrowed as the taxi turned into Shaftesbury Avenue. All around London buzzed and blared with noise from the traffic, garish neon lights from the shops, restaurants and the theatres that lined the road, and the pavements were thronged with people out for the evening. Suddenly it dawned on him. An echo of her terse comment when he'd asked where she lived sounded in his memory.

'I don't like cities.'

Of *course*—that was it! Enlightenment hit him. No matter how carefully he'd chosen the restaurant tonight, it was London itself she didn't care for.

Relief at his realisation filled him. He slid his mobile out of his breast pocket and tapped in an internet search. Moments later he'd connected to the phone number provided and made the reservation he wanted.

He sat back, his shoulders relaxing into the seat. Tomorrow night would be very, very different from tonight. He was sure of it.

He shut his eyes, letting the image of Flavia, in all her beauty, infuse his retinas.

CHAPTER EIGHT

'The limo's here, sweetie. Don't keep him waiting!'

Anita's voice was sugared, but Flavia could hear an acid note in it as well. Her father's girlfriend was making a poor job of failing to conceal both her irritation and her jealousy of her. As she walked past the other woman, Flavia could see Anita, glass of wine lolling from scarlet-tipped fingers, subjecting her to a scornful scrutiny.

'God, I hope he's got a taste for seducing nuns!' Anita sneered. 'Why the hell you don't take my advice on how to dress to impress, I don't know!'

Yes, well, thought Flavia silently, making no comment, *that depends on just what impression one wants to make*. Her eyes flicked dismissively over Anita's clingy leopard-print dress.

She knew what impression *she* herself wanted to make, and the round-necked, sleeveless black shift over which she wore a silk-knit jacket fitted the bill. As she reached the front door, she caught a last jibe from Anita.

'I hope you've got a spare pair of knickers for the morning in your handbag, sweetie. We don't want to see you back here tonight! This time make sure you don't cop out—just do whatever it takes to keep Leon happy. Your father's counting on it. Or ga-ga Granny'll be popping her senile clogs in a council house. And don't think your father won't see to it! If he goes down—*you* go down!' she promised venomously. 'So keep that gorgeous Latino hunk of yours sweet on us, if you know what's good for you!' Her tone changed, becoming barbed and accusatory. 'It's not like it's going to be any kind of bloody ordeal, is it? Going to bed with a guy like that! So stop looking like Little Miss Martyr! Hell, I'd trade places with you like a shot—believe me!' She took another swig from her wine glass, and glared balefully at Flavia.

Face set, jaw as tight as steel, hatred for her father and for Anita biting in her blood, Flavia snapped the apartment door shut behind her, shutting out Anita's crude, cruel words, her sleazy innuendo, and stalking towards the lift. Mortification burned in her—and shame, and anger, and bitter, bitter resentment. All twisting and writhing like snakes.

But as she walked out of the apartment block she crushed her tormenting emotions back down inside her. The evening stretched ahead of her, and there was nothing she could do about it.

Leon's driver was getting out of the car, tipping his cap to her as he opened the rear passenger door, and she stepped inside. But as she sank back into the seat she froze.

Leon was also in the car.

For a moment she felt panic flare in her eyes. She subdued it as swiftly as she could, stiffly returning his greeting as the car pulled away.

Leon gave her time to compose herself whilst, with a catch in his throat, he took in just how stunningly beautiful she looked all over again. The black of the dress, severe though it was, illuminated the pearlescence of her skin, the soft sheen of her hair in its customary chignon. And the faint floral scent she was wearing was winding into his senses. How incredibly beautiful she was! Emotion welled through him, and for a moment he could only drink her in.

But he could see that she was just as tense tonight—there was no lowering of her guard. Determination scythed through him. Well, perhaps this evening would be more propitious...

'You said last night,' he began, 'that you would be happy to let me choose what to do this evening. So...' He took a breath.

'I hope I've made a good choice. Tell me—' he looked at her enquiringly '—have you ever been to Mereden?'

She looked slightly confused. 'Mereden? No. I've heard of it, but...' She paused. 'Isn't it way out of London?'

He nodded. 'Yes. You let slip last night that you didn't care for cities, so I thought you might enjoy somewhere like Mereden instead. It shouldn't take more than maybe half an hour to get there. I hope that's OK with you?'

'Um—yes. Yes. Of course.'

He threw a glancing smile at her. 'Good. While we're travelling there, I hope you won't mind if I use the time to finish off some work. There's some magazines if you'd like something to flick through.'

Relieved that she did not have to make painful conversation with him yet, Flavia took one of the magazines at random while Leon focussed on his laptop. Every sense was super-aware of him sitting there, a few feet away from her, and every part of her mind was leaping with the memory of what had happened the last time she'd sat in this limo with him...

He'd swept away her reserve, her resistance, as if they were nothing. Nothing at all! Melting her with his kiss, dissolving her very bones with it!

It had been the most devastating experience of her life—changing everything she'd been. Making her feel what she had never felt before!

She could feel her heart-rate quicken as the memory seared across her brain, feel her breath catch. Urgently she fought for control, lest he turn his head, see the hectic flush in her cheeks—and know just what had caused it.

Somehow she managed to regain at least an outer semblance of the composure she was trying to hang on to with all her might. Inwardly, her emotions were in turmoil—currents swirling inchoately as she tried not to think about what might lie ahead at the end of the evening...

She was grateful for the journey out of London. By the time the car was making its way off the motorway into the

Thames Valley she was able to take some cognisance of where they were going. They were driving through hilly woodland along quiet, country roads that seemed a universe away from London, only that short journey behind them.

The car slowed to turn through imposing ironwork gates, to move along a drive bordered by rhododendrons in vivid bloom, with glimpses of extensive parkland beyond. Early evening sunshine lit up the landscape, and Flavia could not help but feel its soothing influence over her jangled nerves.

'Better than London?'

Leon's enquiry made her turn her head. He had shut down his laptop and was slipping it into its case.

'Oh, yes...'

There was a warmth in her voice that was obvious by its previous absence. As the magnificent Palladian frontage of Mereden came into view, bathed in sunlight and lapped by manicured gardens, he knew with satisfaction that he had made a good decision in bringing Flavia here. She was no city girl, craving bright lights and crowds. This country house hotel, set in rural parkland, was far more her style!

They drew up in front of the grand entrance and a uniformed doorman stepped forward to open the passenger door. Flavia climbed out and looked around her. She had heard of Mereden, but had never been here before. Once a stately home, now it was a lavish private hotel, set in the exclusive wealthy catchment area of the Thames Valley.

'Shall we go in?'

Leon ushered her forward and she stepped through the imposing double doorway into a high-ceilinged hall beyond.

They were clearly expected, and were conducted out on to a wide terrace overlooking the gardens and the River Thames beyond. Guests were enjoying pre-dinner drinks, watching the sunset. Flavia caught her breath, gazing out over the panoramic vista.

'Worth the drive out?'

She turned impulsively to Leon. 'Oh, yes! It's absolutely breathtaking!'

His expression stilled. Slowly he replied, 'I'm glad you like it.'

'Who couldn't?' she answered, and turned back to gaze over the stone balustrade at the verdant lawns, drenched in golden evening sunlight, reaching down towards the river's edge.

Even without consciously realising it, she could feel some of the tension racking through her ebb a little. It was *so* good to be out of London, away from the built-up streets, in such a glorious place as this, with such a vista in front of her. It was impossible not to respond to it. The warm, balmy air, clean and fresh after the fumes and pollution of London, was like a blessing, as was the blessed quietness all around her. No traffic noise was audible, only the murmuring of the other guests, and the evening birdsong from the trees set around the wide lawns.

'Madam?' A waiter was standing beside her, champagne glasses on a tray.

'Thank you,' she found herself saying with a smile, and took a narrow flute filled with gently fizzing liquid.

Leon did likewise. A sense of achievement glowed in him. He'd definitely done the right thing in bringing her here. He could feel relief easing through him, and hoped it was not premature. But, for all his wariness, at least her reaction so far was proving encouraging.

'To a pleasant evening,' he said.

With only the barest hesitation Flavia clinked her flute to his, then, as if to give herself some cover, turned back to gaze out over the vista, sipping at the champagne. It tasted cold and delicious.

'I don't know how anyone can live in London,' she heard herself musing, her eyes resting on the peaceful scenery before her.

Leon moved slightly and came to stand beside her, taking care not to invade her body space lest she take fright. He rested a hand on the sun-warmed stone of the balustrade.

'Many don't have another choice,' he pointed out mildly. What he didn't point out, though, was that her comment was the first completely unprompted one she'd made to him. He wanted to do absolutely nothing to make her aware of that. If that meant treading on eggshells, so be it.

Her eyes flickered to him, then swiftly away out over the view again. 'Yes. I feel so sorry for them. But some people like the city. My father and Anita, for example.' Her voice was flat.

'I hated London when I first came,' Leon said, choosing not to take up her remark about her father and his girlfriend. 'It was freezing cold, and it rained all the time.'

'A lot of foreigners think that,' she said wryly. 'Quite a few Brits, too—it's why they head south to the sun. But somehow winter is worse in the city, I think.'

'I wouldn't disagree with you there,' said Leon dryly. He paused. 'So, whereabouts in the country do you live?'

Immediately he saw her stiffen. Inwardly he cursed himself. Up till now, ever since they'd arrived here, she'd seemed to thaw discernibly—as if the beautiful, rural surroundings had calmed her. Now the tension was back in the set of her shoulders.

'Oh, in the West Country,' she said, offhandedly. 'Look, isn't that a heron?'

Her voice was animated because she wanted to change the subject fast. It was the second time Leon had asked her where she lived, and it was the last thing she wanted him to know. Disquiet swirled rancidly within her at the reminder of just why she was here—and at whose bidding. For a brief moment there seemed to be a shadow over the sunlit view she was gazing over.

Thankfully, he accepted her change of tack. 'I wouldn't know,' he said. 'Natural history isn't my thing at all.'

'I think it *is* a heron,' she said, eyes fixed on it.

'What are those smaller birds darting around over the river?' If she wanted to talk about wildlife, then he could only be grateful. Anything to keep her mood as it was. The stiffening in her shoulders as he'd asked about where she lived had gone again, and he was thankful. He didn't want to talk about anything at all that might make her tense up again. This visible thawing, slight though it was, was far too precious for that.

'Swallows and swifts, probably,' she replied. 'They like to catch the insects that are attracted to the water.' She took another sip from her champagne flute. It helped to let her speak more naturally, with less awkward stiffness. And besides, sipping chilled champagne, here on the terrace, looking out over so beautiful a vista, seemed an appropriate thing to do in such a setting.

With such a man beside her... A man who set every nerve-ending in her body aflame...

No—she mustn't think of that! Mustn't let herself. She was coping with this whole situation in the only way she could—by taking it minute by minute and keeping that composed, unemotional mask over her face, her mind...

Leon smiled. 'Ah, yes—I've seen them at my villa on Santera, skimming over the swimming pool in the evenings.'

Flavia glanced at him. 'Santera?'

'One of the many smaller islands of the Balearics,' he said.

'I've not heard of it.' She shook her head slightly.

'Most people haven't,' he answered. 'They know about the main islands of the Balearics—notably Majorca—but the archipelago has a host of other tiny islands and islets. Many are uninhabited, kept as nature reserves or just places to sail to and around. A few have villas and resorts on them, like Santera.'

Flavia looked away again. It was safer to look at the view down to the river, to study the birds darting over the water, than to stand looking at Leon. He was talking again, and she was grateful. More about this island near Majorca. She made herself pay attention. Nature, geography, foreign travel—all were safe, innocuous subjects.

'Santera is very flat,' he was saying, 'and the land almost seems to meld with the sea. It's dry and sandy, but to my mind very lovely. The beaches are wonderful, and there is only one metalled road, leading from the small harbour where supplies are brought in. There are only a few other villas there besides mine, so each is very secluded.'

'It sounds beautiful,' she said slowly. There had been a warmth in his voice she had not heard before, and it made her turn her head to glance at him. Just for a moment—the briefest second—their gazes mingled.

Then she pulled hers away and looked out towards the River Thames again, rotating the stem of her champagne glass. Her blood seemed to be swirling in her veins suddenly.

'It is,' he said. An idea was forming in his mind, though he was not sure of it yet. 'But it is not by any means luxurious.'

She gave a small, dismissive shrug of her shoulders. 'Luxury isn't important,' she said.

His eyes narrowed, studying her as she gazed out over the balustrade. She was a child of luxury—born to it—with a wealthy father to lavish her with designer clothes like the elegant outfit she was wearing now.

'Easy to say when you have always had it at your disposal,' he could not stop himself saying.

She turned at that. Her expression was stricken, and Leon immediately felt bad that he'd made such a remark.

'I'm sorry,' she said, 'that was crass of me.' There was a sincerity in her voice that was not there just for politeness.

He would have responded, but one of the hotel staff was approaching, enquiring if they would care to take their table yet.

Their table was by the French windows and gave a full view of the setting sun, its rays gilding the ornate room and glinting on the polished silverware. Menus were presented, their flutes refilled, and whether it was the champagne or the air of the countryside, Flavia suddenly felt hungry. When she gave her order, Leon looked mildly surprised at her choices. They were definitely more hearty than they had been the night before.

'It all sounds so appetising,' she said by way of explanation.

When the food arrived, superbly presented and even more superbly prepared, she found she was eating with real enjoyment.

Something was changing, she knew. It wasn't just the champagne, or even the exquisite food, or the beautiful room they were dining in—all painted Adam ceiling and gilded pillars, opening out on to the terrace and the view beyond. It was more than that.

Her gaze went to Leon.

For a long, long moment her eyes rested on him, taking him in, drinking him in. She felt an aching longing welling inside her. And knew she must answer a question she could no longer avoid, no longer hide from.

If I were free—totally free, without any consideration for anyone but myself—where would I be?

She had fled from Leon once, overwhelmed by him, by the feelings he could arouse in her, seeing only the impossibility of it all, scared and overcome by it. She had fled back home to her responsibilities, to the grandmother who depended on her. Leon Maranz was not for her—he could not be. The inescapable circumstances of her life made it impossible.

But now she had been forced to go to him. Forced to do her father's foul bidding. She resented and hated it. Yet for all that the question came again, refusing to be silenced.

If I were totally free—if I could choose for myself—where would I be?

And the answer came clear, with no possibility of denial.

I would be here. Here with Leon.

Because there has never been anyone like him before in my life and being with him is all I want!

It was a truth she could no longer deny. Yet even as she accepted it she felt the cry come from deep within her.

If only... If only I were here with him without anything to do with my father! Without the hideous pressure he is putting on me! If only I were here with Leon and the threat to Harford, to my grandmother, never existed! If only my father had not tainted and befouled what I want so much! This time with Leon...this precious time!

Because if that were so... If that were so, she knew, with deep, absolute certainty, that she would be here willingly, joyously. With absolute conviction in what she was doing. Giving in to the overpowering need to succumb to what he had lit within her like a flame.

There has never been anyone like him—never been anything like the response he evokes in me! Never before—and never again...

Why it had happened she could not tell. Why this man she did not know. She knew only that it was so—that it had happened—and she could no more deny it or defy it than cease to breathe. The truth of it was as radiant as the sun setting in liquid fire, its last rays streaming all around her, turning the world to gold.

Anguish clutched at her. That what she felt for Leon, this extraordinary flame of burning desire, should be so sullied by what her father was doing to her was unbearable—unbearable that her father should be soiling it with his foul demands and threats! Making something shameful of what should have been so wonderful!

And then, as she gazed at him, her anguish in her face, his eyes met hers. Blazed with sudden desire impossible to veil. And in that moment, as she met the full charge, she felt something shift and change and resolve in her.

So what if her father was trying to exploit her for his own ends? Trying to manipulate her, threatening and blackmailing her, making her feel soiled and ashamed? She was doing what he wanted for her grandmother's sake—and the knowledge seared within her that it was what *she* wanted, too! What she wanted with all her being.

Words formed in her head. Strong—resolute. From the inner core of her.

What is happening is happening. I will not let what my father is doing poison and destroy it. I will not let it taint and sully it.

She would put everything aside but her own feelings for Leon. Nothing her father could do could poison *them*! She would not allow it—would not permit it! She would put aside everything her father had said, and threatened, and insinuated, and manipulated. Because one shining truth was blazing within her, as golden and glorious as the setting sun bathing the world in beauty: she was here, now, because she *wanted* to be, because she would of her own free choice be nowhere else but here, with Leon. Going forward with him to wherever he would take her, on a journey she had never taken before—on a journey into the heart of desire and its burning, incandescent fulfilment.

She would give herself to him and let nothing taint this time—*nothing*!

Like light and warmth, the resolution streamed through her, blazed from her eyes. Her gaze hung on Leon's, and in his dark, beautiful eyes she saw suddenly, like a fire kindling, an answering blaze. For one endless moment it was there—a moment of intensity she had never known before. Then, as if it was overwhelming her, like breathing pure oxygen or gazing into the heart of the too-bright sun, she dropped her gaze, breathless with sudden, extraordinary happiness.

Across the table Leon felt his senses reeling. Triumph—more than triumph!—coursed through him. For the first time he had seen in Flavia what he had so long ached to see: the fire of her response to him acknowledged, admitted—accepted. Relief filled him, deep and profound. The knowledge that finally he had broken through that endless guard she'd held up to him, keeping him at bay, holding him off. Gratitude welled within him, and resolve—resolve that her new-found trust in him would never be betrayed. He would take her only where she herself wanted to go, on the journey that awaited them into the heart of desire—desire fulfilled...

Emotion moved within him, making him pause. A sense of wonder filled him—a sense of gratitude that this beautiful, beautiful woman, as wary as a doe, had been granted to him.

I will not hurt her or let her down. I will be worthy of her. I will not betray her trust in me, so valued because it was so hard-won...

But he must still proceed slowly, carefully, he knew. She must not be rushed or overwhelmed lest she take fright again, hide once more behind that frigid wall surrounding her. He cast about for something easy to talk about—some unpressured, uncontentious topic that would help to draw her out, set her yet more at her ease, build on the fragile trust that had put forth its precious green shoots this evening.

Ironically, he knew that what he wanted was to find out much more about her. There was so little he knew—even where she lived. Well, it was no matter. Gradually, as they got to know each other fully, they would talk more about themselves, have no secrets from each other. Already, the previous evening, he had found himself telling her about his work to help others living as he once had himself—a subject he did not usually dwell on in company. There were those in the world he moved in now who found the thought of such dire poverty uncomfortable, unsettling.

Flavia hadn't seemed to, though—and it had been the sincerity of her sympathy, briefly expressed as it had been, that had shown him she was not the shallow, venal, pampered princess he'd feared she might be, given her wealthy background and given, he thought, with an inward frown, her father's utter lack of sensibility about the plight of others in the world! But Flavia was clearly cut from a different cloth from her father—he trusted that instinctively.

As if catching his thoughts, she spoke, pre-empting his mental search for a safe, neutral topic to converse on with her.

'You mentioned last night you'd set up projects to help those trapped in poverty in the Third World?' she ventured. 'What sort of enterprises are most effective?'

There was genuine interest in her enquiry. Even so, she was conscious that she was seeking a subject that would give him the role of talking the most. Her own thoughts and emotions were in freefall, and she needed time—precious time—to let them settle. Letting him talk would give her that time— time to come to terms with the momentous resolution she had made.

Time, too, to do what she so wanted to do—just sit there and drink him in. Drink in the strong, magnetic features, sit quietly and watch the lean perfection of his body, look at the dark feathered sable of his hair, the quick indentation of his lips, hear the deep accented tones of his voice. All a sensuous, breath-catching delight to her!

A sense of release filled her. As if a hideous burden had been lifted from her, freeing her from the corruptive taint of her father's venal machinations.

Now, finally, she could accept that, whatever the cause of her being here with Leon, *this* was where she wanted to be. And accept freely that it was what *she* wanted, too—to have this time with Leon, come what may.

As he started to answer her she sat, listening to him as they dined. He elaborated on the work he was doing—giving back the fruits of his own hard, long endeavours to drag himself out of the same poverty—and she set her senses free, her passions free. She would give herself joyously, willingly to Leon, to his desire for her—her desire for him.

And she would let nothing taint it, poison it.

She would not allow it.

On wings of liberation she felt her spirits soar, and happiness, relief, anticipation and joy filled her being.

CHAPTER NINE

'SHALL I extinguish the candle? You would see the stars more clearly then.'

Flavia shook her head. 'No, I think the garden lights will still make it impossible to see them well.'

They were taking coffee at the far end of the terrace, where it opened into a stone-paved parterre edged with box into which were inset small footlights. Other guests were dotted around at low tables, seated in wickerwork chairs, taking coffee and liqueurs.

'The best stars I've seen,' Leon was musing, 'are on Santera. Like gold discs cut out of black velvet. One day I'll buy a telescope—though I'll need to hire an astronomer as well, to show me what I'm looking at,' he added ruefully.

She smiled. 'I'm sure it would be a popular job,' she said.

She let her shoulders relax back into the chair, lifting her cup of coffee. Despite the liberating ease with which she now found she could converse with Leon, at the same time she could feel a sensation like a trickle of electricity rippling through her, just below the level of her skin. It was setting her heartbeat just a little more rapid, and her pulse was a little more tangible, her breath a little more uneven.

Her eyes went to the man sitting back in the wicker chair opposite her, and it seemed to her that the trickle of electricity flickering beneath her skin gave a little surge of voltage. Her gaze hung on his face—so darkly planed, so compelling to look at. His whole strong, dominating physical presence was waiting for her.

Waiting for her to be ready.

And I am—finally. That is what has happened. I am no longer fighting what I first recognised in that very first moment of seeing him. At last—despite everything my father has done, despite all my fears for my poor grandmother—this is something that I want...with all my being.

The shadow of her father, his malign presence in her life, his threatening power to destroy the last months of her grandmother's life, still hung there like a lowering cloud, but she set it aside. She would not let it poison this time that had come upon her, which finally she would accept.

Willingly, joyously, desiringly...

Her eyes met Leon's.

He knows—he knows I am ready now.

She thought he might smile, might look with satisfaction upon her, seeing her acquiescence, her acceptance, in every line of her body, the melting of her eyes. But he did not smile, and she was glad. Touched.

This was no triumph, no conquest, no victory over her doubts and resistance.

This was a mutual desiring—a shared acknowledgement of something flaring between them that both of them welcomed.

Embraced.

He got to his feet. Held out a hand to her. She took it silently and let him draw her to her feet.

They walked hand in hand, and it seemed right, and real, and welcome. Strolling beside him, no words were necessary as she walked down to the far end of the terrace, where it was quiet, unpopulated by guests, unlit by floor lamps. Only the stars above glinted and gleamed in their crystal orbs.

He paused and turned, took her other hand. Gazed down into her eyes in the dim, diffused starlight.

'My Flavia,' he said.

And that was all. All she heard—all she wanted to hear.

Needed to hear. She lifted her face, let herself gaze at him, let the warmth of his hands holding hers be all the reassurance she needed.

Why this man?

She did not know. It did not matter. This moment now was all. The reasons she was here were unnecessary. Irrelevant.

'Leon…' Her voice was a breath, an exhalation, a sigh. Accepting everything he offered her. Offering him everything he craved.

He took her mouth as a flower, as the sweetest fruit. The most delicate flavour. The gentlest touch.

He was holding himself in absolute control. He knew it. Knew that this moment was precious, that it was of absolute importance that he not get it wrong this time. That this was the moment that could win him Flavia—or lose her for ever.

There would be no second chance. Not if he screwed it up now. Not if he rushed her too fast, allowed his needs to overwhelm hers.

Besides, he wanted this exquisite moment to last—to stand here beneath the stars and have her warm and pliant in his arms, as tender as the summer's night that webbed about them. Just her and him—as if alone in all the world together.

Gently, delicately, tenderly, he explored the beauty of her mouth with his, has hands cradling her head, fingertips whispering through her hair. She was leaning into him, and he felt the soft wand of her body against his, felt himself responding.

He drew away a little, released her mouth, still cradling her upturned face. There was a dazed look in her eyes, and he found himself lowering his lips to graze each fluttering eyelid.

Then, with a breath, he let his fingers slip from her completely, standing away from her.

There was a puzzled look in her starlit eyes.

'I got it wrong with you once before,' he said, his voice low, his eyes searching hers. 'I made assumptions—rushed you. This time—' he took another scissoring breath '—I won't do that. This time...' He paused, making sure he got it right this time. 'I don't want you running from me.' He paused again. 'So I ask you now: if you would like to go back to London, back to your father's apartment, I will escort you there and no further. But if you would like to stay here, at this hotel, in a room of your own, then that is what will happen. It will be exactly and only as you wish, Flavia.'

It had cost him to say what he had—but he knew he'd had to say it. Had to give her the space, the time she needed. For himself, all he ached to do was take her back in his arms, take her to a room, a bed, and finally possess her.

But this night had to be *her* choice, her choice alone, uninfluenced by him or anything else. Her free, untrammelled choice.

He let his eyes rest on her as she stood, swaying very slightly, as if being released from his hold on her had left her unsupported. He stood still—stock still. It was for her to make the next move—only her, not him. Even though it was taking every last ounce of self-control her possessed.

The expression in her eyes changed. She lifted her hand. Let her fingers graze the edge of his jaw. He had shaved before he had met her, early in the evening, but now, at this midnight hour, he could feel her fingertips encountering the slight roughness of regrowth. Her touch was electric, and he could feel every muscle in his body tense.

She gazed up at him.

'I don't know why this is,' she said, and her voice was still soft, still murmuring, but with a plaintive note in it, as though bemusement was infusing it. 'I don't know why—I only know that it is so. I only know...' Now her fingertips were tracing, with the lightest touch, the line of his lips, and his jaw tensed with the effort not to do what every sensual instinct was pounding at him to do—to catch her with his mouth, fold her into him, his hands spanning her narrow waste, and with his lips lave the slowly questing tip of her slender finger.

'I only know that I don't want to leave. I want to stay here with you.'

His hand snaked to her wrist, drawing her hand slightly away from his face. 'Are you sure—are you truly sure?' There was an intensity in his voice, in his expression, that he could not mask. Would not mask. He would hide nothing from her—as she was hiding nothing from him. He was seeing the truth of her now. He knew absolutely. This was the woman he wanted—and she wanted him. No more masks, no more ice maiden, no more chilling reserve or holding him at bay with every word she spoke. This was the woman he wanted—here, now...

'Yes...' Her voice was a breath, an exhalation.

A promise.

He lowered his head to hers, kissing her mouth lightly, sweetly. Then he tucked her hand into his, never relinquishing it for a moment, and drew her against his side.

'You'll stay with me tonight?' Leon's voice was husked. He needed to be sure—absolutely sure.

Her answer was to lean into him, brushing her cheek against his shoulder. 'Do you think,' she mused, starlight glinting in the eyes uplifted to his, 'a place like this might run to a four-poster bed?'

His mouth tugged in a smile that made Flavia's already strong beating heart catch. He dropped a lingering kiss on her mouth.

'Let's go and find out,' he said.

Hand in hand, they headed indoors.

The hotel did, indeed, have a double room with a four-poster bed. A huge one, draped in blue damask.

'It's beautiful!' Flavia exclaimed, gazing around, taking in the panelled walls, the ornamental plastered ceiling, the thick carpets and the antique furniture, all dominated by the richly hung four-poster.

'And so are you.'

The timbre of Leon's voice sent a thrumming of electricity through her and she turned to face him. Emotion swelled through her. In the low-lit room his face was strongly featured, and she could see, blazing like a dark light in his eyes, the message of his desire for her.

'Leon—'

She breathed his name, came towards him, came into his arms.

They kissed, their mouths entwining, their arms around each other, and longing quickened within her, making her breathless and amazed. When he drew away from her she felt a loss, a parting she did not want, and reached for him again.

But he smiled down at her, a slanting smile rich with promise, his eyes devouring her. 'My beautiful Flavia.'

He said her name low and resonant, and she could only gaze at him, her pulse strong and insistent in her veins.

His eyes held hers and slowly, carefully, he reached his arms around her slender back, slipping off the loose, soft jacket, feeling for the zip at the top of her dress, sliding it slowly, oh-so-slowly, down her trembling body.

As the almost bare lines of her figure were revealed by the lowering dress, his breath caught.

She was so beautiful! So slender and so poised and so perfect…

The dark shift pooled at her feet and she stepped out of it. Then, of her own volition, she raised her hands to her spine and slipped the clasp of her bra, letting it fall. She heard the rasp in Leon's voice and rejoiced in it, sliding her panties to the floor as well. It was right, it was good, it was perfect. It was what she wanted to do and it was a joyous, blessed offering to him. For a moment she just stood there, letting him feast upon her. Then, with a little smile, she lifted her hands once more to the nape of her neck and loosened her hair from its chignon.

It fell in a sensual cloud around her shoulders, and this time

Leon was no longer motionless. He caught it with his fists and lowered his head to her, drawing her naked body against his.

His mouth seared hers like a living flame, and her body was a flame in his arms. Desire surged through him, arousing, quickening his flesh. His clothes were an impediment, and with a groan he held her momentarily away from him whilst he divested himself of them. His hands were like wood, his movements clumsy in his haste and urgency, but he didn't care. He only knew that this was not a time for posed sophistication, for studied seduction. This was about the naked, blazing desire between them, the clean flame burning with the purest fuel.

As he flung his clothes aside on the nearest armchair he clasped her to him again. She gasped, knowing the strength of his desire for her. Her eyes widened in recognition. In shared arousal.

He swept her up into his arms and carried her to the waiting bed, yanking back the coverlet to lay her tenderly upon the pristine sheet. For one endless moment he simply stood and gazed down on her—on her beauteous body, bared and waiting for him, on her lustrous hair spread like a flag across the pillows, on her face, on her eyes gazing up at him with everything in that gaze that he could want.

Her desire for him—her perfect, perfect desire…

He said her name again, emotion working in his face. She lifted her arms to him, welcoming him to her, and he came down on her with all the ardour in the world, clasping her to him.

In the soft light from the low-lit bedside lamp, in the wide expanse of the bed, beneath the silken awning above them, he kissed her. He kissed her mouth and her fluttering eyes, the line of her jaw, the arch of her throat, the hollow at its base. He kissed with softly trailing lips, tender and arousing, possessing the valley between her breasts. He kissed and laved and teased and worshipped the soft ripening mounds and then their cresting coral peaks, questing ever further, down over the silken expanse of her abdomen, his hands shaping the sculpture of her hips to graze with tantalising arousal the line of the dark vee below.

He heard her gasp and felt her hands clutching at his shoulders. He lifted his head and saw hers lifting, too. He slid his strong, empowered body upwards over hers again, so that his thighs pressed down on hers, slid one limb between hers, parting her for him. His mouth sought hers, his hand cupping the nape of her neck, lifting and shaping her head to him.

His arousal was absolute, but her needs must come first. He moved to slip one hand down her breast, her flank, down to the parting of her thighs. But she caught his hand with hers.

'No—'

She gazed up at him, urgency in her eyes, and with a blaze of understanding Leon knew that she was as ready as he— that she wanted exactly what he wanted now.

'You're sure?'

His question hung only for a moment, and it was her eyes, her questing mouth seeking his afresh, that told him the answer.

And her fevered breath.

And his.

He plunged into her, deep and lifting, and she arched to meet him, her spine bowing upwards, thighs quivering beneath his as she took him into her. She cried out and he clasped her to him, his hands around her spine, supporting her. It was glorious—glorious and perfect and wondrously fulfilling as their bodies merged and fused.

He moved within her. He had to move. Could do nothing else. He was overpowered by the burning of his desire, the intensity of his arousal. And as he moved, her face was transfigured.

'Flavia!'

He saw the ecstasy take her, felt it in her body, felt it around him, pulsing like a beacon, convulsing her body. He clung to her, arms wrapped around her, held her against him as surge after surge swept through her, and he could feel the shaking of her body clasped so tight against his.

And then he could feel his own moment come.

Like a tidal wave, sweeping through his body, powerful and unstoppable. Like nothing he had ever felt before. Nothing like this!

He called out her name, his head thrown back, and gave himself to the power and the glory of the moment, feeling her body give one last, encompassing convulsion around him, taking him further than he had ever known, to lands and realms beyond, where only he and she existed...

Slowly, so slowly, their bodies eased, folding upon each other, lowering down upon the cool surface of the bed. Exhaustion came upon him, and a wake of emotion that swirled and eddied through him. He cradled her to him and she clung to him. He soothed her dampened hair, murmuring to her he knew not what, and she was boneless in his arms, her body still containing his, their limbs tumbled and entwined.

He felt the chill of the air around them now, and reaching for the coverlet drew it over them, still clutching her to him as if he would never let her go. Sleep was heavy upon him, exhaustion stilling him. He held her to him and, clasped in her arms, gave himself to sleep.

His last sliver of awareness was of her hands gentling him, her mouth tender at his lips, her voice murmuring his name.

It was all he wanted to hear in all the world.

Her voice murmuring his name...

CHAPTER TEN

'WELL, what do you think?' Leon's voice was slightly hesitant. 'I did warn you it wasn't luxurious.'

Flavia gazed about her. The single-storey villa, built in a traditional Spanish style, with whitewashed walls and red roof tiles, was framed by pine trees and gave straight on to the beach.

'It's beautiful,' she said.

Her eyes moved about, taking in the whole scene, as Leon lifted out the couple of suitcases from the Jeep he'd driven from the little quay on the far side of the island. Flavia walked forward. The low-lying ground was turfed and sandy, and she could see some goats a little way away, grazing near some bushes. There was the scent of sea in the air, and aromatic plants. And it was very hot—but the heat went with the land, and with the pale beach lapped with turquoise wavelets.

'Fancy a swim?' Leon grinned, seeing her longing glance towards the azure sea.

He carried the suitcases inside, and she followed him. The stone walls of the villa cooled the air, and the wood-shuttered windows made the atmosphere dim and shaded. Leon might have described the villa as 'not luxurious' but it was still beautifully decorated, in a rustic style with a simplicity about it that was immediately appealing to Flavia as she looked about in delight.

But then her whole world was a delight. A wonderful, entrancing delight that she had never before experienced. Her eyes rested on Leon, softening as she followed him along a tiled corridor into a large, cool bedroom and he deposited their suitcases on the wide bed. She felt her breath catch, as it did so often in these unforgettable days and nights since she had given herself to Leon.

They had spent all of the following day at Mereden. Leon had ruthlessly cancelled his business meetings to devote himself to her. They had stayed in bed till late in the morning, glorying in their unity of desire, then passed the rest of the morning exploring the beautiful grounds of the hotel, taking in a waterside lunch at the little Thameside marina the hotel provided for guests, followed by a leisurely, meandering cruise along the river in the hotel launch. They had moored under sweeping willow branches, and Leon had kissed her long and lingeringly.

'Come away with me!' he'd whispered to her. 'Come to Santera with me. Be with me completely there. We can have at least a week there—maybe two.'

Flavia's eyes had shone—then dimmed. Could she really leave her grandmother for a week or longer? Yet even while guilt had plucked at her she'd also known, with a heaviness she had long had to accept, that her grandmother would not really know how long she was away, that she would be in good hands with Mrs Stephens. And who knew? A burning longing had swept through her. Who knew how long Leon would want her? Who knew what the future might or might not hold? She could not tell and did not want to ask—wanted only to shut out everything except this bliss that was enveloping her. This joy and wonder.

A more practical objection had threaded into her mind, and as Leon had looked at her questioningly she'd said, 'I haven't got my passport.'

It didn't faze him. 'I'll send a courier for it. It can be delivered to the airport directly, and we can fly straight off tomorrow morning.'

Flavia's eyes widened. Could it really be that simple?

It was. A single phone call from the hotel's front desk had done it. Flavia had spoken directly to the courier company, giving details of where to find her passport at Harford, while Leon had contacted his PA to clear his diary and arrange flights the next day. All Flavia had then had to do was phone Mrs Stephens and arrange for her to stay longer.

'A holiday is just what you need,' her grandmother's carer had said approvingly. 'I'm happy to stay on as long as need be. Your grandmother is as well as she can be, and there is no need at all to worry.'

Relief had filled Flavia, even if there had still been an undercurrent of anxiety, a fear that she was being selfish in heading off with Leon. But as he'd swept her into his arms, and she'd found all over again the magical bliss of being together with him, her anxious thoughts about her grandmother had been swept away as well. For now—for a little while—she would be with Leon, wherever he wanted her to be.

They had paused briefly in Palma on their way to Santera, to have lunch and give Flavia an hour or two to shop for beach clothes, but now their journey was ended—and an idyll awaited them, she knew. The past and the future were held at bay—she would not think of them, would let only this sunlit present surround her, give herself entirely to the moment.

Entirely to Leon.

And she would let nothing of her fears about her grandmother, her revulsion at her father, get in the way of that.

Leon was opening her suitcase, pulling out the bikinis she'd bought in Palma that day, holding them both up.

'I can't decide which one you'll look more gorgeous in,' he told her.

She whisked them both out of his hands. 'I'll surprise you.' She laughed, and disappeared into the *en suite* bathroom she could see opening up from the bedroom.

'You have already,' murmured Leon, watching her go. His eyes were warm, his expression bemused.

But then, bemusement was a key emotion in him now—bemusement that this warmly passionate woman, whose embrace melted him, could ever have been that stiff, reserved ice maiden, holding him at bay, freezing him out. That Flavia had gone—vanished completely. This Flavia was—a revelation!

And when she reappeared a few minutes later in one of the bikinis she was a revelation again. He'd knew—intimately—just how perfect her figure was, but now, skimmed by the brief material of the swimsuit, her body was breathtaking.

Enticing.

Hurriedly he snatched up his swimming trunks and headed into the bathroom himself, adjuring Flavia to make lavish use of the sunblock they'd bought in Palma.

Within minutes they were outdoors again. 'Race you to the sea!' Flavia cried, and hared across the beach with Leon chasing after her, and both of them collapsed into the shallow turquoise waters.

Flavia lolled in the tiny wavelets, letting her head fall back, hair streaming in the water, face lifted to the sun. 'This is bliss,' she murmured, splashing idly with her feet.

It was a phrase she was to repeat over and over again. It applied, she decided, to every aspect of their days—and their nights. It was bliss to wade into the warm sea, to lounge on the shaded patio on a padded sunbed, sipping iced fruit juice at lunchtime and champagne at sunset. Bliss to have late, leisurely breakfasts, and slow, leisurely lunches, and dine on nightly barbecues beneath the starry sky which was, as Leon had promised, every bit as spectacular as he had described.

But bliss, most of all, to leave the stars to heaven and find their own in each other's arms.

They were in their own private world, Flavia knew. A world where the rest of the world did not exist. Her father's vile machinations were vanished as if they had never been. She would not think of them—or him.

Nor would she think of the reason she had succumbed to his threats.

Though her eyes shadowed, she knew she was deliberately not thinking about her grandmother. All she did was check her phone nightly for the reassuring text Mrs Stephens faithfully sent. But apart from that she let the whole world of Harford slip away. Focussing only on Leon. Only on her time with him.

How can it be so good? How can he overwhelm me the way he does? Sweeping me away, time after time, after time, into such bliss?

But it was more than passion, she knew, searingly intense as that was. It was a sense of ease with him. A togetherness. A naturalness.

She could see that he hadn't quite believed her when she'd said she didn't want luxury, but now, here in this simple villa, with only themselves for company, he had realised she had been telling the truth. And he, too, seemed to be taking this simple life as natural for him.

Was it taking him back to his roots? she found herself wondering. Listening to him telling her about the work he was doing in his own country, to help others make a better life for themselves, about the difficulties they faced, the hopelessness so many lived with, even simply hearing him speak his mother tongue Spanish when they'd arrived on Majorca, had brought home to him just how different his background was from hers. How harsh his early years had been, and how much his life had changed since he was a teenager newly come to Britain, trying to make a new life for himself.

She longed to ask him about it—how he had coped with the trauma of settling in a new country, often hostile and indifferent to him. But she sensed a restraint about it and would not force it. She understood it, too, for she herself did not yet want to talk about her life in England—did not want to tell him about her grandmother, the loss of her mental powers, the non-stop care she needed now. It was too emotional, too sad…

And with a darkening in her heart she knew she *never* wanted to tell Leon about the danger her home was in—about what her father had done.

What he had made her do...

Instinctively she veered away from thinking about it. She had resolved that she would not let her father's poison taint this miraculous time with Leon and she would keep to that. Her thoughts were fierce.

He's got nothing to do with it! Nothing! I'm here with Leon because I want to be—because it's the most wonderful, miraculous thing that's ever happened to me!

It could not last. She knew that. Knew it with a tearing helplessness. This brief, blissful time was all she would have. Soon—all too soon, she knew—they must leave. Leon's busy, demanding life would take over again, and he would have to return to work. And she could not continue to abandon her grandmother as she was doing now. When this idyll ended she would go home—back to her life, back to her grandmother. Would nurse her and care for her until the end came. She would never leave her.

Not even for Leon.

'I'm truly sorry about this—I wish to God I didn't have to go—but it's not something I can deal with here. I'll be back tomorrow, I promise—and then we'll come right back to Santera. I'll make sure I can stay an extra week to make up for abandoning you now.'

Leon leant forward and kissed her reassuringly. Flavia did her best to appear reassured, but she felt the thread of unease unwind inside her further, even here in Palma, at the hotel Leon had checked her into to await his return the following day. The outside world had called to Leon, and he was having to respond to it. He hadn't told her what it was that summoned him, only that it was unavoidable, and she knew she had to believe him on that. Trust him. She knew, too, that a man like Leon Maranz would have a thousand calls on his time.

Her eyes shadowed. For herself, she had only one other rival for her time—but it was an overpowering one. One she would never turn her back on.

She still had not yet told Leon about her grandmother, for she had not wanted anything of the outside world to intrude on their private paradise. Not yet. When they were both back in England, when she was ready to let the outside world back in willingly, acceptingly, then and then alone would she tell Leon about the woman had always been the most important person in her life, and how Harford had always been the most important *place* in her life—her beloved home.

Part of her longed to tell him—longed to talk to him about her grandmother, about Harford—but part of her was reluctant. What if he asked her why, if her grandmother was so frail, she had come away with him as she had? And—far more difficult—how could she possibly tell him now about the ugly threat her father had made? How could she possibly confess how her father had blackmailed her into getting in touch with Leon?

When she thought about it an icy pool congealed in her stomach. What had happened between her and Leon had been so extraordinary, so wondrous, that she did not want to sully it in even the slightest way with any taint from her father's vile machinations. Oh, she *would* tell Leon about it—of course she would!—but not yet. Not yet...

Because it was all so new to her—this revelation of how wonderful it was to be with him! How transformed she was by him! She wished with all her heart that she had never met Leon through her father, that he had had nothing to do with him in any way at all. She wanted, now, to separate them totally.

But she did not know how or when. She only knew not yet...

Fears clutched at her, and unease threaded its disquieting skein through her nerves. She wished Leon was not going to London—however briefly. In his arms she felt those fears silenced—but on her own they plucked at her again, making her uncertain and fearful.

She must not let them surface. So she bade him goodbye, returning his ardent embrace on parting and he set off for the airport in a taxi, leaving her to while away the day in Palma.

She didn't really know what to do with herself, and the unease she had felt on parting from him intensified as she meandered through the morning. Everywhere she looked people seemed to be in couples, carefree and on holiday. She told herself not to be morbid and stupid, that Leon was coming back the next day.

Suppose he's delayed? Suppose his business takes longer than he thought it would? Suppose something else crops up he has to deal with? Suppose he has to fly off further afield...?

She tried to put the anxious thoughts out of her head, but still the sense of unease grew oppressively, disturbingly.

She headed back to the hotel. She would have a siesta in her room and pass the time that way.

When something roused her she was initially too groggy to tell what it was. She stirred dopily. Then, with a jolt, she realised it was her mobile beeping. She had received a text.

Leon!

Immediately she sat up, snatching the phone from her bedside, clicking on 'view message'.

As her eyes focussed on the words she froze.

It was not from Leon...

'I would point out—' Leon's voice was icy, barely leashing his anger '—that it was Lassiter who requested this meeting urgently. So why the hell isn't he here?'

'I'm really very, very sorry, Mr Maranz.' Alistair Lassiter's secretary sounded flustered down the line. 'But all I can say is that he left for the Far East this morning. At very short notice,' she finished, her tone attempting to be placating.

Leon's jaw tightened with angry exasperation. Why the *hell* had Lassiter gone overboard to get him back to London to hammer out the deal right now and then promptly disappeared to the other side of Asia?

'*Where* in the Far East?' he demanded of the hapless secretary.

'Mr Lassiter said his plans were fluid,' she replied uncertainly.

Leon rang off, his face dark. Lassiter was up to something. Had he tracked down a late-entry white knight in the Far East? Was he hopeful of better bail-out terms? Well, the deal Leon was offering was the only one he was going to offer Lassiter, whatever the man did. But in the meantime he'd torn himself away from Flavia, and it had *not* been what he'd wanted to do.

Flavia...

Her name resonated in his head, weaving between his synapses like a seductive, sensuous silken flame.

Flavia...

Emotion welled in Leon, washing away all tiresome thoughts of Alistair Lassiter. Focussing on the one person he wanted to think about.

Flavia.

He said her name again in his head, feeling a rush of wonder. She was everything he'd dreamt she might be—everything and much, much more! He had known from the first moment of seeing her that he desired her, but now—oh, now she fulfilled so much more than desire. There was a warmth to her, a sincerity, an ardour, and a passion that was like a bright, true flame. How he had ever worried that she might be the spoilt daughter of luxury he could not now imagine!

I can trust her—believe her—be happy with her...

Happy...

The word resonated in his head like a sweet note of music.

So simple a word. Yet how much it encompassed! This past week with Flavia had been unforgettable—as if his life had become something it had never been before. As if he had found something he had never found before...

Found *someone* he had never found before...

Someone to be happy with.

Happy for ever?

The question hovered tantalisingly, wonderingly. Dared he ask it?

Dared he answer it?

He stared ahead of him, unseeing of the wide expanse of his office, the high vista out over the City beyond that had taken him so many years of dogged work to achieve. He was seeing only Flavia, smiling at him, with all the warmth in her gaze that he could dream of. Holding out her arms for him...

With a start, he got to his feet. What was the point of him hanging around here in London any more? Out in Palma Flavia was waiting for him, and that was all he cared about. He would head back to Majorca, to Flavia, without delay. Waste not one more moment without her. And as for that question—the one he longed to answer—well, there would be time. All the time they needed together to answer it. There was no rush, no urgency. They would take as much time as they needed, being with each other, learning all there was to know about each other, finding all the happiness that lay between them.

His spirits high, on a rush of anticipation to be with Flavia again that very day, he went through to his PA's office and let her know he was leaving again. Would she book the earliest Palma flight possible for him? Then, taking his leave, he headed to the lift, phoning Flavia's mobile as he went. He couldn't wait to tell her he was on his way back to her. Couldn't wait to be with her again—take her in his arms again!

Impatiently, standing by the lift doors, he waited for her to pick up.

But instead the call went through to voicemail. Frowning momentarily, he stepped into the lift as the doors opened, and redialled once he was in the lobby downstairs.

Yet again it went to voicemail. Well, maybe she was in the hotel pool. He tried one more time, still got voicemail, and left a message, duplicating it in a text as well. Then, to be on the safe side, as he settled himself in the car taking him to the airport he phoned the Palma hotel direct.

'Phone up to Señorita Lassiter's room, please,' he instructed the desk clerk.

Her answer was apologetic. 'I'm so sorry, Señor Maranz, but Señorita Lassiter checked out of the hotel last night.' She paused, then said enquiringly, 'Will you be settling her bill?'

CHAPTER ELEVEN

RAIN was beating on the windowpanes, rattling the frame. Flavia had drawn the curtains; the bedside light was low. Her heart was gripped by a vice.

I should have been here—I should have been here.

The words of condemning reproach went round and round in her head as she sat by her grandmother's bed. The nurse had gone an hour ago, saying she would be on call to come back 'at any time' as she'd said tactfully to Flavia.

Flavia knew what that meant. Had known the moment she'd arrived, forcing herself to drive the strange hire-car from Exeter airport through the driving rain eastwards along the A30 into Dorset.

Had known the moment she'd phoned Mrs Stephens back from Palma.

'It's your grandmother...'

Guilt had struck instantly.

I should never have left her—never!

With her head she could tell herself all she liked that she might just as well have been in London, dancing attendance on her father, as out in a paradise she had never dreamt of— but guilt still clawed at her with pitiless talons.

To have been so selfish! To have thought nothing at all of simply disappearing off with Leon! Living out some kind of self-indulgent idyll just because...just because...

She felt the words twist inside her, trying to get out even

as she tried to crush them back in. But she couldn't hold them back.

Just because I've fallen in love with him...

The words sheered across her mind, forcing themselves into her consciousness, jolting through her like an electric shock. But it was a shock that she had to disconnect at the mains—right away. *Now.* It wasn't something she could give any time to at all! Not now—*not now*! Guilt stabbed at her yet again. Worse than ever.

How can I be thinking of myself now? How can it matter a jot, an iota, what my feelings for Leon are when I'm sitting by my grandmother's bed?

Watching her dying...

The vice clamped tighter around her heart, and she could feel her body rock slightly to and fro with anguish. Her hands were clasped around one of her grandmother's hands—hers so strong and firm, her grandmother's so thin and weak. Unmoving.

The pulse at her grandmother's wrist was barely palpable, her breathing light and shallow. The palliative care nurse who had been there when Flavia had arrived, breathless and stricken, had talked her through how the end would come, though she had not been able to say just when it would come.

'It might be tonight—or tomorrow—or a few days. But I doubt it will be longer,' she'd said, her eyes full of sympathy. 'She is easing away from life.'

Tears had filled Flavia's eyes, and she'd turned away, heart seizing. 'I should have been here!' she'd said, her voice muffled with emotion.

'It would have made no difference,' the nurse had said kindly.

Only that I would not have felt so guilty like this, Flavia thought as she sat now in her midnight vigil.

The last weeks of her grandmother's life and her granddaughter had been cavorting on a beach, immersed in a torrid love-affair, thinking only of herself! Caring only about

herself! Not caring anything about her grandmother—the
woman who had raised her, who loved her, who had always,
always been there for her!

Yet when the end of her life had been approaching, her
granddaughter had not been there for her—she had deserted
her for her own selfish self-indulgence.

Guilt stabbed at Flavia again, and self-hatred.

If she had gone to Leon simply to save Harford, simply
to ensure her grandmother could end her days in her own
home, and every moment with him had been an ordeal, then
she might not have felt like this! Then she might have justi-
fied her absence, told herself she'd only been doing it for her
grandmother's sake.

Lie, lie, lie—

Every moment in Leon's arms had been a moment in paradise! Every hour of the days she'd spent with him had been
for *her* sake—her own selfish, heedless sake—not her grandmother's! Even now, here, at her grandmother's deathbed, she
was still thinking about him! Still aching for him and missing him, wanting to be with him!

Just because she'd fallen in love with him...

*No! Don't think about that! It doesn't matter and it isn't
important! Only this is important—now—with Gran—the
last time on earth you'll be with her...*

Silently, tears spilled from her eyes, wetting her cheeks.
Her heart ached with sorrow and grief. She clutched her
grandmother's hand as the life ebbed slowly from her, hour
by hour, during the long reaches of the rainswept night. Keeping her last vigil at her side.

Leon was watching the rain. It was pounding down on the
pavements far below, streaking down the plate glass windows
of his office. Darkening the sky.

His mood was dark, too. Emotion swirled, opaque and
turbid. A single thought burned in his brain.

Where is she?

Where had she gone—and why? *Why?*
What the hell has happened to her?
She had simply vanished—disappeared! The only communication he'd got back after all his non-stop voicemailing and texting had been a bare, curt message.

Leon, I have to go. Sorry. Urgent family matters.

That was it. Nothing more. Nothing since. Just nothing.

Frustration bit like a fanged snake. What the hell was going on? Where was she? Why was she not talking to him? What had happened? He didn't understand—he just damn well didn't understand!

Part of him was desperately trying to find an acceptable reason for her total silence. Maybe she was out of range again. Maybe her phone had broken, got lost, been stolen. But if that were so, he knew there was no reason why she shouldn't have got in touch with his office via another phone. He was not exactly anonymous! And he'd given his office explicit instructions to put her through any hour of the day or night.

But she hadn't got in touch. Hadn't communicated with him in any way whatsoever.

It was as if she no longer existed.

Or as if *he* didn't...

Emotion gripped at him again. Where the hell was she? What the hell had happened to her?

Why is she doing this to me?

That was the worst of all—the question that was like a kick in the guts, a knife in his lungs, stopping his breathing. There had to be a reason—a good one!—why she had disappeared. There just *had* to be...

For the thousandth time he reread the only clue he had—
'*urgent family matters.*'

What urgent family matters?

The only family he knew about was her father, so did Flavia's disappearance have anything to do with Alistair Lassiter's sudden journey to the Far East? But why not tell him? Why simply cut him out of her life—cut him stone-dead? As if there were nothing at all between them!

Why is she doing this to me?

The question tore at him again. That was the heart of it! That was what was eating him alive. Flavia, who had been as close to him as a heartbeat, who clung to him in trembling ecstasy, hugged him in spontaneous affection, held his hand with absolute confidence and familiarity as they walked along, was now treating him as if he didn't exist! Her silence was deafening—devastating.

Frustration gripped him in its vice. How the *hell* could he find out where she was, why she had disappeared, what was damn well going on and why? As if cold gel oozed through his veins, he was chillingly conscious of just how little he knew about Flavia. Oh, they'd talked and talked at Mereden and Santera, talked about anything and everything—easily, naturally, as if they'd been doing it all their lives—but what they hadn't talked about had been their personal lives.

I thought there would be time for that—much more time!

Instead, all he'd ever told her had been the bare bones of where he'd grown up, how he'd come to Britain and found a way to make something of himself. And as for Flavia—what had she told him about herself?

Very little. They hadn't talked about her father, and apart from saying she lived in the West Country, she'd said nothing else. He frowned. The West Country covered a fair amount of territory. He'd already run a search under her name for everywhere west of Salisbury, but nothing had come up.

She could be anywhere! Anywhere!

He strode back to his desk, his mood black and bleak. Those turbid emotions swirled inside him again—part frustration, part anxiety. And one more emotion as well. He knew what it was—knew it but did not want to identify it. Did not want to name it.

But it was there all the same. Like a knife piercing into him.

Hurting him…

He sat down in his chair, closing his eyes. The pain sliced again.

I thought we were happy together. I thought we'd found something in each other that was special—binding us together. Making everything good between us.

That was what made her disappearance, her obdurate silence, so impossible to understand. That she could have gone from the warm, ardent, wonderful woman she'd been to someone who could just walk away without any desire to communicate with him, to let him know what was happening.

If she has things to deal with, I can understand that! I don't demand she comes back to me immediately. I don't expect her to cut out everything else from her life! I only want to understand what those calls on her are—to know she's all right…

It was the blankness that was destroying him. The impotence. He wanted to know where she was, discover what she was coping with and why.

Where is she?

The question rang again in his head, as unanswerable now as it had ever been.

Grimly, he got out his work. He'd been working like the devil, trying to drown out his emotions with hard labour. Give his teeming mind something to grip on to. At least he didn't have the business of whether or not to proceed with bailing out Lassiter to contend with. Alistair Lassiter had gone as silent as his daughter…

No. Don't think about either of them! Don't speculate pointlessly, frustratingly, about whether Flavia's disappearance has anything to do with her father. Just focus on something else—anything else.

But for all his harsh self-adjurations the only question he was interested in kept surfacing.

Where is she and how can I find her?

Then, like a gate opening in his mind, something struck him. Her passport.

She'd got her passport couriered to the airport so she could fly to Santera.

Couriered from where?

His hand moving faster than his mind, he seized up his desk phone. His instructions to his PA were immediate. The courier company the concierge at Mereden had put in touch with Flavia would know *exactly* where they had fetched her passport from.

He sat back. Relief filled him. Finally he could make a start on finding her...

Within the hour he had his answer. Five minutes later, anticipation leaping in him, having keyed in the address, he was staring at an aerial image on his computer screen of the house Flavia called home. His first reaction was immediate.

No wonder she prefers it to London!

It might not be the largest country house he'd seen, and it certainly wasn't what the British called a stately pile, but the substantial Georgian greystone dwelling was lapped by several acres of lawned gardens, girdled with woods and set amongst the fields and rolling hills of deep English countryside.

A little jewel of a place, he could see.

Is that where she is now?

For a moment longer he stared at the image, as if he might see Flavia suddenly appear, walking out of the house. Then, with a start, he reached for his phone, ready to dial the number that went with the address. He felt his spirits leap, buoyed by searing hope. In less than a moment she might be answering the phone, speaking to him—

His office door opened. Leon's hand froze. His PA was standing there, hovering and looking harassed.

'I'm so sorry to disturb you, but Mr Lassiter is in my office—' she said. 'He is asking to see you. I know he doesn't have an appointment, but...' Her voice trailed off and she looked uncomfortable.

Exasperation spiked in Leon. God, the man had lousy timing, all right! For an instant he felt like telling him to get lost, but then, with a steadying intake of breath, he subsided. OK, he might as well see the man. For all he knew Lassiter might have come here about Flavia.

Fear struck him. *Was* that why Lassiter was here? Had something happened to Flavia? Had she had an accident? A disaster?

Even before he'd nodded at his PA, Lassiter had walked in. His expression, Leon could see instantly, was not that of a man come to report bad news about his daughter. There was an air of confident jauntiness that immediately set Leon's teeth on edge. So did Lassiter's equally jaunty greeting, and the way he took a seat without being invited.

Leon's expression lost any sign of the alarm it had momentarily held, and darkened. 'We had an appointment,' he said icily, 'made at your insistence, for which I specifically flew back to this country—and you failed to show.'

Lassiter was unabashed. 'Yes, sorry about that, old chap,' he answered airily, sounding not in the least apologetic. 'I had to fly to the Far East.' He paused minutely. 'Bit of a turn-up for the books on my side, as it happens.'

He looked expectantly across at Leon, who remained blank-faced. Beneath his impassive expression, however, he was wishing Lassiter to perdition. The last thing he wanted was to have to focus on his bail-out proposal. All he wanted to do—urgently—was get his office to himself and phone Flavia's home. Impatience burned in him. But he crushed it down. Like it or not, Lassiter was here, and Leon would have to deal with him first.

Lassiter had pursed his lips. He was looking, Leon assessed, sleeker than usual. Smugger than he had been in their previous exchanges, when his predominant attitude had veered between ingratiating and blustering. Leon waited, irritation suppressed, for Lassiter to continue.

'Yes,' went on Lassiter, as though Leon had made some encouraging remark, 'looks like there's another interested party out in the Far East. Made me a *very* tempting offer, I must say.'

He looked expectantly across at Leon, whose impassive regard remained undented. Lassiter was doing nothing except wasting his time and increasing Leon's irritation.

'Very tempting,' Lassiter went on after a moment. He looked hard at Leon. 'They're not interested in taking any equity. Just offering me a generous line of credit for further expansion.'

'Then I can see the attraction for you,' agreed Leon.

Flavia's father went on staring, clearly trying to read Leon's reaction, and equally clearly taken aback by his statement of agreement.

'So you can see,' he went on, 'why I'm giving them serious consideration.'

'Yes, I can,' was all the response he got.

Leon's deliberate impassivity triggered Lassiter into showing his hand completely.

'So why would I accept *your* offer if I can avoid losing equity by taking this new one that's come up?'

'Why indeed?' Leon agreed again. Then, with a slight lift of his hand, as he was getting bored now, as well as irritated, he simply said, 'I thought I'd made it clear that my deal is the one we discussed. It won't change. If this new offer means you don't accept mine, so be it.'

He'd kept his tone neutral, and the flash of anger in Lassiter's pouched eyes at being unable to hustle Leon into renegotiating his proposal left him unmoved. Any turnaround by him would be on *his* terms, not Lassiter's, and if Lassiter had found another white knight abroad, with less stringent conditions, good luck to him. To his mind, to bail out Lassiter without the control that equity would afford would be financial madness—Lassiter would just squander any loans and continue unabated in his lucrative but exploitative African ventures.

His gaze rested, unimpressed, on Alistair Lassiter.

It's a miracle Flavia isn't like her father—

The thought formed in Leon's head as he levelled his gaze on Lassiter. Flavia's warm sympathy for his *pro bono* work in South America, and her heartfelt indignation at the economic exploitation so many people suffered, was a complete contrast to her father's callous attitude that profiteering out of the impoverished Third World was perfectly acceptable.

Thinking of Flavia made his eyes flicker automatically to the image on the computer screen—the beautiful house in the tranquil Dorset countryside that she lived in and called home. Was she there now? Would a single phone call put him back in touch with her at last? His eagerness to reach for his phone and do so was almost overwhelming. He just had to get rid of Alistair Lassiter first.

He sat back pointedly, indicating there was nothing more to debate. Then, both to expedite Lassiter's departure and because he had no wish for his relations with Flavia's father to be unpleasant just because he wouldn't budge on his rescue package, he said, his tone cordial enough, 'I wish you luck with your alternative offer, and I hope you get the business settled soon. There's a great deal of good value in the company—you hardly need me to tell you that—but I have my own ways of operating, and I always want to take equity.'

There. That was surely sufficiently conciliatory to give Lassiter a face-saving exit. As he finished speaking, for an instant he thought he saw another flash of anger in the fleshy face, but a moment later it was gone. In its place was a resumption of the smiling bonhomie that Leon was used to seeing.

'Well, old chap,' he replied, his manner bland once more, 'I'm sorry you're going to let go the opportunity I've offered you, but there it is. Looks like the other lot get the deal.' He made it sound as though it were Leon's loss, and he got to his feet as if regretfully.

As he did so, he nodded towards the computer screen

on Leon's desk, and Leon realised, to his annoyance, that Lassiter must have been able to see it.

'Ah, I see you're taking a look at Harford. Beautiful place, isn't it? Flavia's devoted to it. Comes to her from her mother's side.' He smiled, as if jovially. 'But of course you'll know all that by now, won't you?'

There was a knowing look in his eyes, but Leon would not be drawn. His personal relationship with Flavia was not something he would discuss with her father.

Lassiter's expression lost its smile. 'Of course,' he went on, shaking his head, his voice rueful, 'sadly—like so many of these upper-crust county families—they ran out of money some time ago. That's why, if I'm absolutely honest about it,' he confided, 'Flavia's mother was so ready to snap me up— self-made as I am. Because I could help finance its upkeep. I still do. It's cost me a fortune over the years, but Flavia adores the place—would do anything to keep it.' He paused. 'Anything at all.'

He smiled. Paused again. 'She's a lovely girl, isn't she? So beautiful! I could tell you were very taken with her, and I'm glad you've got together now, despite her being…well, a bit capricious towards you initially. I don't like to say such things, as a fond father, so you must allow me some prejudice in her favour. I can never see any wrong in her—but that's fathers for you!'

He smiled again, dotingly. 'Her mother was just like her— beautiful and determined. She always knew what she wanted! And how to get it!' He gave a little laugh—an indulgent one. 'Mind you, she could be sweet as pie, too—when she was after something!' Now he looked Leon in the eyes again, an open, frank expression on his face. 'I never thought I stood a chance of winning her—I've never been a handsome chap— but I did at least have money to my name. Some people might say it was wrong of her to take that into account, but I could never hold it against Flavia's mother. She was just as devoted to Harford as her daughter is, and she wanted to save it any way she could—it's very understandable. *Very* understandable.'

He gave a sigh. 'When she set her cap at me because she knew I could preserve Harford for the family she was just too beautiful to resist—I was putty in her hands. And when she died, so tragically young—well, I guess it's not surprising I lavished everything on our daughter.' He shook his head regretfully. 'And I guess it's not surprising that it meant Flavia grew up thinking she could have everything she wanted. I know she can be moody—' there was an apologetic note to his voice '—well, you saw that for yourself, didn't you, at the charity ball?' he acknowledged. 'But I made allowances that evening because I knew how worried she was about my state of affairs.' He held up a hand. 'Not that I've burdened her with them. I would never do that! But she's a smart girl, and must have got wind of how things stood with me.'

He nodded at the image on the computer screen again. 'She'll be *so* pleased you've taken an interest in Harford, I know. Have you been there yet with her?' he asked. 'Mind you, now that you and I won't be business partners after all things may change on that front. It wouldn't surprise me, I have to say. But if you should go down, you'll see why Flavia's so devoted to it and how much she wants me to be able to keep it safe for her—expensive luxury though it is.'

He started towards the door. 'Well, I mustn't keep you. We're both very busy men. I'm sorry we shan't be partners, but of I look forward to seeing more of you with Flavia on the social front,' he answered Leon. 'If the two of you are still together, of course.'

He opened the door and was gone.

At his desk, Leon sat very, very still. Then, slowly, he reached for his phone to make his call to Flavia.

He had one very simple question to ask her.

CHAPTER TWELVE

'EARTH to earth, ashes to ashes…'

The rector's voice was low and resonant. Flavia stood, head bowed, tears running down her cheeks. Her grandmother would lie beside her husband in her grave, as together in death as they had been through all their long married life. Grief buckled through her again, as it had been doing over and over again in the long days and the longer nights since her grandmother's breathing had become shallower and shallower…and then stopped completely.

The committal ended and she lifted her head, blinking away her tears, knowing she now had to get through the ordeal of a reception at Harford for the mourners to attend. It was what her grandmother would have wanted, but she felt she couldn't take one more expression of sympathy, one more person calling the loss of her beloved grandmother a *'merciful release'* before adding *'and not just for your grandmother'* with an encouraging expression on their faces.

One person had even said right out, 'It was no life for you here, buried in the countryside at your age—a young girl—no life at all. You should have been off living your own life. finding romance and excitement.'

Anger and guilt had pierced her, needle-sharp, lancing in and out of the ravening grief that shook her, body and mind. It was like being possessed, blocking out everything else.

Even thinking about Leon.

No! She mustn't think about Leon—not now—not yet. He belonged to a different world—a world she wasn't in right now. She had to blank it out totally because she couldn't cope with it. Even without the guilt spearing her she couldn't have coped with that world now. *With* the guilt, it was impossible!

I should have been here, with my grandmother—I should never have gone off with Leon!

It was no good telling herself that at least she had come back in time to be with her grandmother at the very end—no good telling herself that her grandmother would not even have realised she had gone away.

And no good telling herself, with chill bleakness, that she had done what she had in order to save Harford for her grandmother.

Numbly, she somehow got through the reception, played the role of dutiful granddaughter even though she had betrayed her grandmother at the last, putting herself first, her own desires...

Indulging herself with Leon, and all that he'd offered her.

But she couldn't bear to think of Leon, because guilt racked her on his account as well. She'd abandoned him to rush back to her grandmother, and knowing she had done so crushed her with guilt, too.

Guilt...every way she turned. Guilt over her grandmother for not being with her, guilt over the reasons she'd gone to Leon at her father's malign bidding, then yet more guilt for abandoning him to rush back home again...

The guests were all gone at last, and she finished clearing up after them. She wandered blindly outside, looking back at the house. Never again would she see her grandmother here. Never.

The word tolled in her head and she felt her heart squeeze with grief. The future stretched ahead—a future she would have to cope with somehow. Dealing with probate, with the aftermath of death. She took a shuddering breath. Dealing somehow with what was going to happen to Harford.

The burden of her father's loan still hung like an ugly weight over her head, and now death duties would strike, too. Could Harford survive them both? Anxiety pressed at her. Her plans for the time when her grandmother would be no more had been laid long ago. She would raise a mortgage on Harford and use the money to pay off death duties, pay the mortgage off slowly by turning the house and any outbuildings she could afford to convert into upmarket holiday lets.

Now, though, she would have to raise enough to pay off her father as well. On that she was determined. Her father would be out of her life. Out for good! And when she was finally free of him...

She felt a rush of blood, of longing.

When I'm free of my father—finally, finally free!—then and only then can I be free to seek out Leon again. To see if the magic is still there, to see if that wonderful, blissful time with him can be recaptured. But pure this time, clean and free of any taint by my father!

The power of her longing almost overcame her. To be able to go to Leon without deceit, without pressure, without the malign, corrupting influence of her father. She would offer herself as she truly was, without any of her father's venal agenda, with no hidden motive, no shameful collusion to further her father's interests, no guilt-racked obligations to her grandmother to save her house by any means she must—whatever it took.

Shame flushed through her again at what she had done. Oh, she would have willingly—*so* willingly!—gone to Leon, given herself up to that overpowering response to him she had felt the moment she'd first set eyes on him, had she not had her responsibility to her grandmother, the duty of love for her, to hold her back. Yet even with that knowledge the taint of her father's scheming still haunted her. Even though she knew that she would have done what she had, rejoiced as she had, embracing the time she'd had with Leon, it still had the sleazy shadow of her father's ultimatum to her louring over it.

But now—now she could finally free herself of that sleazy shadow. Now she could pay off her father—free herself for ever from his baleful influence over her life.

Free herself to focus only on what she so deeply longed for. Leon.

I want him so much. I miss him so much.

Like a beacon shining through the pall of her grief for her grandmother, the malign shadow of her father, her longing for Leon called to her.

And now I can go to him. Free—free of my duty of love to my grandmother, free of my father's hideous threats. Free to go to Leon only as myself, what I am, what I truly am...

Hope flared in her and she lifted her bowed head, looking afresh out over the gardens of the house she loved. Resolution filled her, and hope for the future—longing for the man who had opened to her a world of wonder she had never dreamt could be hers.

And it could be hers again...

Memory, rich and golden, glowed in her vision. The starlit terrace at Mereden, the river flowing beyond the lawns stretching away from them, Leon's hands cupping her face, his mouth seeking hers. The warm, cicada-filled nights on Santera, clinging to Leon, her body trembling in ecstasy.

Just being with him! Walking along the little sandy beach among the fragrant pine trees, barefoot, hand in hand. Laughing with him as they made their nightly barbecues. Curled up against him on the sun lounger as they took their daily siesta in the baking heat of the day. Breakfasting with him over coffee and pastries in the cool of the morning, with the little breeze fresh off the water's edge.

Just her and Leon. Easy. Happy. Blissful.

Yearning filled her—an ache in her heart for him…only him…

She took a deep, steadying breath. Her mind raced ahead. Tomorrow she would see the solicitors, get probate moving as swiftly as she could. She would visit the bank manager, too, to set in motion her plans for raising a mortgage, getting liquid funds to pay off her father's pernicious, punishing loan. Plan ahead for readying Harford for the holiday let market in the spring.

And, most precious of all, tomorrow she would write to Leon.

I'll tell him everything! Everything! About my grandmother, how I had to abandon him as I did because she was dying. About my vile father, how he threatened Harford, and how I had to protect it for my grandmother's sake. I will confess everything to him—confess what I dared not tell him before—and beg his understanding, his forgiveness!

As she stood there in the warm summer air, gazing out over the lawns streaked with the last of the afternoon's sun, for the first time since she had rushed back to her dying grandmother's side she felt hope surge through her. Yes, she would grieve for her grandmother, accept her guilt for abandoning her as she had, accept her shame for the way she had had to capitulate to her father, but for all that she would not give up on Leon—she would strive to recapture the bliss they had shared. Make all things right with him.

Make a future with him.

Her heart squeezed with longing.

Oh, please, please let it be so! Let there be a future with him—I long for him so much. So much!

As she stood and felt the emotion of her longing for him seize her, her hope for a future with him sear within her, gazing out over the gardens of the home she loved so much, she became aware of a disturbance in the peaceful tranquillity of the air. A distant, rhythmic throbbing that grew louder and louder still.

She looked up, craning her neck, into the sky. It was a helicopter, its rotors chopping the air like a fearful heartbeat. She stared, hearing and then seeing the machine loom over the trees beyond, coming from the east. A frown warped her brow as she watched it descend. Heading down towards the lawn.

The branches of the trees at the edge of the lawn were whipping frenziedly in the gusts, the tall flowers in the herbaceous borders were winnowed, the grass below the machine flattened. Before her eyes the helicopter landed, setting down on the wide lawn beyond the terrace. Its engines were cut. The whirling, thudding vanes slowed. They had hardly stopped when the door opened and a tall, lithe figure jumped down.

Like a flame leaping inside her, Flavia felt her heart sing out.

Leon! It was Leon!

Leon—here—now. Come to her.

Disbelieving with joy, she could only stand, watching him walking towards her, her heart full.

As he alighted from the helicopter Leon could feel his heart churning. The rhythmic chopping of the helicopter's rotors was still throbbing in his head. Even before the machine had landed he had seen Flavia standing there in front of the house—the gracious, greystone Georgian house that was every bit as beautiful as it had looked on the computer screen, every bit as beautiful as Alistair Lassiter had said it was.

No wonder Flavia Lassiter wanted to hang on to it.

Just as her father had said.

He could hear him talking again in his head, hear what he'd said about her. The words fell like stones. Destroying, one by one, everything Leon had thought he knew about Flavia…

The knife that those words had plunged into his side twisted again.

The moment Lassiter had gone out of his office Leon had seized up the phone, called the number on his screen. Urgency had impelled him—but a new urgency.

No one had picked up the phone. All he had got was an answer-machine, telling him to leave a message. He'd dropped the phone down. No, he would *not* leave a message. He would not wait pointlessly for Flavia *not* to return his call, just as she hadn't any of his calls. The time for that was over. It was time for something much more decisive.

He straightened, seeing her standing there, stock still, on a gravelled terrace on the far side of the lawn the helicopter had landed on. The churning in his heart intensified, his emotions firing like gunshots. As his eyes rested on her, he could hear a silent cry come from him.

Flavia!

Flavia standing there—as beautiful as his memory had painted so vividly—real and close and there in front of him. He wanted to rush up to her, sweep her into his arms, fold her close against him! Feel her heart beating against his!

But instead all he did was quicken his stride towards her, feeling the knife in his side strike again.

I have to know! I have to know whether she's the way her father says she is or whether...

Whether she was the woman he had discovered that night at Mereden, those magical days and nights on Santera. Passionate and ardent. Warm, genuine, sympathetic, generous.

Or someone quite different. Someone who could be as sweet as you like when she wanted something. Someone who set her sights on something and went after it, whatever it required.

Such as deliberately, calculatingly having an affair with a man she thought was going to bail out her father—the father who was keeping her home solvent.

Again, as it had done over and over on the journey here, the question seared in his head. *Was it true—was it true what her father had said of her?*

The knife twisted in his guts again.

His stride quickened and he reached the terrace. For an instant longer Flavia seemed to stand there, transfixed. Then...

'Leon! Oh, Leon!'

She had thrown herself at him, and without conscious volition his arms went around her. Held her to him. Closed around her. Emotion clenched in him. It seemed a lifetime since he had last seen her, last kissed her as he boarded the flight for London, leaving her behind in Palma. But now she was back

in his arms, her face buried in his shoulder. Almost, *almost*
he forgot what had sent him here, heart churning, thoughts
dark as night. Almost he simply cupped her face and kissed
her lips with his, recapturing the happiness he'd felt with her.

Almost.

But then, with a ragged breath, he steeled. Put her away
from him. She swayed, gazing at him, the joyous expression
draining out of her face. Bewilderment, consternation took
its place. Leon wanted to seize her back into his arms, make
her eyes shine again—but he forced himself to resist.

Not yet—not yet. First he *must* know the answer to the
question he would demand of her.

*I thought I knew her—had discovered the real Flavia be-
neath the freezing exterior.*

But if that were a fiction—a lie? What if the damning
portrait her father had painted at was true? What if Flavia
had been running a play the whole time they were together?

The knife in his side twisted again.

He looked about him. Looked down the length of the perfectly proportioned Georgian façade flanked by gardens. *Oh,
yes, this place was a jewel, all right!*

'So,' he said slowly, 'this is Harford.'

His gaze came back to her. She was standing, had paused,
consternation still in her face, but there was something new,
too—a tension netting about her. A wariness.

'How…how did you find it?' she faltered.

Her first joy at seeing Leon—the rush of pleasure in running into his arms—had gone. When he had put her aside it
had been like a douche of cold water. Now she realised that
she had no idea how it was he came to be here.

*He doesn't know anything about Harford! Doesn't even
know it exists, let alone that I live here!*

Yet here he was, standing right in front of her. And with
an expression on his face that was sending cold all the way
through her.

'The courier company you used to fetch your passport gave me the address,' he said.

His voice was distant. Dark eyes rested on her. She could not read their expression, and that of itself made the chill in her veins deepen.

'Why didn't you tell me about Harford, Flavia? Why the big secret?'

She swallowed. 'I…I was going to tell you,' she began, then could go no further.

'But you didn't, did you? Did you think it would scare me off?'

Before his doggedly impassive gaze he could see a dull flush stain her face. Revealing to him that he had hit home.

The knife twisted in him again.

His eyes swivelled away—it seemed easier than watching her colour in front of him, betraying herself. He looked about him.

'It's a gem of a place,' he said slowly. It was, too—a flawless example of a miniature country house, at one with its landscaped gardens, a beautiful, peaceful haven from the world.

He thought of his own upbringing in the fetid, rat-infested *favela*—an ocean away from here! Oh, Flavia Lassiter came from a different world—a different universe! Bitterness filled him, and anger, and a deep, numbing cold that iced all the way through him.

All masked an emotion that went much, much deeper. That bored into him with every twist of that knife in his side.

Flavia was speaking, her voice low and faltering. He made himself listen, made his gaze go back to her, though her image seemed to burn on his retinas. Her beauty assaulted him. She was dressed as soberly as she had been in London: her narrow skirt black, her neat high-necked blouse lavender, a jet brooch at the collar, her hair back in its chignon, her face bereft of make-up. There were dark circles under her eyes, he noted with a strange pang, as if she were not sleeping well.

He thrust the observation aside, making himself listen to what she was saying so haltingly. Was she trying to find words to counter that revealing flush? Was that it? His jaw tightened.

'...so sorry. I'm so very sorry I left you like that. But—'

He held up a hand, silencing her. 'I understand the reason,' he said.

Urgent family matters—and now he knew just what those were...

She looked puzzled. 'You do?'

'Yes. It's very simple, after all.' His voice was expressionless. 'You didn't bother to wait for me in Palma because by then you knew there was no need to. Your father had already contacted you about the new white knight he'd flown off to have discussions with. So there was no reason to hang around with me any more, was there? It wasn't *me* who was going to save his skin—or this place. So you could dispense with me—which you very promptly did.'

She had gone pale. White as a sheet. Leon could feel his emotions lash through him like the tip of a whip.

'What?'

Her astonishment was convincing. Very convincing.

But not to him. It only made him angry—like a wounded jaguar.

'Are you going to try and deny it?' he retorted.

'Yes! Of course I am!'

'And what else are you doing to try and deny?'

'What do you mean?' Her voice was hollow, strained.

'Tell me—what was my main attraction to you, Flavia? What made you stop totally ignoring my calls and get in touch with me? Accept my invitations?' He paused. A deadly pause. 'Have an affair with me...?'

Her eyes were wide, so wide, as she made herself answer. Emotion was storming through her. Making it hard to speak. Impossible to think.

'Because...because I couldn't say no to you...'

Leon's gaze speared her. 'Really? Or because you couldn't *risk* saying no to me…'

That flush came again—a fateful, betraying dull flaring of colour staining her cheekbones. Staining her conscience.

'I have to explain.' It was a whisper. A plea.

'Do you? I don't see why. Your father gave me all the explanation I need.' His voice was chill.

Her expression stilled. 'What did my father say to you?'

Now it was her voice that was chill. Leon's face hardened. 'He said quite a lot.'

Flavia's chin lifted. A cold pit had formed in her stomach. 'What did he tell you?'

What lies has he fed you—and why are you believing them?

She wanted to shout the words at him—but the cold inside her was taking over, freezing through her veins. Paralysing her.

Leon's level gaze never left her face. 'He said that you were determined to hang on to this place—whatever you had to do to keep it.'

She opened her mouth, then closed it again. Leon's eyes were like the talons of a hawk, tearing into her. Cruel and pitiless.

He was speaking again, and she had to force herself to hear him through her faintness.

'You wanted to keep me sweet so I would be likely to bail out your father. Until your father told you he didn't need me any more—then you didn't either. So you left me.'

She shook her head violently. 'No! *No*—Leon—listen. That wasn't why I left!'

She stepped forward, as if to cling to him, but his hands closed over her elbows like a vice. Holding her away from him. His face was dark like thunder.

'Don't lie to me!'

'Leon—listen to me—*please*!'

'No—*you* listen to *me*. I have one question—*one question*—and it's a very simple one.' His eyes skewered into hers, like stakes. 'Did you or did you not finally answer my calls to you and agree to go out with me because I was going to rescue your father's company? Just tell me the truth—yes or no?'

Her mouth opened—then closed. Her face worked.

'Leon, I have to *explain*—' She tried to speak but her throat was closed, stricken. Guilt and shame washed through her.

He thrust her back, letting her go, and she swayed.

'No.' His voice was cold, and hard as steel. 'You *don't* have to explain. Was it to save this place that you came to me? Because I was going to bail out your father? Yes or no?'

'Leon—please, *please*—'

'You don't deny what I've asked—that means it's true. Isn't it? *Isn't it?*'

She could feel her teeth start to chatter. 'Leon, please...' Her voice was a whisper again, forced out past the agonisingly tight cords of her throat.

His hands on her elbows was like a vice. 'Tell me it isn't true. Just tell me that. Yes—no. Very, very simple.'

Her face was working. She was trying to speak. But she was powerless to do so. Powerless to give the answer she so desperately wanted to give him...

'Yes or no?' His voice was remorseless, his face implacable. *'Yes or bloody no, Flavia?'*

'I...I...' She could get no further. Her eyes were anguished, guilt and shame convulsing her.

Something changed in his face. 'Your silence gives me the answer.' His voice was dead. He dropped his grip on her.

'Leon, *please*—let me explain—' She reached a hand towards him—begging. She had to find a way—she had to tell him, explain...confess.

But he'd turned away from her, was walking away from her. She watched him go—helpless, stricken. At the edge of the lawn he paused, looking back at where she stood, frozen.

'There's a word for you, Flavia, for what you did. What you were prepared to do.' He looked around him again for a moment, taking in all the tranquil beauty of the house and its sun-filled gardens, then back at her, his gaze slicing her open, lacerating her. 'And it doesn't matter whether you were doing it to try and save this place, because whatever justification you try and come up with the answer is the same. The name for you is the same.'

He paused, and took a ragged, razored breath. 'I would have given you the world—all I possessed. What we had...' He paused again, then forced the words out. 'What I thought we had was—'

He broke off. Then wordlessly he turned, and strode out across the lawn, back into the waiting helicopter.

The rotors started to turn.

Like a giant bird of prey it lifted off into the air.

Leaving her carrion carcass far below.

Somehow—she didn't know how—Flavia stumbled indoors. Got herself inside her bedroom and threw herself down on her bed. Distraught, fevered sobs seemed to crack her ribs and rack her throat, convulse her whole body.

How long they lasted she didn't know—couldn't tell. She only knew that when they had finally emptied her out she could only lie there, staring at the ceiling, feeling as drained and hollowed out as an empty husk of rotten fruit.

Facing the truth. The bitter, shaming truth.

Leon had every right to accuse her—every right to despise her.

I should have told him the truth! I should have told him on Santera just what my father had done!

But she had been too ashamed to do so. Too fearful that Leon would despise her—too fearful that if he'd rejected her for what she'd stooped to then her father would have carried out his threat and taken Harford from her grandmother...

And fearful for more than that. Much, much more. As she lay, staring, tear-stained, up at the white blank ceiling, she faced the truth within her.

I was scared he would reject me for what I'd done—hate me for it. Hate me just when I was falling in love with him...

And now the truth had come out and he had done what she had feared so much. Thrust her from him, despising and condemning her.

And there was nothing she could do about it—because it was true. The truth had condemned her...

I've lost him and I can do nothing to win him back. Nothing. He's condemned me—rejected me.

Despair filled her.

He hates me now—he hates me and there's nothing I can do to make him not hate me. Because what he accused me of is true.

She could tell herself all she liked that she had had no choice but to collude with her father or he would have forced her grandmother to lose her home—that still didn't take away what she had done to Leon. Deceived him and betrayed his trust in her.

In her head, anguished, she heard his voice, low and intense—*'I would have given you the world...'*

She closed her eyes, feeling wave after wave of pain wash over her, crying his name in her head.

On leaden limbs she dragged herself up, forced herself to go downstairs. Out in the garden, the sun had long gone, and twilight was gathering in the shadows. Limply she sat down on a bench looking out over the silent lawns. How often had she seen her grandparents, sitting here, hand in hand, looking out over the gardens? They had loved each other deeply. With needle pain she envied them with all her heart.

Now they were both gone, and only she was left. She had lost them, one by one, and now she had lost the man she knew she loved.

She did not cry—there were no tears left to weep. Instead she heard a small, anguished voice inside her cry out.

What am I to do—what am I to do?

And as she sat it was as if she could hear inside her head the calm, wise voice of her grandmother.

'When you wrong someone, child, you must put it right.'

She gazed out over the place she loved most on earth. The place she had tried to protect for her grandmother's sake. But her grandmother did not need her home any more.

The cry from her heart pierced Flavia.

But I need it! I need it—I love it so much and it's all I have left! I've lost everything else—only this is left to me! Only this!

Yet the voice in her head came again. *'You must put it right, child—whatever it costs you. Then and only then can your conscience be clear again.'*

Wind winnowed the hairs at the back of her neck. A last songbird called from the high bushes. The scent of roses caught at her.

'You must put it right, child...'

She closed her eyes, hearing her grandmother's voice, bowing her head. A strange kind of peace filled her. Then slowly, very slowly, she got to her feet and went back indoors. She had wronged Leon. And she had lost him. But she *would* put it right—the only way she could.

In her head his voice sounded again. *'I would have given you the world...'*

She did not have the world—but she knew what it was she must give *him*.

CHAPTER THIRTEEN

'THERE you go, Mrs Peters. That's more comfortable, isn't it?'

Flavia's voice was cheerful, and she smiled down at the elderly lady in her bed, whose pillows she had just rearranged, even though Mrs Peters only went on staring ahead of her blankly. But that didn't stop Flavia chatting away to her as she tended her the way she had her grandmother. Carefully she brushed her patient's hair, gave her some sips from the glass of barley water on the bedside table, which Mrs Peters took docilely, if wordlessly.

Her tasks done for the moment, Flavia bade her patient a kindly leavetaking, and went out of the room. Time to look in on her next charge.

It wasn't difficult work, though seeing elderly women so similar to her grandmother could make her heart ache with loss at times, but it took energy, and patience, and endless cheerfulness, and a great deal of kindness and consideration to look after her charges. Given all her experience caring for her grandmother, it had seemed the obvious work for her to do, and the job also had the huge benefit of providing live-in accommodation at a residential care home.

Just how long she would go on working here she wasn't sure—she couldn't think very far ahead yet. It was enough simply to have a steady job and something useful to do each day.

And to be far, far away from everywhere and everything she'd known. And everyone.

It was what she wanted. All that she could do right now. To get right away from her past and leave it all behind her. Eventually, she knew, she would feel strong enough to lift her head up from the daily round and try and think what to do with the rest of her life.

But that time hadn't come yet, and in the meantime this was enough.

She was just about to go into the next room on the corridor when one of the other carers spotted her.

'Oh, there you are. Someone phoned, asking about you.'

Flavia froze. *What on earth...?*

Apart from her grandmother's solicitors, no one knew she was here. Her eyes hardened. If her father were trying to contact her, using them to do so, he would not succeed. She would have nothing to do with him ever again. On that she was adamant. She was free of him now, and he would never harm or injure her again.

Not that he'd made any attempt to contact her before. She'd presumed he'd accepted he had no more hold over her and therefore he could not use her for his own purposes again. So she had ceased to exist for him. What he was up to these days she neither knew nor cared. Presumably Leon had bailed him out, and he was merrily sporting Anita—or her successor—wherever he wanted to be.

She walked down to the office and went inside.

'Did they leave any message?' she asked.

The other carer—Maria—shook her head. 'They just wanted to know if you worked here,' she told Flavia.

Flavia stiffened. 'Did you tell them?'

'Yes.' The other woman nodded. 'Shouldn't I have?'

Flavia gave a quick smile. 'No, that's fine—don't worry.'

But behind the smile she was frowning. Who could it have been if not her father?

She could feel her heart convulse. Heard a name leap in her head. Immediately she crushed it down.

It isn't Leon! He won't get in touch! I know he won't! He's got no reason to—none at all!

She would never see him again. She knew that. Accepted it. Had made herself accept it.

It's over—completely over. I treated him shamefully and though I have tried to make amends, it cannot be mended. Because I can't undo what I did to him. My father pimped me to him and I went along with it. It doesn't matter why I did it—I did it. So all our time together was a lie! How could it have been anything else?

Anguish filled her. Well, she'd been punished for what she'd done. Punished in a way she had never foreseen. With a perfection of justice that was exquisite in its torment.

I went to him at my father's bidding and my punishment was to fall in love with him—and for him to know what I'd done and hate me for it...

She was in love with a man who had every reason to hate her and despise her, and that was something she would have to live with from now on. Until surely, she prayed, love withered and died. For it must eventually—it must wither and die without nurture, without hope.

I made amends in the only way I could and I have to leave it at that. I have to.

She took a razored breath, setting off back down the corridor to go on with her work. As she tended her next charge, washing and bathing her, helping her into fresh clothes, settling her comfortably once again, she almost she found herself envying her patients' dissociation from the world. Wherever their minds were, they did not have to deal with the emotions that knifed through her so tormentingly. They had gone beyond emotion—gone beyond love...

Beyond loss.

Her hours at work passed swiftly enough, for there was never a shortage of things to do. It was a good care home,

Flavia knew, but seeing its inmates she also knew, with absolute conviction and certainty, that her grandmother would
have hated it—however good the quality of care. She had
only been contented at Harford—knowing somewhere in the
depths of her silent mind that she was at home. Safe.

The knowledge was another layer of torment in the vortex
that twisted constantly in her heart now.

*I could only keep Gran at Harford by doing what I did to
Leon—there was no other way. No other way.*

But, whatever the motive, the deed was the same. Shaming her. Damning her.

*So I have to pay the price without complaint, without self-
pity.*

'Flavia!'

The sound of her name broke her reverie of misery. She
looked up. Matron was beckoning her. Dutifully, Flavia went
over to her.

'You've got a visitor,' Matron said. 'Usually I don't allow
such things in working time, but on this occasion I will make
an exception.'

There was the slightest ruffled look about her normally
brisk manner, but before Flavia could speculate, Matron was
ushering her inside her own inner sanctum, which she hadn't
been in since her original job interview nearly four months
ago. But she had hardly got inside the doorway before she
stopped dead. Frozen.

Leon was inside.

Her first reaction was disbelief, followed by a storm of
emotions. She fought for control, clinging to the door handle for stability.

How on earth had he found her?

Had she spoken out loud? She must have, for he was answering her, his face set.

'I bullied your solicitor into telling me.'

'Why?'

'Because he wouldn't tell me willingly,' he replied tersely.

Flavia shook her head as if to clear it. 'No, I mean *why* did you want to know?'

Emotion flashed in his eyes. 'You ask *why*? Did you think I wouldn't want to track you down—find you—after your solicitors had been in touch with me?'

She was trying to get control back but her mind was all to pieces. She was speaking without thinking, without conscious volition. All her consciousness was on Leon's presence here. So close...

Every sense was leaping in her body, overwhelming her. *I thought I'd never see him again.*

But he was here—now—dragging her gaze to him so he dominated her vision, and she could see nothing else at all except Leon. She could feel her heart going like a sledgehammer, her legs weak with shock. With more than shock.

His face was stark, his cheekbones etched like knives.

'You gave me Harford.'

His words fell into the silence. A silence she could not break. She could only stand there frozen, immobile, incapable of speech, or thought, or anything at all other than a reeling of her mind that he was here. Leon was here...

'Why?' His question bit into the air. 'Why did you do it, Flavia?'

She took a ragged breath. 'I had to do it.'

His face darkened. But she did not let him speak.

'I had to do it because it was the only thing I *could* do. All I could think to do.' She took another shuddering breath, her eyes anguished. 'To try and make amends to you for what I did. For deceiving you. Using you. I behaved unforgivably—I know I did. And I am more sorry for my behaviour than you can ever know.' She could hear her voice catch dangerously, and knew she had to plunge on. 'Gifting Harford to you seemed to me all I could do to attempt to make amends,' she said awkwardly. 'It wasn't actually much of a gift, because of the debts on the property, but I knew you would clear some-

'hing once they'd all been paid, and...and I didn't have any-
hing else to give you.'

'Debts?' His voice was blank.

'Yes. I knew the taxman would want his share for death
duties.' She took a difficult breath. 'And that the other claimant would have to be paid back, too.'

His dark eyes were levelled on her. Still expressionless. She
bore their weight pressing down on her, trying not to collapse
beneath it. She could feel the pulse at her throat throbbing.

*Why had he come here? What for? She'd done what she
could—all that she could!—to show him how much she regretted what she'd done to him at her father's behest. So
why had he tracked her down. Just to get her to spell it out
to him like this?*

'The other claimant?' His words echoed hers, but heavily,
like stones. He paused. 'You mean, of course, your father?'

Her lips pressed together again. 'Yes, my father. I'm sorry
about that, Leon, because it was a vast amount of money I
owed him. But there was nothing I could do. The loan agreement was watertight. I had it checked, and there was no way
I could get out of having to repay that final sum because of
the rate of interest.'

'The one set by your father?' The same blank, heavy voice.

She nodded, swallowing. 'Yes. I'm sorry.'

'You're sorry?'

He seemed to be echoing everything she said—echoing it
as if each word weighed a ton.

'Of course I'm sorry! That debt to him ate into the value
of the house hideously.'

'Yes, it did.' He paused, and she felt the world still for a
moment. Then he spoke again. His voice sounded distant,
remote. 'One might wonder,' he said, 'just why your father
should have set such a rate of interest in the first place. Considering the loan was to his mother-in-law.'

'He didn't care for her,' said Flavia.

'So one might surmise, from the terms and conditions of

the loan,' Leon commented. 'Had she done something to injure him that he set such terms?'

'No,' she answered. 'But there was no love lost between them.'

'Evidently.' Leon's voice was dryer than the Sahara. 'And yet one might think it reasonable to suppose—' his voice was deadpan now '—that once his own daughter had inherited Harford that ruinous debt would be instantly lifted. Why would he want his own daughter to owe him money like that? What father would want that? What *devoted, loving* father? Because he is devoted to you, Flavia—he's told me so himself! Several times! So devoted, he assured me, it was *his* money that kept Harford afloat!'

She didn't answer. Couldn't. His eyes were like weights on her, crushing her into the ground.

'Except that it didn't, did it? In fact it almost sank like a stone. That debt was hanging round your neck like a lead weight! The house you'd inherited after the death of your grandmother—who *died*, Flavia, forty-eight hours after you left Palma, whose funeral was the day I confronted you at Harford after what your father had told me—'

His voice was no longer dry. It was no longer expressionless. It was filled with a black, murderous rage.

'You,' he bit out, 'are now going to tell me the truth! Finally and comprehensively. And you are *not* going to escape this—do you understand me? Because I have been through months of *hell* trying to find you, and I will not go through one more hour! Not *one*!'

She was staring wide-eyed, stricken. 'Leon, please...' Her voice was strained, low-pitched. 'I've done what I can to make amends—it's all I can do. I did what I did and I can't undo it. I know it was unforgivable, and I hate myself for it, but giving you Harford seemed to me the only thing I could do! It was because of Harford that I did what I did, and handing it over to you seemed the only way to try and show you just how sorry I am that I behaved as I did! It was shameful and despicable and dishonest, and you didn't deserve it!'

He was looking at her. 'And you did—you *did* deserve it? Is that what you're telling me?'

There was something in his voice that told her he was keeping himself on a very tight leash. Then he shook his head, giving a short, rasping sound in his throat.

'God Almighty, Flavia—why didn't you just tell *me*?' The question burst from him, tearing into his throat.

She could only go on staring, open mouthed. 'Tell you what?'

He swore—she couldn't understand the words, only hear the angry emotion.

'Tell me just why you got back in touch with me after you'd left London! Tell me how your father was threatening to foreclose on you and sending over an estate agent to scare you! Tell me—' his voice shook '—that you'd been nursing your grandmother, and how frail she was, and how you got called back from Palma because she was near death! *That's* what you didn't tell me—and I don't know why the *hell* you didn't!'

He took a sharp, biting breath. 'And I don't know why in *hell* you thought you had to gift me your home because you felt you *owed* it to me!'

She forced herself to her feet, forced her mouth to open. Forced herself to tell him. Spell it out for him.

'Leon, I deliberately and calculatingly started an affair with you because I wanted to save Harford. Nothing can make that not true! *Why* I had to save Harford doesn't matter! How can it? I used…*sex*—' she stumbled over the word but made herself say it anyway '—to stop my father foreclosing on that nightmare loan he'd made to my grandmother, which he was using to make me do what he wanted: use *sex* to keep you sweet, just as you accused me of doing! He wanted the rescue package from you. He didn't want anything jeopardising it—so if you wanted me in your bed, my God, he'd see to it that it happened!'

Her face worked but she made herself go on. Forced herself.

'I told myself I didn't have a choice! That I *had* to do what he wanted because I knew how devastated and distressed my grandmother would be, in her frail mental condition, if she had to leave Harford. So I got back in touch with you and let you take me out on dates—let you…let you take me to bed! And I knew it was wrong—knew my father was pimping me out to you—but I went along with it! I used sex to get what I wanted!' Her voice rasped bitterly. 'And to think I used to despise Anita for doing that—I was doing exactly the same thing!'

He was looking at her strangely. 'That's what you think, is it? That you're as bad as Anita?'

'*Yes*! How could I be any different from her?'

'How about,' he said tautly, 'because your motivations were somewhat different from hers? You wanted to save your home and you didn't want your grandmother to lose hers! The home your own father had saddled with iniquitous debt just so that he could blackmail you into doing what he wanted!'

He stopped, his eyes resting on her. Implacable. Drilling into her. Giving her nowhere to hide.

'And there's another difference between you, isn't there? *Isn't there*, Flavia? Don't try and deny it to me! Don't try and pretend to me that what we had together from that first night, our whole time on Santera, was only because you wanted to save your home!'

She closed her eyes in anguish, unable to bear that merciless gaze drilling into her.

'That made it *worse*,' she whispered. 'Agonisingly worse! To be so blissfully happy with you and yet to know that I was with you only in order to save Harford! I felt so guilty about it—but I couldn't tell you. How could I? Because I wasn't brave enough! I couldn't bear to have you look at me and know what I'd done, what I'd stooped to! And it wasn't only you I felt guilty about.'

Her voice dropped even more, became even more strained.

'I felt so guilty about my grandmother! There I was, so blissfully happy with you on Santera. I'd just abandoned my grandmother! When I got that phone call from her carer, telling me she'd had a sudden deterioration and was sinking fast, it was like a knife in my heart! While I was with you my grandmother had given up the last of her will to live—I'd abandoned her when she was at her weakest! I was with you and my grandmother was dying! If I had stayed at home with her she might never have deteriorated like that—'

Her eyes flew open. 'Guilt—guilt—guilt! It's all I could feel! About you, about my grandmother—however I twisted and turned. Guilt, guilt, *guilt*!' She gave a long, exhausted sigh. 'When you arrived at Harford the day of her funeral, and threw in my face what my father had said to you, I couldn't defend myself. I was exactly what you said I was. And there was no way out of it. No way.'

She inhaled heavily, lifting her head to look at him. 'Except to try and make amends to you in the way I did. It had been trying to save Harford that had made me do what I did. So giving you Harford was the only way I could try and clear up the mess I'd made—salve my conscience. Absolve me from the guilt I felt.'

She fell silent, just staring at him. Drained. He went on standing, just looking at her.

'Guilt,' he said. 'That's a word you use so much. But I am amazed...' He paused, then continued. 'Amazed you even know what the word is. His eyes were resting on her, completely unreadable. 'It's a word that seems totally and completely unknown to your father!'

His eyes flashed suddenly, and Flavia felt herself reel at the fury in them.

'My God, I always knew the man was unscrupulous—his business dealings showed me that! But to do what he did to his own daughter! And then—' his voice twisted in disgust '—to prate to me and pretend he *doted* on you!'

She gave a painful shrug. 'It was part of the act he always

put on when he got me to go up to London—he'd lent me money for a hip operation for my grandmother, and in return I had to go and stay with him sometimes, act as his hostess and all that. I hated it!'

'That's why you were so hostile and prickly all the time?'

She nodded. 'Yes.'

'Especially to me?'

'Yes.'

'Because your father had made it clear you were supposed to be "nice" to me?'

'Yes.'

She was answering monosyllabically because it was all she could do. She could feel the tension ratcheting up in her. Feel his dark eyes resting on her. Unreadable—so unreadable. She wanted out of here. There was no purpose now—none at all—in being here any longer. She'd said everything to him—confessed everything to him. He was free to go now—*surely* he was free to go? There was nothing more to confess.

Nothing more?

She felt the accusation swirling inside her—whispering, dangerous.

Liar...

No! There was nothing more she was going to confess to him! Dear God, she'd laid bare *everything*—the sordid truth of her relationship with her father, what he had got her to do and how he'd got her to do it. Told him about how twisted up she'd felt about her grandmother—about the time she'd spent with him on Santera! There was nothing else to confess to him—*nothing*!

But still that voice inside her whispered—*liar...*

He was speaking again, the words brushing like acid against her defenceless flesh.

'And so had it not been for your father's manipulation of you—had it not been for your concern over your grandmother—you'd never have had an affair with me? Even if your grandmother hadn't been old and frail and dependent on you, you'd never had had an affair with me? Would never have had anything to do with me? Would have been totally indifferent to me.'

'Yes.'

'Liar.'

Who had said the word? Him or her? She stared at him.

'Liar,' Leon said again softly. 'If you had met me with no connection to your father, and if you had had no responsibilities towards your grandmother, what would you have done?'

His voice was changing, sending ripples of electricity trickling along the endings of her nerves. She could feel her pulse beating—insistent, strong.

'I'll tell you what you would have done, Flavia.'

He stepped towards her, cupped his hands around her face. She could feel her skin flush with heat.

'This,' he said.

His kiss was soft. As soft as velvet. His lips caressed hers and she could feel her limbs dissolve, feel her heart leap. Her mouth opened to his, her arms wound around him, clinging and clinging and clinging to his strong, hard body.

Oh, dear God, it was bliss—bliss to have him kiss her again. Leon—her own Leon—the way he had before—the way he was doing now.

He tore his mouth away, his fingertips pressing into her skull, holding her, gazing down at her. His eyes were lambent.

'This is the truth, Flavia! This is what you could never deny—and this is what absolves you! Just as the fact that you did what you did *not* for yourself but out of love and care for your grandmother! You couldn't hide the truth about this— what there is between us—whatever the foul machinations of your father, whatever your sense of guilt about yourself! When you left me, and when your father had fed me his poison about you, it gutted me to think that the time we'd had together had been based on nothing more than an attempt to use my desire for you for your own venal ends! I saw you then as what I'd feared you were when I first met you—a pampered,

idle female who was happy to live off her father's wealth. On Santera I thought I'd got that completely wrong—because you truly seemed happy in such a simple place, happy only to be with me! Then afterwards I thought *that* was the lie—and it gutted me! Gutted me because I'd thought—'

His voice choked suddenly, and Flavia could feel her arms tightening around him instinctively, protectively.

'I'd thought you were feeling about me what I had come to feel about you.' His gaze, dark and glowing, poured into her. 'But that time on Santera was true—wasn't it? *Wasn't it*? That was the true time between us—away from your father's machinations, away from your concerns about your grandmother—just you and me together. Happy. *Blissful.*' He used the word she'd used fondly, smilingly.

Lovingly.

That was what she could see in his face now. Impossible to deny—impossible to hide.

As impossible for him to hide it as it was for her...

'I made such a mess of things,' she whispered.

He shook his head. 'It was an impossible situation.' He took a heaving breath. 'I only wish that you had told me on Santera about what your father was truly like, about how you were the carer for your grandmother, about the way he was holding that debt over your head—I just wish you had told me all that.'

'I didn't dare to. I was scared you might be so angry you would call off the deal with my father, and then in revenge at my spoiling things for him he'd foreclose on that debt anyway! And my grandmother would still have lost Harford! So I didn't dare tell you—I didn't dare!' She took a shaking breath. 'And I didn't *want* to tell you—didn't want you looking at me knowing I'd let my father pimp me out to you.'

He shook her—gently but angrily. 'You did it for your grandmother! Did you think I would condemn you for that?'

'I was scared you might! And I didn't want to lose what we had because...because I knew it couldn't last. I knew I had to go back to my grandmother, that I wasn't free to have a relationship with you. So I...I just blotted it all out, blanked it all out.'

He kissed her softly. 'Never again. You understand me, Flavia?' he said admonishingly. 'From this moment on you trust me—you trust me with everything! I can't go through again what I've been through—wanting you from the first moment I saw you, being endlessly rebuffed by you, then you bolting from me and leaving London the way you did, having to tread on eggshells to win you, and then—dear God—losing you again after Santera and all the hell that came afterwards. Missing you, mistrusting you, accusing you and hurting like hell every moment of that time!

'And then the bombshell of the title deeds of your home landing on my desk! Telling me, once I'd found out from your solicitors, not just about the ruinous debt your father held over you, but about how you'd been your grandmother's devoted carer and how recently she'd died—all that slamming into me like punches to my gut. I'd been totally, totally wrong about you, about my accusations! I set off to try and find you after you'd yet again disappeared off the map! Hell, Flavia—nothing but hell! Right up till today,' he said feelingly, 'when I phoned this place and finally tracked you down!'

He kissed her again. Devouringly, possessively. Wrapping her in a bear hug that enveloped her completely.

'And now I've got you!' he said. 'And I am never, *never* letting you go again! So get your things and tell your boss you're leaving. Tell her to hire as many agency staff as she needs to cover for you and send me the bill! Because I am taking you away with me *right now*.'

He straightened, holding her elbows, looking down at her. Then, abruptly, he frowned.

'You're crying,' he said. His frown deepened. 'Why are you crying?'

His answer was a convulsive sob, and Flavia threw herself into his arms again. He held her as she cried, weeping out the tears inside her, weeping out all the guilt that had racked her for so, so long. Held her and soothed her, his strong, protective palms smoothing down her back, his lips brushing her eyelids. When all the tears were shed he kissed her again gently, so gently.

'All done?' he asked, his eyes as soft as his voice.

She nodded. All she was capable of doing.

'Good,' he said. 'Let's go.'

He led her towards the door, taking her hand. She would go with him to the ends of the earth now, and never leave him again.

Gratitude, wonder—love—filled her like light pouring through a window.

'Where to?' she asked, gazing lovingly up at him.

He smiled down at her. 'Where do you think?' He paused to kiss her nose. 'I've recently become the extremely satisfied owner of an exceptionally beautifully country house.' He paused again, this time to brush her lips with his. 'I think you'll like it,' he said. 'It's a place filled with love—a place where a beautiful, brave girl once lived. She did the wrong thing for the right reason and then found it was the right thing after all. And as her reward—' he smiled '—she got to live there happily ever after...'

He gazed into her eyes. 'Does that sound good?' he asked.

She lifted her mouth to his.

'Blissful,' she whispered. 'Because it comes with the one thing I want more than anything in the whole world—the one thing I can't live without.' She kissed him softly, with all the love in the world in it. 'You,' she said.

EPILOGUE

'How would you feel,' Leon said, with a slightly tentative questioning note in his voice, his arm around Flavia's shoulder as they stood on the terrace at Harford in the autumnal air, 'about having a helipad here? It would mean I could commute to the City and so spend more time here.'

Flavia leant into his shoulder and smiled warmly up at him. 'It's a brilliant idea. The lawn really isn't a good place to land.'

He gave a rueful laugh. 'No, I can see that. Not good for your herbaceous borders.'

It was Flavia's turn to sound tentatively questioning. 'Are you sure you want to be based here, Leon? You're not used to country living…'

'Cities are overrated,' he said dryly. 'Even now that I can live in penthouses and not on the streets. But even though I would love to be based here at Harford, there will still be more times than I would like that I have to travel abroad. Especially when I'm checking up on my South American *pro bono* projects.'

Her eyes warmed. 'Will you let me come with you?' she asked. 'I'll learn Spanish, I promise, so I won't be a total waste of space! I'd love to see all the good work you are doing.'

'I would love to show it to you. My endless concern is how few the projects are, compared with the need for them.

So many lives need to be transformed to lift people out of poverty.'

She heard the frustration in his voice and kissed him softly on the cheek. 'You're a good man, Leon Maranz. A better man than so many who have made it in this world. Think of men like my father, who's used people all his life for his own selfish ends, caring for no one but himself!'

Anger was etched into her voice. Leon looked down at her.

'Maybe there is a cosmic karma after all. His Far Eastern bail out came to nothing, and after I'd made it crystal clear to him my offer was off the table because of the way he's treated you and your mother's family he lost everything. Including the lovely Anita, who wanted a more solvent protector.'

Leon's voice changed from harsh to reassuring. 'But you needn't be afraid that he'll try and contact you. I've done a deal with him. While he leaves you totally alone and stays out of the country I'll pay him a modest monthly pension. He's taken himself off to Spain, and the last I heard he was trying to set himself up as a property developer. Don't worry,' he said caustically, 'I've got someone keeping tabs on him, and if his business ethics veer towards the dodgy I'll be leaning on him painfully. He won't intrude into your life any more.' He paused. '*Our* lives,' he amended.

He turned her towards him, gazing down at her uplifted face. Flavia felt her heart squeeze and melt with love, as she was bathed in the love-light in his dark, expressive eyes.

'Our lives, my beautiful, adored Flavia. Our lives together from now onwards. Never to be parted again.'

Softly he lowered his mouth to hers, kissing her gently with sweet, possessing passion. He cupped her face with this hands.

'I wish I could have met your grandparents to tell them how wonderful a granddaughter they raised. To tell them how grateful—how profoundly and eternally grateful I am to have found you. And to tell them—' he glanced around at the autumn splendour, framing the house in a blaze of colour

'—how beautiful their house is. How wonderful a home it will continue to be for you and me—'

'And for our children?' There was a wistful note in Flavia's voice.

He gave a warm laugh. 'Oh, yes, for our children. Definitely, *definitely* for our children. You were happy here when you were a child, and you know all the secret places in the house and in the grounds. Our children can roam wild here, be happy and carefree. And you and I—' he kissed the tip of her nose, sliding his arm around her shoulder and strolling with her towards the open French windows leading into the drawing room '—will watch them grow well and strong, and safe and loved. All our days. All our years together.'

At the entrance to the drawing room he paused and looked out over the lawns. 'We'll make a happy home. A happy family.' He drew her fast against his heart. 'A blissful, perfect marriage. Wouldn't you agree, Mrs Maranz?'

She clutched him close, radiant with happiness. 'Absolutely,' she breathed.

He laughed, happiness in his voice as in his heart. 'Then let's crack open that waiting bottle of champagne and drink to our marriage! And then...'

The expression in his eyes altered and Flavia felt a quickening of her pulse, a breathlessness in her lungs.

'And then, my beautiful, beautiful bride, I'm going to carry you upstairs and remove you from that exquisite but really quite unnecessary bridal gown you look so breathtaking in. We shall have a wedding night that will melt the very stars in heaven!'

She frowned. 'I don't think stars can melt, can they?' she queried.

'Whatever,' he said airily, and hefted the champagne bottle out of its ice-bucket. Then he paused. 'On second thought...'

He scooped up two flutes, hooked his fingers around the neck of the champagne bottle, and then, with effortless strength, scooped up Flavia as well. She cried out in laughing surprise and he grinned down at her.

'The champagne can come with us,' he said.

'Whatever,' she answered airily.

He grinned again, kissed her nose, and carried her and the champagne upstairs.

* * * * *

MILLS & BOON

MODERN

Power and Passion

Prepare to be swept off your feet by sophisticated, sexy and seductive heroes, in some of the world's most glamourous and romantic locations, where power and passion collide.

Eight Modern stories published every month, find them all a

millsandboon.co.uk/Modern

t might just be true love...